Dear Reader,

It is with this book that we wrap up our time in Rose Hill—
and what a time it's been! Thank you from the bottom of
my heart for joining me on this adventure.

This town and these people have become something of a
comfort blanket to me. Unlikely friends from all walks of
life becoming what feels an awful lot like family.

And I think that's the thesis of this series, really. Family
isn't just the one you're born into. It can be found and it
can be created, and I think there's something especially
beautiful about that.

I hope you all fall in love with the family that Gwen and
Bash create for themselves. I think their story is the perfect
one to close out this series. One that will leave you with
all the best warm, fuzzy feelings and one I'll think about
for years to come.

So without further ado, please enjoy one final Dads' Night
Out!

Love,

WILD CARD

ELSIE SILVER

Bloom books

Copyright © 2025 by Elsie Silver
Cover and internal design © 2025 by Sourcebooks
Cover design by Mary at Books and Moods
Cover images © BigAlBaloo/Depositphotos, Hermit Crab Designs/Shutterstock,
Sven Taubert/Adobe Stock, Neillockhart/Adobe Stock, Sayhellonan/Adobe Stock,
Pikisuperstar/Freepik, LiliGraphie/Depositphotos, Aerial3/Getty Images
Map illustration by Laura Boren/Sourcebooks

Sourcebooks, Bloom Books, and the colophon are
registered trademarks of Sourcebooks.

Published by Bloom Books, an imprint of Sourcebooks
1935 Brookdale RD, Naperville, IL 60563-2773
(630) 961-3900
sourcebooks.com

Cataloging-in-Publication data is on file with the Library of Congress.

Printed and bound in Canada.
MBP 10 9 8 7 6 5 4 3 2 1

For the ones who were told their dreams were too dreamy but who went on to make them come true anyway.

And for my awful high school English teacher, Mr. C, who looked me in the eye at sixteen years old and told me I'd never be a good writer. Thanks for the motivation.

THE ELSIE SILVER UNIVERSE

BRITISH COLUMBIA

ALBERTA

SASKATCHEWAN

Vancouver Island

Ruby Creek

Emerald Lake

Blisswater Springs

Rose Hill

Chestnut Springs

N
W E
S

READER NOTE

This book contains mentions of weight stigma and reflections on fatphobia. It incorporates brief discussions related to body shaming. I would like to thank the early sensitivity readers and clinical therapist I employed throughout the writing and editing process for helping me ensure that these topics were handled with the care and attention they deserve.

Please be advised that one main character is a firefighting pilot and as such there are detailed scenes that explore natural disasters and related subject matter.

CHAPTER 1

Bash

ONE YEAR AGO...

I'm stuck in an airport, and everyone is annoying me.

"We're delayed again, but it's so beautiful outside that I don't even mind," a voice singsongs from the row of blue pleather chairs behind me. It's a nice voice. Rich and calm and, based on the way she's chatting away on the phone, not at all frustrated by being stranded in a snowstorm. "I feel like I'm living in a snow globe or something."

I scoff, flexing my fists beneath my crossed arms. We've been waiting to board for three hours, and this woman doesn't even mind.

And I believe her. I don't bother looking in her direction, but I can tell by her tone, the awe seeping into every word, that she's never seen snow and would describe this nightmare as "cozy."

"Yeah, honestly…it's cozy."

Yep. There it is. Whoever she is, she's enjoying this.

Must be fucking nice because I'm ready to crawl right out of my skin. People sneezing without covering their faces, babies crying, the smell of stale bagels. I've walked laps like a tiger pacing his cage, and even that isn't taking the edge off anymore.

Leave it to Vancouver to be the only place in Canada that doesn't know how to handle a snowstorm. And it's not even *that* bad.

The crackle of the speakers filters through the low hum of Gate 82's waiting area. "Attention all passengers awaiting boarding for Air Acadia flight 2375 with service to Calgary. We regret to inform you that your flight has been canceled and rescheduled for tomorrow morning. You should receive an email shortly with updated flight information. Please see a booking agent if you require further assistance. We appreciate your patience and understanding and look forward to serving you tomorrow."

A communal groan rolls through the space. What follows is a string of announcements delivering the same message to neighboring gates: no one is getting out of here tonight.

My head drops back against the chair's metal top and I let out an exhausted sigh. It's been a crappy week, and this is just the bread that makes the whole thing a shit sandwich.

I'd empty my entire bank account just to sleep in my own bed tonight. To be alone with some fucking peace and quiet. To decompress.

Instead, I am fully compressed. Every muscle feels tight,

and my jaw hurts from clenching it. Even my lungs feel constricted.

This was the last thing I needed after having my entire world turned upside down.

"Yeah, canceled." That too-happy voice floats through the air toward me. "It's okay. It is what it is. I'm going to make the most of it! When life gives you lemons…"

It squeezes the acid right in your fucking eyes.

I push to my feet.

A peek over my shoulder reveals a shock of wavy, platinum hair draped over the woman's face as she rifles through an oversize bag, her phone pressed to her ear.

My brows scrunch low as she laughs at whatever the person on the other end of the line has said. I shake my head as I turn away and heave my bag onto my shoulder, deciding she's altogether too happy. It's not normal.

For some reason, her cheerfulness sours my mood even further. So with my heavy footfalls echoing on the polished concrete floors, I head toward the booking agent's desk to see if there's a way I can get the hell out of here.

Waiting in line doesn't ease my annoyance. As it turns out, I'm not the only one in a foul mood. An angry middle-aged man ahead of me has gone from agitated to a full-blown meltdown. He points his index finger at the frazzled customer service representative, demanding she fix this—as if she personally created the snowstorm.

He's mad about his bags. He's mad about the lack of available accommodations. He's mad about the new early flight time.

I'm mad too, but I'm not punching down over it. And the longer I watch, the more I'm just mad about what a royal asshole this guy is.

The girl's cheeks darken, and her bottom lip wobbles. When her eyes fill as she shrinks back from his tirade, I've had it.

"My man." I project my deep voice toward the desk. "Shit happens. No need to speak to her that way."

Heads swivel in my direction, including the one belonging to the red-faced man. "Excuse me?" His jowls vibrate with fury, his lip beneath his thick mustache curling as his eyes home in on me. I get the sense that he's not accustomed to people telling him off.

I shrug. Looking nonchalant is the ultimate affront to someone who wields their power in such a belittling way. "Take a walk," I say in a low rumble. "It is what it is."

"It is what it is?" His eyes bug out, his pie face turning an even deeper shade of red.

I can't believe I just used that woman's line on this guy, but I'm getting a kick out of confronting him, so I borrow another sentiment from Miss Happy.

"Yeah, it's like when life gives you lemons, don't be an asshole to the service staff. Or something like that."

The man stares at me, and I stare back. His gaze sweeps over my favorite plaid flannel shirt, then down my black jeans and leather boots. I'm bigger than him, and while it's been a few years since I threw a punch, I'm not above it. I may be pushing forty, but I'm in great shape, and it might feel good to release this tension.

His beady eyes skitter across the hushed crowd, as though assessing how embarrassed he should be (the answer is very embarrassed). He must realize I'm not an easy target because he turns back to the woman behind the desk—who looks suitably shocked—and swipes his paper ticket off the counter before storming away as fast as his furious little legs will carry him.

Watching him waddle away in a huff makes my lips twitch.

And here I thought nothing could make me smile tonight.

Though her shy *thank you* pulls on my heartstrings a bit, my polite exchange with the agent behind the desk doesn't make anything any better—the closest hotels have no availability because of other cancellations and our flight has been rescheduled for a 6 a.m. departure.

It's currently 11:08, which means by the time I get through the hellish traffic in and around the city to a place with a vacancy, I might as well turn right back around since I'll need to clear security all over again. The only reasonable solution is to sleep on a bench in the terminal.

Everything about tonight sucks, but I swallow my frustration like a real man and thank her for her help before leaving to find a place to hunker down for the night.

Tired legs carry me through the airport as I scan for a spot where I can go horizontal for a few hours. Years of battling active forest fires have left me with the uncanny ability to doze off almost anywhere and function with little sleep. Wildfires don't care about your bedtime and often like to do their worst after dark, so I'm no stranger to catching some shut-eye in uncomfortable places.

Except, I'm not the only person who seems to have resigned themselves to sleeping at the airport tonight.

I stand in place, hands on my hips, searching for even a free corner, but the place is like a fucking hostel, people and bags splayed all over the place.

The only place my eyes land on that has a free spot is the bar. One lone table for two at the edge of the seating area, tucked right next to the walkway that leads to the bathroom. It's not glamorous, but it's something. And a drink sounds pretty damn good right now.

I don't bother asking if it's available. I just march past the deserted hostess stand and stake my claim. And just in the nick of time, based on the stream of people who walk up and peer around the restaurant like they can will an open spot into existence. But their wishful thinking is futile. The bar top is packed, shoulder to shoulder, with a mess of bags cluttering the floor. Frantic waitstaff hustle between the tables, struggling to keep up with the unexpected Monday night rush.

I feel bad for them too, so I pull my phone out and scroll as I wait—it's not like I have anywhere to be. The news about the snowstorm and all the chaos it's causing across the Pacific Northwest makes me shake my head. In almost any other Canadian city, this wouldn't be an issue. But here? Not enough plows. Not enough deicing machines.

As I internally scold a major airport, a voice catches my attention.

The sound of it pulls me right out of my downward spiral. I glance up, and there she is. The lemonade girl.

Woman.

Because there is nothing girlish about her. She carries herself with a confident ease, wearing soft, feminine curves like she invented them. And that voice? It's the furthest thing from girlish. That voice is all grown-up. It's not giddy or overly bright. It's all honey and spice, smooth with a hint of heat—borderline sensual without even trying.

"Not a single spot in the entire place?"

There's a kid at the front now who looks barely old enough to be working here. He stares back at her, and I can tell he's not immune to the heart-shaped face with matching heart-shaped lips. He looks ready to build her a chair himself, just to give her somewhere to sit.

As her gaze searches the restaurant, he watches her raptly. And I follow suit.

No wonder he's practically panting. He's just encountered a modern-day Marilyn Monroe—but she's even more buxom. Loose, platinum waves fall next to full cheeks and a button nose. But it's her big blue doe eyes that are a fucking kick to the gut. They're so vibrant, I swear they trend toward a lavender tone.

I shift in my seat and focus back on my phone. I'm too damn old to be gawking at a pretty girl in the airport. Scrolling the news is far more appropriate.

"S-sorry. I wish I could—"

I hear him trip over his words and chuckle.

Poor fucking kid.

"Oh, don't be sorry. I see a spot over there, actually. I appreciate your help."

I scoff under my breath. Help. That's generous of her.

"Something funny?"

I hear that voice again, closer this time. And when I look up, she's standing right in front of me.

And fuck me if for a moment I don't feel as tongue-tied as the kid I was just laughing at. I stare back at her, feeling like I could squirm under the weight of her soulful gaze.

I grumble out an irritated-sounding no to cover for my otherwise-stunned reaction.

I deemed her pretty before, but I was wrong—she's fucking gorgeous.

Her lips tug up in an almost-knowing smile. "Good. I'd hate to sit with a stranger who's laughing to himself over nothing."

"Sorry?" I ask, confused.

But any confusion vanishes when the woman slides the chair opposite me back from the table and takes a seat.

Uninvited.

"You don't mind, do you?"

I straighten, a little put off by her…familiarity? Friendliness? I don't know how to define it, but it throws me off. I'm not the guy who strikes up conversations with strangers. Hell, I barely like striking up conversations with the few people in my life that I consider friends.

"What if someone else is sitting there?" I grumble, not particularly comfortable with the unexpected nature of this run-in—or how attractive I find her.

She sets her bag on the floor with a husky, amused laugh. When she straightens, she doesn't look remotely uncomfortable, resting her elbow on the table and propping her chin against her palm. "No one else is sitting here."

I cross my arms and lean back, creating some space between us. "How do you know?"

Her head tilts, the overhead lights highlighting the apples of her cheeks. "No bag. No phone. And you are giving off some serious stay-the-fuck-away energy."

I quirk a disbelieving brow at the woman. "Stay-the-fuck-away energy?"

She hits me with a conspiratorial smile. "Yes. If you were a house, I would sage you."

Ah, more granola, woo-woo, make-lemonade, salt-of-the-earth shit. Exactly what I'm in the mood for.

I bite the inside of my cheek to keep from laughing, and I suspect she picks up on my cynicism, but she just reaches across the table. That same tattoo I saw earlier catches my eye as dainty vines and leaves unfurl in my direction.

I frown at her hand, which gets me a throaty laugh followed by "Hi. Thanks for inviting me to join you. My name is Gwen, and you are?"

I glance back up, and her sparkling eyes flit between mine, a dimple deepening on her right cheek the longer I glare back. I swear to god, she's getting a kick out of irritating me.

So, to ruin her fun, I reach for her hand with a brusque "Hi. I'm Bash. And I think our definitions of *invite* might be wildly different."

Gwen lifts one shoulder in a gentle shrug. "Maybe this seat was meant to be empty."

My lips flatten. "Yes, exactly. It was."

She laughs softly, head shaking as though I fascinate her. "Yet here I am. And you know what they say… When life gives you lemons…" She winks at me, and my jeans feel the slightest bit tighter across the front.

My jaw flexes but I give the woman seated across from me my best bored look in a pathetic attempt to cover for my downright boyish reaction to her.

"What if I wanted limes?" I ask, right as a flustered server pops up at our table with a breathless, "What can I get you?"

With her eyes fixed on mine and that pretty mouth curved into a knowing smile, Gwen—the interloper—doesn't miss a beat. "Oh, thank goodness you're here. This man desperately needs a lime margarita. Extra sour."

CHAPTER 2

Gwen

THE SERVER RUSHES AWAY BEFORE I'VE EVEN FINISHED SAYING, "Make that two." When I turn my focus back on the man across the table from me, I am met with a look that could kill.

And if I hadn't seen him be so damn nice to that poor customer service agent, I might buy it. Except I was there. From a few spots back in line, I watched him speak up for the woman without hesitation.

Hell, he'd even used a fresh and amusing spin on one of my favorite sayings.

So, no, Bash, the grump whose dark, heavy brows are tugged down tight with an adorable little wrinkle at the top of his nose, does not put me off at all.

I know what a truly mean expression looks like—the kind that precedes words sharp enough to wound. This isn't it. Instead, he looks like all bluster and chiseled features.

If I had to use one word to describe him, it would be *masculine*. From head to toe.

Chunky black leather boots, no-nonsense Levi's, and a soft, boxy flannel shirt give him a total lumberjack vibe. A grumpy lumberjack.

But it's his face that's most eye-catching. Not traditionally handsome, not conventionally pretty. His nose is strong, his jaw square, and his thick beard is neatly trimmed. Streaks of silver dust through his dark-brown hair that's trimmed close on the sides and styled neatly on top.

"Did you just invite yourself to my table and then order for me?" His deep voice rumbles but there's no bite.

"Oh, is this *your* table? My apologies. I didn't realize you owned the airport."

A vein on the side of his neck pulses. One that I know is only visible because this man is tense as hell. "No, but it's a known rule that when someone is sitting at a table, the other chairs are also taken."

My lips form into an O as I pretend to be enlightened by this new information. "Gosh, I had no idea. I haven't read the rule book to being stuck in an airport overnight. Do you have it on hand?"

He glares back at me, tongue swiping over the front of his teeth.

I smile, offering an innocent shrug. "Strikes me that we're all fucked tonight, and any open chair is fair game. If you don't like me, then I fear I cannot help you. But if you just don't like margaritas, then I'm happy to help you out by drinking both. I don't have anywhere to be tonight, and I do love a good margarita."

His full mouth pops open as though he's about to say something, but no words come. He just stares back at me like I'm an exotic bird he's never seen before. Finally, he mumbles, "I like you just fine."

"Wow, high praise coming from you. Thank you for blessing me with your approval," I tease, watching his eyes roll and a muscle in his jaw twitch like the implication annoys him somehow.

"I didn't mean it like that, and you know it."

With a satisfied smile, I lean back, crossing my arms to mimic his position. "Do I? All I know about you is that you prefer limes to lemons and have a strong moral compass."

His head tilts ever so slightly. "Strong moral compass?"

"The booking desk."

Understanding flares in his eyes. "Saw that, did you?"

"In all its glory. And it really was glorious."

He grunts as he shifts, his eyes flicking away like he's uncomfortable with the compliment. "It was no big deal."

My head joggles as I consider that. "I mean… No one else did anything. I suspect, for that woman, it was a pretty big deal. It's quite the phenomenon that men like that are all fire and brimstone when they're talking to someone they can intimidate."

Just ask my dad.

He'd wanted to send me out into the world meek and obedient.

And he failed.

The only thing he sent me into the world with was a defiant backbone, unfailing optimism, the desire to chase my dreams…and a few daddy issues. But none of those issues are *actually* him. Because I haven't spoken to the man in eight years.

Bash scoffs at my assessment, fiddling with the napkin of rolled-up cutlery before him. "Yeah, that guy was a fucking loser. I can tell you that much."

I nod my agreement when I hear Bash mumble, "Maybe you should sage him instead."

My eyes widen as I take him in, not finding a single other sign that he just deadpanned a comment like that. So I play along. "Absolutely. I'll take that under advisement. Maybe if we track him down tonight, I could offer a two-for-one deal and get both of you cleansed up."

That earns me another scowl, which only makes me laugh.

"So where you headed?" the man asks.

"Toronto. You?"

"Calgary." I nod, remembering his gate was just beside mine. One quick glance down and my eyes catch on the tag attached to his bag. It would appear "Bash" is short for Sebastian Rousseau.

Even his name is hot, I think to myself distractedly.

Just then, coasters slide across the table in each of our directions and two margaritas unceremoniously plunk down in front of us as the server basically does a drive-by.

Bash glares at the glass of bright-green liquid suspiciously before lifting his dark eyes in my direction. "They're very… neon."

I nod solemnly, gazing down at the drink. It's definitely not reminding me of the margaritas I was enjoying on the beach in Mexico at my yoga retreat only a day ago. "This looks like it's the from-concentrate juice off the soda gun. It's a margarita but not a *good* margarita."

Bash winces. "This is gonna be sweet as hell."

"There *is* some good news." His dark gaze flicks to mine, and an airy flutter in my chest distracts me for a beat. "The good news…" I lick my lips. "The good news is that there is tequila floating around in all that sugary juice."

He nods, not looking away. And though I'm not usually one to squirm under a man's attention, I feel my cheeks flush as this one looks me over. His gaze is appreciative, and I revel in it.

"That's a great point. And when stuck in an airport over-night, some tequila is better than no tequila."

I straighten, propping my forearms against the table as I lean closer. "Absolutely. I'm certain this will make us feel better. What with life giving us limes and all that."

His stubbled cheek twitches before his fingers wrap around the glass.

His large palm dwarfs it, and I can't help but notice the signs of physical labor on his hands. There's a coarseness to them. Calloused on the palms, the odd scar on the backs. One nail with the dark-blue tinge of a deep bruise.

Yeah, this man works with his hands.

I swallow quickly and follow suit, lifting my glass to the middle of the table. "Cheers. To limes."

Bash gives his head a slight shake before lifting his glass and clinking it against mine. "To limes."

We both take a sip, and I try not to wince because it really does taste like liquid sugar. Each sip tastes better than the last though, and soon I barely notice that I'm drinking glorified limeade.

A companionable silence settles between us as we nurse our drinks, watching the world go by. But the more margaritas we down, the more that silence morphs into a tipsy, friendly sort of companionship. At the very least we partake in some mutual rubbernecking, tossing the odd comment each other's way as we take turns pointing out the night's mayhem—a couple arguing, a child toppling off a seat they were climbing, a man staggering out of the restaurant with bloodshot eyes.

But it's the father and his young-adult daughter sitting at the bar together who continue to catch my eye. The way she said "Daaad" and tossed her head back when he'd cracked a joke drew my attention, and the friendly ease between them keeps me coming back. They're each drinking a beer, watching the sports highlights on the screen. Laughing. He even squeezes her shoulder at one point.

Watching them is like digging a finger into an old wound. One that just won't heal, no matter how hard I try. No matter how much work I put in.

I yearn for that relationship.

And I'll never have it.

Eventually, the crowd in the bar thins. Other patrons have the foresight to find a place to hunker down for the night. The man and his daughter leave too.

But not us. No, we just keep ordering the shittiest margaritas I've ever tasted.

When we're officially billed and the staff begin to close up shop around us, we still don't rush. I have too many questions floating around in my head, ones I want to ask Bash now that tequila and sugar have softened him up.

"So what is it you do for a living?"

His tongue runs over his teeth like he's considering whether to answer me. Then, with a shrug, he answers in a gruff voice. "I'm an aerial firefighter. But during the winter I—"

My palms slap the table as I pitch forward, breasts pressing against the edge. His gaze drops to my chest briefly, but I don't call him on it. My boobs *are* pretty damn big and they're constantly in the way. "I'm sorry, what? You're not just a regular firefighting hero? You fly actual planes into actual fires and drop water on them?"

"Depends on the fire. And the strategy. Sometimes it's retardant."

I can feel my cheeks flush as my eyes rake over him with a whole new appreciation. "So you're like a *hero* hero," I say, leaning back in my chair to get a better view of the man before me.

Poor guy looks uncomfortable with the praise. I bet he doesn't see himself that way at all. He's all gruff and matter-of-fact. I bet he's about to say that he's *just* "doing his job."

"That's the tequila making you exaggerate."

I scoff. "Okay, Top Gun. I'm sure someone whose home was saved by your perfect aim and huge set of brass balls would describe your contribution as 'exaggerated.'"

He snorts and looks away. "You've got a way with words. That's for sure."

I flip my hand in a rolling motion and tip my head forward in a dramatic bow. "Thank you, thank you. I'll be here all night." My head pops up, and I wink at him. "No, literally, I'm fucking stuck here."

A ghost of a smile touches his lips, and god, I bask in it. I'm certain that when I sat down, he found me annoying, and now I have weaseled my way into an entirely different territory. Which is a huge relief because I can't handle people not liking me. That's the stuff that eats away at me and keeps me up at night.

"And what do you do, Gwen? Is it stand-up comedy? Palm readings?"

My tongue pops into my cheek. "No. But I did go through a tarot phase."

His eyes roll, but there's no malice in the movement. "Of course you did."

I chuckle softly and take another sip. His gaze lowers again, but this time to the tip of my tongue as it darts out over the salt rim.

"I'm a yoga instructor."

His eyes widen, snapping away from my mouth. "That makes so much sense."

That tiny critical voice that sounds an awful lot like my father pops into my head. *That makes so much sense* could be interpreted in many ways, but years of explaining my career choices make everything sound like a backhanded slight.

It puts me in defense mode.

"I'm really good at it too," I say, explaining myself. "I have hundreds of teaching hours. Have trained all over the world. I even do contract work with professional sports teams."

Bash nods, one sure dip of his stubbled chin. "I meant what I said. I can totally see it. And I have no doubt you're excellent at it."

Relief drops my shoulders, and I release a breath I didn't realize I'd been holding. "Yeah, no. I'm just used to people…" I trail off with a light laugh and glance away. "You know what? Never mind."

"No, tell me."

My gaze trails back to the man across from me. The one watching, listening. Really listening. He's leaned forward a bit, shoulders square, attention locked on me. Like he actually wants to hear what I have to say.

So, with a shrug, I forge ahead. "I don't know. For starters, I don't look how people expect a yoga instructor to look."

His gaze rakes over my body, chin tipping down and then back up. And the only thing I see in his eyes is appreciation. "What do you mean? You look like a yoga instructor to me."

He says it so simply and with a slightly confused tone. It's…endearing. *Refreshing.*

I lift a shoulder, playing his response off casually. "I meant my size."

At that his brows furrow. Confusion morphing into irritation. "People are stupid," he grumbles simply.

A happy hum vibrates in my chest and I bite down on a smile. Then I forge ahead. "And then people often sort of pat my head when I tell them what I do. Like, *That's so cute, but what do you plan to do when you grow up?* Or *but what about university?* Very patronizing. It's tiring having to justify that what I do has value."

His brows furrow, and for a flash, he looks…fierce. Perhaps I'm imagining it, but he appears almost offended on my behalf. When he speaks again, his voice borders on stern. "Again, people are stupid. Plenty of us make great livings and have fulfilling careers without attending university."

I smile my thanks and then slam back the rest of my margarita to cover any blubbering I might do. "You should tell my dad that," I mutter before dropping my glass like a gavel on the table.

Internally, I berate myself for dumping my personal baggage all over this hot stranger just because he's being nice to me and saying things I desperately want to hear.

Then, I push to standing and change the subject. "All right, too serious. Let's go do something."

CHAPTER 3

Bash

I BLINK UP AT HER, WANTING TO GO BACK TO THE PART ABOUT her dad. Or the comment about her size. Because I barely know her, but I'm pissed off that *anyone* could make her feel that way about herself. I've been in her presence for just over an hour, and I can tell she's got a knack for helping people. For making a dark room feel just a little bit brighter. And that's not something you can learn in the pages of a book.

But I can tell by the way she quickly hefts her bag over her shoulder and glances around that she's practically running in the opposite direction of that conversation.

So, I let my agitation go and ask, "Do something? Here?"

"Yeah." She shrugs. "Where else? There's gotta be something to entertain us."

"I was thinking of sleeping."

"Pfft." She waves me off. "Please. How many times in your life are you going to be stuck in an airport overnight?"

"Hopefully only once?"

"Exactly! This is a core memory. A night we'll tell our kids about one day."

I wince. *Kids.* That's a sore spot tonight, but she doesn't notice the sobering effect her words have on me. She just carries on, unruffled.

"And if the story ends with *I lay on a dirty floor unsuccessfully trying to fall asleep for hours*, it's going to be the worst story. Don't live life with regrets, *Sebastian*."

Fuck me. It's like she's found my fresh wound and is squeezing her limes right into it.

Her arm shoots out, hand stretched toward me. "Come on. Don't quit on me now. I have a deep inner need to make you like me, and I feel like I'm getting close."

With a roll of my eyes, I toss back the last of my margarita. "I like you just fine, Gwen," I grumble as I reach for her hand.

"That's what you keep saying. But I'm not settling for fine," she volleys, giving my arm an eager tug.

It feels strange to be holding hands with a woman I only just met. And yet, as she leads me out of the restaurant, I don't pull away. I let her thread her dainty fingers through mine, as though we've done this a thousand times before. Heat hums through my hand, racing up the veins in my arm.

She warms me. And a cautious optimism surges from within. It makes me think that maybe—just maybe—despite my surliness and sour mood, she might be enjoying my company.

I hope she is. Because I know I'm enjoying hers, bewildered as that might make me.

She turns and leads us into the long, open hallway, pulling me along on her adventure.

My eyes drop to her round ass—jeans hugging her hourglass shape perfectly, curved hips swaying confidently with every stride.

Yeah, she's hot as hell. She's fucking *trouble*.

I let my hand fall away as I take a couple of longer strides to catch up with her. Walking side by side seems more appropriate now that I've taken a few breaths of fresh air and looked at something other than her unusual eyes and soft lips.

Gwen glances over her shoulder at me, her expression almost disappointed. Which is impossible. So I brush the thought away with a question.

"Where are we going?"

She shrugs, gazing around with an expression of wonder on her face and a flash of amusement on her features. "I don't know. Do we need a plan? Maybe we'll just walk along, and something will catch our eye."

My Adam's apple bobs in my throat as I regard her and wonder what the hell was in those margaritas. Because my mind is consumed by one thought: *something* has *caught my eye*.

She peeks at me. "I know what you need."

I flush, feeling like a kid caught gawking. *I sure hope not.*

"You need a pick-me-up before we go on our adventure."

"I think all the coffee shops are closed."

She just laughs and leads me toward a stretch of darkened windows that faces out into the snowy night. I watch as she kicks off her shoes, sits down cross-legged, and lays her palms over her knees.

She doesn't call me over, but I go all the same, intrigued by the woman and her zest for life. I could use a little of that zest, and I know it—I just don't know how to find it. Not when it feels like the last several years of my life have been one big cosmic joke.

"What are you doing?"

"Meditating." I can hear the smile in her smooth voice.

"Why?"

"Because it can be just as restorative as sleep. And I don't want to waste my night sleeping." She pats the space beside her, a silent invite for me to join.

"I'm not really a meditator," I grumble, though I still fold myself down beside her while wondering what the fuck I'm doing. My knee brushes the tips of her fingers, and I stare at her hand before shifting away to leave a few inches of space between us. I'm stiff as hell and must look like a busted-up pretzel trying to match her position. I don't think I've sat cross-legged since grade school.

"Okay. Well, just sit here for a while then."

I sneak a glance in her direction to see that her eyes are now closed and her lips are tipped up in a soft smile. "And do what?"

Her smile widens, but her lashes stay down, casting shadows over her apple cheeks. "Nothing."

"Do *nothing*?" Doing nothing is not my forte. I pride

myself on staying busy, on always having a project on the go. Hell, I could take winters off since I quit going overseas to fight fires. I have enough money saved up to spend the season in Mexico, sipping margaritas on the beach. And yet, here I am, building up a contracting business and taking odd jobs over the winter months.

She peeks out of the eye closest to me. "It's harder than it sounds."

I bristle at that. "I know it is. It's impossible."

Her chin tips up as that one eye draws shut once again. "It's not impossible. It's good for you. But it takes practice. See if you can let your mind be blank."

Blank? I scoff. Not after this week. "*That's* impossible."

She doesn't respond to my feelings, though. Instead, she says, "Stare at the snow out the window. Watch it fall. Pick a single flake and watch its course. Then pick another one. Do it all over again."

"What's the point?" I ask, out of genuine curiosity. The way her brain works is...refreshing. And I want to know more about it. I think I'd like to spend some time in her brain just so I can get the hell out of mine.

"It's beautiful, isn't it? The snow. Each flake has its own unique shape. That hush of quiet it brings to the world. You have nowhere to be. You're safe and warm. Peaceful." She sighs the last word, chest rising and falling.

Peaceful.

I turn and face the window, considering her words.

Peaceful.

It's the last thing I've felt lately. But as I stare at the snow, falling thick and soft, I have to admit I feel a glimmer of it stir within me—a soft corner amid all my rough edges.

My gaze latches on to a single flake, following its gentle descent.

Then another.

And another.

I lose count of how many I watch fall or how much time passes. I wouldn't say that my mind is blank, but it's… soothed. And it's only Gwen moving beside me that draws my attention away from the window. She's shifted onto her knees and folded forward, her elbows propped on the floor with her hands held up in a prayer position.

"You can follow along if you want to do some energy-boosting poses."

"That's okay. I suspect I'd injure myself if I tried to do that."

She chuckles and carries on, breathing deeply, moving between yoga poses I recognize but couldn't name.

I watch her without shame. Her body moves with effortless grace, every curve on display. I force myself not to leer, shifting my attention instead to her fingers splayed on the floor, the way her bright hair falls in soft waves when she drops her head. The smell of her shampoo when it hits me—rosemary and mint.

She's borderline hypnotic. Flexible and feminine. And there's something incredibly bold about her doing this right here and now, beside a man she barely knows.

She doesn't give a fuck what I think. Nor should she.

And I admire that about her.

This night has been one surprise after another. I don't know how I got here, but it almost feels like I'm having fun.

Stuck in an airport.

With a fucking stranger.

And what a stranger she is. I'm not usually taken with new people I meet. I usually have my guard up, reinforced and sky-high. Rock and ice.

But Gwen has blasted right through.

Eventually she stops, her shoulders held tall but soft. Then her lashes flutter open, and those unusual irises focus on me.

"Were you watching me the whole time?"

I feel my cheeks flush, but what's the point in denying it? She could probably tell anyway.

"Yes."

She searches my face before tilting her head. "And?"

I swallow, mind racing with all the different ways I could answer that question. Commenting on how fucking incredible her ass looked when she was on all fours is definitely creepy and off the table, so I shrug and tell her something else that's true. "I knew you'd be good at your job. The snowflake thing almost worked."

She brightens, like a ray of sunshine in the middle of a dark winter night. Her entire body lifts with the simple compliment, and she clasps her hands together in front of her chest. "Yeah?"

I give her a firm, reassuring nod, wanting to leave no doubt in her mind as to the sincerity of my comment. "Absolutely."

Her face breaks into the most heartrending smile.

And all it does is make me want to pay her more compliments.

CHAPTER 4

Gwen

It's eerily quiet in the airport, the lights dimmed to a soft glow. We've walked the entire terminal, read every placard detailing the area's history, and admired every photo of Vancouver from over a century ago. Now, we've come across a special, limited-time display of tiny Disney figurines.

"Oh, look at this Minnie Mouse!" I point at the glass. "She's doing yoga."

Bash comes close, his thick shoulder brushing against mine as he bends at the hips to inspect the one I'm referring to. The unexpected contact makes my heart skip a beat.

"I think she's just sitting cross-legged."

The low gravel of his voice doesn't help my heart rate either, and I realize that, for being an absolute stranger, I like him far more than I have any right to.

"No, she's in Seated Pose or Easy Pose," I say with a roll of my eyes, even though I'm amused. His surliness doesn't put me off. Strangely, it charms me. "Like we just were."

"First, that pose wasn't easy. I think I dislocated my hip." I try not to smirk. I did sneak a peek at him all folded up, looking stiff as hell. The man is strung *tight*. "Second, these figurines are probably as old as me. I promise you no one was making figurines of Minnie Mouse doing yoga back then."

I give a solemn nod, still staring ahead at yoga Minnie. "Right. In the olden days."

That gets me a snort. "Something like that."

"How old *are* you, then? Like, do you just look phenomenal for someone born in 1928? Because the sign says that's when they were created."

His beleaguered sigh as he straightens has me clamping my lips down tight to cover my amusement. I turn to face him, watching his eyes scan my face. He looks at me with such intensity that I almost squirm under his attention.

"I'm thirty-nine."

He slides his hands into the pockets of his jeans, as though going through the motions of acting casual when facing each other in this deserted hallway feels…not casual at all.

"Well, color me relieved. If you were born in 1928, you'd be altogether too old for me."

He doesn't react to the quip. Instead, he just keeps staring me down.

"How old are you, Gwen?" His dark eyes spark, and the question drips with—I don't know what to call it. Promise? Knowing? He has to know I'm younger, but I'm also not so young that I'm afraid to take him by the hand and drag him out of the bar just to get him alone.

So I don't slink away. I just tilt my head and let my eyes flit down to the grim line of his mouth. "I'm twenty-seven, Bash."

He says nothing.

I swear I can see the gears turning in his head, but I don't want him to use this as a reason to leave me tonight. I'm enjoying his company too much.

So I forge ahead before he can overthink it. "Glad we cleared that up. Let's go." I take his hand again and turn away as I do. His arm is rigid, and he resists, but a quick glance over my shoulder has him softening.

And following.

"Aren't you tired?" he asks, not dropping my hand this time.

"Sure." I shrug. "But tired is kind of relative. I have been more tired. And there are worse things to be than tired. I'll let my body rest tomorrow. Tonight, we make memories."

"Like debating whether Minnie Mouse does yoga?"

My eyes latch on to the moving sidewalk before us. It's going the wrong direction for the way we're headed. But I don't let that deter me. I hop on anyway, the movement constantly pushing me back toward him.

"No. Like drinking bad margaritas, meditating in Terminal B, and racing on the moving walkway."

"Have you never walked on one of those bef—"

I turn so I'm walking in reverse, facing him, and grin. "It's just an added challenge."

He stops, those thick, dark brows drawing together. "That sounds like a bad idea."

I drop my tote bag on the ground beside me and lift a hand to my ear. "Sorry, what was that? Did you say that you're scared?"

"Gwen."

"Don't Gwen me."

A dimple on his right cheek pops up. "Gwenyth?"

"Nope." I continue taking slow steps back toward the conveyor.

"Gwendolyn?"

I wink at him. "Nope. Sorry, that's first-date information."

He blinks. And blinks again. He looks so floored by what I've just said, I can't keep myself from smiling.

I'm about to turn from him, ready to face the walkway, but his words bring me up short.

"What are we calling tonight, then?"

Blood rushes in my ears. I expected him to grumble and balk at my teasing, but here he is, arms crossed, stance wide, calling me out.

I can hear the threads of hope in his voice, which brings heat to my cheeks.

"Oh, tonight? Tonight is just our meet-cute. It's the night we'll tell our kids about one day. Remember?"

He quirks a brow, and I realize how what I just said sounds given the context. Embarrassment hits me hard and fast. If my cheeks were warm before, they're downright boiling now. My entire face feels like lava.

God, he must think I'm totally nuts. Maybe he already has children. I could be lusting over a perfectly happy family man.

My eyes drop to his left hand. No wedding band.

"Respectively," I clarify quickly, pointing a finger back and forth between us. "Our respective children. Separately."

His expression remains unchanged.

Things are already awkward, so I add one more parting shot with a little shrug for good measure. "Or not."

His head bucks back as though I've hit him, and I revel in even the most subtle reaction. But not for long. Recovering quickly—and partly because I'm eager to put some space between us—I turn away and call out a rushed, "On-your-marks-get-set-go!"

Then I turn and take off.

For several seconds, I can only hear my own footfalls as I struggle against the opposing motion of the walkway. A small giggle spills from my lips. Because honestly, I'm being ridiculous, and I'm well aware of it.

This stoic, almost-forty-year-old man will not want to do the equivalent of trying to go up the down escalator.

But I don't let that stop me.

My arms pump as I work my way farther down. This is me. I still want to be silly sometimes. I love to explore. I like to look at the glass as half-full. Hell, I will happily make lemonade.

I've worked too hard in recent years at accepting and loving myself to let one random, grumpy guy in an airport make me second-guess who I am—

My thoughts come to a screeching halt. Because I hear it. And I *feel* it.

Heavy footfalls. The change in the air around me—it's warm, and it hums as he pulls closer.

I let out a loud, unladylike guffaw when I hear his breathing behind me. "Sorry, this must be hard for someone your age," I call back.

And for the first time, he laughs. It bursts from his throat like it's a relief to let it go.

It gives me the fucking giggles.

The end of the walkway is in sight, and I'm already out of breath, but laughing like this? All breathless and grinning like a loon? It takes me out. I slow down. Bash is close, and I know he's going to pass me and win.

But that's okay. He kind of seems like he could use a win today.

Ten feet from the end of the belt, I give up and drop my hands to my knees, doubling over. I prepare to eat his dust and get my laughter under control.

But he stops beside me, mimicking my position. The space is narrow enough that we end up shoulder to shoulder again. The ramp continues moving, slowly taking us backward, the odd laugh spilling from our lips between heavy breaths.

"Fuck, Gwen. You…" I peek over at him, and his eyes are trained on the belt below us as he shakes his head before settling on, "You have no idea how badly I needed this."

"What? To race some weird girl in the airport?"

He chuckles, and my spine tingles. "No. To blow off some steam."

I glance back down and nod. "Rough day?"

"Rough week."

"Those are the worst," I reply, curious but not feeling comfortable enough to ask him what happened. That seems bold, even for me.

Bash shakes his head. "Found out I have a kid I never knew about. Met him for the first time yesterday."

I stop breathing for a few seconds before pushing myself upright and groaning. The heartache in his voice is downright palpable, and I feel sick for a man I barely know. "Fuck meee. And you just let me fumble around all over the place with that awkward joke about kids?"

Bash straightens, and I'm struck by his height. Not only does he have that heavy set to his shoulders that comes from hours of manual labor, but he's also got to be well over six feet.

"Different things." He shrugs, the ghost of a smile still dancing over his lips. "He's twenty-four."

I blink. "Oh shit."

"Yeah." He grimaces. "Oh shit."

"Listen, I'm no mathematician, but that means you were—"

"Fifteen and in high school? Yeah. Haven't seen her in decades, but I ran into her brother at a fundraiser, and he let it slip."

"And she never told you? That's just…"

Some evil bullshit is what I want to say. I'm not even living the story, and it's a punch to the gut. But looking at his face makes it so much worse. I see it now. He's not just tired and grumpy.

He's grieving.

He sniffs and looks away. "We were both fifteen and clearly stupid. I was the kid from the wrong side of the tracks, and she was very much from the right side. It sounds like her family played a heavy-handed role in sending her to a private boarding school. They even moved to a different city. I remember that day like it was yesterday. I showed up for class and she was just gone. Broke my fucking heart."

I want to say that she's known for twenty-four years, which is plenty of time to make it right. But I don't. I settle on a weak "I'm so sorry."

His gaze slides over to mine. "What's that saying again? *When life gives you lemons?*"

I tap a finger against my lips. "Hmm, I'm not familiar with that one. The only one I know is *When life gives you limes…*"

His lips turn up in a faint smile as he nudges his shoulder against mine. Sensing we're nearing the end of our ride, we both turn to face the spot where we dropped our bags. There's something ominous about it. It feels like we've been living in a happy little bubble and the moment we step off this conveyor, reality will come crashing back down on us.

In silence, we draw nearer. And I find myself counting down.

Three.

Two.

One.

With a heavy swallow, we step onto solid ground. We reach for our bags, pulling ourselves back together after what feels like a shared moment of insanity. When I've righted myself, I finally look over at Bash. He's staring at his watch. "I've only got about an hour," he says.

"Is that all?" The words come out softer than I intend. It seems like the night went by in a flash, and a heavy weight settles in my gut over the impending cutoff.

I don't want tonight to be over yet.

"Yes. Only an hour to ask for your number."

My eyes snap to his, red-rimmed and clearly tired. "Me playing chase on the moving walkway didn't scare you off?"

He shoves a hand into his pocket and pulls his phone out, hitting me with a gravelly "Not at all."

I feel like a teenager again—that hot, fluttery feeling unfurling in my chest because a cute boy just asked me for my number. But this is so much better because he's a hot *man*. With big fucking hands and a deep fucking voice.

"There's no accounting for taste," I volley, falling back on self-deprecation because there's this little mean, vain part inside me that still feels unworthy of this kind of attention.

You're too big.

You talk too much.

Your optimism is obnoxious.

They're hard insecurities to shake, especially when they were planted so young, reinforced by the words I grew up hearing. But I've come to embrace these parts of myself. Most days, I believe they are some of my best qualities. Other days, I hear my dad's voice in my head. And I hate it.

"Gwen. Your number." Bash watches me carefully, phone in his hand, ready to input my contact information.

I give my head a shake and stop coming up with reasons I might not be worthy of his attention. "555-555-7699."

He nods along, inputting the numbers with an excruciating level of focus. The broad pad of his index finger types on the screen as he repeats the numbers back to himself.

It's adorable.

"Last name?"

I flush. Last names feel serious. And yet, there is something serious about what happened tonight. A connection. It's hard for me to wrap my head around the fact that I've met a lot of people in my life but they don't get under my skin the way Sebastian Rousseau has.

It's borderline unnerving. It has my sleep-deprived brain reaching for reasons why we shouldn't get our hopes up about meeting again.

"I'm kind of nomadic and move around a lot. I don't have a home base."

It's almost easier this way, to bow out gracefully. We could part ways and leave this one dreamy night in the past. A perfect memory, untarnished by any outside forces.

He just shrugs, clearly not feeling the same. So sure. So direct. "I don't care. I'll figure it out. I want to see you again."

I giggle, the punch-drunk feeling of having pulled an all-nighter settling in to accompany my giddiness over this entire situation.

All I can offer him is a nod and a "Same." Because what else does a girl say to that?

We spend the next hour wandering the terminal, drinking coffee—the coffee shops now blessedly open—to keep ourselves from fading. He tells me about his contracting business, and I tell him about my dream of opening a yoga studio one day. All the while, I do my best to ignore the growing sense of dread in my gut.

Eventually our clock runs out.

He boards his flight, and as I watch him leave, I see the way he glances back over his shoulder, brows drawn low as he searches for me. A thrill races down my spine at the stoic parting wave he gives me.

And I tell myself it's just goodbye for now and not forever.

Because the world works in mysterious ways, and it would never squander a meet-cute like ours.

CHAPTER 5

Bash

Bash: Hey. It's Bash.
Bash: From the airport.

I'm not a big texter. But I text Gwen as soon as I land.

Fifteen years ago, I might not have. Now, I'm too fucking old to play mind games. I'm interested. Simple as that.

I don't know her last name. Or if she lives in Toronto or was just visiting. I only know that she was on her way back from a yoga retreat in Mexico and that I had more fun with her than I have with anyone in a very long time.

And I want to do it again sometime. Hell, we could just meet and hang out in another airport for all I care.

With that thought in my head, I drive the three hours to Rose Hill, trudge through the door of my custom lakefront home, fall face-first into my king-size bed, and drift off into a dead, dreamless sleep.

When I wake up, the first thing I do is reach for my phone. When I see a text notification, I sit up, leaning against the head of my bed frame, and take a deep breath before sliding it open.

> **West:** When are you back? We suck at bowling without you. We need our daddy back.

A disappointed sigh rushes over my lips. Weston Belmont is one of my closest friends, and even though I pretend to be irritated by him, I'm actually pretty attached to the guy.

Despite the fact that he's taken to jokingly calling me *daddy*.

I suppose that's how I ended up on a bowling team with him. Leave it to West to turn a casual night of beers and bowling between a few friends into a recurring event that requires a lot more commitment than I wanted to offer.

But he's a persuasive motherfucker. So here I am. Committed to what has become a dads' night out bowling team ever since I told the guys about my surprise son—Tripp Coleman.

Our other member is Clyde or, as everyone refers to him, Crazy Clyde. It's a nickname he's embraced with gusto. Sometimes I think he just says wild shit to get people talking, to live up to the name.

Either way, he's another stray I've adopted along the way.

A loner with no family who—for as bonkers as he is—has become something of a father figure to me. Or a paradoxical boomer child, depending on the day.

We're a ragtag crew of three who are constantly on the hunt for a fourth. West brings in random people to try on for size, but they never make the cut. I usually have to tell him afterward how much I hate them and why.

One guy ate hot wings and stuffed his fingers into the bowling ball without washing them and I walked out mid-game to show my displeasure. Another one smiled too much. Like constantly. It was unnatural and creepy, so he had to go.

I'm pretty sure Clyde scared off the others with his zany conspiracy theories.

Aside from those two clowns, my life is simple. Fight fires all summer, pick up contractor jobs in the winter to keep myself busy. Plus, I enjoy working with my hands, so it keeps me sane.

Or at least it keeps me distracted from spending too much time in my head.

Bash: I will be there on Thursday.
West: Cool. How'd it go with Tripp?

How did it go with Tripp?

It went? It was weird? It felt like an out-of-body experience to be faced with a grown man who is supposedly my son. Hell, he looks enough like me that the DNA test is probably entirely unnecessary.

He looks like me, if I were a twenty-four-year-old NHL

star who grew up in the lap of luxury. And his mom? She can barely look at me at all.

If I wasn't so furious with her, I'd feel bad for her.

But I am, in fact, furious. I hate to admit it, but I'm *bitter*. I've spent the better part of my adulthood wanting to be a father. I'm sure I wouldn't have been a good parent at fifteen, but I'd have shown up the best way I knew how. And considering my dad went to the grocery store when I was nine years old and never came back, there's no doubt in my mind that I would have been better than nothing.

But Cecilia and her family decided it was better if I wasn't around at all.

And that stings like hell.

They robbed me of the opportunity. Now I'm left feeling like I missed out on something I never even knew was within reach. And it's only made worse by the fact that I've wanted a family of my own. That yearning cost me my marriage. I wanted something she didn't. So we parted ways, and I've been too shit-scared to try again.

But now I'm faced with what I wanted but not at all in the way I expected it.

So how did it go with Tripp? We met in Vancouver so I could watch him play a game. We had dinner and exchanged contact information. It was nice enough…but the fact remains that I'm just a stranger to him.

Still, I left there with a determination to be more. I missed out on twenty-four years, but I get to be around for the next twenty-four. I told him I could be whatever he wanted me to be but that I'd love to be part of his life.

He'd seemed amenable to that, so we shook hands and left it there.

It was equal parts awkward and incredible all at once.

It left me feeling…I don't know. I'm not sure how I'm supposed to feel. Deep down, I'm worried. He comes from so much—what could I possibly have to offer him? Especially when he already has a man who's been a father to him.

The entire week has left me feeling low.

Until Gwen sat her fine ass in the chair across from me and made herself at home.

She made me feel better.

But now, her lack of response gnaws at me, leaving a pit in my stomach and a sour mood I can't seem to shake.

I don't feel like hashing this out with West right now. I'm not ready for his brand of unshakable positivity. So I text him back, and I lie.

Bash: It was the best.

CHAPTER 6

Bash

Bash: Hey, Gwen. It's Bash. We drank shitty margaritas together two weeks ago. I sent a text when I got home, but I don't think it went through.

EIGHT MONTHS LATER...

I EYE GWEN'S CONTACT IN MY PHONE AS I SIT AT THE CALGARY airport. It's been eight months since that freak November snowstorm. Thirty-two weeks since I sent the first text to her. Thirty weeks since I sent that follow-up. And I still come back to our very one-sided chat.

I look over the messages for what feels like the millionth time. All marked as *delivered*.

Since she didn't respond to either, sending another now

just seems pathetic. The answer is probably to read between the lines. And with the way my life has been turned upside down in the last year, I'm not sure I need to volunteer myself for a full-on rejection. I'm already grappling with heavy feelings of inadequacy.

Making a hot twenty-seven-year-old spell out that she's avoiding me might just be my killing blow.

So I decide to keep it simple—do my mental health a favor. She ghosted me, and I don't need to be the creepy dude who can't let it go.

Simple.

Still, it stings.

I put my phone away and stare at the moving walkway at the end of the terminal.

And I think of her.

I think of that night.

She wasn't wrong about it becoming a core memory. I should be focused on heading to my newfound son's birthday party but, fuck, if she's not perfectly burned into my mind.

"Cecilia." I force my lips into a smile, but I'm sure it looks more like a grimace. I'm trying not to hate the woman standing in front of me.

But it's fucking hard.

Which is probably why my "nice to see you" sounds like code for *you're a piece of shit*. This is the second time I've seen her, and she's been nothing but cool, distant, and awkward.

Not an explanation or an apology as far as the eye can see.

Her lips are pursed, and it feels like she's looking everywhere but *at* me. Beyond me to the road, down at the rosebush beside her front door.

Coward.

"Yes, well…" Her hand floats up to her throat, a diamond the size of a large grape adorning her finger. "You know, Tripp is a good boy. He wanted you here. And what the birthday boy wants, the birthday boy gets." She smiles, but it's pinched, like she finds the sight of me distasteful.

I glare back at her, running my tongue over my teeth. At least we have that in common. Because I find the sight of her distasteful too. I thought that this whole thing might feel easier today, but it doesn't. I've had *months* to stew in my bitterness. It's thick in my chest and tight in my jaw.

I don't know how a person is supposed to feel after finding out they have an adult son whose existence was intentionally kept from them.

Some parts of me are happy. I'm trying, and to his credit, Tripp is trying too. As in, we exchange the odd text. Usually, it's me congratulating him on his game—because I watch all of them now. Hell, I even bought a jersey with his name on it. I guess I'm a fan now. Even if I'm not a fan of his mother.

A bigger part of me feels paralyzed by the injustice of it. The missed years. The missed opportunities. I suppose some people might take this total fiasco and make margaritas or what-the-fuck-ever. But me?

I've spent the last several months torturing myself over

it. Squeezing that lime juice right into my damn eyes like some sort of masochist.

Because I want so much more. I want all the birthdays I missed. I want the first steps back. High school graduation. His NHL draft—the one I looked up on the internet, only to watch his name be called and see him hugging his mom and stepdad. It was the happiest of moments.

And I was nowhere to be seen.

"Okay, well, if this meet and greet from hell is over, I'm just gonna…" I point over her shoulder and into the palatial house, where music and chatter filter toward us.

Cecilia's eyes narrow, her mouth popping open as though she's about to say something. But before she can, her husband, a tall, broad man with salt-and-pepper hair and a kind, dopey face, rounds the corner. His tucked-in powder-blue collared shirt reveals a slightly thick midsection over his khaki trousers. He reminds me of an aged, all-state quarterback who still meets up with teammates to relive their play-by-plays.

The grin he hits me with is genuine, though.

I've only met Edward once before, and just like then, the guy is impossible to hate.

"Sebastian!" His deep voice booms across the foyer, and his arms go wide as he greets me with a genuine excitement that his wife couldn't even pretend to muster. "Get in here. What are you doing, Ceci? Let the man in."

She steps away as Edward reaches forward to shake my hand. "Great to have you here," he says, following up with a firm handshake.

"Edward. Beautiful home. Thank you for having me. But please, call me Bash."

He laughs, stepping back and gesturing me through. "Well, in that case, call me Eddie. I mean, hell, we're all family here."

From the corner of my eye, I see Cecilia flinch. Then she covers for it by holding her willowy frame tall and tense.

For a flash, I feel a pang of sympathy for her. I'm certain this is not how she envisioned her son's twenty-fifth birthday party.

But then, she did this to herself. And as much as I like to consider myself a good person, I'm not the soft, doting type. If she needs someone to feel bad for her, that person can be Eddie.

He leads me through the house, spouting off about Tripp's statistics from last season and practically overflowing with pride. And why shouldn't he? He raised Tripp as his own. Tripp plays with Eddie's last name on his jersey.

He's his dad.

"Tripp will be so pleased you're here. And everyone is just out back…" Eddie carries on enthusiastically, going through everyone else who is in attendance as though he thinks I'll know who he's talking about.

I'm hit with the stomach-sinking realization that I'm an interloper here. The scruffy, surly guy who lives in the mountains, who works two jobs and has no family. If simply driving through the neighborhood in West Vancouver made me feel out of place, actually walking through their massive, modern home is a flashing sign telling me I don't belong.

I never did. Even at fifteen, I didn't fit—and Cecilia's parents knew it.

My molars grind, and I suck in a deep breath, lifting my shoulders. I might not be one of *them*, but I'm proud of who I am, and I'm not in the habit of letting ridiculously rich people make me feel small.

So I move through the open sliding doors onto the back deck with my head held high. Tripp spots us and rises to greet me. "I'll leave you to it," Eddie says before making his exit.

Then my eyes are back on my son.

He may not look like Eddie, but the mannerisms are all his. The copper tinge to his hair and the heart shape to his face are all Cecilia. I think the dark eyes might come from me, but it's hard to say when, in so many ways, he feels like a perfect stranger.

"Bash, hey!" We start off with a handshake, then he pulls me into a hug. Hard slaps land on my back, and the affection in his greeting surprises me. He's always been friendly enough, but I wouldn't call our interactions warm. More stiff than anything. "So glad you could make it."

He reeks of gin and cologne, so I wait until I step away to take a breath of fresh ocean air.

Tripp shifts to the side, and the view beyond him unfurls. Just over his shoulder, I can see the rocky, wild coastline that graces this neighborhood's shores.

My gaze scans the horizon, where the humid August air shimmers in undulating waves above the water. Farther up the grass, a catering station stands next to a large white tent, complete with a checkerboard floor, and then—

Beautiful doe eyes, more lavender than blue. Eyes I haven't seen in eight months.

All the air leaves my lungs in one rough exhale. Because I'd know those eyes anywhere. I've dreamed of them.

I stand frozen, heart racing as quickly as my mind as I soak in the woman before me.

She looks just as shocked as I am.

What are the chances?

Tripp smiles like a politician and gestures toward her with a look of fondness on his face. "Bash, I'd like you to meet my girlfriend, Gwen. Gwen Dawson."

The word *girlfriend* falls through me, landing hard and heavy in my gut.

Yeah.

What are the fucking chances?

CHAPTER 7

Gwen

Blindsided.

That's what I am.

Tripp nudges me with his elbow. "Babe, this is my biological dad. Sebastian."

Sebastian.

The full name feels too formal for the night we shared. A night I think about more often than I should. A night during which we barely touched, and yet it rivals the intimacy of any night I've ever spent with a man.

I stare back at Bash, his hawkish, dark eyes slicing through me from beneath heavy, furrowed brows.

My stomach is in knots. My pulse is in my throat. My heart falls somewhere down near my feet. Words fail me.

In a desperate attempt to make this introduction look a hell of a lot less awkward than it really is, I wipe one sweaty palm on my silky kaftan dress before outstretching it toward Bash.

His gaze flits down to it, and his expression tells me he'd rather do anything but shake my hand.

And he does.

He shoves his fists into his dark-wash jeans and hits me with the world's tightest smile. "Nice to meet you, Gwen."

Awkwardness be damned, I guess.

It feels like someone just slapped me. He shows no signs of recognizing me, and the warm rasp I remember in his voice is notably absent. His body language is as closed off as a fucking prison cell. He doesn't even tell me to call him Bash. It appears he's relegated me to *Sebastian* terms.

Which honestly pisses me off. Ire surges through me as the shock of the moment wanes.

"Sure is," I spit out, letting a little venom seep into my voice.

Because how dare he?

There's a kind way to let a girl down, and it isn't by letting her constantly check her phone like a desperate teenager hoping that the cute boy she's obsessed with might text her.

For *months*.

I stayed positive and "glass half-full" and all those things I pride myself on being while I waited for him to reach out.

And he didn't.

Even a simple *I had a wonderful time with you, but it's best we go our separate ways* would have sufficed. I'm a big girl—I could have dealt with that kind of rejection.

But this? Tripp's dad? The universe really decided to fuck me on this one.

"I'm gonna go make some introductions. You good if I

leave you here?" Tripp tosses an arm over my shoulder, tugging me toward him in a side hug before dropping a casual kiss on my hair. But all I can do is watch Bash. Slashes of heat appear on his cheeks as his gaze follows his son. He flinches when Tripp kisses me, then he turns his head away from us.

I try to will the tension out of my shoulders. I don't want Tripp to notice how uncomfortable I am. It's not as though I've done anything wrong, but explaining that night to him? Any explanation would seem trite—it wouldn't do it justice.

"Of course." I nod quickly, a light tremor in my voice.

Bash's brow lifts, and I see him peek at me out of the corner of my eye. Tripp doesn't notice my discomfort at all. Instead, he just grips Bash's shoulder and leads him away into the crowd.

To the outside observer, it would appear that I'm staring at the guy I showed up here with.

But they would be wrong.

I'm staring at his dad.

I flit through the party, making small talk with strangers whose names I won't remember when I wake up tomorrow morning.

It's beyond painful. This couldn't be further from my scene if it tried. I'm wearing a thrifted silk dress with no label, while across the lawn, there is literally a woman in a Chanel pencil skirt and matching blazer. Her heels sink in the grass with each step, and I watch her adjust her stride, walking on her tiptoes to make it look like the ground isn't swallowing her feet.

Everything about these people and this place is an illusion.

Luckily, my leather slides do me just fine as I make my way toward an empty cocktail table on the lawn. It's covered in a stretchy, pale-blue tablecloth, which makes it feel like a party for a little boy, not a grown professional athlete. But then, the way his mom treats him is downright childlike. Like she shot him out of her vagina to songbirds chirping, a double rainbow arching across the sky, as the hospital staff erupted into a celebratory flash mob dance.

Before today I didn't realize that Tripp is a full-fledged mama's boy. And not in the way that means he respects and speaks highly of her. No. Instead he borderline reverts to being a little boy around her.

Suffice it to say, it's been a weird day. I chuckle dryly as I sit, taking in the party around me. There must be over a hundred people here, and I feel like a total outsider. But it doesn't bother me. I take it in all the same. I love to travel, to learn and experience different cultures.

And this is just that. *A cultural experience.*

Tripp and I have been casually seeing each other for a few months. We met when I taught yoga and mindfulness classes for his team during the playoffs. He was charming and determined and seemed like a fun time. He asked me out after every class, and I finally caved on the fifth attempt and said yes.

During the season, he was frequently on the road, and

that worked fine for me. I don't want or need to spend every waking hour with him. I've always had a wanderer's spirit, moving from city to city and filling in at different studios. Settling down is low on my to-do list, and Tripp seemed like a perfectly passable Mr. Right Now.

But now the season has ended, and he's around. A lot. Possibly too much for my taste.

This always happens to me. I meet someone who seems great, and then they slowly start to annoy me. They get attached more quickly than I do, and I end up feeling locked in, tied down, *stuck*.

I start envisioning myself as my mother, trapped in a house with her babies and no possibilities on the horizon.

And I run.

At twenty-seven years old, I have figured out this much out about myself. I know it's not healthy, but I own it all the same. Which is why I've been clear with Tripp about where we stand. He knows I have no intention of staying in Vancouver, that I'm here for a good time, not a long time.

So the way he's trotting me out and introducing me to everyone as his girlfriend feels strangely performative.

Before today, I hadn't met his parents, and truthfully, there's been nothing relationship-like about our setup. Him introducing me as his fuck buddy would be a lot more accurate. But instead, he picked me up in his expensive sports car with a laundry list of rules about how to act around his parents.

It would seem that, with the Colemans, perception reigns supreme.

Especially considering he told me his biological dad was a deadbeat who left his mom when he found out she was pregnant.

I glance toward the sprawling house to see Tripp and Bash walking back in my direction. Side by side, I can see the similarities.

It makes me think of that night. My shoulder pressed against Bash's, gliding backward on the motorized walkway as he recounted the story of the child he never knew existed. Now that story sours my stomach. Because despite all my hurt feelings around Bash…I know what I saw that night in the airport. The grief that touched every square inch of his body.

And the sanitized storyline Tripp fed me is too damn convenient. Turning Bash into the villain makes the Colemans look mature and gracious, downright hospitable to even welcome him into their home. I know that was my first thought when Tripp told me his biological dad was coming today. And now he's parading him around, introducing him to people and acting like including him makes Tripp worthy of nomination for sainthood.

It's bizarre. It's cruel. And it's a *lie*.

It's a lie that shines a different light on Tripp Coleman— and a bad one. A small part of me wonders if he even knows the real story or if he's been lied to as well. There's something off about the way he acts around his mom, I just can't quite put my finger on it.

I'd call him out on it here and now, but I think it would gut Bash to hear it. So I decide to bite my tongue and save it for later.

A tray full of champagne passes by, and I swipe one with a quiet "Thank you."

The caterer smiles back with a subtle nod. She looks nice. And normal. I'm probably better suited to hanging out with her and her colleagues behind the tent.

Instead, I'm stuck pretending I belong in this viper pit. What I thought was going to be a fun party has devolved into an awkward, secret-fueled, rich-person alternate universe.

I toss back a mouthful of chilled champagne just as the two men approach.

Am I using alcohol as a coping mechanism today? Yes.

Do I care? No.

My heart races, and my blood feels sluggish in my veins as I take another drink, my gaze darting toward the ocean. I'd rather be sitting on the shore, meditating. Feet in the sand, finding some semblance of solid ground.

Earlier, when I tried to head down there, Tripp specified it would be more "appropriate" to keep my shoes on, as though I planned to go skinny-dipping in front of his parents' friends.

That should have been my first clue from the universe that today was destined to go sideways.

To anyone else, it might seem like nothing happened between Bash and me. Like I'm making a mountain out of a molehill by feeling as off-kilter as I do.

But for me? That night? Something happened.

I can't put my finger on it, and god knows I've spent many a late night staring at the ceiling, trying to figure out why I haven't been able to shake his memory.

Maybe it was the way he looked at me or the way he listened to me. Hell, it could have been the way we laughed together. Or maybe it was the spark I felt when his hand enveloped mine. I've wondered if it was one of those moments in the universe where all the stars align—where every little choice made in life led us to that airport on that exact night.

Maybe it was just a little bit of magic. Inexplicable and undeniable all at once.

What I do know for sure is that it's been eight months, and I still think about Sebastian Rousseau every damn day.

I gnaw on the inside of my cheek as they approach the table. Bash looks stoic, his jaw clenched so tight it's going to be sore tomorrow from all the teeth-grinding he's doing. Meanwhile, Tripp appears affable and polished as the sun glints a rusty tone off his auburn hair.

"Hey, babe, how you doin'?"

I smile, but it's forced. "Great. I'm great."

Except I'm not. Bash won't even look my way. His gaze stays locked on the water.

The awkwardness gnaws at me. He's clearly *pissed*.

Anxiety swirls and the sinking realization that he might be angry over my relationship with Tripp hits hard and fast.

Another caterer passes by, drawing my gaze away from him. "Arancini?" she asks, holding out a tray of bite-size golden fried spheres.

Tripp and Bash pass, but I jump at the opportunity. "Hell yes," I say as I reach for a cocktail napkin. Partly because I'm hungry, and partly because I figure if my mouth is full, it will give me something to do and possibly spare me from the awkward lie of a conversation that's about to occur right in front of me.

I take one, then tip my head, considering. They're small, so I select another and offer the girl a friendly smile as she departs.

Tripp leans close and drops another casual kiss on my hair with a light chuckle. "Easy, girl. Don't eat too much."

Easy, girl?

I pause, my brows furrowing as I stare down at the two bite-size pieces of food on the napkin in my hand, wondering if I misheard my "boyfriend."

Did he really just tell me not to eat too much?

"The fuck did you just say to her?" Bash's voice is cold as ice from across the table.

I can't bring myself to face him, but I do look up, eyes tracing Tripp's svelte physique as I make my way up to his face.

"All in good fun, right, babe?" He winks at me, like I'm in on his joke, and turns his attention to his dad, who is staring daggers at him.

"No. Not in good fun," Bash says. "That was plain rude."

Tripp scoffs and waves him off. "It was a joke. I just meant save some room for dinner. Don't make it into something else."

I shift away from Tripp, not liking the version of him that comes out to play around his family.

It *was* rude. And manipulative. An unwelcome commentary on what and how much I'm eating disguised as a joke—a tactic my dad employed masterfully when I was younger.

"Hilarious," I say sarcastically before popping one ball of rice into my mouth. "A real knee-slapper, *babe*."

Tripp winces, and I can see the apology in his eyes. I shake my head subtly back at him. If today has proven anything, it's that he acts like an asshole around his family.

It's like I'm dating Dr. Jekyll—and Mr. Hyde has just come out to play.

He says nothing, so I give him a thumbs-up before lifting the second one in a salute. "Cheers, boys." I stand and add, "I'll be back. Gonna go see what other snacks I can track down to fill up on."

As I depart, their staccato murmurs trail behind me, but the hum of the surrounding party swallows any words I might be able to make out. What I can tell is that, for the first time today, Bash is pissed *at* Tripp rather than just in general.

I finish chewing the arancini, but I don't taste it. And I don't bother looking for more snacks. It feels like every pair of eyes here is trained on me—the curvy, hippie chick Cecilia's golden boy randomly brought home.

I slip into the house and make a beeline for one of the many bathrooms on the main floor. It's a small powder room and not the closest one to the backyard, so I'm hoping it's a private spot to hide out for a few minutes. Once inside, I shut the door behind me, lean back against it, and drop my chin to my chest, letting out a heavy sigh.

"Fuck me," I mutter quietly, a disbelieving laugh spilling from my lips.

But the vibration of a knock, followed by a deep voice

that makes my stomach flip over on itself, cuts my amusement short.

"Gwen? Open up."

Bash chooses *now* to follow through? Infuriating. He's got no business.

"I don't think that would be very appropriate" is what I say back.

But Bash isn't deterred. "Too bad. I'm coming in." The weight of him pushes on the door, like he thinks he's just going to blast his way in here or something.

Not wanting to cause a scene, I step away and turn the handle. "What the hell, Bash? Someone is going to see and—"

He steps in with authority, crowding me into the small room, before spinning and locking the door.

"What are you doing here?" he asks quietly, still not turning to face me. His broad shoulders heave as he breathes.

He knows damn well what I'm doing here. "I could ask you the same thing."

"Visiting my son for his birthday. And you knew about that." He whirls around, accusation flaring in his eyes as his index finger jabs the air in front of me. "You knew I'd just found out about my son. We were in the Vancouver airport for crying out loud. He told you about me, and you thought, what? That it would be funny to ignore me and date him instead?"

My jaw drops. "Excuse me?"

"You heard me, Gwen. What kind of sick joke are you playing?"

Bash is riled up—his chest rising and falling, his hands shaking—but as furious as he seems with me, I don't feel threatened at all. No, I press my shoulders back, cross my arms, and square off, meeting his blazing gaze with my own.

But as I stand my ground, I try not to slip down the rabbit hole where I fixate on our night in the airport. A safe place I like to sink into when I feel like torturing myself.

"I should ask you the same thing. You didn't care enough to contact me, but now you're going to stomp around all mad because I'm dating your son?"

His jaw works. "Are you—?" He stops and averts his gaze from me, shaking his head tightly. "Are you fucking kidding me?"

His look of disbelief, as though he's offended, washes over me, leaving me chilled.

"No," I whisper, the sinking feeling that something is very, very wrong suffusing my body.

"No, you know what? Here." He pulls out his phone and jabs the screen with his finger like he's trying to break it. Then he hands it to me. "*You* ghosted *me*. So don't bother playing dumb. I can handle the rejection but not being treated like I'm an idiot."

I stare at the screen, showing a few texts sent a couple of weeks apart. Delivered but never responded to by me. A growing sensation of panic takes root in my gut.

"I never got these."

I never got these. I never got these. I never got these.

He scoffs, and my eyes flit to the contact name. *Gwen Margaritas.*

Tears spring to my eyes as my shaking finger taps the icon. I read the number. 555–7669.

Six-six-*nine*.

"Honestly, you don't owe me anything," Bash rants on as realization settles in my bones. "But this is just fucking weird. And what's worse is he's out there disrespecting you to your face, and that makes me want to break something..."

Without thinking, I reach for him, my palm landing flat on his chest to still him. Every muscle in his body tenses. "Bash."

"What?" He spits the word, glaring down at my hand like my touch offends him. But he doesn't shake me off.

"The number is wrong." He blinks as I hold his phone out, open to the contact card. "It's six-nine-nine not six-six-nine."

His sharp inhale launches the small powder room into silence. You could hear a pin drop. I don't think either of us is breathing.

"I never got your messages, and if I had..." I swallow, trailing off and licking my lips. "I..." A frustrated groan lurches from my throat when I see the devastation etched on this man's face as he looks beyond me, staring blankly at the perfectly white wall.

He's gutted. I see it on his face. I feel it in his body.

Hell, I can feel it in my own. This is a cruel, cruel joke. Because I may not know him well, but I ache for him all the same. I would have chosen *him*.

I curl my fingers, gripping his cotton T-shirt—trying to get his attention, to drive my point home. "Bash, I waited months for you to contact me. If I'd gotten those messages... You have to know I would have responded."

My voice turns almost pleading as I repeat, "I would have."

His eyes scour my face as though checking for any signs of deceit. He looks how I feel.

Sucker punched.

He takes the phone from me, gaze boring into the incorrectly entered number. An understandable mistake for someone who stayed up all night.

I should have taken his number.

We should have planned better.

His lips twitch, and his Adam's apple bobs, but he doesn't look back up at me.

Instead, without another word, he turns, yanks the door open, and storms out.

I stand there, frozen—shaken. And that feeling is only made worse when, several seconds later, I hear a loud, "Fuck!" followed by what sounds an awful lot like a fist going through a wall.

CHAPTER 8

Bash

FOUR MONTHS LATER...

"Are you okay?" is the first thing I say when I pick up the phone.

Last night, I watched the TV with a boulder in my stomach as Tripp was helped off the ice. He hadn't rejoined the game, and I caved to instinct, sending him a message asking if he was okay.

It took him a day to respond, but he called. And that's something.

"Yeah. I cleared the protocol. They said I'm fine. A little banged up, but I'll be back on the ice tomorrow."

I listen to my son casually recount the fallout of a dirty cross-check he was on the receiving end of and grapple with an unfamiliar feeling. It's protective and enraged all at once. My stomach sinks and my ire rises.

Even though Tripp is an adult, I'd like to march down to the league headquarters and demand an explanation for how they can keep letting their top talent get rag-dolled like this.

"And is that goon going to be suspended?"

He chuckles now. The sound is a blend of amusement and disbelief over my demand for justice—like somehow he expected less from me.

"Probably. I can't imagine him not getting a game or two."

"I'd give him ten," I grumble, irrationally hating the other player.

Tripp laughs again now. "Missed your calling working in player safety, Bash."

I grumble at that, still not impressed. "I'll be checking the news" is all I respond with as I head up the mountain toward Clyde's property. "I'm going to lose reception right away here, but stay in touch, okay?"

A beat of silence passes between us. There's still something surreal about talking with him at all. He already has parents to keep in the loop, and I can't help but feel like it must be inconvenient to add another one to his busy schedule.

Still, he responds, "You bet." And it's only slightly awkward.

Progress. Or at least that's what I keep telling myself every time we have a remotely normal conversation.

The line goes dead right where I figured it would, and I drive up the winding gravel road worrying about Tripp *and* about Clyde. The thought of him living up here alone with his current health scares me.

I never know what I'll find when I pull up to the small log home. Today is no exception.

"Clyde, what the fuck are you doing?"

I watch as the older man hobbles around my black pickup truck, bending over stiffly to inspect god knows what. "Hold yer horses! Kids these days are so impatient." He shuffles across the snow, a smattering of wiry, white facial hair covering his stubborn jaw as he pants from the simple walk to my truck.

It's taking all my self-control to not get out and help him. But the thing about Clyde is that he doesn't want any help. Convincing him to give dialysis a go was the challenge of my life.

The passenger door opens, and he heaves his short body into the seat with a grunt. He's got a wiry but strong build, topped with deeply lined, leathery skin from years spent in the sun (and not believing in sunscreen). It's actually weird that his kidneys are the issue and not some type of skin cancer. But his doctors assured me that, aside from the kidneys, he's as healthy as a horse.

I'm worried about him, though. I can't help it. I've grown attached to the ornery old git.

"What are you waiting for? Me to die while you stare at me?" He crosses his arms and shoots me a petulant glare from beneath his trucker hat.

I just sigh. Anyone who thinks I'm hard to handle should try helping Clyde. "I'm waiting for you to put your seat belt on."

"Pfft. I don't need a seat belt. I grew up in cars that didn't even have 'em. And look at me." He holds his arms out wide. "I turned out fine."

My brows drop. "I think our definitions of *fine* might be different."

Clyde's lips twitch. "You're so crabby. Still stewing over the wall-punching incident?"

Now *that* is something I don't want to talk about. So I don't answer. I just glare at him. He doesn't reach for the seat belt, and I'm out of patience. "Fuck it," I mutter, shifting my truck into reverse and throwing a hand over the back of his seat to maneuver down the long driveway.

If he refuses to wear a seat belt, then it's not my hill to die on.

"Oh, so we're still pretending that didn't happen?"

My molars clamp down on each other. "I'm not pretending shit, Clyde. I'm just internally berating myself for even telling you about it."

Of course, the loud noise and the hole in the wall hadn't gone unnoticed. People came running—Cecilia included. So, of course, Tripp found out too.

Obviously, I couldn't admit why I'd had a completely out-of-character outburst.

Sorry, I've been obsessing over your girlfriend for months, blew my shot because, in the fog of pulling an all-nighter, I missed one fucking number, and now I'll never have her.

I had to cover and said my frustration over all the years I missed got the best of me. It wasn't a total lie. It was a frustrating position to be in, but it wasn't why I lost it and punched a wall.

Tripp looked shocked. His mom turned and walked away—which was just so fucking fitting. And Eddie tried to placate me.

I gave Tripp his gift and saw myself out with my tail between my legs and my dignity left in the powder room.

I headed straight to the airport to come home, thinking my luck couldn't get any worse. But I'd been wrong. Because there in the terminal, I ran into my ex-wife for the first time in three years.

She looked happy, healthy, remarried, and *very* pregnant.

Pregnant. Something she told me she never wanted to be. Something she clearly just didn't want to be *with me*.

Our greeting was brief and awkward, and once the shock of it passed, the run-in only pushed me deeper into the hole of despair that I'd already been calling home. Since then, I've done my best not to analyze how I feel about it. And I certainly haven't told anyone about it. Not even Clyde got that piece of information.

Instead, I may have fallen back on venting to Clyde about other things. About Tripp and Cecilia and the mess that comes with this whole new chapter in my life. And in my most distraught moment, I may have even divulged my misery over the Gwen bombshell.

Things may have been tenuous between Tripp and me after I put a hole in his mom's wall, but with persistence, we've managed to forge something of a connection. Even if we only talk about work.

Work is safe. Personal lives are dicey. Gwen is personal.

And I sure as shit don't want to talk to him about her. I don't even want to think about her.

With him.

Clyde's raspy voice interrupts my spiral. "You should call her."

Her.

I don't even need to ask who he's talking about. I scoff and roll my eyes as I pull the truck around to head down the back road.

Of course, Clyde has to live way the hell and gone—up the back side of the mountain. Something about fewer cameras tracking him. As if anyone wants to track Clyde and his daily puttering around his land.

"Absolutely not. That would be beyond inappropriate."

"According to who?"

"Everyone, Clyde. Everyone. Especially my son—her *boyfriend*—who I'm trying to be friendly with. I'm trying not to totally fuck everything up with him, so it might be best to steer clear of that ticking time bomb."

He sniffles, wiggling back against his seat. "Seems to me that little prick could use some fucking with."

I let out a heavy sigh, but I don't respond. The worst part is, I agree. Although I barely know Tripp, it's clear he has his mother's family's fingerprints all over him. He's not all bad, but the silver-spoon, image-obsessed genes are there. I could tell by the way he introduced me to people and the way they patted him on the back with that knowing look in their eyes.

Like he was downright heroic for welcoming me back into his life.

Truthfully, I didn't care. They can all say what they want about me. But teasing Gwen about her eating habits felt like a backhanded way of criticizing her body.

And that set me off.

Because her fucking *body*. I've dreamed of it. Of her. I know I shouldn't—especially now—but my subconscious is having a grand old time torturing me over what could have been. What I could have had.

Clyde yammers on about the jet trails in the air, spraying the mountain with chemicals, poisoning the water and the animals. He suspects this is the reason his kidneys are in such rough shape. *Chem trails*.

I let him talk. I could explain the science of what he's seeing, but he would just inform me I'm brainwashed and all too happy to believe every lie the government feeds me.

He comes by his moniker "Crazy Clyde" pretty honestly. If anyone were going to wear a tinfoil hat, it would be him. I find a comfort in it, though. The world around me can get turned upside down, and Clyde just…stays the same.

And who knows? Maybe he's right. Maybe I'm the idiot in this equation. Lately, it definitely feels like I am. The butt of every joke. The perpetual runner-up.

I pull up to the hospital's front entrance, and Clyde ambles out of the truck. Our routine is that he heads inside to get started and I find parking before wandering back in there to keep him company. It's a rhythm that wouldn't work in the summer months while I'm constantly away and fighting fires. But it does now.

Something about him doing it all alone, with no one in

his corner, doesn't sit right with me. So I continue to show up for him. I promised I would, and if there's one thing I am, it's loyal.

Before he can slam the door, he pauses and turns back. Watery, blue eyes narrow in on me, more perceptive than he has any right to be.

"I know you don't want to talk about it, but I'm going to anyway. So listen up. Just because you got horny at fifteen and that kid has half your DNA, it doesn't mean you need to let him treat you like shit while you constantly beat yourself up over his existence. And for what it's worth, when doomsday hits, he's not invited to my bunker. But you are."

Then, with a firm nod, he slams the door, leaving me feeling a mixture of amusement and—strangely—affection.

Bowling is a success.

For once.

And I suppose that's why West dragged us all to Rose Hill Reach to celebrate with "the girls" as he calls them. Rosie, Skylar, and Tabby have paired off with my teammates, which firmly makes me the seventh wheel of the friend group.

What started as a casual bowling night with West and Clyde has become a hell of a lot more organized. Over the past several months, we've picked up two more regular members—ones I don't hate. Ford, West's childhood best friend, and Rhys, a stray that our local bistro owner dropped off one day. Don't know much about the guy, but I like him a lot. He's not annoying, and he doesn't ask a bunch of questions. We've struck up a friendship that mostly consists of rolling our eyes at West and exchanging to-the-point text messages.

He reminds me of my friend Emmett, a professional bull rider on the WBRF circuit. He travels a lot, so we don't see each other often, but when we do, we just pick up where we left off.

Now and then, I get a message from him that says, "You still alive?" I give it a thumbs-up. And then, a couple of months later, I'll check the standings on the WBRF website and give him shit for not being number one. I get back a "fuck you," and I also give that a thumbs-up.

It's a solid relationship in my books. And much like Emmett, Rhys keeps things simple—something I like about him.

The guys walk in ahead of me but draw up short once they get inside because Doris, the owner of the Reach and longtime bartender, calls out, "Last question. It could be a tiebreaker since we have two teams with the same number of points right now. What is a group of unicorns called? A herd, a flock, a blessing, or a rainbow?"

Ford's brows knit together as he whispers, "What the fuck?"

"Oh, a blessing. Duh," West says with an eye roll.

I shoot him a scornful glare, which only makes him laugh.

"You're just mad you were thinking rainbow, aren't you?"

I sigh. "You're an idiot."

"A happy one," West volleys with a wink. He bounces on the balls of his feet like a boxer, craning his neck as though he'll be able to make out the answer from here. "I swear Skylar knows this one. She's got this. When did they start a trivia night? And why does it have to conflict with bowling? This would be so fun."

I cross my arms. "This would not be fun."

"Rosie would kill me if we started crashing girls' night," Ford adds.

West doesn't seem put off at all, though.

Shaking my head, I turn and take in the bar, gazing at the massive floor-to-ceiling windows facing the lake. If it weren't already dark, I'd be able to see the water, the mountains, and the floating dock that serves as a patio in the summer. Inside, the lights are warm and sporting goods plaster the walls for decoration. At each table, groups of four huddle together with a bunch of tiny pencils and small scraps of paper littered between them.

Beside me, Rhys stares at his wife, Tabitha. He's already an intense guy, but when his gaze lands on her, that intensity ratchets up even further. Just watching them makes me feel like I've stumbled into something private.

It hits me with a pang in my stomach. Makes me realize all the domestic milestones I've missed out on in my life. Not because I'm averse to them, but because I've been thwarted at every turn. To avoid any further rejection, I've turned my focus to my career, and now it's like half my life has gone *poof* before my eyes.

Watching these boys makes me feel like I've missed out

on something integral. Something I don't know that I'll ever have.

It's feeling like that ship has sailed.

"Who's that?" Ford asks, though I don't pay him any mind. He's new in town and still learning the ropes. I'm too lost in my head to pay much attention to what the guys are saying. Until one single sentence out of Rhys's mouth stops me in my tracks.

"That's my yoga instructor, Gwen."

My head snaps toward the table, and my gut drops to the floor beneath me. Because, sure as shit, there is Gwen from the airport.

Tripp's Gwen.

Sitting at a table with my friends.

In my town.

The guys rib Rhys about doing yoga, but I'm frozen, mind racing with why she might be here. What she's playing at. Why this keeps happening to me.

My heart races uncharacteristically. I'm too fucking old for this shit. My molars grind against each other as I watch Gwen stand to let Tabby back into the booth. As Gwen slides in beside her, the guys head over there, and my feet move to follow, even though I'm dreading facing her again. Especially after my meltdown at Tripp's party.

I stand stiffly as introductions are made, Gwen smiling graciously each time. That captivating twinkle in her eye takes me back to gazing at her over too-sweet margaritas. Then, the moment I've been bracing for arrives when Tabby gestures in my direction.

"Gwen, this is Bash."

My lips turn down as I realize I don't know how she'll spin this. How are we supposed to explain that we know each other? The last thing I need is the guys knowing this much detail about the cosmic joke that is my personal life. The silver lining is that Clyde isn't here tonight to spill the beans.

Gwen glances up at me from beneath a thick fringe of lashes, that plush mouth just slightly parted as she nervously tucks platinum hair behind her ear.

"Yeah, actually… We've met."

I can't tell if it's just me or if the entire bar suddenly becomes quieter.

Rosie, Ford's fiancée, goes wide-eyed, already sinking her teeth into the moment like a dog with a bone. She's a force to be reckoned with—I know because she's bargained with me, talking me into taking offseason contracting jobs I didn't need. If she starts sniffing around, it's only a matter of time before all the dirty details of my and Gwen's missed connection will come spilling out.

"You have?"

Yeah. Rosie sounds *far* too intrigued for this to be safe.

So I opt to jump ship.

"Yup," I reply brusquely, trying not to cave under the weight of everyone's stares while also trying not to gawk at Gwen. "Good to see you again. I'm going to head out. You kids have fun."

And with that, I flee.

Like the down-bad coward I am.

CHAPTER 9

Gwen

I watch Bash go with my heart in my throat and my eyes on his ass. I don't even think I'm being subtle about it. Which is probably why Rhys pipes up with, "Do you know him from yoga?"

From yoga. It takes me back to that night in the airport. The heat of his gaze on my body as I flowed through some of my favorite poses. I'd felt sensual—desired—in that moment, like I could sense his appreciation humming in the air around me. It's something I've never felt before.

So you could say that I know him from yoga, but it's become so much more than that. And saying that I know him because the universe keeps pushing us together would probably get me an eye roll.

Plus, I'd be lying if I said I didn't know he lived in this town. I'd tried looking him up online with little success. It was only when I read the job offer that a memory surfaced of Tripp telling me his dad lived in Rose Hill.

I got an email straight to my inbox asking me to take on a one-year contract in this exact town. But the studio's owner, Kira, didn't know that—she only knew she wanted to travel around Asia for a year and needed someone to fill in. The bonus was that her furnished apartment above the studio was rent free.

Apparently, a former employer recommended me, which is exactly how I keep getting gigs like this. I'm almost always ready for a new adventure, especially ones where I can work, learn, and save up to do some traveling of my own. What I love most is studying yoga abroad and learning from experts in other parts of the world. I'm on a mission to gather as much knowledge as possible, with the dream of one day opening my own studio.

So room, board, studio hours, and a consistent paycheck made for the perfect combination.

It all feels like something bigger is at play, so I settle on a quiet "No", ignore the lingering silence, and allow the conversation to flow in another direction.

The truth is, I knew Bash would be around at some point, but I didn't know when we'd run into each other.

When I came into Rose Hill Reach tonight, my plan was to sit at the bar, have a drink, and enjoy a little people-watching. But that was before I met Doris, the shrewd, overly direct bartender who owns this place. She talked to me for a while and then marched me over here to team up with Tabitha, Skylar, and Rosie. Like she just *knew* we'd hit it off.

And we did. We were a good trivia team. They were welcoming, fun, and down-to-earth. Rosie, outgoing. Tabitha, more sardonic. And Skylar—a country pop star known all over the world—quiet and completely grounded.

It was everything I love most about starting fresh. Meeting new people, trying new things. Yeah, so far, Rose Hill has been pretty damn perfect.

Cool women.

A stable job.

Mind-blowing mountain views.

The guy I met a year ago.

The one I haven't been able to forget. The one who still hasn't reached out to me, even with the correct number. The one who probably hates me now for having dated his son.

And that all stings just a little more than it should.

The small charm above the studio's front door jingles, pulling my attention from the computer screen. A short man with scraggly, white facial hair, a cap perched on his head, and a cane clutched in his hand enters the room. Knobby knees peek out between loose shorts and clunky snow boots, an odd choice considering snow hasn't fallen in the valley yet. My brows furrow, curiosity piqued.

"Hi. Welcome to Bliss Yoga."

He mumbles something indistinguishable under his breath.

"Can I help you?"

The man eyes the space carefully, taking in the pale-pink walls, wicker cabinetry, and neutral fabric draped artfully across the windows almost critically.

"Are you Gwen?"

My head tilts. "I am."

"Are you a yoga teacher?"

"I am."

He stomps his boots, nods, and points his cane toward me. "Good. You're the one I've heard about, then. I want to take a yoga class with you."

I hold my head high, careful not to preen too obviously. Stepping into someone else's established studio always comes with added pressure. I need to keep regulars happy while offering classes that feel both fresh and familiar. And his wording makes me feel like there has been some good word of mouth happening in recent weeks.

"Well, I'd love to have you in a class, but the next one on the schedule isn't until four p.m. Would you be willing to come back then?"

He waves me off with a little scoff. "No. I'll take a private lesson."

I blink. He knows what he wants, and he wants it now. "Okay. Do you want to look at our price list?"

His cheeks pinch like I've offended him. "Can't put a price on quality."

A small chuckle escapes me. "That's fair." I pull out a waiver. "Can I get you to fill this out for me? Just so we have some of your information on file."

The man steps forward, grumbling something that

sounds an awful like *that motherfucker is going to owe me* as he reaches a shaky hand for the pen on the counter.

I watch as he scratches in all caps, skipping entire sections, marking other ones with NONE OF YOUR GODDAMN BUSINESS.

Woof. I can tell he's quite the character. And tense from head to toe.

"Have you done yoga before? What's your experience level?"

"Never. Sounds like a bunch of baloney to me, but I'll try it anyway."

He pushes the incomplete form back to me, and I let out a genuine laugh at his blunt honesty. My gaze drops to his name at the top of the paper. CLYDE GIBBONS. What a bizarre little man.

"Nice to meet you, Clyde. I appreciate your honesty and openness. It's one of the most important components of a solid practice."

He stares at me with a blank expression. "Well, you've got your work cut out for you then," he grumbles, before removing his boots near the front, just like the sign asks. When he turns back around, he eyes the welcome area warily. "You got any cameras up in this place?"

His eyes land on the dark bubble in the corner just behind me, and I turn to look at it as well. "Only that one out here. None back in the studio."

His lips work, eyes narrowing like he might be able to laser the device right off the wall. "Don't like bein' watched."

I wait a beat, considering what to say to that, gauging the

best way to approach this man. I'd be lying if I said I'm not a little thrown off by him. Part of me wants to tell him not to worry about it, but that feels dismissive in a way.

"Can't say that I blame you. It's unnerving, right?"

He freezes for a moment, like I've caught him off guard. Then he nods, and I seize on his small show of agreement.

"And really, if you think about it, there isn't much to see up here. *But* if someone came in while we were in the back and tried to steal, say..." I trail off, glancing around, before my eyes land on what are a damn nice pair of winter boots. "Your boots. Maybe I wouldn't be able to get out front fast enough to greet the person, but the camera would capture it, you know?"

His scraggly, gray brows furrow as he assesses me. "You know, that's a great point. Plus, you're here all alone. Don't want any weirdos wandering in."

I smile brightly to cover the laugh that's lodged in my throat, but I'm also relieved to have put him at ease. I wave him forward and start heading toward the back room. "Well, good then. Follow me back. And we'll—"

"Though you know, if someone was desperate enough to steal my winter boots, it strikes me they might need them more enough than I do."

His response brings me up short, and I peek back over my shoulder. He's the most unusual combination of cantankerous and thoughtful.

I figure he can't be much older than my father, but there's a stark difference. My father would have spat some venom about tracking that person down and serving them up a little street justice. He lives in a constant state of forced machismo.

And who am I kidding? My dad wouldn't be caught dead in a yoga studio, the place where I choose to *waste my life*.

My nose wiggles as I push the painful thought away. "That's very thoughtful of you, Clyde."

He just harrumphs and follows me back into the studio, the soft shuffling of his socked feet interspersed with the clunk of his cane.

Once in the room, he removes his coat, and I see it then, a heavily distended abdomen. Based on the shape of his socks, I'm assuming his ankles and feet are swollen too. "Clyde, I know you weren't keen to write down your medical history—especially in front of the camera—but do you think you could tell me about any major health issues you might be facing?"

"Yeah." He hangs his coat on a hook and turns to face me. "I'm in kidney failure, and according to the white coats at the hospital, that's pretty major."

I nod, processing the information. The fluid retention makes sense. My brain cycles through the best poses or asanas that could benefit kidney health, liver support, and energy flow to keep the swelling from getting worse. I'm well aware yoga has its limits. I won't be able to make him better, but I'm confident I can make him *feel* better.

I can help Clyde Gibbons be comfortable.

Turning away, I quickly grab a purple mat to help stimulate his crown chakra, a bolster, and two blocks to set up a station against the wall. "Okay, Clyde. Come on over, and I'll help you get started lying on your back."

And so begins my mission to help this funny, strange, oddly thoughtful little man feel better.

WILD CARD

A jingle at the front door takes my attention away from sanitizing the mats after my last class. "Be right there!" I call out, setting the spray bottle and rag down before pushing myself to my feet.

I'm shaking my hands dry as I round the corner, my gaze lifting to see Clyde standing there. Back again after yesterday. It makes me smile.

But when my eyes slide up behind him, the smile falls off my face.

Bash. Looking like he could kill someone. And also looking hot as hell in black jeans, work boots, and flannel jacket, sherpa collar flipped up to beat the chill.

I ignore the nervous flutter in my chest—and the way my stomach flips like one of those dreams where I'm free-falling—and focus on Clyde. "You're back."

He shrugs. "Turns out I like yoga."

Bash groans and rolls his eyes so dramatically that his head practically follows their motion. I can't help but wonder what he's doing here—especially since he can barely look at me.

But me? I beam because I knew yesterday's stretching would make Clyde feel better. "I'm thrilled to hear that. Maybe we can make a more regular appointment?"

"Sure. I'll make it for right now."

Bash glares at Clyde. "Whatever you do, you can't just drive down the mountain yourself like you did yesterday. Your legs don't bend well enough after dialysis to push the pedals. You know this. I'll slash the fucking tires on your car if you do that again. First responders don't need to deal with the aftermath of your stubborn bullshit."

My eyes bounce between them as Clyde scoffs and waves a dismissive hand in his direction. "I'd like to see you try."

"Are you two related?" I blurt, entertained by the grumpy-man face-off.

"Fuck no," Bash mutters, but Clyde lets out a high-pitched giggle, like he's amused by the other man.

"Sometimes it feels like we are, though, doesn't it, Bash?"

"In the sense that I wish I could get rid of you, but I can't? Yes. Yes, it does."

My lips twitch.

"How long will he be? I'll come pick him up," Bash says to me, but he directs his gaze to the clock on the wall.

"An hour."

Bash nods, but his eyes don't move.

It kills me that he won't make eye contact. I feel like I'm silently begging him to just *look* at me. To see the way I look at him. To talk.

God, what I'd give to talk the way we did that night. Honest and open and unexpected.

But I also know there's now an ocean between us.

Two little numbers.

One man.

And not just any man—his son.

Had I known…

I shake the thought away, not wanting to feel guilty over things I couldn't have predicted. What's done is done. We're both grown-ups. I desperately want to bridge the gap, but based on the way Bash addresses the wall, I'm thinking I might be the only one.

It taps straight into every hurt I carry with me. I grew up feeling like I had to bend over backward not to anger my father. *Seen but not heard* is what he requested of me.

And I was.

It can be my default now when I'm feeling off-kilter. It's a hard habit to shake. So when Bash starts in with, "Okay, I'll be back to get you—" I cut him off.

"It's okay. I can drive Clyde home."

He looks at me now, but the glance is so fleeting that it's almost dismissive. Further proof that I don't need him back here, sullying my good mood with his immaturity. Or this grudge he's holding. Or whatever this awkwardness is between us.

"He's way up the mountain. The road's rough. Not well tended. You probably can't even—"

"Cool," I bite out evenly, more irritated by the second as he stands there acting like I'm some incorporeal voice.

Can't. That word fires me up. It's the word that had me walking out of my parents' house at seventeen and never looking back. My dad told me I *can't* live a "proper" life as a yoga teacher, and if I wasn't going to university or getting married, I wasn't living under his roof.

And I said, *watch me.*

"I'm a big girl. With a big truck. And above-average driving skills. You can take your bad energy elsewhere, Bash."

His head snaps up as Clyde chortles. "Bad energy?"

I lift my chin and wave a hand over him. "Yes. It's time for you and your fully blocked crown chakra to go."

Clyde nods. "Oh, you're right. His crown chakra is fucked."

Bash glares at his friend. "Why are you pretending you know anything about the crown chakra?"

"Gwen told me about the chakras yesterday. She said one has to do with enlightenment. And you are certainly not acting very enlightened."

I blink while Bash scowls.

"Well, forgive me for not taking lessons in enlightenment from a guy who believes Tupac is still alive."

"Tupac *is* st—"

Bash barks out a disbelieving laugh as he turns to leave. "You two have fun together."

I'm a bit stunned by him storming out, but Clyde doesn't seem affected at all. Instead, he shouts after him, "Go look at something purple! It'll help support your crown chakra!"

Bash leaves without a backward glance, stomping out into the chilly afternoon air. At first, I'm concerned that their bickering constituted an argument, but when Clyde turns to me with a toothy grin, I'm not so sure.

"All right, let's go do your weird stretches, followed by that Savasa-whatever-you-called-it. It made me feel a lot better."

His words warm me down to my bones. Knowing he came hobbling in and left feeling even a little bit better—that's why I started teaching in the first place. I may not have any higher education, and I may not be settling down and playing house, but I've come to believe what I do has value all the same.

"Savasana?" I gently correct, naming the resting pose we finished with yesterday.

"You say Savasana, I say nap," he tosses over his shoulder as he marches back into the studio.

And I can't help but chuckle as I follow him, ready to guide him through my "weird stretches" and nap. I lead him through a similar practice as yesterday, slipping into the headspace where all I focus on is breathing and alignment.

Except my attention is not as absolute as usual.

Because my thoughts keep circling back to Bash.

CHAPTER 10

Bash

Bash: Three games. Seven too few, if you ask me.

Tripp: Lol. I hear ya. Gonna celebrate anyway.

Bash: With who?

Tripp: Just some buddies.

Bash: Not the girlfriend?

Tripp: Nah. Just a few of the boys.

Bash: Have fun.

"Seriously? Yoga again?"

Clyde stomps his feet, spraying snow all over the footwell of my truck. My teeth clamp together, but I say nothing. I'm too busy beating myself up for trying to get information about Gwen out of my own son. I know she's here, but that doesn't mean they aren't together. Tripp didn't confirm or deny shit via text. And not knowing is irritating me.

"Feels good. And as I've always said, 'If it feels good, do it.'"

I glare at Clyde. He's got that shit-eating grin on his face. I swear he's like a child sometimes.

"Clyde, that's not something you've always said. That's a Sloan song."

He grumbles. "Huh. Maybe it was, 'If it makes you happy, it can't be that bad.'"

I sigh and drop my head to my palm. It's not worth telling him that's a Sheryl Crow song.

"Whichever one it is, you should take my advice," he says. "A private yoga class would be good for you."

Shaking my head, I pull away and drive him down the mountain. Anxiety builds in my stomach the closer we get to the yoga studio because having to see Gwen here—so close and yet so fucking far away—is its own special brand of torture.

Go look at something purple, Clyde teased yesterday. And all I could think was, *I can't. Not when everything purple reminds me of Gwen's unusual eye color.*

And looking at Gwen makes me want that first date she teased me about, the one where I finally learn her full name. It's been a year, and try as I might, I can't shake her. Or what could have been. I blew it when I entered that one number wrong. And the brutal truth is that I can't act on it with me and Tripp still trying to find solid ground.

The injustice of it all just stokes the constant spark of

fury that's been burning in my chest since everything got turned upside down.

I hate feeling like a victim.

And yet here I am, playing one. Stuck in a rut I don't know how to get out of. I work on Ford's property, finishing up the inside of the guest cabins at his recording studio. I bowl on Thursdays and try to have a good time. And even though he irritates me, I help Clyde with medical appointments and ferry him into town.

But every other night, I'm home alone, consumed by what could have been, knowing Gwen from the airport is staying practically down the street. Nothing happened between us, and yet her mere presence eats me up inside.

I've never been known for my enthusiasm, but I'll admit, even by my standards, I'm dark these days.

Clyde and I drive into town in silence, and it's not until we pull up in front of the yoga studio that Clyde looks my way. "You're acting like a sullen teenager," he says plainly. Then he gets out.

I'm annoyed to realize he's right. And I have no clue how to stop.

So I decide my best course of action is to avoid Gwen at all costs.

Months pass of Gwen and I skirting each other.

Much to my dismay, my friend group has slowly become her friend group. Clyde has become yoga obsessed, and if it wasn't actually making him more comfortable, I would accuse him of taking private lessons with Gwen to terrorize me. On top of that, Rosie, Skylar, and Tabby have taken to inviting her to group dinners and family get-togethers.

I appreciate how inclusive they are, but I also fucking hate it. It's like I can't escape her, no matter how hard I try.

So like the mature adult I am, I stick to the opposite side of the room when we wind up in the same place at the same time. I make conversation with literally anyone other than her, while also listening in on her conversations, desperately lapping up any droplets of information I can get.

Truth be told, I'm listening for any mention of Tripp. On one hand, I hope like hell she dumped his ass. On the other, I hope they're making it work because Gwen is a catch and that's what a good dad should want for his son.

But I make a point of never asking. Of making sure I don't seem *too* interested.

Tripp hasn't been forthcoming about his personal life, and I haven't pushed him. Instead, I've settled for what he's been willing to give me.

One bright spot is that he's taken a sincere interest in my start as a wildland firefighter and how it led me to wildfire aviation—something we've ended up talking about during the odd phone call. His questions on that topic are always thoughtful and give me hope that we might still be able to forge a genuine relationship.

Slowly but surely, Tripp Coleman is starting to feel less like a stranger and more like someone I'll know for the rest of my life.

Still, I think about Gwen. Even though I know I shouldn't.

My contracting business has been slower than usual, leaving me restless. Between my psychological torment and my hyperfixation on summer—when I can get back up in the air and feel needed for something—I'm in a weird headspace.

Bad as it sounds, I'm desperate for forest-fire season just so I can get out of here. And wishing for natural disasters has to be a new all-time low.

Maybe I'm just in a bad mood because of the lousy, green beer I'm drinking across from Clyde at a narrow high-top table.

"I don't think you should be drinking," I say.

The man ignores me, taking a healthy guzzle of his beer while looking around the Reach. Doris has decorated, and it looks like a bunch of leprechauns exploded all over the place. Even the windows have slimy, green jelly cut-outs on them. They're gross.

"Meh. You only live once, Sebastian. And I don't think it will be that long for me. Let me enjoy my swamp beer. Can't make my kidneys any worse than they already are."

Clyde has been on the transplant list for some time now—and it's not looking good. As much as I grumble about the guy, the prospect of losing his annoying ass is more than I can take right now.

I swallow hard and glance away. My eyes catch on his wheelchair in the corner. He's gotten so weak that walking has become difficult. I can tell that he's tired.

For his sake, I try to stay positive.

"I still think a donor could come through."

Clyde shrugs, a soft smile curving his lips. "Maybe," he says noncommittally. And I don't like the way it sounds. The way he's watching everyone, taking it all in as though this might be his last St. Patrick's Day.

Suddenly, his request for me to take him out tonight feels…bleak. It makes me realize that there probably will be a last time I pick him up. There will be a last beer we share. A last eye roll he shoots me. And I might not even recognize the moment for what it is.

I don't know if it's because I've been wallowing in misery for months or if it's a reaction to the toxic levels of Green No. 3 in my beer, but I blurt out my next words without thinking.

"I think we should see if I'm a match."

Clyde laughs and slaps me on the shoulder. "That's a mean joke, ya little shit. I like it."

I blink, gears turning in my head, before shifting on my stool to face him. "I'm not joking. I've got two working kidneys and nothing but time on my hands right now. Wouldn't hurt to check."

Clyde spins the pint glass between his hands, assessing me from beneath furrowed brows. As though searching for some proof that I'm bullshitting him. "That's ridiculous," he grumbles.

I shrug. It probably is, but here I am, offering it all the same. "I could use a little good karma, Clyde."

He rolls his eyes. "Only you could make giving me a kidney about yourself. *Oh please, Clyde, let me give you a kidney so I can feel better about myself,"* he teases in a whiny voice.

I scoff. "You know what, maybe I should just let you die."

"At least then I wouldn't have to spend all my free time with a guy who cries as he masturbates while thinking about his son's ex-girlfriend."

My head falls back as I glare up at the ceiling. "Get fucked, Clyde." Then I pause and turn back to meet his watery, blue eyes, the whites of which look awfully yellow these days.

A word sticks in my head as I stare back at him. In an instant, my throat goes tight, my palms sweaty.

"Did you say *ex*-girlfriend?"

Now the older man laughs and shakes his head, like I amuse him greatly. "Caught that, did ya? You little pervert."

I should be embarrassed by how quickly I latched on to this tidbit, but my desperate curiosity prevents me from overthinking it.

"Clyde, for fuck's sake, I'm trying to give you an organ, and you're sitting here shit-talking me to my face."

He smacks his lips. "Someone's gotta do it. You're more depressing than I am, even though I'm the one who's dying. Surprised you're not offering me both kidneys with how god-damn emo you've been lately."

I freeze at that, jaw working as I assess the man. "Wait. Are you hanging out with me as some sort of good deed?"

Clyde glances away. "Why else do you think I'm out drinking stupid green beer with you? There are security cameras all over this place, and I'm pretty sure Doris is an undercover agent."

My mouth pops open and stays that way. I thought I was here doing Clyde a favor when he's the one extending a pity invite to his loner friend on St. Paddy's Day.

I don't want to fixate on that part, so I parry it aside with, "You think Doris *what?*"

He takes a swig and glances around. "You heard me. Don't make a scene—she's probably watching. Reporting."

"Clyde, you say the wildest stuff sometimes. I don't even know where you come up with it. What would she report?"

He grins. "That you'd miss me if I died and that you desperately want to save your best friend's life."

My eyes roll. *Best friend.* "No kidney for you. I take it back."

"I'll talk to Doris. She can arrange to have it harvested against your will."

"You would too," I grumble.

Clyde just cackles, all raspy and amused. "You're so obnoxiously loyal, you'd still be my friend if I did."

I scoff at the idea. I'm not *that* loyal.

Still, I stay and have a second (and third) beer with the man while we guess what different patrons do for a living.

And the next day, through the haze of too many green beers, I call my doctor to schedule a donor evaluation.

CHAPTER 11

Gwen

CLYDE LIES ON HIS BACK WITH HIS LEGS UP AGAINST THE wall. And I stand above him, watching his chest rise and fall, trying to ignore the light rasp in his breathing. It makes the thought of leaving him even harder.

Because I *am* considering leaving.

Kira, the studio owner, contacted me over the weekend to let me know she'd need her apartment back by the end of the month. She offered little explanation, just something about a family member needing a place to stay. To me it sounded far-fetched. Especially when she told me she wanted me to keep teaching.

Now, I have to find a new place to live—and rent (and pay rent for)—which is less than ideal for my savings plan. But I didn't tell her that.

I've buried my anxiety over the upheaval, not ready to leave yet. I'll figure something out. I always do.

"So now we'll take one regular breath in through your nose and then another quick one at the top of that. Fill your lungs as full as possible before you slowly breathe out through your mouth."

Trying not to stare at the increasingly yellow tinge to his body, I demonstrate the breath a few times before letting Clyde take over breathing on his own.

Over the past several months, I've spent a lot of time with the man. It's too remote where he lives. The roads are bad. And the hospital is too far away for comfort. And he needs too much help with day-to-day tasks.

Which is why I was both grateful and relieved when he offered to hire me to help around his house. Now I spend a couple of days a week up on the mountain—meal prepping, shoveling snow, and doing general chores that have become harder for him as his kidneys weaken.

In all honesty, spending time with Clyde fills something in me that I didn't realize I've been missing. The way he calls to me when I enter his home—*That you, kiddo?* in his raspy voice—makes me smile every time.

He always asks about my yoga classes and how they're going. Always checks if I've been sleeping well and eating properly. He always lights up when I walk in, and he always, always listens when I speak.

Yes, Clyde pays me for my time, but if he stopped, I'd continue to show up. Hell, I've even offered to do it for free, which, in hindsight, I think offended him. He'd hobbled away and come back with a handful of cash, shoving it at me brusquely. Then he looked me straight in the eye and told me to never work for free. To never sell myself short or question my value.

I cried in my truck after that and never brought it up again.

So we keep doing our regular private classes for cash payment. Bash drops him off at the studio's front door in the big black Denali pickup truck he drives, and I try not to crane my neck too far, straining for the smallest glimpse of him. He never comes inside, but he never fails to get Clyde here on time. He also never fails to get Clyde to his doctor's appointments. He just…never fails to show up for the man, *period.*

Between the two of us, Clyde gets a daily check-in. Bash might act like an awkward dickhead around me, but I admire the relationship he and Clyde share. It's heartwarming, endearing, and—unfortunately for me—I find his reliability and loyalty to be incredibly attractive.

We don't even have to see or speak to each other for Sebastian Rousseau to occupy space in my mind. My meditation practice is a struggle, constantly interrupted by flashes of surly brows, a square jaw rough with stubble, and big, calloused hands.

When Clyde's breathing transforms into a coughing fit, I drop to the ground beside him, gently placing my palm on his sternum. Because after months spent with the funny, quirky old man, I have grown attached to him. And watching him deteriorate is, well… It's brutal.

"Soften your chest," I murmur. "It will pass."

"People can't soften their chests, Gwen," he grumbles between coughs from behind closed lids.

Always arguing with me.

"I can. So you can too."

"I don't want to be an old pervert like Bash, but I need to point out to you that our chests are very different."

I bite down on a laugh and just end up snorting.

"Plus," he continues, "I don't need to soften my chest. Because my new kidney is on the way."

I freeze and stare down at Clyde. "What?"

"I must have forgotten to tell you. Bash is giving me a kidney tomorrow."

My lips pop open. "Sorry?"

A raspy smoker's laugh spills from his lips as his eyes finally flick open. "Yeah. Couple weeks ago, he brought it up over beers. Went and did all the testing. Turns out the two of us are a match made in heaven."

My heart swells with joy, and my eyes fill with unshed tears.

"Gwen, if you get all sappy on me, I'm leaving. All this universe and energy yoga shit is already toeing the line for me."

I smile and swallow the lump in my throat. He always claims he's skeptical about yoga, but he keeps coming back, sullenly admitting that it does, in fact, make him feel better. So I don't take his threats to heart.

"I bet Bash loves being referred to as your 'match made in heaven.'"

A mischievous grin curves across his wrinkled lips. "He hates it. Still giving me a kidney, though."

My head shakes as I gaze down at the frail man, feeling a weight lift off my chest, replaced by an overwhelming sense of gratitude.

Fucking Sebastian Rousseau.

His name plays on repeat in my head as I guide Clyde through a "nap"—what he continues to call the Savasana. My words come slow and steady as I lull him into a state of meditation. I've tried to tell him that dozing off defeats the purpose, but he's so exhausted these days, I figure if he's relaxed enough to drift off, then comfortable sleep might be one of the most restful things we can do for his body.

I watch his chest rise and fall, his breaths slowing and lengthening as he slips from consciousness into what I hope is a peaceful dream state.

The blocks prop up his thin limbs. His fingers unfold as the tension melts away. I blink a few times as I watch over him, hoping he finds rest.

Relief.

Relief that he might make it through this hits me hard and fast. I might still have someone to visit. Someone who looks forward to having me around—who takes an interest in me.

As emotion wells in my tear ducts, I swipe at my eyes and head to the basket in the corner. I pull out a thin fleece blanket, then return to Clyde's resting form, draping it over him gently. Just to make sure he doesn't catch a chill.

I dim the lights and slip out of the studio, sniffing as I meander to the front, where I know there's a box of tissues.

What I don't expect to find there: Bash.

He's lounging in a chair, one ankle slung over his knee as he casually flips through a yoga magazine wearing his typical hypermasculine boots-jeans-flannel combo.

My heart thuds when he glances up and meets my gaze.

For several moments, we watch each other in silence. His eyes taking a leisurely cruise over my bright-pink matching leggings and crop top. My skin prickles under his attention so I pull my oversized, cream cardigan tighter around my shoulders.

"What are you doing here?" I ask, my voice quavering as I force myself back into motion and round the front desk, heading toward the small table in the corner.

He never comes in, and he never *looks* at me. But right now, he is, and it has me squirming under his attention.

There's also a little part of me that feels like this is a step toward forgiveness. Like maybe he can finally stand the sight of me again. And the prospect of that makes me feel almost relieved. Like a weight lifts from my shoulders because I can't stand the thought of anyone—especially him—disliking me.

"Clyde seems weak today. Figured I'd be here early to help get him—" Bash starts, but his sentence cuts off as I let out a watery sigh, followed by a sniffle. "Sorry, are you crying?"

I press my shoulders back and tip my nose up as I snatch a tissue from the box. "No."

Bash's skeptical gaze sweeps over me.

"Just have a runny nose," I add, dabbing at my nose right as a stray, traitorous tear tumbles down my cheek.

His eyes track the droplet, like the tear itself has done something to offend him. Then my other eye betrays me, and his gaze moves over my face, sharp and assessing. Jaw popping, he pushes to stand, his tall, broad form towering over me.

"What did he say to you?" His voice comes out rough, edged with something fierce.

I blink, dabbing at my stupid, leaky eyes as I shake my head. "No. No. It's not—"

He goes to step past me, his focus like a laser down the hallway where Clyde is resting. "So help me, if Clyde made you cry, I'll—"

"Bash." My hand darts out to stop him and lands flat on his chest. Just like that day in the bathroom at Tripp's party, I can feel the hard lines of his toned body beneath the soft weave of his flannel shirt.

His head jerks down, eyes snapping to the contact as we both still.

I should move my hand—snap it back like I've touched a hot stove. Because this fire between us is bound to burn someone eventually.

But I don't.

Instead, I tip my face up and let my fingers splay.

His dark eyes lock with mine and the air between us thickens. If I wasn't choked up already, the sheer intensity of Bash's expression would be the thing making it hard to breathe.

"Thank you," I murmur, voice still watery.

His gaze searches my face again, attention flicking between my eyes, like he's looking for more information.

"Clyde's asleep. But he told me about the—the kidney." My voice breaks, and more wetness springs up in my eyes. "And just...*thank you*. I'm so relieved."

"You're crying because you're happy?" The bite that was in his tone has morphed into a soft rumble.

I smile up at him and nod. What can I say? I'm a sensitive gal. I've always felt things just a little more deeply.

Bash lets out an exasperated groan, his eyes closing for one long beat as he gives his head a subtle shake. "Please don't cry. It's just a kidney."

A weepy laugh lurches from my throat. "Only you would say it's *just* a kidney. He's…he's been so sore. So resigned. This is…" I suck in a trembling breath. "Bash, this is a new lease on life. You're saving him."

A whimper spills from my lips as I continue to think about it, my breaths between sentences growing more emotional as I go. "This is so selfless, so brave. You're giving him a piece of yourself. Do you not see how deeply generous this is?"

"For fuck's sake," Bash growls. "You're killing me."

And then he stuns me by reaching forward, his fingers cradling my jaw as calloused thumbs sweep my tears away with a touch far gentler than I would have expected.

His palm slips down, softly cradling the side of my neck. I'm pretty sure I stop breathing altogether. But then I force myself to look up at him, and it's like the world shrinks down to just us. Then his eyes meet mine before dropping to my mouth. His throat bobs and I suck in a breath.

The scent of him wraps around me—something woodsy mixed with something sweet, like cedar dusted with vanilla.

It's just a little too easy to imagine his hands on me. Holding me like I'm his before dropping his lips to mine.

It's silly. Frivolous. And unlikely, considering the fact

that I'm quite sure he hates me for dating his son. Something I'm sharply reminded of when he stoops just slightly, bringing his face to the same level as mine. The simplest motion feels warm and reassuring with him.

"Stop crying, Gwen. I can't stand it. Everything is fine."

His broad palm slips from my neck, rubbing over my upper arm reassuringly. Up and then down. I can't help but shiver at the unexpected contact. And I know he notices because he steps away, creating more space between us.

His tone changes when he speaks next. Confident and sure, but the softness of mere moments ago evaporates at once. "It's all going to be good. You'll see. Nothing to worry about."

I blink away any wetness and try not to laugh at his brusqueness. Then I consider if I should cry again, just so it will bring him closer.

But I don't get the chance.

"Oh, good. You two have kissed and made up," Clyde rasps as he hobbles down the hallway.

"We didn't kiss," Bash snipes, right as I say, "There's nothing to make up about."

We both look at each other, eyes locking for a beat. Then Bash steps even farther away, hands raised, like Clyde caught him red-handed, while I wipe any lingering dampness from my face.

Clyde chuckles, not bothering to inspect us too closely, instead heading straight toward his boots near the front door. "One of my best naps, Gwen. Thank you. I'm glad Bash stopped sulking and invited you to his party tonight."

Awkwardness descends between us because he most certainly did not. And based on the smug twist of Clyde's lips and the murderous scowl Bash hits him with, we all know he didn't.

And yet, like a scolded child, Bash turns to me. "Gwen, would you like to come to the annoying party that West is hosting for me tonight?"

He's clearly only inviting me to be polite. The look in his eyes is practically begging me to decline. But beyond him, Clyde is nodding enthusiastically.

I shrug. "Sure. I love annoying parties."

I tell myself I'm only saying yes to make Clyde happy. And that it has nothing to do with spending more time around Sebastian Rousseau.

Absolutely nothing at all.

CHAPTER 12

Bash

Bash: I know this is random, but giving you a heads-up that I'm donating a kidney to a friend. So if I'm MIA for a bit, I'm probably just in the hospital.

Tripp: Jesus. When is this happening?

Bash: Tomorrow.

Tripp: And you're just telling me now?

Bash: Didn't want you to get all sappy on me or something.

Tripp: Well, I do think it's pretty cool that you'd donate a kidney to a friend. I don't think I like anyone that much. Lmao.

Bash: One day you will.

Tripp: Maybe. For now, I will just admire your generosity from afar.

Bash: Okay. Good luck with the end of the season. Catch you on the flip side.

Tripp: Ugh. Yeah. End of the season is looking like it will be sooner rather than later. Maybe I'll come visit you sometime. See your place.

Bash: I'd like that. Drop me a line.

West strides out of his kitchen with a shit-eating grin on his face and a kidney-shaped cake in his hands.

He stops at the head of the table, right beneath the banner that reads *We're going to miss you, Daddy!* "Bash, congratulations on finally finding your perfect match," he announces to the dining room full of our friends. "None of us expected it to be Clyde, but sometimes the heart wants what the heart wants. And I, for one, could not be happier for you. Or him."

A ripple of laughter rolls through the room as he sets the white cake on the table for everyone to see. It's covered in… veins? Capillaries? I don't fucking know. The decorative icing has done an incredible but disturbing job of making it look like an anatomically correct kidney. In perfect script it says *Bon voyage, Kidney!*

And all I can do is groan.

Only West.

Beside him, Skylar shakes her head but stares up at him with stars in her eyes. Like no matter how ridiculous he is, he still hung the moon for her. I sometimes wonder if it's *because* he's so ridiculous that she's found peace with him.

Rosie has dropped her face into her hands, and Ford has his arm slung over the back of her chair—the only thing he gives West is his typical dry eye roll.

Rhys's deep, rumbling chuckle filters in from the other side of the table. Arms crossed over his broad chest, he looks downright amused.

Amused enough that his wife, Tabitha, shoves an elbow into his ribs along with a threatening sounding, "What are you laughing at? I made that cake."

He turns his smirk her way with an innocent shrug. "And? That just means that even though it looks disgusting, it will taste delicious."

The warmth between them—the teasing and prolonged eye contact—makes me feel like an interloper.

It makes me think of Gwen.

And finally, I let my gaze flit to the opposite side of the table. To her.

Gwen's cheeks are rosy, her smile bright and genuine. Her eyes sparkle as she appraises the horror that is my cake. She has her lacy white blouse unbuttoned far enough to show the slopes of her ample cleavage. Those buttons stood no fucking chance, and she owns it. Her subtle confidence might be the most attractive thing about her.

Still, she looks different now than she did earlier, when those big doe eyes welled with tears.

Tears for *me*. Happy tears.

It threw me for a fucking loop. I hated it, but a part of me loved it too. Because for a moment, it felt like someone in the world really saw me—and liked what they saw.

When Gwen looked at me today, I hadn't felt like a second choice.

"Tabby, I think it's beautiful. How could a healthy kidney be anything but?" she gushes in her typical Gwen way. I swear she can find beauty in anything.

"See?" Tabitha pokes Rhys. "Gwen thinks my kidney cake is *beautiful*."

I shake my head and look back toward West, who is watching me, eyes lit up like a kid on Christmas. "So? Do you like it?"

I roll my lips together, trying to keep from laughing. "You're an idiot, Weston."

He brightens further. "Calling me an idiot is your love language, so I will take it. I love you too, man. Stay safe tomorrow." Then, glancing around the table, he lifts his champagne glass and waits for everyone to follow suit. "Here's to Bash and his kidney," he says as everyone raises their glasses. "You just might be the most thoughtful asshole I know. Cheers, to you and that big soft black heart of yours! And to Crazy Clyde!"

I give in and chuckle now. West will wear a guy down like that, and after looking around the table at all my friends here today, it didn't feel as hard to let that amusement trickle out. The others laugh, and we all gently tap our rims in a salute around the table with a shared murmur of "To Crazy Clyde."

Clyde needed to check into the hospital early for surgery prep and couldn't be here tonight. But tomorrow morning I fully intend to tell him that everyone gave a toast for *Crazy Clyde*—I think he'll get a real kick out of that.

Gwen and I toast last, and it feels like everyone is watching us. I don't think it's lost on anyone that after months of avoiding her like the plague, I'm the one who extended the invite today.

I did it to be polite. This isn't an elementary school birthday party. Hell, I'm forty years old. I don't need to exclude someone just because I'm all tangled up over her.

I'm mature, dammit. I can totally be around Gwen. This invite was a peace offering.

Our eyes catch and hold. For one beat and then two. Even as chatter breaks out around us, I can't look away.

And though Gwen is younger, she's no little girl. She holds my gaze back just as boldly. I've thought that maybe she's angry, going out of her way to be polite but secretly resenting me.

After all, I'm the one who got the number wrong. I'm the one who didn't try harder to track her down.

I don't know why she and Tripp broke up. He never told me, and I sure as hell haven't brought it up with Gwen. But I can't shake the thought that I caused the demise of that for her too.

Yet looking at her tonight, I don't get the sense she's irritated by me at all. Have I been beating myself up in my head for no reason? It's on the tip of my tongue. To ask her. To just spit it out so I can stop torturing myself wondering.

But the moment slips away when West slides a slice of cake in front of me. "Dude. You have *got* to try this. Our Tabby Cat outdid herself."

Gwen shoots me a small quirk of her lips and a second silent toast, then she turns away to chat with Skylar.

I watch her as I hold the glass to my lips but put it back down without drinking. I know alcohol consumption before this procedure isn't recommended. But I didn't want to ruin everyone's fun. Then I regretfully turn my attention to West and the cake.

It's delicious.

But not delicious enough to steal my wandering thoughts away from the woman seated across from me.

As is fairly typical for me, the large group atmosphere becomes more irritating than fun. The music plus the chatter makes it loud, and being the center of attention is pretty much my worst nightmare.

There's a reason I keep to myself. There's a reason I built on a private piece of property. And it's because I like my peace. I enjoy my time alone. In fact, I don't even usually feel all that lonely. It's doing me no favors in the dating department—but there's a large part of me that's avoiding that scene altogether. Especially considering what happened the last time I felt a spark of connection with a woman.

Still, there's something about coming home from a long stretch away working a fire and finding space and silence. I'll sit out on my balcony and decompress. The birds, the lake, the swish of the breeze through the trees—that's how I rejuvenate.

Not by surrounding myself with friends.

No, I do this for them. They need this. They wanted this, and as much as I love to see everyone together, my social battery drains rather quickly.

It might also have something to do with the fact that everyone else is drinking while I've officially hit the point in the night where I need to fast before surgery.

I've retreated to the kitchen for some breathing room, and everyone else is huddled in the living room playing an old game of Operation that West dug out of his crawl space "special for this party." The buzzer is going off a hell of a lot more than it has any right to, which is resulting in a chorus of laughter each time.

It makes me smile even though no one is here to see it.

Seeking some quiet, I slip from the house during one of those more raucous moments. Spring is in the air, and the nights are growing warmer. Still, it's spring in the mountains, and I rub my hands roughly over my arms for the friction.

West has a stunning property. A sweeping stretch of land near the lake, just outside of town. His old farmhouse sits back in the trees—not along the shore, like mine. But I know that just down a narrow, winding path, it opens up to a panoramic lake view.

Drawn by the sound of the water lapping at the shore, I shove my fists into my jean pockets and head toward the lake. Dense pines line my path as I pass a small guesthouse on my way. Warm, dim light filters from inside, and I peek in through the window, wondering why it would be lit up at all. The space looks tidy but unused, not lived in.

Except for the small, gray mouse in the corner. It's

nibbling on a piece of cheese that looks suspiciously similar to the Manchego on the ornate cheese board Tabby laid out earlier. My brows furrow, but I decide it's not my issue. I can mention the mouse to West later.

I continue toward the lake, the inky ripples highlighted by the bright moon. I haven't let myself think much about the fact that surgeries go awry sometimes, but taking the last steps down the short drop to the shore, it hits me I might never see this view again.

The sand shifts beneath my boots as I approach the shoreline. Rocking backward and forward, I suck in a sharp breath, the first inkling of anxiety twisting in my gut. Entirely unwelcome.

"Fuck." My heartbeat picks up momentum in my chest. "You picked a hell of a time to get cold feet, old boy," I mutter, chastising myself for doing this now.

As I shake my head into the night's darkness, a soft rustle comes from my right. If she wasn't wearing a bright-white blouse, she might be harder to spot.

But she is.

Gwen tiptoes toward the trees, clearly trying to creep away silently. And failing.

I sigh and turn to watch her. All it takes is one peek back over her shoulder for her to drop the ruse and face me with crossed arms.

It does nothing but prop her tits up, the moonlight bouncing off them in the most alluring way.

God, I might never see those again either. What a fucking shame.

"Don't give me that look, Rousseau. I was here first. Can't use that weaponized sigh on a girl who was just trying to give you some privacy."

At least she misread the look I was giving her. Small victories.

"It's fine," I grumble, letting my eyes trail down her body. Because why the fuck not? I could die tomorrow. Might as well look my fill.

A wide, ornate western belt cinches her waist, highlighting the feminine curve of her hips and thick thighs—hugged by jeans that flare out into a wide-legged shape.

Jeans I'd happily tug off if she asked me to.

I shake my head. *No*. That ship has sailed.

My gaze drops lower, to her bare feet, her pink toenails wiggling in the sand. She holds her socks in a loose fist at her side.

"What are you doing out here?" I ask, confused.

"It was loud inside. I have to teach a hot yoga class early tomorrow morning and I would rather not be sweating champagne for all my students to smell. So I can't really treat it like a night out, even if it is a Friday." She glances at the water with a soft shrug. "Plus, I'm a sucker for going barefoot in the sand, so I snuck out for a breather."

I nod. "Same. Minus the yoga part."

She quirks a brow but doesn't call me on it. Then her expression softens. "Want me to leave?"

Do I want her to leave?

"I can get out of here. I wanted to go check out that little guesthouse. That's my dream spot for yoga. Maybe bigger windows. Private. Quiet. A view of water. Just lock me up in there and I'll be happy. Actually, bring me food too."

I almost smile at her ramble. Despite the way I've behaved around her lately, Gwen doesn't annoy me. Not in the least. She's a go-with-the-flow free spirit, and I'm laced up tight—fighting against the flow a lot of the time. But she just...doesn't.

"No," I murmur, keeping my face turned toward the lake. "Just stay."

I feel her approach, coming to stand beside me quietly before asking, "Are you nervous?"

"A bit."

"Take your shoes off."

I turn to glance at her now. "What?"

"Just trust me. It'll help you feel better."

I'm already kicking my boots off when I ask, "How?"

She closes her eyes, and her lips curve up. "It will help ground you. Feel the pulse of the earth on your bare skin."

I scoff, and she peeks out one eye. "Shut up and lose your socks, Sebastian."

Her snapping at me like that makes me chuckle. It's so out of character. And yet, I'm reaching for my socks and soon standing barefoot beside her.

"Now what?"

"Push your feet into the sand." My head tilts as I watch her, ankles rotating, toes wiggling as she slowly works them down into the cold grains.

I follow suit and a wave of déjà vu hits me even though I can't specifically remember the last time I did this.

"It's fucking cold," I mutter.

Gwen smiles, eyes fluttering closed once again as she sighs deeply. "Makes you feel alive, right?"

I don't respond to that. I'm not sure what to say, because, as ridiculous as it sounds, yeah, it does make me feel alive.

"Now turn your palms toward the water and press your middle finger to your thumb."

A small part of me wants to roll my eyes, but a bigger part of me trusts that she might actually know what she's doing. So I go along with it, positioning my hands the way she instructed.

We stand like that for a while before she speaks again. "It would be weird if you weren't nervous, Bash. It's normal to let your brain wander down every path of possibility. So long as we don't let it go too far. You have to come back to that feeling of knowing yourself better than anyone. Of being so in tune with yourself that your mind always comes back to center. You need that stability. Grounding."

"You have a lot of practice with that, do you?"

"I do."

"You seem pretty at peace with almost everything."

Her head tips softly. "I practice a lot."

"How do you practice?" I ask, genuinely curious. Because I should start practicing pulling myself out of this hole of self-pity.

She breathes in deep through her nose, letting the air breeze back through softly parted lips. "For example, right now my thoughts start to turn to *what must you think of me?* I was often told growing up that I'm too much—"

"Who the fuck told you that?"

She doesn't respond at all to my outburst even though all I want to know is who had enough nerve to say that to her face so I can set them straight. "And I allow myself to acknowledge that I am not every person's cup of tea. Maybe I *am* more than they can handle. And that's okay because I'm quite fond of myself and no one can take that away from me. I'm at peace with who I am, so what you think of me doesn't matter."

I think you're just right is what I want to say. But I don't. Instead, I go with, "I don't think you're too much."

She turns and winks at me. "I don't care." Then, her head tilts my way. "Now you go. Close your eyes and quit staring at me like you're going to beat someone up to defend my honor."

I roll my eyes and then close them, letting the peaceful sounds of night settle in around me and that spark of anxiety ignite.

"Where are your thoughts turning?" Gwen asks.

"What if I die tomorrow?"

She's silent for several beats. I get the sense that's not what she expected me to say. Still, I hold my position. Feet in the sand, thumbs against my middle fingers, trying to feel whatever this is supposed to make me feel.

I start slightly when her cool fingers slip over mine, dusting over my skin until she's holding my hand. Just like we did that night in the airport. My palm hums with the contact, and my entire arm feels warm. I should shake her off, but it's a friendly gesture. A gesture of support.

And truthfully, I'm feeling a little too flayed to not take it.

"Okay," her smooth voice starts. "We can acknowledge that's a possibility. In all reality, any of us could die at any moment. Nothing is ever promised."

I nod at that. It's true. I've seen the fury of a wildfire turn people's lives upside down, destroy towns, decimate nature. And no one could have seen it coming.

"But, Bash, what if you live?"

Her question echoes in my head as her warm palm molds to mine. I feel her pulse. It thrums through my body. Hell, maybe I even feel the earth beneath my feet a little differently.

All I know is that the first thing that comes to mind is, *If I live, I'm coming after you.*

But I bury it as quickly as it pops up. Because I know I won't let myself cross that line. So I release her hand with one grateful squeeze and try to force myself to think about all the things I'm *actually* going to do once I recover.

Things that aren't just a fantasy.

CHAPTER 13

Gwen

"Knock, knock!" I call out, rapping my fist against the open door of Clyde's hospital room.

"Why do people say 'knock, knock' while actually knocking?" he grumbles. "It's totally redundant."

His snark just makes me smile. Because it means he's feeling like himself. He's propped up in bed, watching TV, with an abundance of cords and lines surrounding him. But he already looks brighter than when I saw him before his surgery.

A relieved sigh spills from my lips as I look him over. I promised myself I'd give him a few days to recover before barging down here…but I lasted two.

Tabitha kept me up-to-date throughout the surgery and the first day of Clyde's and Bash's recoveries, since she and Rhys stuck around to help. But I think my asking for constant updates annoyed her. She finally asked me what the hell I was waiting for, so I caved.

"Nice to see you too, Clyde," I singsong brightly as I sashay into the room. "I brought you flowers."

His gaze flicks to the vase of cheerful, yellow daffodils, soft pink ranunculus, and deep purple hyacinths in my hand. "For what? I didn't do anything."

"You didn't die. Congratulations. A huge accomplishment," I fire back with my sweetest smile, already feeling better for being able to make him smirk.

"Guess so, huh? Just need a few more days, and I'll be back to yoga."

I place the vase of flowers on the windowsill before turning back to him and leaning in, dropping a quick, friendly kiss against his stubbled cheek. "I miss you, Clyde, but you won't be back to yoga until we get clearance from your doctors."

He responds with a petulant eye roll. "These fuckin' clowns don't know shit. Did you know they had to write on me with a Sharpie saying which side the kidney needed to go in on? A big X to mark the spot." He shakes his head as he crosses his arms, disappointment dripping from every motion. "Over a decade of schooling, and these kids don't even know right from left."

I bite down on my lip and nod along. "Yeah, I think that might be more of a precaution than anything? I'm certain your surgeon would know right from left. And they must have gotten it right—you look so much better already!"

He grumbles something about not being convinced, but I glaze over it because he's not yellow anymore. "How are you feeling?"

Clyde looks longingly out the window before turning big blue puppy dog eyes on me. "Like I want to go home. I will hire you to break me out of this place."

I take a seat in the chair beside him and pat his hand. I don't know where Clyde gets all his money from because he's always wearing the same dusty overalls and stained trucker hat. His truck is a relic and constantly sounds like it's taking its dying breath. But he throws around cash for personalized services like it's nothing. And truth be told, I can use the extra income, so I never say no.

"Hospitals have a strange energy. I totally get it. Maybe I can come help you at home once you're discharged? We could do some breathing and *napping* and things like that since I'm already there helping with other tasks."

He goes still for a moment, brows lifting as his head tilts in consideration. I swear it's as though I've just seen a light bulb flick on in his head. "Yeah. Yeah. That would be great. I might need more help than usual."

"In the beginning, maybe. But I know you'll bounce back quickly."

He turns toward me, an earnest expression on his face. "Would you be able to visit daily to start? Or even do overnight? There's an extra room. I really think that would be helpful. Apparently, the hospital wants to know that I have someone to assist me in order for my discharge to go through. And I don't trust many people. We could work out a good salary for full-time."

I almost laugh in relief. I've been looking for a place in town to tide me over until I can find my next gig. Clyde doesn't know about my upcoming housing crisis, but I guess the universe works in mysterious ways. "Would it be okay if I still taught at the studio?"

The prospect of having both jobs is too good to not ask.

He shrugs. "Sure. I don't want you sitting there staring at me all the time. You'll annoy me."

I laugh, thinking about the practicality of adding this responsibility to my plate. It feels like the universe has guided me through my life this far, and I've taken the opportunities that have presented themselves. And, to this point, it hasn't led me astray. So I go with that energy. The positive *watch me* energy that I know so well.

"Actually, yeah. This will be great," I say with a soft nod. "You know I'm saving up to travel, but now I unexpectedly need to be out of my apartment by the end of the month."

His forehead scrunches. "You didn't tell me that."

I just shrug. "It's fine. I didn't want to burden you with that hiccup."

"Well, good. You'll move in with me. No rent necessary."

He looks so pleased that I can't help but smile. It makes me feel all glowy and warm to see how happy my presence makes him. It's a reaction I've never been able to garner from my father. Instead, I seem only to exasperate and disappoint him.

Which is why I'm here—out in the world, carving my own path, my own life, exactly the way *I* want it. And with that goal in mind, I offer Clyde a smile and a firm nod. "Count me in."

He brightens exponentially. "Do you promise?"

Does he brighten just a little too much?

There's something suspicious about his reaction. I scan his face for clues. The glint in his eye reminds me of a little boy who knows something he shouldn't. "You want me to promise?"

"Yeah." He nods solemnly, grumbling as he shifts in the bed. "I know I'm a lot to handle sometimes. People get tired of me. Then they stop showing up."

I swallow roughly, feeling like I relate just a little too easily. It's why I keep moving. If I leave first, no one can stop showing up for me. I don't give them the chance to get tired of me the way my dad did.

Poor Clyde, though. He can't keep up with that lifestyle. He is certainly…an acquired taste, but the thought of him being left all alone after a major surgery breaks my heart.

"Yeah, of course. I promise. I'll be there."

"Great." He melts back into the pale-blue pillows with a grateful smile on his face. Then he asks, "Now that we're allied, will you bring me a burger? With bacon? And french fries! They're starving me in he—"

"Clyde, for fuck's sake, you already know you can't have fast food." A voice filters from the door. And before I even see its owner, I know who it is.

I'd recognize that voice anywhere, and a wave of relief hits me when I hear it. *He lived.* I already knew he had, but seeing him in the flesh adds a layer of relief.

Since that night standing on the beach, I've been worried about Bash. We didn't talk much after he let my hand go, and I couldn't help wondering if I'd gone too far. Stuck my nose where it didn't belong. But he told me to stay. So I did.

Bash walks into the room but stops short when his gaze lands on me. He doesn't look entirely thrilled about my presence. I wince and offer a small wave.

I get why he stays away from me, but that doesn't stop me from hating it. There are times when everything between us feels so perfectly natural. And other times, it's like a comedy of errors, where we're avoiding one another but keep crashing together anyway. I hate how awkward things are with us in those moments. It's like the ultimate missed connection topped off with a huge amount of baggage. And longing. And…regret.

So much regret. Should have, could have, would have.

Why didn't I take his number?

Why didn't I try to find him?

Why did I automatically assume I wasn't good enough for him to stay interested?

I wish they didn't, but those questions keep me up at night. And just like when I'm lying awake, the hospital room is quiet. Too fucking quiet. I squirm under Bash's stare, not sure where we stand right now. Sure, we shared a nice moment on the beach, but it doesn't change everything else that's happened.

I half expect him to pretend I'm not here at all, but he acknowledges me with a stiff nod and a terse-sounding "Gwen."

Like I said, *awkward*. But then, I grew up tiptoeing around my dad's moods, hoping to fly under the radar, so fading into the background is old hat. I can go unnoticed with the best of them.

Bash turns his attention to Clyde, moving closer. I look him over, wanting to ask how he's recovering, but other than the light hitch in his step, he appears mostly fine.

"I'm discharged, but you need to stay for a bit still for monitoring and occupational therapy," Bash starts in, while I do my best to pretend I'm not here.

My gaze snags on the front of his sweatpants as he props his hands on his hips and talks. The gray sweats. The ones that leave almost nothing to the imagination.

"They agreed with me that your house is too far from the hospital to be safe or to conduct proper follow-up care. So in about ten days when you get discharged, you'll stay with me—like we talked about—and we'll have to hire a live-in aide. They can take the spare room upstairs since you'll be on the main floor."

My attention moves from Bash's big dick to the words he just said. My head turns slowly in Clyde's direction as I piece it together.

He stays focused on Bash, like a puppy who's done something naughty and is avoiding eye contact. "Oh, thank you, Bash. That's perfect."

My jaw unhinges as I watch Clyde…play him. His voice is all soft, his shoulders just slightly hunched. "I actually hired someone already."

A beleaguered sigh slips from Bash's lips. It's like he expects Clyde's going to say he's hired a dancing penguin or something.

Little does he know, it's so much worse.

Fingers woven together in my lap, I can't help but twist

and wring them as the silence stretches on. Bash just stares back at the older man, like he's waiting to be enlightened.

His dark eyes slip to the motion in my lap, and I stop immediately.

The fidgeting is an easy tell, and based on the way his brow furrows, he knows it.

"Clyde, who did you hire?" he asks slowly, with intention.

In response, Clyde's eyes go comically wide and innocent. And with one shy tip of his head, he says, "Gwen, of course."

Bash tilts his head back, big hands propped on his hips as he looks up at the ceiling like he might find an extra dose of patience tucked behind one of the terribly unflattering lights. He heaves in a sigh so deep that I can see his chest expand beneath the soft fabric of his white T-shirt, filling his lungs to the brim. Based on what little I know of him, it's probably a great exercise for calming his nervous system. Except he doesn't let the air out slowly.

"Clyde." He sighs the man's name, sounding exasperated.

I try not to take it personally. Rising above is second nature by now, which is made easier by the fact that Bash avoids me like the plague. Most times, the man gives me little more than a glance. He clearly can't get past me dating Tripp, and while it used to bother me, I've let it go. I can't change the past. I can only control my own feelings, and unfortunately for me, those haven't changed either.

Bash just does something to me. Even now, when agitated with Clyde and me, a delicious pressure curls behind my hips, and I try to keep my lips from curving up in a smirk.

Much like that night in the airport, his surliness amuses me. It lacks venom. It's like a mask.

Sure, Bash and I are mostly strangers, but I can tell he's all bark and no bite. I grew up with bite. And this? This isn't it. This is stern on the outside and soft on the inside. This is a man who bristles and grumbles but folds when it matters. And if I had to bet, I'd put money on Clyde's little heist working—and Bash won't even stay mad at him.

Clyde adjusts in the bed, moaning like he's in pain, one sun-spotted hand reaching across to lie across his abdomen. "She's already been helping me," Clyde says with a wince. "I don't trust anyone else."

I chuckle now because I'm going to give Clyde a goddamn Oscar later. He knows *exactly* what he's doing. But I quickly swallow my amusement when Bash's head snaps in my direction.

Clyde isn't the least bit put off, though. He carries on unperturbed. "Just because you gave me a kidney doesn't mean that you're the boss of me now."

"Thank god," Bash grumbles. "That's a terrifying fucking prospect."

I bite my tongue. I really, really should not laugh right now.

"She's got nowhere to live. Nowhere to go. You'll be working—gone, with fire season starting soon. You won't even notice us."

Bash's gaze bounces between us. "Nowhere to live?"

I shrug. "I need to be out of the apartment here by the end of the month and haven't made plans for where I'll go next. I've put out some feelers and have started looking online, so I doubt I'll be around for longer than a month or two. The timing is probably perfect if you really do need someone to help with Clyde."

He glares at me like I'm a problem that needs fixing. And that feeling I've spent years running from—the one where I worry that I'm an inconvenience—rears its ugly head.

Of course Bash doesn't want me in his home. If I stop and think about it, it's unfair to even ask. He's just forged a relationship with his son. Me living at his house? Red freaking flag.

So I tell myself what I always do.

On to the next stop.

Maybe this was meant to happen.

When life gives you limes...

"You know what? It's okay. I can probably find something right away." I slap my hands together as I turn to Clyde. "I'm very self-sufficient. I always land on my feet, and this will be no different."

Clyde is about to interject, but I hold my finger up to silence him. "You will find someone more appropriate. I don't want to burden you or Bash with—"

"No. You'll stay." Bash's deep voice cuts off my awkward ramble, and I freeze. For that matter, so does Clyde. In time, we both turn to look at him. Flushed cheeks, downturned lips, and crossed arms. "Two months. Not more."

It's not so much of an offer as a demand. One I don't know how to respond to, nor do I get the chance. Because before I can come up with any other words to say, Bash gives a sharp nod and marches out of the room, filling out his sweats just as well from behind.

"Quit gawking at his ass," Clyde whispers, making me snap my gaze away.

"I'm not. I'm looking at his back."

He *giggles*. This grizzled old man giggles. Like a little girl.

My eyes narrow, and now it's my turn to cross my arms and look down my nose at him. *Suspicious*. "Are you in pain?"

"Me? No. I'm on more drugs than I've taken in my entire life. I can't even feel my face."

I suspected before, but the truth of it dawns on me at once. At best, he's stirring the pot. And at worst, he's trying to play matchmaker. "You're being a little shit-disturber aren't you?"

The man's lips twitch, and he waves me off. "I'm just a frail old man, not long for this world. Let me get my kicks in where I can." I shake my head at him in disbelief and he peeks my way with a wink. "Plus, his shit could use a little disturbing."

CHAPTER 14

Bash

THE DOORBELL RINGS AND I HAVE TO TALK MYSELF INTO walking toward it. Because I know who's on the other side.

Gwen.

Airport Gwen. Beach Gwen. *Tripp's* Gwen. Gwen, who Tripp never so much as mentions.

I scoff, shaking off the way that thought makes my stomach turn and stride toward the door. As my hand wraps around the handle, I steel myself because every time I lay eyes on her, it's this full-body, visceral reaction.

I freeze up like a fucking teenager. My heart pounds. My hands get clammy. And I have to clamp my molars together to keep from sighing like an awestruck little boy.

Because Gwen isn't just hot as fuck. She's kind. And fun. And thoughtful. And *flexible*.

How do I know? Because I found her social media channels. I couldn't keep myself from looking at her when

I woke up from surgery. *Alive.* Just like she reassured me I would be.

And honestly, it's fucking embarrassing.

Holding it together around her is hard enough, but then I went and invited her to live with me. I'm not oblivious to the shit Clyde pulled, but that's not why I said yes.

It's the way she flippantly wrote herself off as a burden. The way her smile fell and her amethyst eyes went flat. Her quiet voice at the beach when she so casually mentioned that she's been told she's too much.

I didn't like it. Didn't want to contribute to it.

We barely know each other, but I know the woman isn't a burden. Like she said, she's self-sufficient. She lands on her feet. And I didn't want to be one more obstacle for her to overcome.

So I decided to be mature about it. Even though, thanks to Gwen Dawson, turning regret and self-loathing into an erection appears to be my new superpower.

I yank the door open with that galling thought on my mind, and just like I predicted, I take one look at her and the world around us stands still.

"Hi!" She waves meekly. "Sorry I'm early. Guess I'm still not used to how close everything is in a small town."

It hits me all at once that Tripp's ex-girlfriend is moving into my house and I haven't told him. Part of me thinks I should text him immediately and explain myself. If he finds out, it will look bad. But the other part of me knows this is only temporary—a month or two—and what he doesn't know won't hurt him. Not telling him just seems…easier.

"It's fine," I choke out through an embarrassingly dry throat.

Then we just stare at each other—me gripping the door so hard that my knuckles turn white and her hugging her duffel bag against herself like a shield.

Because me being a surly dickhead all the time is probably not super reassuring. But the truth is, I don't know how to act around her.

I fear if I soften up even a smidge, I'll cross a boundary I shouldn't. Take something that isn't mine. Irrevocably fuck up my relationship with the son I've always wanted. It doesn't matter that they aren't an item anymore. It would still be a betrayal. An incredibly unfatherly one at that.

Even just having her here in a professional capacity, living under the same roof as me, is a dangerous temptation.

"Bash? Are you feeling okay?" she asks hesitantly, because I'm still blocking her entry like a big dumb statue.

I step aside, internally chastising myself for being so fucking awkward, and gesture through the open doorway. "Yeah, fine. Sorry. Come on in. I'll show you your room."

Her lips roll together and she ducks her head as she enters the house, peeking around from beneath heavy lashes. She draws up short when she gets a good look at the wall of windows that face out to the balcony overlooking the water. "Wow. That view," she breathes. "You have a beautiful home."

I turn to face the lake, a spark of pride flaring in my chest. I love this house. Buying the lakefront lot was a gift to myself. I lived in a trailer on the property while I saved, knowing building on the rocky slope wouldn't be cheap.

Watching Gwen stop and stare is satisfying as hell. Those plush lips, slightly parted. That impressed expression sparking ideas in me.

It's all trouble.

"Did you build this?"

"A lot of it. Or a lot of the interior, I guess."

She turns in a slow circle, taking it in with total admiration. I step closer and take the heavy duffel bag from her. She hands it over silently, still gazing around the open living space and lofted ceilings with awe.

"I don't think I've ever lived in such a nice house."

"No?" I ask, hefting the bag over my shoulder and trying not to gawk at her.

"Nah. Army brat. And the houses on base weren't even close."

"Mom or dad?"

She finally turns to face me. "In the military? My dad."

"Impressive."

Her head joggles, like she doesn't quite agree with my assessment. "Almost as impressive as the depth of my daddy issues and the uniform kink my upbringing sent me out into the world with."

She barks out a laugh, and I try not to choke on my own saliva. "Jesus, Gwen."

Her responding laugh is light as she lifts a hand while placing the other over her chest. "Your Honor, I only speak the truth."

I shake my head and turn away to lead her upstairs. It feels like I'm walking to the gallows because living under the same roof as Gwen Dawson is sure to be the death of me.

"Even this stairwell is nice," she remarks from behind me. "Like the tiles on the face of the steps? The curve in the banister? It's beautiful, Bash."

"Thanks, I made them myself." I glance over my shoulder when I finish the stairs, watching her dainty fingers flutter over the rounded woodwork at the top landing.

She doesn't even look my way as she muses, "Goddamn, you must be good with your hands."

We freeze in time, and I watch pink splotches pop up on her round cheeks as she slowly turns her head in my direction. Fuck, she's so pretty, I can't even stand it.

Eyes wide and pleading, she adds, "I mean, you must be handy."

"I'm both."

My molars clamp down hard and fast, as though that might help me take back the two words that slipped out all too easily. Too late. My gaze drops to her mouth, watching her lips part on a sharp intake of air. Her tongue drags over the seam as she slowly quirks one disbelieving brow at me.

I've had too many quiet days spent recovering thinking about her. And I hate it. I hate it because what I want to do is close this gap between us. Shove her up against the wall. Peel those tight fucking yoga pants off that perfectly round ass.

But I can't.

And I hate it.

In fact, my desperate craving makes me hate myself a little bit too.

So, without another word, I walk down the hallway and drop her bag in the spare room—painfully close to mine.

Then I leave her there to get settled before I can get myself into more trouble than I already am.

As I jog down the stairs, I promise myself I'm going to create some space between us.

It's only when I reach the last step—a safe distance away—that I call back up, "Leaving for the hospital in an hour!"

"The energy in this truck is fuckin' weird." Clyde's beady eyes bore into the rearview mirror from the back seat.

Gwen and I worked expediently to get Clyde formally discharged, coordinating with the porter to get him arranged in my truck. When there's a task to do right in front of us, Gwen and I get shit done well enough.

But when you take the task away, the tension seeps back in. That's probably what Clyde is referring to—the way we're both sitting stiffly in the front like two kids forced to share a bench on the school bus.

Weird? Absolutely.

But not as weird as the drive to the hospital. That was one for the record books. Even my go-to '90s grunge playlist couldn't quell the deafening silence between us. Gwen stared out the window, strumming her teeth over her bottom lip while I squeezed the hell out of the steering wheel, trying to forget that I looked her in the eye and told her I'm good with my hands.

Right now, everything is much the same. Except Clyde is shit-talking us from the back like a snarky teenager.

"Just focusing on the road, Clyde. I've got precious cargo in the back seat," I deadpan, drawing a snort from Gwen and an eye roll from the older man.

"That's rich," he grumbles. "We all know I'm only here because you're a big, broody, dutiful motherfucker."

I sigh. He's not wrong. I am those things. In fact, I pride myself on being dutiful—*reliable*. But with Clyde, it's more than that. I care about him.

I mean, I haven't told him that. But I gave him my fucking kidney. What more does he want? A tattoo across my forehead?

"Clyde, if I didn't want you to live with me while you recover, I wouldn't have offered."

"Heartwarming," he mumbles, turning his head to look out the window. "You're just so nice."

From the corner of my eye, I see Gwen's head taking on a considering tilt. "Bash isn't nice—"

"This is going to be a long couple of months," I mutter as I turn off the main drag onto the quiet lakeside road that leads toward my house.

Gwen's head snaps in my direction. "If you'd let me finish, you wouldn't have to be having a big cry over an incomplete sentence."

My jaw works. "Comment stands."

She turns in her seat so she can look back at Clyde. "What I was about to say is that Bash isn't nice—he's kind. The two are not the same."

I watch in the mirror as Clyde squints at her. He fuckin' hates being told he's wrong. It's the source of most of our disagreements. "I'm pretty sure those two words are syn-onyms, Gwen."

She shrugs. "Perhaps. But I still think they're different. You don't have to agree." Then she turns back and faces the front, ending the conversation without giving him the satis-faction of an argument. I could learn a thing or two from her.

Silence stretches in the truck, and I can see Clyde's lips working, twisting and scrunching like he's chewing that over. Maybe even waiting for her to say something. Eventually, her lack of engagement pushes him to break.

"How do you think they're different?"

A ghost of a smile dances over her face, barely perceptible before it disappears. She doesn't turn around this time—instead, I feel her gaze on my profile.

"Well, I think being nice has more to do with behaving in a way that's driven by social expectations. Whereas being kind is behaving in a way that's driven by a concern for other people's well-being. And the two are not necessarily mutually exclusive. I'd be rather wary of someone who is nice but not kind."

I fight the urge to squirm in my seat as her words hang in the cab of my truck. It's a compliment, but I don't know what to do with it. So I keep my eyes on the road, seeing my driveway ahead like a portal to freedom and escape from being stuck in a small space with these two.

"Ah," Clyde drawls, as though understanding is dawn-ing on him in some grand fashion. Then, he grins at me in the mirror, and I just know he's about to toss a grenade and metaphorically run away giggling. "So it's like how he's being generally not *nice* to you in an attempt to be *kind* to his son?"

My foot instinctively taps the brake in shock as I choke on absolutely nothing. The truck jerks and then carries on as I cough to clear my throat.

Over the sound of Gwen laughing.

Head thrown back, hand on her full chest, *laughing*.

Yeah, this is definitely going to be a long couple of months.

CHAPTER 15

Gwen

"Okay, how's that?" I ask as I release the button that adjusts the angle of the mattress.

Clyde shifts, wincing ever so slightly as he tries to get comfortable on the home-care bed that's been set up for him. "My lower back is still sore from lying in the same goddamn position all the time. I knew they shouldn't have taken me off the morphine."

Bash scoffs, his shoulder propped against the doorframe of Clyde's temporary bedroom. "Funny how a little pain brought you around to the merits of modern medicine so quickly."

I shoot him a glare. "Can you not antagonize him for one day? I know this is your love language or whatever, but I want to make sure everything is okay."

All I get in return is an irritated glare. One I give right back. Because I'm not in the mood for Bash's shit right now.

I've stacked the pillows behind Clyde's back, being borderline obsessive about getting him propped up just right. Since getting him through the front door, the weight of taking care of him feels…heavy. Like I signed up to care for this man who I've grown quite fond of, and if something goes wrong, I'll hold myself responsible.

If I'm anything, it's hard on myself.

I stand back and eye him carefully before sliding one extra pillow under his knees to take any extra pressure off his lower back.

"Oh, yup. That's better, I think." Clyde's tired eyes flutter shut, and he sinks back. He may be dramatic sometimes, but I can see the tension that comes with pain and exhaustion on his features. His already weather-worn skin looks more deeply lined than usual, though the color seems to have improved in a matter of only five days.

"It's a miracle I've survived this many days post-surgery without someone propping me up with every pillow in this house."

I turn back slowly to face Bash, who clearly just can't help himself.

"Do you want me to come upstairs and get you settled as well? If you keep this attitude up, I can hold a pillow down over your face to make it stop."

Bash swallows roughly while continuing to glare at me but says nothing.

"Careful," Clyde interjects with a raspy cackle, "some people are into that kind of shit."

Bash's cheeks heat as he watches us impassively, otherwise

completely unfazed. "We're gonna need to lay out some ground rules for this arrangement. Because I'm already annoyed by you two."

"That's a compliment coming from him," Clyde whispers conspiratorially as he leans toward me.

I try not to laugh, because Bash looks serious as a heart attack when he begins to speak again. "I know this arrangement is best for everyone, so I'm tolerating it. I wouldn't change it, but I don't love it. This isn't some happy-family dynamic. We're roommates. You do your thing. I'll do mine."

I do my best to nod seriously, but Bash is downright sexy. It makes me want to needle him just so he'll crack a smile.

I lean toward Clyde with a stage-whisper loud enough that Bash can hear. "He reminds me of Oscar the Grouch sometimes." Then I turn back to face Bash, wanting to reassure him that I understand. "I love how honest you're being with us about your expectations and what you need. Clear communication will make sharing the space easier for everyone."

Clyde nods solemnly. "Bash, we understand. This is your trash can, and we're just living in it."

Bash's jaw twitches. "The two of you are really annoying together. Do you know that?"

I flash him my brightest grin. "Just think of us as the two annoying kids you never wanted."

"Oh, pfft," Clyde scoffs, landing a playful slap on my arm. "Ain't no way Bash is thinking about you like a kid."

Bash groans, and before I can even lift my eyes back his way, he's turned and left the room.

"Clyde, you really gotta ease off on him with that."

The man turns to me with a blank expression. "I don't know what you're talking about."

My head tilts, and I prop my hands on my hips. "Stop playing, silly fucker."

"He likes it."

"I don't think he does."

Clyde drops the pretense with an annoyed grumble as he reaches for the book I unpacked and placed on the bedside table for him. It's a compilation of firsthand accounts of alien abduction and, hilariously, exactly the type of literature I'd expect Clyde to consume.

"Well, then he needs it."

"What?"

He doesn't look up—just opens the book as he responds with, "Something that makes him happy."

My brows furrow. "Which is what?"

Now it's Clyde's turn to hit me with a head tilt. "Gwen, stop playing, silly fucker."

Once Clyde drifted off for an afternoon nap, I made my way out to the grocery store, using the card he gave me to purchase each item on the list he also provided. Of course, I accidentally forgot some of the less healthy items and replaced them with more nutritious options.

Clyde grumbled about it when I returned, but I just told him, "We're taking good care of this kidney because no one else likes you enough to give you one."

He rolled his eyes, but his lips twitched. Funny, ornery old man that he is.

Now I crack a window and get to work preparing a healthy meal—whether Clyde approves or not.

After months in a small studio apartment, it feels good to spread out over the butcher-block countertops. Light trickles in through the expansive windows and makes the gold hardware on the green cabinets shimmer. My bare feet are warm on the wide floorboards and I feel alarmingly at ease in the space even though it's all new to me.

Bash and I cross paths briefly, wordlessly preparing food side by side without him so much as sparing me a sideways glance.

I wish I could say the same for myself. Instead, I find myself fixating on the smell of him, willing him to look my way. To say something. To throw all that loyalty and commitment that I admire about him out the fucking window and cross a line.

I daydream about it. Him, swiping all the chopped vegetables off the counter and lifting me onto it. Him, taking me out onto that balcony and bending me over the railing. Waiting until Clyde's asleep and then sneaking into my room next to his. Covering my mouth with his hand to keep me quiet while he makes me come.

But my dreams aren't meant to come true.

Because Bash isn't that guy.

His morals barely let him *look* at me. And maybe I should be more concerned about my own morals because, when he retreats upstairs with his sandwich while I finish making chicken noodle soup for Clyde, I'm downright disappointed.

Dinner at the long dining room table feels strange knowing Bash is one floor above us all alone. I'm sure I don't imagine the way the Clyde keeps checking the stairs, as though expecting to see Bash relent and join us.

After we eat, I clean Clyde's incision and tuck him in, rolling my eyes when he tells me to stop hovering because I'm not his mother.

I think it's because Clyde doesn't make demands of me that taking care of him is so satisfying. Not once has he asked me when I plan to settle down, find a steady job, or start a family. I grew up with this feeling of never being good enough, never trying hard enough. Never *quite* fitting in. I'm sure the unrelenting questions were my dad's way of motivating me—it was the drill sergeant in him—but they only stifled me.

I was—and still am—too soft to hold up under that brand of motivation. It wasn't until I got away, saw the world, found yoga that I felt like I might actually be good at something. That I discovered passion. That I learned to love my body. That I found helping others is what fulfills me.

It's with those thoughts in mind that I shut the house down. I double-check the locked doors and turn off almost all the lights—I leave a few on just in case Clyde needs to get up, something he assured me he doesn't need any help with—before I head upstairs. I look back over the living room, illuminated by the glow of the outdoor lights. Vaulted wood panel ceilings make the room feel big but not sterile. And the warm white walls make it feel airy but still rustic.

I turn away with a soft smile touching my lips. I can so perfectly imagine Bash building this place. It's soothing and masculine and brimming with thoughtful touches—just like him.

Upstairs, I enter my room and let out a dreamy sigh. My room is beautiful, and I'd be lying if I said I wasn't excited to go enjoy the space. Be still. Stare at the lake. Meditate. Stretch.

The rounded bay window with a cushioned bench makes this the bedroom of my childhood dreams. A queen-size memory-foam bed—with a door just to the right that opens to a small balcony overlooking the lake—makes this the bedroom of my adult dreams. And after months of winter spent in the apartment above the yoga studio with zero outdoor living space, that balcony is where I want to be.

It's still early spring in the mountains, so I grab a fleece, a pair of slouchy wool socks, and my yoga mat. I slip from my room, shutting the door quietly behind me.

The dead bolt on the outside of the door catches my attention. It gets the wheels in my head turning, speculating on why Bash would possibly want to keep someone locked *inside* the room. Too many crime podcasts filter into my thoughts, but I shake them away, telling myself to quit being so distracted.

But that proves to be impossible when I notice Bash mere feet away. He's sitting out in front of his room. And until I fully stepped outside just now, I hadn't realized the balcony runs the full width of the house.

He doesn't look my way. Instead, he tips his head back against the Adirondack chair, letting out a deeply tired sigh.

It's dark, but the outdoor sconces drench the deck in a warm glow. Straight ahead of us, the lake moves in soft, undulating waves. The soothing, steady sound of it lapping against the rocky shore calls to me.

But I know when I'm not wanted somewhere, so I begin to turn away, whispering a parting, "Sorry. I'll go back inside."

I see his eyes close as he subtly shakes his head. "No. It's fine. I'll go."

"That seems silly. It's your house. I'm intruding. I can meditate inside just as easily."

"Gwen. Clyde argues with me enough as it is. Can you just…not?"

I swallow at that. Everything about Bash right now screams exhaustion, and guilt nips at me for interrupting his quiet moment. "Sorry. I didn't mean to bother you."

His head rolls along the back of the chair and his dark eyes land on me. I try not to squirm under the intensity of his stare. "You don't bother me, Gwen."

I give him my best disbelieving look. I don't want to argue, but I also don't buy it.

He just sighs, turning to stare back at the water. "Not in the way you think."

Perplexing—that's what Sebastian Rousseau is. Inconsistent too. His moods shift like the tides.

"You're confusing, you know that?" I toss my mat down, deciding to honor his wishes and stay outside. "And kind of exhausting," I add as I take a seat and cross my legs.

"I know" is all he says back.

But he doesn't leave.

I go inward anyway, not caring if he stays and watches. It might inspire him to do a little meditating of his own. God knows that nervous system of his could use it.

Doing my best to ignore his presence, I close my eyes, letting the sound of his breathing mingle with the echoes of the night. The hush of the lake, the call of a loon, the wind slipping between the needles of the pines that surround the private lot.

Unlike the main strip in Rose Hill, where I've been living, everything out here smells fresh and wild. Like amber and cedar and that bright mineral scent of rain on warm pavement.

My breath flows, and I let the tension of the day slip away into the mat beneath me. My shoulders drop and my hips soften. My neck unlocks and—

Why is there a lock on the outside of that door?

Fuck my brain. It just won't let me go these days. It's like years of working on stilling my mind are shot because I have a crush I can't shake. And I know myself well enough to realize the question will niggle at me. So instead of forcing myself through it, I quietly ask him, "Why is there a lock on the outside of that balcony door?"

Several beats of silence follow my very random question. I peek one eye over at him, wondering if he's drifted off in the few minutes of silence.

Though that seems out of character for what I know of him. There's something watchful about Bash. Guarded. And falling asleep beside someone who makes him as tense as I do would just be plain unnatural. Fight-or-flight—it seems like I usually make him want to fly away as fast as he can.

Unlike him, I don't find it difficult to relax when he's near at all, despite all the true crime podcasts I've consumed. In my stalwart dedication to not irritating him in his own home, I decide to let it go. Or at least try.

I close my eyes and rest the pad of my thumb against the tip of my middle finger. I breathe again, imagining fluidly wiping a mess of writing from a whiteboard and leaving behind a shiny, clear expanse. Letting all my jumbled thoughts and feelings be wiped away—if for only fifteen minutes. Because I know it will make me feel better.

"I thought I'd have kids."

Bash's gravelly words cut through the silence and stop me in my tracks. My head turns slowly in his direction. I keep the rest of my body still, like I'm approaching a wild animal. Worried I might spook him if I do too much too soon.

I say nothing. Instead, I just listen. Give him room to talk if he wants to.

And he does.

"When I built this place, I thought I'd have kids."

I swallow and nod softly.

"The room you're staying in was supposed to be the perfect kid's room. The bench. The window. I figured by a certain age, they'd want to use the balcony too. But then I worried that when they were small, it might be a safety issue. So I put a dead bolt on the outside so my wife or I could—"

He trips over his own words, stopping midsentence with an irritated twist of his lips before forging ahead. "Whatever.

I just figured I could lock it from the outside, then head back into my room from the shared balcony and not have to worry about a curious toddler wandering out."

Everything he's saying makes so much sense. Except for the *wife* part—my brain trips up on that word.

"I can take it off if it makes you uncomfortable. I didn't even think."

I glance over my shoulder at the pewter circle adhered to the door. For some reason, that one little touch feels monumental somehow. It's endearing to think he planned that far ahead.

"No, that's fine. You should keep it up for when you do have babies."

He snorts at that.

"I think that ship has probably sailed."

"Why?"

"I'm forty and a bachelor. And I'm not sure if you noticed, but I'm not exactly great company these days. The thought of wading back into the dating world is exhausting and daunting. The clock is ticking, and my options have dwindled."

Options. The sentiment rankles me, and I have no right to it. Pushing the feeling aside, I shimmy my shoulders, drawing my spine up tall as I stare out over the moonlit water. "I enjoy your company."

"Gwen." He sighs my name like I exhaust him, his palm scrubbing over his stubbled jaw.

"Oh, quit constantly flattering yourself. That statement doesn't need to mean more than it does." I swear I see a dimple flash in his cheek, so I forge ahead. "I just meant that I'm not put off by all your snarling."

He finally looks my way. "Snarling?"

"Yes. Barking and growling too."

"Am I a dog now?"

"A big, dumb one who's been living tied to a post for too long and doesn't know how to interact anymore? Yes. You are."

His cheek twitches quickly, once, before smoothing, and the responding grunt sounds suspiciously similar to a chuckle. I take satisfaction in thinking I may have lightened his mood for even a moment. I watch him raptly, his expression growing thoughtful, his gaze moving back out to the water.

"I wasn't always like this. It kind of snuck up on me, I guess."

"Well, we're all constantly changing. Evolving. Growing. I don't know a single person who is the same as they once were. I know I'm not. And how boring to just…know who you are and think there's nothing more out there for the rest of your life."

He shrugs. "I might have changed too much."

I inhale deeply, a soft smile curving my lips. "Impossible."

Bash scoffs. "Not if you ask my ex-wife."

There's that word again. I ignore the sudden tightness in my neck and jaw. *Wife*. But no, *ex*-wife.

Swallowing, I forge ahead with something suitably vague. "Maybe she was wrong."

"Nah. She wasn't wrong. And I don't blame her one bit."

He scoffs. "You know, actually, due to recent developments, maybe I do."

My eyes lead my head in his direction again. "Listen, I want to respect your privacy and not annoy you and all that, but I am way too snoopy to sit here and pretend that talking in code about this is the least bit satisfying."

Our eyes meet across the ten or so feet that separate us and my stomach flips over on itself. *Fuck, he's handsome.* I never—not once in my life—had this kind of physical reaction to another person. Several beats pass, and I'm transported to a quiet corner of an airport with a handsome stranger who makes butterflies erupt in my stomach.

That feeling of being alone with him is impossible to shake.

"It's not an exciting story. We got married young. It was impulsive, but we had a lot of fun. Both of us had good jobs and too much disposable income. In a lot of ways, we were very compatible. Life was great."

He pauses for a few moments, then continues. "Then one day adulthood snuck up on me and I realized I wanted a family. She didn't. We tried to work it out. For a few years, I thought I could go along with it. Thought maybe she'd change her mind. But…" He shrugs, dropping my gaze and looking off into the distance. "Resentment grew anyway. And I *really* wanted a family. We were at an impasse, and neither one of us was happy. So I left and built this place as therapy, thinking maybe I'd be able to meet someone new and have it all one day."

I let a breath rush out through my lips. That's…a lot.

The disappointment of it. But then he hits me with the killing blow.

"The really hilarious update is that I ran into her when I left Tripp's birthday party all those months ago. I was waiting around at the airport, hoping to get onto a flight, and *bam* there she was. Remarried. With a toddler. And very, very pregnant. So now I know it wasn't that she didn't want a family. She just didn't want it with *me*. And all I've done is spend years licking my wounds, wishing for something I'll never have. Too scared to even try."

The pain in his voice is like a spear to my chest. It aches for him.

I ache for him.

"You can. You should. Try, that is. You're a catch. Someone will happily snap you up." I work to keep my voice neutral and my face passive, but my tone feels frantic—a little desperate. Like I want him to believe me just a little too badly.

He laughs, a flat, biting chuckle. His jaw flexes, but he doesn't respond immediately. Eventually, he turns his attention my way, dark eyes boring into mine. "Turns out it's not that easy to find a person you actually connect with."

My throat constricts and my mouth goes dry because I can read between the lines. Hear the bitterness in his voice. Pick up on the thing he just can't bring himself to say. The elephant in the room that neither of us knows how to talk about.

We connected. *We* had that spark. The one you can't force. The kind that sneaks up on you when you least expect it. And the worst part is, we both know it.

Who knows where it could have gone? It could have been nowhere at all, but I still feel the loss of that possibility. Acutely.

Tripp doesn't have to be here for his presence to loom between us. We both know it's there, but we don't talk about it.

I turn my body, rising to face him. "I broke up with him at his birthday party. Right then and there. If I had known…"

Bash goes deathly still as I trail off. It's almost as though he stops breathing.

"You left me in that bathroom and—"

"Gwen, just don't."

But I don't listen. "The way he spoke about you? The way he spoke to me? I went straight back to him and ended it on the spot."

"Gwen—"

"I left," I say, forging ahead. I want him to know. No, I *need* him to know. "I wasn't even that far behind you. I thought maybe I could catch up. I tried to find y—"

He sits up, spinning to face me, a pained look of fury on his face. "Gwen. Stop."

"That night something happened between us—"

"Stop!" His harsh voice cuts through the night air, and I still, watching as he wipes a trembling palm over his mouth in frustration. "I can't have this conversation with you. I *can't*."

Eyes wide, I just blink back at him. He looks pained and desperate all at once. But his voice leaves no room for debate. This isn't a conversation. It's a demand. A plea to stop even *thinking* about us.

My throat aches as the reality of our situation crashes against me in a sudden wave. It bowls me over. The sharp bite of cold water stealing all my warmth, drowning all my unfailing optimism.

"Don't you get it?" he implores, propping his elbows on his knees and holding his hands out like he's begging me to understand. "Tripp might have some glaring character flaws—I won't argue that with you—but he's my *son*. And I've wanted that. Maybe not like this. But it might be my only opportunity to have even a sliver of this thing. My dad was a piece of shit. Walked out without a word and never came back. I've always wanted to…I don't know…*fix* that wrong. Do better one day. Prove to myself that while I might have half his DNA, I'm not him. It's why…it's why your being here has to be for Clyde. For professional reasons and nothing more."

His breathing is rough as he pierces me with a scorching gaze that would normally make me squirm. Tonight, it just hurts.

"Gwen. I can't fuck it all up. I can't cross that line, no matter how tempted I am."

His reasoning hits me like a ton of bricks. It feels as though this entire conversation has been building toward this exact moment. Like the universe is a lawyer presenting its case in court, slowly laying a trap that I waltzed right into.

My breathing turns shallow, and I press my lips together to keep from saying anything. Because what is there to say? And I don't trust my voice not to break if I speak. I hug my arms around my torso, feeling like I need to cover up, even though I'm fully clothed.

He shifts forward, drawn toward me, and I swear he's about to stand. But his motion stops abruptly, his fingers gripping the armrests of his chair as though holding himself back.

He makes no other move and I'm more disappointed than I have any right to be. My eyes sting as I push to stand. The weight of having to be mature about this whole thing feels impossibly heavy, but I get to my feet all the same.

Then I offer Bash a sad smile and a whispered, "I'm sorry," as I turn and head back to my room.

And he doesn't stop me. Doesn't offer me a single other word.

A familiar feeling stirs inside me. The one where I'm in the way or not good enough—a burden. I know it's not true. I know that's not what he meant.

But I feel the sting of it all the same.

I wash my face, telling myself the wetness on my cheeks is just tap water, then crawl into the pillowy, soft bed with a heavy heart and a busy mind. Our confrontation keeps me awake for hours. I think myself in dizzying circles. Turning every possibility between us over in my mind again and again.

The entire mess feels monumentally unfair. Because I like Bash.

I *really* like Bash.

Unfortunately for me, I like Bash enough to keep my distance.

It shouldn't be too hard. I was never planning to stay anyway.

CHAPTER 16

Bash

Bash: Hey, just letting you know that I'm all good. Back home and healing well.

Tripp: Better than my news, which is that we didn't clinch a playoff spot. I'll touch base when I'm in a better mood.

It's Dads' Night Out at Rose Valley Alley, and I'm sidelined. Forced to watch and not partake, even though I'm a founding member of the Ball Busters.

But I don't care. After a couple of weeks spent recovering slowly, lying in bed for too long, and constantly dodging Gwen in my own home, I really needed a night out.

"That was fucking terrible," I tell West right to his face as he saunters back to our team's table. My text exchange with Tripp rubbed me the wrong way. Truthfully, it hurt my feelings. He didn't reach out to ask how the surgery went, and when I told him I was okay, he instantly turned it into a conversation about hockey. Like making the playoffs was more important than my survival. And maybe it *was* more important to him—and that just makes me feel worse.

West's brow furrows as he turns to look back at the bowling lane. "Did we see two different turns there? I got you a spare!"

I grunt and sip at my boring-ass water. Because apparently mixing alcohol and prescription painkillers isn't recommended. "A spare isn't a strike, West."

Ford, West's best friend, chuckles from beside me, and Rhys just shakes his head. He and I have grown closer over the past several months. He's a man of few words but many facial expressions, and I can tell he's amused.

"Well, have someone better take your turns for you, then. Not sure who made you the dictator of this entire team," West teases.

I haven't been medically cleared to bowl since my surgery, but I have been medically cleared to go for light walks. And I figure sitting at bowling, hydrating, and coaching this ragtag team can't be any more strenuous than a light walk.

It's a hell of a lot healthier than sitting at home trying to avoid Clyde's off-color jokes and Gwen's mere presence. Since our talk on the balcony last week, we've avoided each other like the plague. It's different this time because *she's* avoiding *me.*

And I hate it.

"I'm not a dictator. I'm coaching you. And I know you can do better than that."

West rolls his eyes at me before hitting me with one of his signature smirks. "No. You're a *dick*…tator."

Ford drops his head to his hands. "Jesus, West. How old are you?"

"Age is just a number, fella," West quips as he slaps his friend on the shoulder. "And, Bash, if you don't like me bowling your turns for you, why don't you ask Rhys? At least he could use the practice."

Rhys's cheek twitches, but he says nothing. He doesn't need to defend himself—he knows he's the worst on the team by a long shot.

He's just not as fun to pick on as West.

"Don't insult him. He's a professional athlete. He's mastered *something*, and here you are, pretending spares are something special."

West just laughs. He's impossible to piss off. "Man, you're even more miserable than usual. Were all your good moods in the kidney that you gave away? Are you stuck with the bitchy kidney?"

"My kidneys are both exceptional. The doctors told me as much," I mumble defensively.

"No, seriously. Who pissed in your cereal and why is it Clyde?"

I bristle at him assuming Clyde is the one who's under my skin. "Clyde doesn't bother me. Mostly." He's been at the hospital daily for follow-up appointments, but otherwise, he's fairly bedridden. Gwen takes care of him, and while she's at the yoga studio, he usually sleeps or dozes in front of the television.

"Wait. Does that mean Gwen pissed in your cereal?" Rhys finally pipes up, curiosity dawning on his dark features.

"Is there a different metaphor we can use?" Ford sighs, taking a deep swig of his beer. "I don't love the mental imagery with this one."

West grins, no doubt about to add something he thinks is funny to the conversation. But he stops mid-breath and shifts his gaze to me. Analyzes me. And though he's a big old goofball, he's also great at reading people. I think it's a skill he's honed as a horse trainer, picking up on subtle cues and body language. And the way he's staring at me makes me feel like I've given him a tell.

"No, wait. That makes so much sense."

Rhys chuckles. "Is she bugging you about your chakras? Is one of them blocked?"

I scowl, wondering why everyone is talking about my chakras lately. She must be indoctrinating Rhys during his classes too.

"No. She's fine."

West's mouth pops open. He looks like a fucking dog with a bone right now, and I don't like it one bit. "Like, fine or...*fine*?"

"Fine. Like I don't notice her at all."

I look back at three sets of eyes, all fixed on me. Even Ford, who usually stays out of this shit now regards me with pity.

"What?"

"Bash, old boy, you've got a crush," West announces eagerly, making me wince.

I whip around and take in everyone around us, hoping upon hope that no one is listening. The small-town gossip network is fucking vicious, and I don't want to be its latest subject.

"I do not," I say. But it sounds unconvincing, even to me, so I add something that I am convinced of. "Plus, she dated Tripp. That's a line you just don't cross. Even if I saw her first."

If I had known.

I ended it on the spot.

I tried to find you.

I'd cut her off, but I know that's what she was about to say. I could piece it all together. I wasn't blind to the way she looked at me. The way she *looks* at me. Gaze licking over me like flames over kindling.

"Saw her first?" Rhys asks, looking confused.

I wave a hand casually. "We got stuck in an airport overnight together over a year ago."

West gasps. "Wait, she's that girl? Didn't you get her number?"

My stomach drops hard and fast. I never told West that story. "How do you know that?"

"Clyde told me."

Fucking Clyde.

I find myself wondering if it's too late to take my kidney back when Terence—who likes to go by Too Tall and is the most universally hated guy at bowling—pops his head over to our table. "Is one of you going to take your turn? Like this year? Or are you forfeiting?"

"Fuck off, Stretch," all three of my teammates say at once.

Rhys turns to glare at him, making a twisting motion with his hands as though he's wringing the water out of a dishrag.

The guy leaves, but not without muttering something offensive under his breath.

Or…it would be offensive if any of us cared what he thought.

"Okay, wait," Rhys starts up. "You're telling me that you met Gwen first? And hit it off first? And *then* she dated your son?"

Ford hisses out a breath. "That's so weir—"

I correct his train of thought before he can even go there. Because I went there at first too. So now I admit to them what I haven't even admitted to myself. "I don't think she knew Tripp was my son, so don't make it sound like that. And I took her number down wrong after pulling an all-nighter, so in her defense, she thought I ghosted her."

West elbows Rhys. "See that? Falling all over himself to protect her honor."

Rhys smirks in response, but Ford looks downright thoughtful. "That's actually—"

"Kind of romantic?" West guesses with amusement twinkling in his eyes.

"No." Ford shrugs. "Sad."

Fucking Ford. Direct to a fault sometimes. "Thanks, I'm really fine, though," I reply grimly.

Fine.

"So you're saying that it *is* Gwen who pissed in your cereal, but you're fine with it?" West asks while stroking at his chin like he's some sort of old-school philosopher.

Rhys rolls in with his deep, authoritative voice. "You know, as someone who grew up without a dad, I don't think this would bother me."

"You mean if your dad came around and started dating Tabitha, you'd be cool with that?"

Rhys turns a fierce glare on West. "Fuck no. That's my wife you're talking about."

West laughs, holding his hands up in an amused *don't shoot* gesture.

"I just mean," Rhys continues, "if my dad showed up and dated a casual ex of mine that he met before I did? I don't know. I'd have no relationship with the guy, so I doubt I'd care. It would be like any random dude dating an ex of mine. Unless I was hung up on her."

I know he's trying to be comforting, but it doesn't work. Instead, it just stresses me out to think my already tenuous relationship with Tripp isn't salvageable.

"But what if your dad wanted to have a relationship with you?" I blurt, hoping the big, broody man before me has a magical answer.

Rhys shrugs before shooting me an apologetic glance. "I don't know. Our situations aren't the same. But I'd probably have some shit I needed to work through before I could do that. And him dating my ex would be the least of the grudges I'd be holding against him."

I swallow and glance away, trying not to spiral. Because it feels like I'm damned if I do pursue Gwen and damned if I don't.

But beneath my layers of anxiety, he's planted a seed, one that gets me thinking. What if Tripp wouldn't care? He doesn't seem to care all that much about me anyway. It begs the question: am I holding myself back for no good reason?

All three of them are staring at me like they expect me to respond, but I'm done talking about this. "Somebody take your turn before Stretch throws a full-blown temper tantrum," I bark, effectively ending the conversation. I cross my arms, shuttering my emotions.

I'm not sure when a fucking bowling team turned into heart-to-heart chats and relationship advice with these guys, but it catches me off guard. I simmer and stew over my opening up for the rest of the night.

And against my better judgment, I order a much-needed rum and Coke. Just to take the edge off.

CHAPTER 17

Gwen

Gwen: Hihi. Got your number from Tabby. Just checking in. I'm headed back. How was Clyde when you left for bowling?

Bash: Sometimes I regret giving him my kidney.

IN THE DARKENED BACK SEAT OF OUR CAB, I SMILE DOWN AT my illuminated screen because I know he doesn't mean it. He's just being surly. Going out for dinner with Tabitha, Rosie, and Skylar was fun, but I'd be lying if I said I didn't worry about Clyde while I was out. Checking in feels good. The fact that Bash wrote back feels good too. So I text again.

Gwen: No you don't.

Bash: His new lease on life is a lot more gross than I

anticipated. He shares too much. Did you know there are dating apps for people who want to prepare for zombie apocalypses? Because he told me all about them.

Gwen: I think it's sweet. He'll need someone like-minded to pass the time in that bunker.

Bash: I don't want to be in his bunker then.

Gwen: You can come get eaten by a zombie with me.

Bash: What?

Gwen: In all those zombie movies and shows, I will never understand those people's obsession with staying alive. For what? Living in a zombie world where everything sucks and all is lost? No, sir. Not for me. Peace out, bitches. It's been a slice. On to the next.

Bash: Zombies aren't real.

Gwen: Well, you're the one who keeps bringing them up.

"What's the deal with you and Bash?"

Tabitha is leaning across the center seat, staring at my screen, and I didn't even notice. I go still now, flipping my phone over in my lap and peeking out the cab's windshield.

Bash's place is just a little farther beyond hers, so we split the ride. We've had a fun night. I needed it after the intensity of Clyde's post-op care. And after sharing two bottles of wine with the girls, my brain is just a little too foggy to properly respond to such a direct question.

"What do you mean?"

"I mean that you're sitting here texting him with a creepy smile on your face. And Rhys told me that you"—she drops her voice and leans toward me with a dramatic whisper—"dated his son."

My heart rate accelerates like it always does when this topic comes up. I feel guilty over Tripp, even though I had no way of knowing. If I could go back in time and un-date him, I would.

"Yeah. But it's…complicated."

Almost as complicated as dodging Bash every day in his house. Trying to keep away because he asked me to.

"Pfffffft." Tabitha blows a drunken raspberry as she flops back in her seat. "Complicated is just an excuse. Ask me how I know. Rhys and I were complicated once."

My lips press together. She and Rhys are a different story. They were made for each other, where Bash and I were apparently made to torture each other.

"You know what's complicated?" Tabby's head rolls toward me. "Life. Life is complicated. And short. Gwen, life is too damn short not to wade through all the complications. And you guys are too hot not to bang. I've seen the fuck-me eyes you give each other."

I bark out a laugh. "Tabitha. You've had too much wine."

The tiny woman just waves me off. "You heard me. If you're allowed to tease Rhys and me about chakras, then we get to talk about Bash. He needs chakra 911. The only cure is doing naked yoga with the hot teacher."

I slump back and throw an arm over my eyes to hide from the embarrassing conversation. Sex doesn't make me uncomfortable—but the thought of everyone around us knowing our sordid history does. "Bash wants to settle down," I counter. "I'm not the right person for that."

And it's partially true. Bash does want to settle down. He straight-out told me as much.

"Why not? You act like he's looking for a woman to keep pregnant and barefoot in the kitchen or something."

"Rose Hill is a temporary stop. I like moving around. I like to travel. There's a lot I want to see and do still. I can't be tied down—it stresses me out. I watched my mom do it. It's not for me."

What I don't tell her is that this morning I received a job offer that would take me to Costa Rica teaching yoga at a resort for the winter. It's the perfect combination of travel and professional development. It's an escape from Canadian winters.

It's an escape from Bash.

And yet, I didn't instantaneously accept the position.

"You can't leave. You love it here. Our trivia team would be fucked without you. And I'd miss your big titties." Her gaze drops to my chest, where my breasts are indeed pressed against my thin black sweater. She sighs wistfully. "You sure there's no way to share just a little of all that with me?"

I laugh. "My titties and I will miss you too. I'll definitely have to come back and visit."

Tabby shrugs. "Why do you have to be tied down? I tend to think the right person would be happy to go on those adventures with you. Or not. Rhys and I do lots of things on our own. Having a partner doesn't mean being tied down."

My head wobbles, but I don't respond. I don't know

what to say to that. I've never seen that kind of relationship in action. My mom was always rushing to get dinner on the table before my dad walked through the door. Packing his lunch in the morning. Pressing his clothes for him like she was a maid and not a partner.

If I tiptoed around him, she *catered* to him. No savings, no education, no job experience.

No way out if she even wanted it.

Yeah, no. I won't let that be me.

When we pull up in front of Tabby's craftsman house in the center of town, she pats my leg. "The world is your oyster, Gwen. But eating oysters with someone else is the best. Do you know why?"

"Why?"

"Because they make you horny." Tabby winks at me over her shoulder as she flicks the door open. The cabdriver just sighs, and I can't help but wonder what he must think of us.

She gets out of the car but bends at the waist, popping her head back inside. "Gwen, I just want you to know that if I were you, I'd fuck my ex-boyfriend's dad, and I wouldn't even feel bad about it because that other guy sounds like a fucking loser."

A choked sound filters from the front seat, and my cheeks go hot.

"Anyway, bye!" Tabitha calls as she slams the door on me. The driver pulls away slowly, but not before I see my friend approach her front porch. The one where her husband sits on the steps waiting for her.

He greets her with open arms, and she moves in to

straddle his lap before dropping her mouth to his.

It's sweet. But more than that, it's...appealing. I bet they'd want to stay alive in a zombie apocalypse just so they could have more time together.

It makes me wonder if maybe, just maybe, I could find comfort in a partnership like that. In a place like this.

If I was ever inspired to try...it might be now.

CHAPTER 18

Bash

FORD DROPS ME OFF AT HOME, AND I TIPTOE QUIETLY—IF somewhat unsteadily—through the front door, not wanting to wake anyone.

But I can hear chatter filtering in from the kitchen. When I drop my gaze to take off my boots, I see dirt tracked across the floor. Immediately, I know it's from Clyde. He's always walking around with his fucking shoes on.

"Clyde!" I yell. "Does your occupational therapist recommend sweeping as an exercise? Because you need to clean up the dirt you tracked in. I'm not your goddamn maid!"

His raspy cackle is the first response I get. Followed by "But you'd be a good one! Being neurotically tidy comes so naturally to you!"

I toe off my shoes, pull the broom and dustpan from the front closet, and clean up the clumps of dirt he left behind.

With broom and shoes properly put away, I head toward the kitchen, grumbling and shaking my head.

I find Gwen and Clyde seated at the dining room table with playing cards and plastic chips spread between them. There's a pot of lavender I've never seen before pushed off to the side.

"Raise."

Clyde pushes more chips into the middle, and Gwen laughs, sipping at a glass of white wine. "You can't just raise every time, Clyde."

The older man scoffs. "I can if I want to."

"It's not a great strategy," I say by way of announcing myself as I wander into the kitchen. Both of their heads snap in my direction—Gwen's eyes wide, Clyde's narrowed.

"You're just mad because I'm the one up playing poker with her," Clyde says. "Plus, giving me a kidney doesn't mean you get to tell me what to do. That wasn't in the contract."

My lips wobble. I'm too inebriated to keep my amusement at bay right now. "I'm not telling you what to do. Just offering a little advice."

Clyde rolls his eyes at me and pushes himself up with a stiff motion. "Here's my advice. Stop being such a chicken-shit and take over my hand. I'm going to bed."

With that, the older man punches my chest—hard—on his way past. "You kids have fun."

"You should stay," I try feebly. Mostly because the prospect of being alone with Gwen is daunting and thrilling all at once. And I'm far too unencumbered right now to make good decisions.

But Clyde is already hobbling down the hallway. "I'm sick of your company. You're extremely negative, you know?" He turns and glares at me over his shoulder. "Allergic to fun these days. It's like living with Eeyore."

I choke back my laugh. "I thought I was Oscar the Grouch!" I call back, pulling out his vacated chair to take a seat.

"If this were really a trash can, your panties wouldn't be so twisted over a little dust on the floor."

"You're a slob, Clyde," I volley good-naturedly.

The only response I get is Clyde flipping me the bird without looking back, and this time Gwen wheezes a laugh from behind her fist.

"I'll sweep up the dirt."

I peek at her with a wink. "I already did." Then I scoop up his cards—a two of diamonds and a three of clubs.

"*That's* what you kept raising on?" I blurt, turning back toward the hallway with a look of genuine shock on my face. "That's arguably the worst hand in poker!"

Clyde's already rounded the corner into his room, but it doesn't stop him from calling back, "You're just lucky we weren't playing strip poker!"

"You're right. I'd rather not see you naked because that's what you'd be raising with hands like this."

"I'd like to see you do better! Now stop talking to me. I'm turning on my white noise machine so I don't have to hear your stupid voice!"

"Oh my god," Gwen whispers. "You two are ridiculous."

I drop my head into my hand and smile down at the table. If I weren't drunk, I'd be mortified.

"Why do you even bother getting into it with him like that?"

I snort a laugh and smile up at Gwen, swaying ever so slightly in my seat. "Honestly, it's fun."

At first, she looks stunned, and then a grin takes over her face. "You guys are like father and son bickering over the dumbest shit. You both take each other's bait. Every. Single. Time."

I shrug, another chuckle spilling from my loose lips as I check down the hallway, half expecting to see Clyde eavesdropping.

My eyes catch on the lavender as I turn back to Gwen. Pretty flowers and pretty Gwen. The color reminds me of her eyes.

"You like? I bought it for the house. I hope that's okay. I didn't want to break any rules by talking to you in order to double-check."

I look up from the small purple flowers toward Gwen. "That's not a rule."

She pushes the pot closer, ignoring my response. "Rub the flowers between your fingers and then smell. Nothing better than fresh lavender. Especially when you're hammered."

I reach for a flower, running my fingers over it. "I'm not hammered."

"Oh-kay," she singsongs, like she doesn't believe me.

When I wave my hand in front of my nose and inhale, my eyes fall shut. It *does* smell good. Good enough that I confess, "I'm only regular drunk. Not hammered."

"Drunk enough to play strip poker?" she asks, waggling her brows.

I laugh and cast her a faux glare. "Probably."

She throws her head back and laughs, the sound rich and warm—one of the first things I noticed about her. My eyes soak in the elegant curve of her throat before she looks back at me and says, "Or go fish. Whatever floats your boat."

My cheek twitches. "Do you know how to play poker? Or were you just humoring him?"

Gwen's head tips to the side. "I understand the concept."

It's a bad idea. I know it is. Sitting here, after dark, across from her. *Drunk.*

But Rhys's words are fresh in my mind. So I stay.

With a firm nod, I reach across the table and collect the cards to shuffle. "I'm not starting off with Clyde's shitty hand. Fresh game."

"Works for me," she says matter-of-factly, as she reorganizes the chips.

Within minutes, we're all set up again. Me at the head of the table and her slightly down one side at a right angle to me.

I take her in. Teeth pushed down onto her pillowy bottom lip as she gazes down at her two new cards. A loose, cropped sweatshirt draped off one shoulder. Tight fucking yoga pants that show off every goddamn curve. Fuzzy socks with little raccoon faces all over them.

I've dreamed of this. Her. Having her here.

"You have to place your blind, Gwen. That means match my five."

Her lashes flutter up to me. "Oh, whoops." She giggles and reaches for her stack of chips, counting them meticulously before sliding them next to mine.

I glance down at my hand. It's good, not a throwaway. But I don't want to womp Gwen. I could toss a couple of hands just to be nice. But not this one.

"Bet," I say, sliding in a few more chips.

She stares at me, a smile dancing on her pretty mouth. Then with an innocent shrug she says, "Bet," and matches my chips again.

I quirk a brow at her, trying to make sense of her giddy demeanor, then lay out three cards face up for the flop.

It makes my good hand a great hand. I have a straight. Glancing up at her, she's still looking at me like the Cheshire cat.

I know I'm just regular drunk and not hammered, but I can't quite make sense of her expression.

"Bet."

She nods, taps the table, and responds with "Call."

I turn the blind card, and it changes nothing for me, but her face lights up like it's Christmas morning.

It makes me want to fold. Shovel my entire stack of chips her way and lose it all to her.

But I don't. I burn another card and flip the final one so that five cards are laid out between us.

"All right, let's see 'em, Dawson."

Her baby blues go wide. "My cards, or…?"

My heart stutters, and my eyes fall to her chest. She smiles and takes a deep swig of her wine, then turns her cards over, not even giving me a chance to fall all over myself with that innuendo.

I watch her face. The flush on her cheeks. The twinkle

in her eye. I may not know much, but I'm pretty sure she's flirting with me.

And it's the first time I'm hit with the realization that I don't know how many glasses of wine she's had. That I might not be the only one here who is "regular" drunk. Having a rum and Coke while still taking painkillers was a monumentally stupid decision.

Not wanting to gawk, I drop my gaze to the table.

Her hand is fucking terrible.

I flip mine. "Straight."

"Shoot, I guess I lose," Gwen says, smiling against the rim of her wineglass.

"Gwen, that was a terrible hand. Were you taking advice from Clyde on how to—" My train of thought dies off, because Gwen has pulled off one raccoon sock and tossed it over her shoulder.

My heart thuds heavily. "What are you doing?"

"We're playing strip poker. I lost. Had to take off an article of clothing."

I swallow. What I should tell her is that we *aren't* playing strip poker. That was a passing joke. But I don't know what else we're playing for. Chips? Participation trophies?

I eye the sock. It's just a sock—no lines crossed. This is my chance to course correct this entire thing right here and now.

Tell her to put it back on.

Tell her to put it back on.

"I don't think you can account for socks separately" is what I say instead.

Her eyes light up as she slides the wineglass across the table carefully. "I can see the merit in that," she says, nodding.

Then, with one casual flick, her other sock comes off. Her innocent eyes land back on me. "Next round?"

We play again, and I try to keep my eyes from straying to her feet, her heels pressed against the chair leg, the graceful curve of her arch on full display.

She loses again.

She seems unperturbed again.

And I find myself both eagerly awaiting her next move and dreading the implications of her removing another piece of clothing.

Gwen, though? She seems unfazed. With a bubbly laugh and a saucy wink, she yanks off her sweatshirt and sits before me wearing a white sports bra with small black polka dots all over it.

My mouth goes dry.

Obviously, being attracted to her is nothing new, but seeing her body on display is the cruelest temptation.

"Hang on," she says, pushing to stand. "I need more wine before the next round. I'm not teaching tomorrow, so I can enjoy myself."

I sit woodenly, watching her curved hips sway, the roundness of her ass on full display through skintight leggings, her tits propped up high.

She makes me fucking insane. That's the only reason I could possibly be sitting here playing strip poker with the one woman in the world I shouldn't want.

When she returns, her eyes scan me carefully. "You doing okay over there? Sobering up a bit?"

"That's one way to put it," I grumble, shifting in my chair and rearranging myself in my pants without being overly obvious.

She just laughs. She *knows*. And all it does is egg me on because I am a glutton for punishment.

As she deals out the next hand, I rationalize that I'm only looking, not touching, and that's fine.

Gwen wins the next round, and I'm relieved that I have some more time before I have to endure watching her take off her pants.

I ditch my socks.

But then Gwen wins again.

I tug off my T-shirt and pretend I can't feel her gaze skating over my torso as we play another round. My upper body is still built and heavy from hard labor, but it's not toned like it once was. Like Tripp's would be.

"Oh, dang. Would you look at that?"

I blink out of my train of thought and stare down at her cards.

I blink again and flip my own cards. Absolutely obliterated by her royal flush. Hearts across the board.

Gwen is all giggles and coy winks. I thought for sure she had no hand. All her tells were—

"Gwen, are you a fucking card shark? Did you play me?"

She lays a dainty hand across her cleavage in fake indignation. "Me? I would never. But also, playing poker is the only way I could get my dad to pay attention to me. So I got rather good at it."

I make a mental note to cuff her dad upside the head if I ever meet him.

"But I thought—"

"You *assumed*. And you know what they say about assuming."

"That it makes an ass out of you and me?"

She shakes her head and leans back in her chair, arms crossed under her full breasts. "No, that you need to take your pants off and show me the goods."

I bark out a laugh now. Gwen always manages to make me laugh. Head shaking as I push to stand, I resign myself to the fact that I am doing this. I don't even feel that buzzed anymore.

But I am a man of my word. And I lost that hand fair and square.

Towering over her, I pop open the button of my jeans and watch her lips fall open on a sharp inhale. When I pull down my fly, she licks her lips.

My dick hardens and I know it will be visible through my boxers. But I can't help myself with Gwen here watching.

Her eyes flash to mine, a little glassy. She crosses her legs and nudges her chin in my direction, urging me to get on with it.

"You that fucking eager, Gwen?" I taunt.

"Yeah. I am," she breathes.

I bite the bullet. Holding her gaze, I slide my jeans down, stepping out of them and in her direction with my cock at full mast.

Her eyes drop, and the little moan that vibrates in her throat only makes me harder. The way she sits up straight, leaning closer, gives me ideas I shouldn't have at all.

Her fingers dig into her knees as she tilts her chin back up to me. "What now, Bash?"

My blood heats and my skin sizzles. I can see her hard nipples pressing against her sports bra. I can imagine everything so easily. Stepping forward and feeding my bare cock into that pretty fucking mouth. Lifting her onto the table, fucking her so hard that those cheap plastic chips fall all over the floor.

"Next round?" I rasp.

Her tongue darts out, wetting her lips. "I can't decide if I want to keep winning or lose a few hands just to watch you work for it."

Fuck.

I can feel my carefully placed tendrils of control starting to snap. Without thinking, I step close, my bare toes butting against hers as I reach forward and gently grip her chin. "Careful what you wish for, Gwen. I've got a laundry list of ways I'd like to watch you work for it, and none of them involve poker."

"Fuck," she whispers, her fingers drifting to the side of my thigh, the sharp points of her nails trailing up slowly.

My molars grind, and I get lost in her eyes for a beat. It would be so easy. It would be so worth it.

"God. I really should not want you this badly," I finally confess, all my jumbled, inebriated, complicated feelings floating to the surface. Gwen's opposite hand lands on the waistband of my boxers, eyes still latched to mine like I hung the moon. "But look at you. You're fucking perf—"

"You know what I hate?" Clyde's voice filters from down the hall, the soft thud of his slow, shuffled footsteps shocking us both into stillness. "How thirsty I am all the time now."

We fly into action. I scoop up my clothes and dart for the back door as Gwen scrambles for her sweatshirt.

"I must be the most hydrated man in the world," I hear him say right as I quietly shut the door behind myself. "Where's Bash? And why are your socks over here?"

My heart thuds wildly, relief and shame pounding at me as I realize how fucking close that was. I shake my head. I'm a grown-ass man sneaking around in my own home. With my son's ex.

It's pathetic.

"Oh, I tried to play strip poker with him. But I took my socks off and he got a massive boner, then acted all weird. Ran off to bed."

Then she *laughs*. A high, manic giggle.

My jaw unhinges. *Is she fucking kidding me?* She's going to pay for that one.

Clyde scoffs. "That tracks. He *would* have a foot fetish. Anyway, good night for real this time. Actually, since you're still up, can you come help me set the pillows up that way I like? I can never get them as good as you do, and I'm a little sore."

Her voice comes out soft now. "Yeah, of course. Let's go get you settled."

Through the window, I watch Gwen follow him down

the hall, and I stay outside, letting the chill seep in. Letting reality seep in too.

Eventually, I sneak back inside and dart upstairs, into the safety of my room, where I lean up against my door and try to wrap my head around what just happened.

CHAPTER 19

Gwen

WHEN I RETURN TO THE KITCHEN AFTER HELPING CLYDE GET settled, Bash is nowhere to be seen. The remnants of our poker game are scattered all over the table, my glass of wine sits innocently next to the pot of lavender.

Hands on my hips, I take a deep breath, head just a little fuzzy, skin just a little hot, heart still beating fast. Because I'm pretty sure I was about to blow Bash in the kitchen.

A smile quirks my lips. Fucking Clyde. Total cockblocker.

I quickly dump my wine, deciding I've had about enough of that for one night, and tidy the table while perseverating on the things that Bash said to me in the heat of whatever the hell that moment just was.

You that fucking eager, Gwen?

I've got a laundry list of ways I'd like to watch you work for it, and none of them involve poker.

I really should not want you this badly.

By the time the kitchen is tidy, I'm hot and bothered.

Deciding I have a date with my vibrator upstairs, I shut off the majority of the lights, check the locks on the doors, and head up to my dreamy room.

I pad softly down the hall, not wanting to make any noise. My gaze drifts to Bash's door as I pass it, half expecting to see light filtering from beneath it. But I don't.

He's clearly not waiting up for me, but that was probably very wishful thinking. I shake my head at myself as I continue to my room. The man might want me, but he definitely hates that he wants me. I'm not oblivious to the fact that he's torn up about it.

And still I wonder if he dreams about breaking the rules the way that I do. He's locked up tight, but if he let himself feel something—feel wanted—maybe he'd see things differently.

Maybe he'd feel like I was worth the risk then.

It hits me, as I enter my room, that we're both scared. Afraid we're not enough. We live in fear of the same type of rejection, and eventually, one of us will have to take a chance or this ship is going to sail.

And I'm not sure I'm ready to give up hope just yet.

With that in mind, I turn and walk back out of my room. Only a few steps down the hall to his. My fingers wrap around the doorknob and then I think better of just marching in. My opposite hand lifts to knock but a noise brings me up short.

I lean closer, pressing my ear to the door.

A groan. A labored breath. The whispered brush of skin against skin. "Fuck yeah," he murmurs roughly.

Heat crawls up my chest and flares down through my hips, curling deliciously in my pelvis. Because I suspect I know exactly what Bash is doing.

But knowing isn't enough. The need to see him drives me forward.

I blame the wine for what I decide to do next. My hand twists before I can even think twice. As silently as possible, I ease the door open, just a sliver.

Silvery moonlight streams into the room, highlighting the harsh lines of Bash's naked silhouette. I can see him in full profile. He's standing at the end of a massive bed, posture slightly curved as he fists his dick. Pumping and breathing in time.

I shouldn't stay and watch, but I also can't look away. I'm entranced and lean closer.

I watch as his palm twists over his length crudely. He moves from base to tip with harsh, jerky movements. The head of his thick, throbbing cock flares out, a drop of wetness glistening at the end.

I lick my lips and heat suffuses my entire body as my eyes catch on the tendons that flex in his forearms as he works himself into a frenzy. My core clenches as I take him in, my own breathing growing ragged as I watch a fantasy play out right before my eyes. I can't decide which view is the best. My eyes jump from his face—all furrowed brows and con-centration—to his cock, to his hand that's dropped to grip the sheets as he holds himself up.

But it's his round, well-muscled ass flexing as he thrusts that's enough to put me over the edge. I now know what I'll be thinking about every single time I finish for the rest of my life.

Roughly hewn muscles. Masculine angles. The way he's panting.

It's primal. It's hypnotic.

And it only gets better.

His body seizes, going still for a beat before he lifts his discarded T-shirt, fucks his hand a few more times, and blows while moaning *my* name.

"Gwen."

It's a breath, a rasp. A fucking prayer. And it will play on repeat in my head until the end of time.

I move to cross my legs, to dull the ache between them, but the awkward position and my blood alcohol level do me dirty.

And I stumble straight into Bash's room.

His shirt is still wrapped around his dick when I straighten. But his dark gaze? It's on me.

Furrowed brows, set jaw, the glint in his eye say he wants to take me over this knee. And honestly, I wouldn't be mad at that. Still, he says nothing.

I'm half expecting him to scold me, kick me out, and tell me how awful I am for invading his privacy like this. Except the way he's regarding me tells a different story. He's looking at me like fucking his hand while imagining us wasn't enough.

Like he needs the real thing instead.

But I'm not so drunk that I don't realize what a huge invasion this is. He says nothing. He doesn't need to. Embarrassment pummels me from every direction.

What have I done?

Reality seeps in—no, humiliation seeps in. "I…" I pause, not totally sure what to say. "I am *so* sorry. I promise this won't happen again."

I back away as he stands there, glaring at me. It's hard to make out his exact expression in the darkened room, but I can feel his energy, and it's dangerous.

When I reach the traitorous doorway, I can't help but add, "You know, unless you want it to."

"Gwen, what the—" He sounds exasperated but cuts off there. Like I've left him at a loss for words. Probably because both Clyde and I have really fucked with the peace of his bachelorhood tonight. The poor guy can't catch a break in his own damn house.

"I'm out!" I squeak, closing the door. "Going to bed! Good night! Sleep tight!" I call from the hallway, my voice painfully bright.

Then I dart back to my room to die from embarrassment privately.

But once that feeling passes, I slip a hand down my pajama bottoms and think about Bash.

I wake up in the morning feeling slightly fuzzy and very guilty. Sober and in the light of day, the weight of my shame for spying on Bash feels especially heavy. I'm a more respectful person than that.

So I prepare to face Bash and apologize to him.

I shower, shave, do my skincare routine, and slick my hair

back into a neat, battle-worthy bun. I'm going for wholesome, proper, girl next door. A polite young woman who would *never* be a creepy, filthy little voyeur while you rub one out.

When I finally make my way downstairs, Clyde is nowhere to be seen. He's probably gone back to bed again if he had a rough night. He's definitely on the mend, but I know he still has a hard time getting comfortable at points. It keeps him up, and he crashes in the early morning hours.

Bash, however, is sitting at the dining room table. In the exact chair he sat in last night. Images of our game pummel me, flashing in my head like a flip-book.

I freeze as I take him in. He looks so different in the morning light. Well rested, stubble trending just a little more toward a beard, hair perfectly gelled. He looks perfectly at ease—downright put together. Especially compared to how I saw him last night.

He doesn't even look irritated with me. In fact, all he does is take a deep swig of his coffee and…smirk at me?

It's unnerving, but I forge ahead anyway.

"Listen." I start toward him but stop short, propping my hands on the island countertop. It seems safer to keep a buffer between us. "I really need to apologize for last night. I was way, way out of line, and I—"

"For which part? Failing to mention that you more than just"—his free hand lifts, fingers curling in air quotes—"'understand the concept' of poker?"

My head joggles before I fix my gaze on him. "Okay, well, sure."

He pushes to stand and begins taking slow, casual steps

in my direction. "Or is it for making me—a forty-year-old man—sneak around in his own house?"

My lips purse. He's really milking this. And his slow approach is doing nothing to calm my nerves. "That part takes two, ya know."

All I get in return is a lifted brow as he rounds the island toward me. Okay, maybe I had been a little forward with the strip poker pressure, but he wasn't exactly begging me to stop either.

"Mostly, I'm sorry for invading your privacy. That was entirely out of character and definitely morally questionable."

He stops before me, props one side of that well-muscled ass I spent the night dreaming about against the counter's edge, and takes another steaming sip of his coffee while nodding absently.

He's too much.

I drop his gaze, watching his Adam's apple bob as he swallows and leans in close, closing the distance between us and coming almost chest to chest. I swear I can feel him inhale as all the air around me is instantly pulled out of reach.

"The thing is, Gwen, next time you want to watch me, you should just ask."

My brain function stutters as my eyes snap to his. "Pardon me?"

"You heard me."

My heart thuds in my ears, pulse rushing heavily through my entire body as my brain wraps itself around what he just flat-out said to me.

"I…" My jaw opens and closes. He's officially caught me

off guard. I was expecting a scolding, not an invitation. A soft, warming sensation takes root in my chest. This teasing, it feels borderline familiar. It takes me back to a snowy night in a dark terminal. To a version of myself who wasn't afraid to say what was on her mind.

It's with that girl in mind that I respond. "I did hear you. And I heard you whisper my name when you came too. So maybe if you wanted me to watch, you should have told me."

Bash swallows as his gaze heats. I can see he's about to say something back, his body coils—like he's on the prowl.

I find my shoulders tipping toward him in anticipation. My tongue darts out and a fluttery feeling bubbles up in my stomach. I'm hanging on to the moment with a sense of eagerness I've never felt before. Until the doorbell rings and the world around us comes crashing back into focus.

Both our heads whip toward the front door.

"I'll get it," Bash grumbles, sounding annoyed by the interruption.

He walks toward me, the smell of amber and cedar floating over his skin, and as he passes me, he squeezes my hip. Then his hand trails over my lower back. Fingertips skimming over the strip of bare skin between my baby tee and baggy jeans. Gooseflesh breaks out over my arms at the contact. And I watch him walk away, his round ass hugged by a pair of faded black Levi's.

Looking like that should be illegal is all I can think. It makes me wonder if he really had been about to get up and put his money where his mouth is.

But when he opens that door, all my wishful thinking dies a fast, fiery death.

CHAPTER 20

Bash

I SWING THE FRONT DOOR OPEN, QUELLING MY RISING IRRI-
tation over the fact that whoever is here is pulling me away
from Gwen. They're interrupting an important conversation, and I'm ready to tell them to fuck off.

But shock renders me silent when I come face-to-face
with my son.

"Tripp," I say blankly, taking in his casual attire of jeans,
a plain gray hoodie, and a team cap.

He shifts awkwardly, hands shoved in the front pockets of his jeans. "Hey. Sorry to just drop in on you. I
just… Well, my schedule opened up, and I know you had
the surgery, so I figured I'd whip out here and check on you."

I keep my face impassive, disguising my shock over his
presence as I search for words that aren't *your timing is shit*.

"You know, like I said I would," he adds for context.

"Unannounced?" I ask and then add a wink, hoping to

hide the thread of defensiveness in my tone. Because I'm instantly swallowed by guilt.

He chuckles good-naturedly. "I don't know, man. It felt more casual this way. No pressure or whatever. I'm trying, okay? Kept thinking that I'd be there for my parents so..." Tripp trails off, trying to cover his wince. "I know we don't know each other all that well, but... It's cool for me to check on you, right?"

Parents. A term I'm not included in and one I'm not so sure I deserve after the way I've been behaving. "Yeah, totally cool."

Except I just told your ex to come watch me next time I jerk off, so anytime except right now?

"Can I come in? Or, like, take you for a coffee? I don't know what you're up for. But I got a room in town for a couple of nights. Figured you're probably still recovering, so I wanted to make it as easy for you as possible."

Easy? There is nothing easy about having to explain to him that his ex is living at my house—has been for weeks—and I chose not to tell him when I had the chance. I think about Gwen, sipping coffee in the kitchen, and my chest tightens. One part of me is relieved he's here, talking to me. The other part is dreading having to explain.

His wide, earnest eyes get me right in the heart. He's here, *trying.* And I'm fucking it all up. Again. I open the door wider and step aside, ready to give a vague and inaccurate explanation of what he's walking into. "Listen, you should know that—"

"Okay, you are taking way too long..." Gwen says as

she rounds the corner into the foyer before freezing midstep when her eyes land on Tripp.

Fuck.

Tripp goes rigid on the front doormat, arms limp at his sides as he eyes her. "Gwen?"

She just stares at him like a deer in the headlights—round face pale, full lips slightly parted, even her eyes look colorless in this moment.

"Tripp?"

Tripp's head tilts. "What are you doing here?"

His gaze darts to me, more in confusion than accusation.

"That's what I was about to explain to you," I start in, wanting to explain this away as quickly as possible. "Gwen randomly ended up in town because she took over the yoga studio here while the owner was away. But then she met Clyde—the man I donated my kidney to—and started helping him out with tasks while he was sick. He moved in here after the surgery, for better proximity to the hospital, so she came with him. To take care of him."

I suck in a breath when I finish my long, overly wordy explanation. I worry it sounded awkward. Because it *was*.

"Sorry." Tripp's eyes shift between us, finger flipping back and forth. "You guys are living together?"

"Yeah." Gwen waves a hand dismissively. "But barely. Ships in the night and all that. I just asked Bash to grab Clyde's meds from my truck so I could organize them and wondered what was taking so long."

I know she's lying. But she gives nothing away, other than possibly smiling just a little too brightly. Then she steps around us like we're in her way and reaches for her key chain on the wall near the front closet. "I'll just do it myself. You two have fun. Just pretend I'm not even here!"

With that, she waves over her shoulder, slips a pair of slides on, and slinks out the front door.

Leaving me to deal with Tripp.

Tripp, whose bewildered eyes stay glued to Gwen as she hustles down the driveway.

"I wasn't expecting to see her, and now it's like… Coming face-to-face with her makes me think I should try again. You know? I still feel like maybe there's something there."

I sit across from my estranged son, sipping a soda water I don't even want just so that I have something to do with my hands. And my face. Because I can barely look at the kid.

He spent the day around the house, and I showed him my property. Hell, I even took him out to the airstrip, pulled out my old plane, and went for a rip.

I didn't know what else to do with him, but after the odd phone conversation about my job as an aerial firefighter, I do know boys like planes. And the ride was a hit. The picturesque valley-and-mountains view stretched below us, and he seemed genuinely impressed. Maybe even a little in awe over what I do.

But now we're at the Reach, having a drink and a bite to eat, and he's unloading on me like I'm a trusted confidant.

About Gwen.

Guess I did a little too well at the dad thing today because, after months of bare-bones communication, he seems eager to tell me all kinds of stuff.

For example, his unresolved feelings for the woman living under my roof. The one who watched me beat off while thinking about her less than twenty-four hours ago. His ex-girlfriend. The one I told to ask next time she wants to watch—mere seconds before he knocked on the door.

Talk about awkward.

But worse, talk about feeling like shit.

Yes, I, Sebastian Rousseau, feel like a giant pile of steaming dog shit for even thinking about crossing that line with Gwen.

It would be like any random dude dating an ex of mine. Unless I was hung up on her.

Those were Rhys's words. And I've thought about them a lot. Those words started my brain down the path of thinking things might be okay between Gwen and me.

But the "hung up on her" part has really fucked me over.

"But today at your house, she didn't even come around." He looks like a sad puppy dog, head hung over a pint of gold beer.

"Have you spoken since it ended?"

The question sounds supportive, but I'm really only asking out of my own morbid curiosity. It's felt inappropriate to ask Gwen about the demise of their relationship, but somehow squeezing the details out of Tripp seems easier, if slightly more distasteful.

His hand slaps the table as he straightens and looks

across at me. "That's the other thing. *She* dumped *me*. I've never been dumped before, let alone by someone like her."

My hackles rise. "Someone like her?"

His hands grip the brim of his hat, folding it into a curve. "You know, like, older. More established. If some young puck bunny dumped me, I wouldn't care. But Gwen knows what she wants, you know? And it's obviously not me. She was so decisive about it. Kinda embarrassing. Which is why I haven't really talked about it."

No one has ever spoken a truer sentence. Gwen certainly does know what she wants. And I can see how that rejection might have stung—especially for someone with a sense of pride like Tripp.

"Rejection is tough, man. I know that feeling well," I say, being supportive, even though a part of me wants to tell him to grow up.

"It's like… She hasn't even called me. And they always call."

I let out a beleaguered sigh and try to remember that, at twenty-four, I was pretty stupid too.

"Have you called her?"

He scoffs now, leaning back and crossing his arms. "Nah. I can't just roll around groveling for a second chance. I'm not that guy."

My eyes hurt from the effort of keeping them from rolling. It strikes me that maybe I'm not cut out for parenting after all because talking to Tripp about this makes me want to grab the fork beside me and stab myself in the face—anything to end this conversation.

With every word he says, my agitation builds. Partly because I'm realizing that my son might be a bit of a douchebag. And partly because, even if he is a douchebag I sure as hell can't pursue Gwen after hearing all this.

I shrug, feeling defeated. "Sometimes that's what it takes when we mess up. And maybe Gwen isn't the right one if you're not willing to grovel. You'll know when it's right because you'll be willing to do absolutely anything to get her back."

"Yeah, but I didn't mess up." He takes a swig of his drink and shakes his head. "She has no idea what she's missing, how good we could be together."

I marvel at his lack of self-reflection, wondering what it must feel like to move through life without questioning every choice and misstep. Meanwhile, I'm dissecting all the places I've gone wrong, all the turns I've taken to get me where I am today.

I'm paralyzed by it. And he's just…coasting.

I can't fathom what it's like to possess his level of confidence and nonchalance.

He goes on to tell me about his team. His summer training plans. The Lamborghini he plans to buy.

I try to enjoy it and soak up his company. After all, I'm the one who wanted a place in his life. And now he's here, practically handing it to me on a silver platter.

But I feel sick and miserable the entire time. He was a fool to let her get away in the first place and his sentiment about how good they could be together eats at me.

The more he talks, the more agitated I become.

All I can think about is...*how good* they'd *be together. Not as good as she and I would be.*

Tripp and I part ways. He mopes back to his hotel room with Gwen on his mind while I opt to grind my teeth the entire drive back to my place—with Gwen on mine too.

I'm about to enter the house when I hear a clicking noise filtering around the side of the property. I'm immediately alert. My property isn't in town, but it's not quite rural like Ford's or West's. I have neighbors dotted along the lakeside.

It could be an animal, or it could be someone trying to steal my boat. So I alter my route and take the stepping-stone pathway around the side of the house that leads onto the back deck.

I find no thief. Only Gwen, sitting on the steps of the back deck, arm outstretched, clucking at a raccoon with a piece of bread in her hand.

Having her under my roof has been a mindfuck. But tonight, after enduring Tripp's reflections on their relationship, is a special brand of torture.

I've spent weeks slowly convincing myself that it would be okay for me to pursue her. I was seconds away from taking that leap. I felt confident that it wouldn't matter if I did.

And then, in one fell swoop, Tripp waltzed in and fucked it all up.

So now, while hiding in the shadows, I soak her in. She's beautiful. More than that, the way she sees the world is beautiful. She's good for me. Hell, she makes me laugh. Living in my head feels like a constant battle sometimes, but standing next to Gwen with my feet in the sand makes everything feel a little bit better.

Tonight, she's peaceful, wrapped in a long, coarsely knit sweater, her platinum locks in a loose mess around her face. The twinkle of the midnight-blue water behind her makes her glow even brighter.

It makes me want…it makes me *want*.

But I can't. Frustration builds as I admire her. And jealousy too.

He had his chance, and he squandered it. Tripp doesn't realize how fucking lucky he is that a girl like her gave him the time of day.

With that frustration bubbling inside of me, I lash out.

"The fuck are you doing?" I ask, startling them both and ruining the moment exactly like I secretly intended to. It will be easier this way. Or at least that's what I tell myself.

The raccoon turns his beady eyes on me, then bolts into the darkness.

Gwen, however, does not share that instinct. Her gaze snaps to mine, incensed. "What the hell! I've been sitting here for thirty minutes, convincing him to come that close."

I should apologize, but I say, "Raccoons are vermin. They carry diseases."

She tilts her head at me.

"What? Are you going to tell me there is a raccoon chakra I don't know about that you're tapping into? They're pests. If they start coming around because you feed them, they'll—"

"They'll what? Lay siege to your castle and take over the entire property like small, furry Vikings?"

I tip my chin up. When she puts it like that, I sound ridiculous. "They can carry rabies."

"That raccoon wasn't rabid."

I sigh. I can't believe I've cornered myself into arguing about rabid raccoons just to get her attention. Apparently, any sort of attention will do where Gwen is concerned.

"Okay." I hold my hands up in surrender. "You know what? It's fine. Feed all the raccoons you want if it makes your energy flow or whatever, but if they come around and make a mess, you'll clean it up."

"Oh, cute. Mocking my beliefs and career. Very original. No one has ever made that joke before," she volleys back before turning and tossing the piece of bread into the trees. "There you go, Larry! Let the carbohydrate energy flow through your raccoon chakras to achieve full enlightenment!"

Then she spins on me, eyes narrowed. "Thanks, Daddy Buzzkill. You just chased him off for no good reason."

The way she spits the word *daddy* makes me realize she's just as irritated by Tripp's unannounced arrival as I am.

I step out of the darkness and into the flood of light that illuminates the backyard. "No good reason?"

She pushes to stand, giving a defiant nod as she wipes her hands against her flowy cotton pants. "Yes. Just to be a dick, no doubt."

I rear back ever so slightly. I hadn't expected her to bite back to this degree. "*Just to be a dick?*" My tongue pops into my cheek. "Is this the famed gentle approach you take with everyone who practices yoga with you?"

I catch myself drifting toward her, drawn in her direction. Forcing myself to stop, I prop a hip against the railing at the top of the steps, crossing my arms like a barricade against the urge to move any closer.

A dry, unamused laugh lurches from her throat as she pads up the steps toward me like she's ready to square off. She comes right to my level. Face-to-face. "Bash, whatever we're doing, it's not yoga. I don't owe you anything. And if you thought being in touch with my mind and body means I have to be a soft-spoken pushover just to accommodate your shit moods, then you thought wrong."

I blink, watching the gears turn in her head.

She reaches forward, pressing her pointer finger into the center of my chest above my crossed arms. "I've done nothing but respect your wishes and your home. I have stayed as far out of your way as possible. Minded my own business. Done only what I was asked here to do. So it's really very simple. If *you* have a problem with *me*, then don't seek me out. Because from where I'm sitting, I was minding my own business, and you popped up out of nowhere to scold me."

She sucks in a breath, like her rant is over. But then she hits me with a killing blow. "I've already lived in the type of household where it was preferable for me to be seen but not heard, and I'm not signing up for that again. So get your shit together and let me have a moment to myself. Maybe you should go take one for yourself too. The sand is that way." She points down at the water. "Go get grounded."

I should back down, but I don't. She's right. I'm being a raging dick, and she's seeing past it all.

"Nothing about my chakras now? Which one is it again? My crown chakra?"

Gwen scoffs. "I mean, to be frank, all your chakras are fucked."

"Oh yeah?"

"You're repressed and lashing out."

My molars clamp as I gaze down on her.

"And bitter. And so tense that I don't think your body would let you take a proper deep breath even if you tried."

"Wow. Encouraging. Please enlighten me. Tell me more about the ways that I'm fucked."

She tilts her head and purses her lips, assessing me. Her eyes trail over my body in a way that makes my skin hum. "Your throat chakra is fucked because you can't, for the life of you, say out loud what's in your head. Never mind your heart chakra—you definitely won't acknowledge anything going on in there. But based on your current behavior, I'm going to go say that one is positively brimming with jealousy."

I roll my eyes, a feeble cover. "Is that so, Gwen? And what would I be jealous of?"

She smirks now, crossing her arms to mimic my motion. "I don't know, Bash. What *would* you be jealous of?" Her toe nudges the tip of my boot. "Could it be Tripp? You mad he had what you want?"

My lungs seize. I didn't expect her to spell it out quite like that.

"I think I've made myself pretty clear. I told you what I'd

have chosen, and you told me to back off." She bumps my toe again, leans in close, and whispers, "So now you'll just mope around feeling sorry for yourself because the timing is all fucked up and you feel like you owe him something you don't."

I incline my head toward her, close enough to feel her breath fanning across my jaw. "Careful, Gwen."

She chuckles, but there's no humor in it. And she doesn't back down. Instead, her lips move closer to the shell of my ear. "Or what? You might man up and take something for yourself for once?"

I snap.

I take something for myself for once.

My hands dart out and grip Gwen's waist.

"You know what?" I snarl, yanking her toward me, staring at her plush mouth as her lips softly part—no doubt to say something infuriating. But I don't let her get a word in edgewise.

"Fuck it," I mutter.

Then I kiss her.

CHAPTER 21

Gwen

In a flash, Bash is on me.

His hands on my waist. His hips pressed against mine. His lips claiming my mouth.

My head spins, my body surging to catch up with him. Sure, I'd been taunting him, but I really didn't know if he had it in him to pounce.

There's nothing soft or seeking about the way he kisses me. He ravages me. We attack each other with fervor. A desperate moan vibrates in my throat as I kiss him back. My palms slide up his chest, squeezing his shoulders, fingers trailing over the back of his neck before slipping into his hair.

His tongue sweeps into my mouth, tangling with mine as he turns us roughly, shoving me against the porch railing before his hands drop, gripping my ass. He squeezes once, a hungry groan spilling from his lips as he grinds his hard length against me in one sensual rotation of his hips.

"Fuck yes," I murmur, hiking a leg up around his waist. Desperate for more.

His broad palm slides over the curve of my ass, gliding under my thigh while he continues to kiss me senseless. He grinds against me, and it's all too easy to imagine us. Like this. With nothing between us. I lose myself to the fantasy. There's a desperate edge to our kiss—it's the first drink of cool, fresh water after months stranded in the desert.

"Again," I beg against his lips, wanting another feel of his cock pressing against my core.

For a moment, I think he's going to give me what I want. He lifts me like I weigh nothing and sets me on the railing, stepping between my legs.

But then he pulls back to take me in with dazed eyes. My lips feel swollen and my body hot as his scorching gaze rakes over me, leaving a path of fire in its wake.

"Fucking look at you," he says, his breathing labored. "Fucking perfect. And so fucking off-limits."

I reach forward, tugging the front of his plaid jacket. "I'm not off-limits."

He lets out a gruff chuckle. "Yeah. You are."

Bash's fingers grip me hard, pulling me tight against his front. He kisses my neck, teeth grazing over my jaw. I shudder, pressing my chest into him. Wanting more. The feel of his stubble on my throat. His hands on me. My clothes feel too constricting, too hot. I want them off. I want *him* to take them off.

I try to explain myself, wanting so desperately for Tripp to not be a factor. "We were never really a thing. And we've been over for—"

"That poor kid waxed poetic about you all night," Bash cuts me off, speaking between languid kisses down my chest, his tongue darting out over the tops of my breasts. "For all the wrong reasons but still. I had to sit there and pat his back over it. And do you know what I was thinking about the entire time?"

I blink. I had no clue Tripp was still upset over our breakup. "What's that?"

"That he was a fool to let you get away. But that it was just as well because I could fuck you better."

I suck in a breath as Bash's dark eyes bore into mine.

"Listening to him talk about you made me want to come home and take you just to prove to myself that I could. Does that make me jealous, Gwen?"

My heart hammers against my ribs, and I lick my lips, meeting his wild gaze. "I think it does."

His hand slides up my side, palming every curve before slipping to the back of my head and fisting my hair. "And what the hell am I supposed to do about that, huh?"

The way he manhandles me with such authority has my body fucking singing. *Begging.*

I wiggle my hips closer, panting.

"What am I supposed to do with you, Gwen? We're just starting to figure this thing out. He'll never forgive me if I do this. I'm damned if I do, and damned if I don't."

Then let's be damned together is what I want to say. But the tug of one strand of hair provides just enough of a sting that reality finds its way into the lust-filled moment. One tendril sneaking through a crack.

My chest hurts for him. I know in my bones that he's trapped in an impossible position—we both are. And that if I'm the one who pushes him to act against his better judgment, he'll hold me responsible when it all blows up.

I can't ask him to make this mess. Not when he'll have to face the fallout. It means he has to be the one who doesn't care. He has to come to me and say *mess be damned*.

But Bash cares a lot. Beneath that stony exterior, he has the biggest heart.

It's one thing I've come to love about him.

Which is why I won't stomp all over his morals just to get what I want. It's also why I draw away. He reads the motion, eyes shuttering as his hands go loose and he steps back.

It hurts my heart that he reads everything as rejection. It's written all over him.

"Bash…"

"No." He shakes his head, looking away. "No, it's fine. I shouldn't have done that."

"That's not what I was going to say."

He sighs, sounding tired, and runs a large hand through his hair, tugging at the ends in clear frustration. "What were you going to say, then?"

"I was going to say that I don't want to be the thing that damns you. It's not fair."

His eyes search mine, flitting from left to right. He's probing for something, and I'm not sure he finds it.

Finally, he steps all the way back, leaving me chilled and missing his nearness.

"No, it's really not," he says before turning and walking away from me.

Again.

And me? I do us both a favor: I walk inside and respond to the job offer from the resort in Costa Rica.

I tell them I'll be ready to start on August first.

The heavy weight of dread presses on my chest before I've even opened my eyes.

My run-in with Bash last night kept me awake. Tossing, turning, thinking. Wishing that things were different.

But I know, from the moment my lashes flutter open, I'll be faced with the reality that nothing is different at all.

The day will start, the sun will rise, everything about Bash and me will feel just as impossible as it did when he left me on the back porch last night. But now I have an end date in sight, so at least I know there's a way out.

When I do finally brave lifting my lids, I'm proven right. There's a heavy stone in my stomach and a weight on my chest that I can't seem to shake. I know I should head downstairs and be the chipper, happy, go-with-the-flow version of Gwen that everybody expects.

But this morning, I don't feel like that version of myself.

I'd rather hide—from reality, from the fact that I basically served myself up to Bash on a silver platter. A man who clearly wants me, yet I still backed down.

I spent half the night figuring out whether I turned him away for some deeper reason. Of course, the constant worry that I'm not good enough sat on my shoulder in the dark, sabotaging me as always. But more than that, I realized that if it had been any other man, I wouldn't have retreated at all. The difference is, I like Bash—I *really* like Bash. And I don't want to damn him with my carelessness. Deep down I know this isn't some meaningless fling.

It scares me. And the thought of losing him scares me too.

Still, I drag myself from bed and start my day, stalling at every turn to avoid what's waiting downstairs. I take my time, even roll my yoga mat out on the front balcony, hoping a few sun salutations will provide some semblance of balance before I have to face Bash downstairs. And Clyde, in front of whom I'll have to continue pretending that nothing is off.

I flow through the poses, feeling every stretch, every ache, and every tender spot. I let myself sink into it, not pushing too far, not letting my mind wander too much. Just feeling my body, feeling the air, and feeling all the complicated emotions coursing through me.

Just when I think I've found a little corner in my brain that resembles balance, I'm thrown off by a voice that I recognize all too well.

One that sounds like nails on a chalkboard.

Tripp.

Low rumbles of conversation between him and Bash drift from the front door. I catch the odd occasional clear word: "swing by…coffee…come on in."

Before I know it, the click of the front door closing ends the conversation, making facing what's downstairs even worse. Eventually, I've primped, changed my clothes, read a chapter of my book, and done everything I can think of to avoid making my descent.

Until my phone buzzes with a text.

> **Clyde:** Will you make me those special scrambled eggs? You do them the best.

Alas, my tenure as a burrowing owl has ended. Because the man paying me to help actually requires my help. Maybe if things get awkward downstairs, I can try my hand at impersonating a fainting goat.

I tell Clyde I'm on my way and force a smile onto my face as I head out of my room. The bitter aroma of coffee wafts up to meet me, and the sound of low voices conversing filters in my ears. I make my way downstairs, and right before I enter the kitchen, my phone buzzes. I pull it out of my pocket to see another message from Clyde. When I click it open, I laugh.

> **Clyde:** I can't believe you dated this guy. He's a full-blown douchebag.

I can't help but smile down at the screen as I type back. Clyde isn't wrong. Tripp isn't all bad—people usually aren't—but when that less-charming side comes out to play it is very...less charming.

Gwen: I know. ;)

I hit send, wipe the humor from my features, and shove my phone into my back pocket. Then I plaster another fake smile onto my face and round the corner into the kitchen as I singsong an overly bright "Good morning!" to everyone in the room.

Tripp's face lights up like a kid on Christmas morning.

Bash scowls at him and then at me.

And Clyde just leans back in his chair, shaking his head with an amused smirk on his face.

Yeah, he's getting far too much enjoyment out of this.

"Gwen," Bash replies matter-of-factly, tipping his chin once in my direction. It's a simple, no-nonsense, no-feelings, I-never-told-you-I-could-fuck-you-better-than-your-ex type of gesture.

Tripp gives me a smooth "Hey, Gwen, you look beautiful this morning."

It takes monumental effort not to roll my eyes.

I can feel Bash's energy without even looking at him. It's a flashing red light. I finally brave looking over at him and can read him like a page out of my favorite book. He hates everything about this situation.

But he'll never say anything.

Clyde, on the other hand, looks me straight in the eye and announces, "This one can't stay in my bunker when the apocalypse hits."

Tripp misses the sentiment entirely, laughing like Clyde is joking.

Leaned against the counter, Bash doesn't laugh.

I take a moment to figure out my next move, how to act naturally. Keep it casual. I try to not to let my eyes linger on Bash for too long or give too much away.

But it's hard.

Especially when he's wearing something that looks like a uniform right now.

Navy-blue cargo pants hug his thighs in a way that I should not be openly admiring. Above a utilitarian black belt, strapped around his narrow waist, a matching navy T-shirt stretches across his broad chest. A crest printed with *BC Fire Service* sits over his heart.

At his feet, a duffel bag.

My heart lurches.

He's leaving.

When I drag my vision back up to his level, I blurt, "Why are you dressed like that?" When I really mean *You have no right looking so good wearing that* or even *Please don't go.*

"Fire," he says gruffly. "Got the call early this morning. Heading out right away."

My brows furrow. "Are you cleared to work?"

Bash just shrugs. "Close enough. I'll be sitting in a plane, not doing anything on the ground. I've taken a few weeks off since the surgery and I flew with Tripp the other day, no problem, so I don't need you being a mother hen about it."

I bristle at that and clamp my molars together to keep from saying something I shouldn't. Clearly, we're back to the be-an-asshole-as-a-defense-mechanism strategy that he tried to employ the night before.

But I'm not in the mood to play that game. I don't hide the venom in my tone either. "Fair. Not my monkeys, not my circus." Then I turn to Clyde and point. "You are my monkey, and this is my circus, and I'm here to make you your scrambled eggs. Right?"

Clyde eyes me suspiciously as Tripp inserts himself into our conversation. "I may not be your monkey anymore, but I'd really like to be part of this circus too."

He says it so affably, so smoothly. But I know that's how he is. I know how calculated he can be. I know how *fake* he can be.

Clyde shoots Tripp a dirty look and crosses his arms, but he says nothing else.

Not even when Tripp adds, "Maybe I could take you to lunch later, Gwen? Or dinner? Before I leave tomorrow?"

From the corner of my eye, I see Bash go eerily still.

In fact, it feels like everyone in the kitchen goes still. Suddenly, the attention on me feels hot and heavy, like something I'd like to peel off and escape.

All three men wait with bated breath for what I might say. I blink once, then twice, weighing how best to respond to his public request.

There's nothing like being asked out by your ex-boyfriend in front of his dad, who you were making out with not twelve hours earlier.

But before I can respond, Bash makes a move. He drops his cup into the sink with a loud rattle before pushing off the counter. Muscles bulge in his arms, flexing in time with the tendons in his neck.

He dusts his hands together like he's removing some invisible dirt from them, definitely trying to appear more relaxed than he truly is. "Well, on that note," he announces, "I'm going to hit the road. Get out of your hair. This grass fire in northern Alberta is moving quickly. Time is of the essence and all that." He smiles tightly, avoiding meeting my eyes, before grabbing his bag and striding out. I watch him leave the kitchen, heart limping along until it falls with a heavy lurch at my feet.

A part of me wants to rush after him, assure him that nothing's happening here, that nothing will happen here, but he's off and moving before I can get a word in edgewise.

He doesn't even look back at me, taking my breath with him as he goes.

"I'll see you out," Tripp says, jumping into motion and walking his dad toward the front door of his own house.

I hear them exchange gruff goodbyes along with the back slaps that come with those manly, one-armed hugs. It makes me wonder if that's the first hug they've ever really exchanged.

Before I hear the front door even click closed behind Bash, Tripp calls back to the kitchen, "So what do you say, Gwen? How about that lunch?"

God, I wish he'd knock that off.

I hurry toward the front foyer, not wanting Bash to leave with the impression that I'd go out with Tripp again after everything that's happened between us. As I round the corner, I say, "You know, I actually…" But the door slams.

Hard.

Hard enough that Tripp turns and furrows his brows toward where Bash just stood, as though he can't figure out what that was all about.

All I can think is that Bash has left. We never got a chance to talk. I don't even know how long he'll be gone for. Suddenly, him leaving to fly a plane into a fire feels monumentally dangerous.

Suddenly, I miss him.

Suddenly, I regret accepting that job offer.

And even though he's not here to hear it, I look Tripp in the eye and tell him bluntly, "I think it's better if we don't."

CHAPTER 22

Gwen

Gwen: Stay safe out there.

"You shouldn't be watching this much news. Rots your brain," Clyde announces as he enters the open living space. He was quiet on his feet this time, which might mean he's getting better—or else I was just too absorbed in the TV to notice him.

Either way, I feel like a thief caught in the act. On instinct, I scramble for the remote and flick the screen off before I even consider how fucking bizarre that is.

Clyde stops and quirks a brow at me, suspicious—then he continues walking into the kitchen. He definitely looks more comfortable this morning. "Dang, girl, you must be taking that brain rot seriously."

"Yeah. My body is a temple and all that." I force a smile, turning to look at him over the back of the couch.

He reaches for the coffeepot but stops again. "Gwen, you're creeping me out. Is this what it's like to have a teenager and catch them doing something they shouldn't be?"

"I'm just checking in on you. How are you feeling?"

He shakes his head, pouring himself a steaming mug of black coffee. "I feel like you're changing the subject."

I scoff. "Nah. Me? No."

His watery blue eyes are alert and I try not to squirm as he shuffles to the living room and takes a seat on the armchair set ninety degrees from me. He takes a deep sip, closing his eyes briefly and sinking back into the cushions. "Oh yeah. That's good."

"Nothing quite like—"

"Now that I'm caffeinated," he cuts me off, "do you want to talk about how you were trying to spot Bash on the news?"

I freeze but only for a beat. "I have no idea what you're talking about."

Yes, I do. Bash has been gone for three days, and with each day, my worry has grown. I check for updates about the fire. The containment levels. The evacuation alerts. Any statements from government officials.

And more than that, I worry about Bash. I worry that he's out there doing something dangerous. It doesn't matter that he has thousands of flight hours and years of experience. It doesn't matter that he seems nothing short of capable in every single thing he does.

I mean, hello, that kiss? That mouth? Those hands?

Capable.

But then, on top of that, I worry that he hasn't entirely healed from his surgery.

And then I worry about the fact that it was probably me who chased him out of town. So if anything happens, it will be my fault.

Basically, I'm a giant ball of anxiety over the guy, and it's entirely possible that I am exaggerating my role in the situation.

Maybe it wasn't me.

It probably wasn't.

That's his job. I bet I haven't even crossed his mind.

"Okay, sure," Clyde drawls. "Is this the game where we pretend there's nothing going on between the two of you?"

Fucking Clyde. "You're not supposed to be this snoopy."

He scrubs a hand over his wiry, gray stubble. "Sorry, sorry. It's just that I'm invested. I worked really hard to get you both under one roof."

My head snaps in his direction. "You *what?*"

I suspected something at the hospital—but hearing him so bluntly confirm it still shocks me.

"Don't act so surprised. I love that big doofus like he's my own, and to be frank, you're feeling an awful lot like my second doofus."

My heart swells. I never thought being referred to as one of Clyde's doofuses would be so heartwarming.

He chuckles now, eyes taking on a faraway look. "They don't call me Crazy Clyde for nothing. Sometimes you gotta be a bit out there to see what's going on. And with you two,

I've seen it since he came back from that night stuck in the airport and wouldn't stop bringing you up. Never seen the guy check his phone as much as he did in the weeks and months after that. He tries to be all bland and grumbly, but I know he never gave up hope that you might contact him."

Now my heart squeezes. Somehow, I didn't realize Clyde was this in the loop.

My shoulders sag, and I drop the pretense. "I would have. I planned to. I checked my phone a lot too. The universe kind of fucked us. And now…" I trail off, gazing out the expansive windows toward the lake. I've lived here for a month, and strangely, that view never gets old.

Strangely, this place that isn't mine at all has started to feel like home.

"Now with Tripp and just *everything*… I don't know, Clyde. I think that ship might have sailed. I don't want to make an issue out of it. It feels like the universe is pitted against us—"

He scoffs. "Quitter talk. The universe isn't stopping either of you from doing anything."

I shoot the older man a disbelieving look.

"Gwen, I know you believe in all this stuff, and that's great. I also believe in a lot of things that other people don't, but don't let that stop you from going after what you want. Sometimes things won't just fall into your lap because the universe provides or whatever."

I snort at that. I don't think I'm that far gone, but I do have a habit of trying to go with the flow and avoiding causing any ripples. "Harsh."

"Good. You both need it."

"Clyde, that's his son. He really wants a relationship with him, and that will be infinitely more complicated with me in the picture."

"So? All the best things in life are complicated."

I sigh. Wise words from the most unlikely source.

I can't believe I'm having this conversation with Clyde. If someone had told me months ago that he'd be the man giving me a fatherly pep talk, I'd have laughed in their face.

"Gwen, listen. I've known him for years now, and he might be one of the best people I know. Prickly and ornery and set in his ways, but *good*. He's been hurt. He's been told a few too many times that he isn't good enough. Between his ex-wife and Tripp's mom, he's learned the hard way that people use him as a stepping stone to the life they really want. He *expects* to be left behind."

Clyde pauses for dramatic effect or to sip at his coffee—I'm not sure which. What I do know is that my stomach has twisted into another knot with each of his sentences.

"And those are tough wounds to heal. Especially for a man so paralyzed by all his own regrets. He's stuck. I see it, and I bet if you looked hard enough, you'd see it too. But when he met you? You shook him up. It changed something. It changed him. And I reckon that if you have the fortitude to keep at him, he might just soften up for you. It won't be easy. But nothing worth having ever comes easy."

I roll my lips together, considering Clyde's assessment.

"But, Gwen, if you aren't serious about the guy, you should leave sooner rather than later. Find that next gig.

Keep chasing those dreams. Because this is harder on him than he'll ever let on."

Nausea crawls up my throat, that churning, dropping feeling in my gut hitting hard and fast. It's the same one I felt when he turned and stormed out three days ago, expecting the worst of me.

Am I serious about him?

I mull over the question, but it doesn't take long. I am. There's a reason I took the position in this town, a reason I moved on from Tripp immediately. And there's a reason I'm sitting here sick over him.

I don't tell Clyde any of those things. But I do nod.

And then I turn the TV back on right in front of him, determined to catch sight of Bash.

CHAPTER 23

Bash

I'M DEEPLY, DEEPLY EXHAUSTED. MY BODY IS SORE, AND MY mood is low.

Surprisingly my incision is fine. But the mental and emotional toll of fighting a fire as destructive as this one never fails to knock me on my ass.

And as much as I hate to admit it, I wasn't ready to take this job. Not physically anyway. Emotionally, I was fucking desperate for it.

I hip check the motel door open and suck in a lungful of filtered air. Outside feels downright apocalyptic. The sky is dark now, but it has an eerie, orange glow.

We got called down while in the midst of laying out fire retardant, trying to cut some lines in the fire's sprawl.

But the winds weren't cooperating and there weren't any natural water sources a convenient distance away.

Gwen would say that the universe was working against

us, and I don't know that she'd be wrong—that's exactly what it felt like.

A hard day on the job and the sinking feeling of wishing I hadn't left the way I did haven't helped my mood.

I tell myself I did the mature thing. The right thing. But usually when I do the right thing, it gives me a warm, fuzzy feeling inside.

Being mature to Cecilia? Satisfying.

Giving Clyde a kidney? Satisfying.

Helping Rhys get an alarm system set up for Tabby while he was away? Also satisfying.

Walking out and leaving Gwen to Tripp? I fucking hate myself.

A hot shower to wash away the smell of ash doesn't improve my mood. It's not until I flop down onto one of the double beds and pick up my phone that I feel better.

Because Gwen's name is on the screen. I swipe it and open the surprise.

In the past, we've exchanged text messages about Clyde. They've been mostly business.

This one, though? This has nothing to do with Clyde, and it feels nothing like business.

> **Gwen:** Hi. I've been trying not to bug you, but I need a
> sign of life.

I read it a few times, like my eyes are deceiving me. I wasn't sure how she and I would interact with everything out on the table. Especially not with Tripp hanging around.

Asking her out right in front of me.

I'd wanted to give him a shake, tell him not to go after her just because he wants what he can't have. I may not have a great track record with relationships, but I know he only started thinking about her because he came face-to-face with her. He didn't light up or stumble over his words—he didn't even try.

If nothing else, I'm offended by how careless he's been with her. I'd feel worse for him if I bought his heartache. Instead, he reminds me of a little boy throwing a tantrum because he can't get the toy he wants at the store.

I know what it's like to not be able to stop thinking about someone.

I know because I've been there with Gwen. Even during an active fire, I think about her. Even when I know I shouldn't, I think about her.

That's how I justify writing her back. Before I thought not answering her texts was the right thing to do. But tonight? I'm weak.

Bash: Consider this a sign of life.

She writes back instantly.

Gwen: Oh, thank god. I've been watching the news, trying to catch sight of you. But it hasn't worked. There are videos of the planes, but how am I supposed to know which one is you?

Bash: You've been watching the news?
Gwen: Yeah.

She says it so plainly. Like, of course, she's been watching the news and looking for me. I smile at my phone like some lovesick loon.

Gwen: Is it as bad as it looks?
Bash: Yeah. It's pretty bad. Early for fire season too.
Gwen: How long do you think you'll be gone?
Bash: Hard to say. Why? Does Clyde miss me?
Gwen: No. I do.

The thrum of my heart comes stronger and faster. She shouldn't be able to make me feel like this with a simple text message.

Gwen: I don't have anyone to play strip poker with. ;)

I chuckle into the quiet room. I shouldn't be this amused by her. Hell, she shouldn't be cracking jokes like that. I kind of thought we both agreed we wouldn't. And yet, here we are, unable to stop. After three days of darkness and destruction, teasing Gwen feels too good to turn away from.

Bash: You could always play with Clyde?
Gwen: Too far. Clyde is basically a cool, weird dad. And trust me, I've seen enough helping him post-op.

The mention of *dad* has me wondering about her back-story. Her life. I want to know so much more about her. I've never asked because it's never felt like my business, and it always seemed like a bad recipe for growing far too close to her. So I've tuned out every mention of her dad and her family life.

Now doesn't feel like the right time, either, so I deflect with a sad little dig about what has been irritating me since I walked out the front door.

Bash: Maybe Tripp will play with you?
Gwen: Oh, I bet he would.

My molars grind. I've instantly set myself on edge.

Bash: Well, problem solved then.
Gwen: No, Bash, not "problem solved." I don't want to play with Tripp. Plus, I sent him packing three days ago, which is what you really wanted to know, isn't it? If you'd stuck around long enough to even say goodbye, you'd know that.

I bristle, propping myself up against the pillows. Then I peer around the empty room as though someone might be watching me and chaperoning this text conversation.

Bash: I wanted to give you guys space.
Gwen: Oh, fuck off. You're being a petty little bitch. Just admit it.

I sigh. I am, but I'm not prepared to admit in writing that I'm jealous of my own son. That I felt a quick thrill of satisfaction knowing she turned him down—maybe even turned him down *for me*.

Bash: He's not good enough for you.

I regret sending it the moment it's gone. *That* was petty. Or maybe it wasn't. At the very least, it's true. If Gwen only remains a friend, I would stand by that assessment.

Even though she can't end up with me, I like her enough to want it to be someone better than Tripp—or at least this current version of Tripp. He's got a lot of growing up to do before he can even hope to handle a woman like Gwen.

Gwen: I know.
Bash: Good.

There. That was fatherly of me. I've steered our conversation into appropriate territory and feel almost good about it. Until Gwen comes in with the last word.

Gwen: I've decided to be patient. Wait for someone better.

Frustrated by the thought of her dating anyone else, I put my phone away and flick on the TV. I haven't been able to sleep much anyway.

Which is probably why it feels like I stay up all night thinking *I could be better.*

On day five of the job, we seem to have reached some level of containment. Homes have been decimated, wildlife has been lost, and even though I should feel satisfied with our accomplishments, my heart is heavy.

So much loss.

And somehow the sentiment of "it could have been worse" rings hollow. Sure, it could have been worse, but for so many people, so many animals, this was the actual worst.

Yesterday, I watched a husband console his wife as she sobbed about losing the only photos she had of her deceased parents. It broke me. I went numb just to get through the rest of the day.

And when I got back to the hotel, I'd texted my mom just to say hi and tell her I love her. She retired and moved to Mexico five years ago to be near her sister and brother-in-law. I'm happy for her. She raised me all on her own, working long and hard to provide the best life she could for us.

I don't know a single person who deserves a peaceful, warm retirement more than her. As her only child, I make a point of visiting her as much as I can—but in that moment, I *missed* her. It made me realize we don't have forever.

It made me ache for a family of my own even more than usual.

It's an ache that hasn't left me today as I hop out of my

single-engine air tanker. My boots hit the ground with a heavy thunk, and I feel it reverberate in my bones.

"Rousseau!" the local fire chief calls from near the hangar. "Great work out there. Again. We've got it from the ground now. You can go home to your family."

A pang hits my throat, and I work to cover my flinch.

But then I think of Gwen. And yes, even Clyde. My strange, complicated, ragtag little family. Or at least the only people who will be there, waiting for me when I get back. Which is better than no one.

"You sure?" I approach him, removing my helmet and outstretching my arm to shake his hand. "I can stick around for a few more days."

Our palms clap when they meet.

"Nah, we'll keep the local guys on call. You go on and get back to British Columbia. Hopefully they won't need you this year."

I nod, my mouth twisting. It's a nice sentiment, but it's wishful thinking.

"You look tired. A little pale. You all right?" His brow furrows as he looks me over.

"Yeah, yeah. Just been a big few days," I say, but the truth is, I don't feel well. I feel monumentally tired.

So I don't fight him on his decision to scale back on the aerial approach. I take the out and head back to Rose Hill.

CHAPTER 24

Gwen

THE LIGHT SNAP OF THE FRONT DOOR SHUTTING startles me from sleep. It's not loud enough to be disruptive, but my body fires awake all the same. I sit straight up, heart pounding, and listen carefully.

A thud. Followed by footsteps.

I reach for my phone, knowing that I set the alarm system just like Bash showed me to when I first moved in. It says it was disarmed one minute ago, which can only mean one thing.

I tiptoe down the hallway and make my way to the stairs, taking them quietly just in case it isn't Bash and I'm walking straight into my murderer's trap.

But once I turn the corner and peek into the darkened kitchen, I see a frame I'd recognize anywhere.

Bash has his palms propped on the countertop and his head dropped like he's catching his breath. He hasn't even taken his boots off—something out of character because this man keeps a meticulous house.

"Bash?" I ask carefully.

He doesn't lift his head. The only sign he hears me is the tensing of his broad shoulders.

"I didn't know you were coming home."

Now his shoulders drop, but he still doesn't respond.

"You okay?" I ask, moving closer to him. Reaching for him. Letting my hand trail over the curve of his upper spine. "What's wrong?"

I can just tell. Sure, usually he's surly and ornery, but this is different.

"Just really not feeling well."

My forehead scrunches, mind running through all the things that could be wrong so soon after donating an organ. "How's your abdomen? Should we go to the hospital? I knew it was too soon—"

"The surgery was laparoscopic, Gwen. I'm fine. I have a really bad headache, and I feel nauseous. I'm just tired."

My fingers press into the divots between his vertebrae, working their way down until I hear him sigh.

"I'm really, really tired." He shakes his head almost sadly. "Like exhausted. Gwen, I'm just *so* tired." His voice cracks, and it does nothing to convince me that he's okay.

"That's okay. You just have to honor that. You're allowed to be tired. It's normal to be tired."

He nods this time but makes no other motions.

"Here." I reach down, sliding my hand over his, linking our fingers. "Come on. Let's go. You need to rest."

He turns now, dangerously dark eyes peering into mine from over his shoulder. They look tortured. He *does* look tired. And downtrodden and...sad.

"You got this," I say softly, not sure what's wrong, only knowing that I would do anything to make him feel better.

"I don't know if I do," he says back, voice rough like gravel. It makes my chest ache.

"I've got you, then," I murmur, giving him a tug as I turn away to lead him upstairs.

I expect him to resist. But he doesn't.

He follows.

The fact that he still doesn't remove his boots sets me on edge. I may not know him all that well, but I know he would never walk through his beautiful home—across these meticulously finished hardwoods—with a pair of work boots on.

I stop and turn to him. "Sit," I say, pointing at the stairs.

He looks stunned, but he complies and drops to a step stiffly. I swallow the lump in my throat before coming to kneel before him. Silently, I lift his foot and unlace the leather boot. I can feel him watching me, but he doesn't speak. My palm squeezes his ankle as I set the boot aside and move on to the next one, one hand massaging rhythmically at his muscled calf while my fingers deftly weave through the tight laces.

With both boots set neatly on the mat, I reset the alarm and take him by the hand again, urging him to stand.

We walk up the stairs, hand in hand, and straight to his bedroom. I lead him over to the bed and give him a gentle push, forcing him to sit while I click on the bedside lamp before turning to study him more closely.

Dark smudges beneath his eyes make them appear even darker than they already are. The shadow of his stubble makes his cheeks look just a little extra hollow. Even his hair doesn't look as perfectly gelled as usual. In fact, it appears entirely unbrushed.

Without thinking, I reach up and cup the side of his face. His eyes flutter shut, and his Adam's apple bobs. Softly, I let my fingers trail over the ridge of his cheekbone, before fluttering over his temple, and then trailing behind his ear.

"Have you been sleeping?"

He opens his eyes. "Not much" is his gruff response. "It just hasn't come to me. Probably sick."

This big strong man who shows up for everyone around him, who always does the right thing, looks beaten down, and I can't handle it.

I give him a firm nod and squeeze his calloused hand as I take in the room around me. The expansive bed with crisp, white sheets. The mountain-scape art on the walls. The plush chair in the corner, tucked beside a standing lamp with built-in bookshelves surrounding it. The perfect spot to curl up with a book.

"I'll be right back."

I move to leave, but his hand squeezes mine harder, a silent plea for me to stay. "Hey." I squeeze back, bending at the hips to try and meet his gaze. "You change and get into bed. I'm coming right back."

His responding nod is stiff as his fingers slowly go slack.

It has me peeking back over my shoulder at him curiously as I walk away. The sight of him looking so small and defeated on the edge of his bed twists my heart. I get the sense that he needs me right now, so I make haste.

I leave the room and head to mine, searching for any tools I can think of that will help him relax. Because I don't think Bash is sick—I think Bash is burned out.

When I get back to his room, he's under the covers, flat on his back, hands laid over his stomach, almost like a corpse, while he stares up at the ceiling.

I swallow down my anxiety at seeing him like this, looking so detached. It makes me wonder what he saw while he was away that pushed him to this point.

Quietly, I set up my Bluetooth speaker and turn on my favorite calming playlist—Tibetan singing bowls.

"Gwen," he sighs my name like it means something. Like he knows he should tell me to stop but can't bring himself to.

"Bash," I reply, my way of telling him to back off about it and let me take care of him. Because someone needs to.

I draw the heavy curtains before padding back toward him. His eyes follow me, but every other part of him is still.

My knees bump against the edge of his mattress on the opposite side of the bed as I hold up my glass vial of lavender oil. It's clear, and the actual sprigs are suspended within. "I'm going to kneel on your bed and rub this into your temples. Please try not to get a boner."

The laugh he coughs out is sudden, and genuine, and something of a relief. "Okay, Gwen. If that makes you feel better."

With a soft smile, I crawl onto his bed. "Yes, I'm doing all this to make *me* feel better."

His lips are upturned when he closes his eyes, and it strikes me that Bash has never let his guard down around me like this. Actually, I don't think Bash lets his guard down around anyone at all.

He's been hurt.

Clyde's words echo in my head as I realize it's more than that. I've been hurt. But this? Bash is actively hurting. It's different, and I hate it.

I draw close enough that my knees press against his arm. Then I squeeze a few drops of the oil onto my fingertips, I rub them together to heat it before tentatively reaching over him and gently pressing my pointer and middle fingers onto each of his temples.

He tenses at first, but then he softens. I work in gentle circles, slowing slightly with each rotation, as though I might unfurl the tension within him with my fingertips alone.

"You've had a big year, Bash," I say softly. "You've been through a lot."

His cheek hitches. "Not really."

"Yes, really. You've endured intense emotional upheaval. Tripp. Your ex. A major surgery." I'm quiet for a few beats, the other thing that has caused him strife at the tip of my tongue.

"Me," I finally say.

His eyes snap open, landing on mine as I continue to massage him.

"You're crashing. Your nervous system has got to be in

overdrive. And yes, your incision may be healed, and physically you might feel fine, but those six weeks they recommend might be accounting for more than that. How is your mental health? How is your emotional health? Stress is often the spark for starting illness."

He watches me, lids slung low. He says nothing, so I carry on.

"If I were you, I don't think I'd be okay. You need to take care of yourself, not just everyone else. Or it will come back to haunt you."

"I know," he whispers, eyes drawing shut once more, like he's just too tired to even keep them open.

"Does this feel okay?" I ask, not wanting to carry on gently scolding him.

"Yes."

I pause for a moment, adding more oil before moving away from his temples, letting my fingers pulse softly on the lymph nodes in his neck.

"You're good at this," he murmurs, dropping a hand on my thigh like it's the most natural thing in the world to just casually touch each other.

I clear my throat, trying not to fixate on the contact.

"Thank you. Clyde likes it as well." I can't even mention the older man without smiling. I never imagined my relationship with him would bring me such fulfillment. It feels serendipitous that he strolled into the yoga studio that day. "He's doing better, you know. I think he'll be good to go around the timeline we agreed upon and if his occupational therapist agrees."

Bash hums deeply as I touch him. "That's good. What about you, though?"

My tongue darts out over my lips, a burst of nervousness tightening my chest. "I accepted a job at a resort in Costa Rica, so I'll be out of your hair in no time. Figure I'll go a little early and spend some time traveling to other parts of the country. I'll be due for a new adventure anyway."

Silence hangs between us, heavy and awkward. I can't help but wonder if my words sound as hollow to Bash as they feel in my head. Several beats pass, and I turn my focus back to the task at hand, pressing harder to mask how self-conscious I suddenly feel.

I sneak an uneasy peek down at him, eyes catching on the flash of silver in his sideburns and the dark stubble that dots his cheeks. His lips part and the anticipation of his response sends my stomach hurtling off a cliff. I don't know why I care so much about what he thinks, but I do.

And I expect him to say something about my upcoming plans—to give an opinion—but he catches me off guard when he asks, "What's the deal with your dad?"

My breathing hitches as I incline my head in thought. It might be the first personal thing Bash has ever asked me, not that I've volunteered much information. But it has me realizing I know a lot more about him than he knows about me.

"Well, we're estranged."

He grunts as I pull my fingers up behind his ears and then down over his throat.

"He kicked me out when I was eighteen. Which isn't really all that bad. I mean, I was an adult. But it was mostly because I wouldn't do what he wanted me to. He's incredibly old-fashioned."

"What did he want you to do?"

"Marry my high school boyfriend and start a family or *maybe* go get a degree—but mostly just so that I could meet a husband. Alas, I wanted neither. I decided I would have fun, casual sex, meditate with my feet in the sand, and rub lavender oil on people instead. He hasn't spoken to me since I walked out with all my belongings in one suitcase. Sometimes I think I haven't stopped moving around just to spite him, just to prove that I have control over how I live and when and where I do eventually settle. To prove I can live a happy, fulfilling life without abiding by his rules."

I chuckle, trying to cover the absurdity of the whole thing.

"He still won't talk to you? Ten years later?"

"It was less about yoga—though he made it clear he thinks it's stupid—and more about control. He hated the fact I wouldn't just do whatever he wanted. My mother embraced the homemaker role, which would be totally cool, except with them it was toxic. If dinner wasn't on the table when he walked through the front door, the passive-aggressive bullshit started. Shirt not pressed perfectly? Then he'd joke about it being too complicated of a job for her. But there was nothing funny about it."

"I hate him," Bash practically growls, his fists clenching before my eyes.

I smile at that, a tightness squeezing my throat. "I wish I could hate him. The comments about my weight should be enough. It fluctuated so much through my teen years and he always let me know that he noticed. Hormonal changes, yo-yo dieting, emotional eating—he'd comment on every phase. Once, he even got me a treadmill for my birthday. Told me he thought it could help with *that extra little bit* I'd been carrying lately."

I laugh, but it's humorless.

Bash's fingers curl to grip my thigh, firm and reassuring. I drop my chin to revel in the sight of his hand on my body. His silent support.

It's comforting.

Not wanting to gawk, I swallow the lump in my throat and carry on. "Obviously, he really fucked with the way I saw myself. Nothing I did was ever enough. And the feeling that no matter what I did, my body was fair game for commentary—for notes and feedback—was inescapable."

Bash's jaw tightens, his teeth clenching, but he doesn't comment. So I carry on. "Then I left. And my world opened up. I realized the way he treated me wasn't healthy or even normal. That I could live a full life *and* find peace in my body. And I did it. I'm there. But I…" I pause and then push through. "I guess I'm still grieving a relationship I'll never have. I've spent years making peace with the fact that no matter what I do, he'll never give me the approval I want. Because I defied him, and for him, that's the ultimate insult. So I focus on loving myself. And most days, I do. Especially my ass and side boob. I'm a big fan of them," I add, to lighten my gloomy monologue.

"Fuck. Me too," Bash mutters with a little groan.

I chuckle, retreating into my head for a beat, reflecting on my childhood and how far I've come.

The air around us vibrates with the ringing of the glass bowls before I speak again.

"The little girl in me will always wish it were different, though. Knowing I won't have him there to walk me down the aisle or be a grandparent or just...any of those things. I've had to make peace with that." I shrug. "Well, I guess I'm still trying. Some days are better than others. Like I said, daddy issues."

Bash peeks at me from beneath heavy lids. "What about your mom?"

"We talk on the phone. It's strained because I know he probably gives her shit for it and she'll defend him until the day she dies. I don't think it will ever change with those two. It's hard to watch. Promised myself a long time ago that I wouldn't end up like her."

"You won't," he murmurs in confirmation, sounding sleepy and relaxed.

I smile down over him, the satisfaction that comes with helping people all warm and gooey in my chest.

"I won't let you," Bash mumbles sleepily. That feeling in my chest goes hot and achy. It leaves a spark of hope.

I don't respond. There isn't much to say to that. I just want to take the sentiment and cherish it.

As I move to roll away, one of his hands shoots out, wrapping around my forearm. "I don't want you to leave, Gwen," he says, his voice rough with sleep.

My heart skips. Because does he mean tonight? Or to Costa Rica?

He doesn't open his eyes to gauge my reaction—like he's hiding from it instead.

His hand slips away, not forcing me to do anything I don't want to.

My heart thuds, heavy and languid, the rhythm of it humming in my veins. My head spins with the possibility of spending the night beside him.

Or more? Could he mean more?

I turn away from his still form, place the oil on his bedside table, and flick off the light, plunging us into a lavender-scented darkness.

Should I? Shouldn't I?

For a girl who's accustomed to running, the decision to stay with Bash is all too easy to make.

With my back to him, I confess quietly, "I don't want to leave either."

And when I turn back to face him, he's pulled the covers open—a silent invitation for me to join him beneath them.

I stare at the spot where I know I'll fit so perfectly, wondering if I'm crossing a line I shouldn't.

I decide I don't care. I decide that where Sebastian Rousseau is concerned, I'll take what I can get. It might not be forever, but I'll settle for right now.

So I slip under the duvet and let him hold me.

CHAPTER 25

Bash

I WAKE LIKE I'VE JUST BEEN JOLTED BACK TO LIFE—HARD, fast, and alert all at once. A strip of bright light slices across the room from the split in the blackout curtains as I check my watch—it's 10 a.m. A time I never sleep to.

I must have needed it. A hard reset.

Beside me, the sheets are rumpled—proof that Gwen did, in fact, spend the night in my bed.

It was something I needed. Something I always wanted when I came back from a job. And she didn't hesitate.

The intimacy of last night satisfied a craving I didn't even know I had. Gwen had known what I needed without me having to explain it to her. Then she'd told me more about herself than ever before.

I understand her better now.

More than that, I feel attached.

I don't want any awkward tension between us. I want the

gentleness of last night. And when my feet hit the floor, I tell myself that today is a new day. If I want things to be like that between us, I can do my part to keep them that way.

A new day where I can try being nicer.

No—kinder.

Ever since that conversation, the distinction has stuck with me. I don't know if I can force myself to have a nicer, more palatable personality, but I can always be kind.

In the bathroom, I brush my teeth and study my reflection. I look tired, but not as worn down as yesterday. I feel a bit blue but not depressed and cynical like yesterday.

It makes me wonder if she was onto something when she asked about my mental and emotional well-being. Truth is, I've ignored both lately.

The prospect of facing Gwen this morning has me unsettled. Without my surliness to hide behind, I feel vulnerable. Soft, sensitive, and easily wounded.

It's also harder to convince myself I don't want her when I'm feeling this exposed. Propping my hands on the counter, I stare back at myself in the mirror.

I can be safe and kind.

I can be mature and kind.

I can be kind to Gwen without fucking her.

Of course I can. I'm a grown man. I'm a highly skilled pilot. I kick ass under pressure. I'll even apologize for my past behavior, really own my shit.

"I can do this," I mutter as I rinse off my toothbrush and turn to head downstairs.

When I get there, it's quiet. I expected to hear chatter

or laughter like I do most mornings since Clyde and Gwen came here and took over my life. It's inexplicable how well they get along. Thick as thieves, the two of them. And it's been nice to watch. Especially knowing what I do now.

He appreciates her and respects her expertise. Sees value in all the things about her that her own dad shamed her for.

And she's the same with him. Clyde gets lonely, whether he wants to admit it or not. Many people can't handle his shit, but with Gwen, he can be the most unhinged version of himself, and she just smiles, letting him ramble on.

I have to confess—I could learn a thing or two from Gwen.

Like how to let things go. How to get over perceived wrongs that I carry with me. Missed opportunities that keep me up at night.

She said I was repressed, and she wasn't wrong. I just don't know how to stop.

Following the smell of freshly brewed coffee, I head into the kitchen, where I expect to be alone. Except Gwen is standing with her back to me, hair tossed up in a messy bun, a mug clasped between her hands. The golden light illuminates her.

It makes me wish we could have woken up together. Left the curtains open, so I could lie in bed and watch the morning sun dance across her upturned nose, watch its rays highlight the tops of her full cheeks.

She'd be warm and soft, and she'd smell like lavender. I'd pull her closer and stare at her for so long that when I closed my eyes, the shape of her would be burned on the back of my lids.

The possibility of it hits me hard in the chest. I'm past pretending I don't want this, at least—someone to wake up with. To share a coffee with. To enjoy the view with.

It's not even the sex I miss. It's companionship. The comfort of knowing that if I'm sick, someone will be there to help. That when I get home from working a brutal wildfire, I won't have to sit with it alone. That at the end of the day, I'll have someone to hold for the night, letting my breathing fall in time with theirs.

It's the simple things.

It's building a life with someone.

I'd settle for just that.

But it can't be just *someone*. I think deep down I want it to be *the one*. I've been hurt too badly for it not to be.

And when I think of the one, I think of her.

Biting down on my cheek, I head toward the coffeepot and pour myself a mug. If Gwen notices my presence, she doesn't show it. She stays facing the sprawling back deck—practically another room added to the house if you were to open the sliding doors.

"Good morning," I finally muster, needing to break the silence. I can't have her feeling like she can't even speak.

Seen but not heard, she'd said when referring to her dad. That sentiment had rankled me. Now it infuriates me.

She peeks over her shoulder, those unusual eyes landing on me. The soft sage green of her sweatshirt and matching leggings does nothing but amplify the purple tinge in her irises.

Lavender. Lilacs. The color of the sun when it rises over heavy wildfire smoke.

"It is…some kind of morning." Her smooth voice is like a balm, and the light curve of her mouth holds not a single shred of awkwardness.

My head tilts as she looks back out the window with a light giggle. Coffee in hand, I cross the expansive kitchen. I pass dark-green cabinetry, with gold hardware and stained wood countertops, as I follow the pull toward Gwen.

Her curves are on full display. I itch to touch her. But that thought comes to an abrupt and screeching halt when I catch sight of what she's looking at.

Because it's not the lake.

It's Clyde. On the deck. Naked.

My jaw unhinges as I come to stand next to her, chin dropping in shock. He's seated facing away from us, legs spread and in the air, with his arms hooked behind his knees.

"What the fuck is he doing?"

Gwen looks up at me, amusement dancing on her face. "Oh, that?" she replies with a little smirk. "He's, uh…sunning his perineum."

Confused as hell, I glance back at the man. He's scrawny and wiry looking, all lean muscles and sun-worn skin. I know he spends a huge amount of time outside to keep his home on the other side of the mountain running. Chopping wood, growing herbs and vegetables, reinforcing his roof, and building his zombie shelter or whatever the hell it's supposed to be for.

Truthfully, if there ever is an apocalypse, Clyde would be the friend to have.

But this? This is too much.

"Sunning his perineum?"

Gwen snorts a laugh, her shoulders shaking with the effort of restraining herself. "That's what he called it. In my head, I've been calling it *tanning his taint*."

I can't help it. I chuckle. Gwen's eyes widen in surprise. Her gaze lingers on my mouth before sliding back toward the tall windows. And a very naked Clyde.

"Is this a yoga thing?" I ask seriously before taking a sip of my coffee. I was bad enough last night. If this is a thing, then I can be respectful about it. Or at least pretend to be.

"Mm-hmm. Taint tanning is all the rage these days. You'll have to try it."

I keep my expression neutral because I don't want Gwen to think I don't respect her expertise. But the tone of my voice gives me away as I ask, "Really?" with some level of disgust.

"No. Not really," she says with a blinding smile.

"So, he's just…" I don't even know what to ask.

"Trying out things he read about on the internet? Yes. Indeed, he is."

"But where is this a thing? And *why?*"

"He sent me a blog post about it. You know, all the best medical professionals hang out on WordPress."

Of course he did.

"According to the article"—she holds one hand up to make air quotes—"it has 'a whole host of benefits. It helps with longevity, vitamin D levels, circulation, and libido.'" She waggles her eyebrows as she says *libido*, and I'm struck dumb.

"He just had a kidney transplant. Why is he worried about his libido?"

She shrugs. "New lease on life, maybe? He's old, not dead. His sacral chakra is flowing. It's pretty normal for him to be thinking about sex. God knows he spends enough time on that doomsday-preppers dating site."

I cringe and take a deep swig of my black coffee, hoping to cleanse my mind of any imagery that combines Clyde and sex.

"Does he know you can get vitamin D at the store?"

"Yeah, but, Bash"—Gwen drops her voice into the perfect imitation of Clyde—"that shit is synthetic and nothing like the real thing."

"Good god, that does sound like something he'd say." I shake my head, eyes fixed on this man whom I've essentially adopted. Who currently has his ass spread in a sunbeam on my deck. "Is it safe?"

She shrugs, hands cupped around her coffee as she takes a thoughtful sip. "Some of his medications are supposed to cause sun sensitivity. But the sun is still mild right now, so I gave him five minutes and told him I'm timing him. I don't think he's hurting anything except our eyes. And maybe if he starts now, he can build up to doing it in the summer. Like a base tan, ya know? Avoid burning."

"I hate this conversation so much" is all I can think to say, and it makes Gwen laugh. Throaty, velvety laughter that never fails to be a shot straight to my dick.

But it's so much more than that. It's the realization that she's everything I want.

CHAPTER 26

Bash

AFTER WATCHING CLYDE ON THE DECK, I DECIDE TO RESTART my day.

I shower, hoping the water will wash away the mental image of him on my patio. Even after a full night's sleep, my body still feels sore, and a dull ache still thrums at my temples.

Under the hot spray, I mull over Gwen's words and consider whether these symptoms could stem from my mental health rather than simply being run-down.

In the privacy of the shower, it feels easier to confess that I'm not at my healthiest, but perhaps not only in a physical way.

As I dress and prepare to head back downstairs, I take a step back mentally and examine myself as if I were an outside spectator. I think about all my years as a wildland firefighter, all the things I've seen, all the men and women I've worked alongside.

I think about how I would react to seeing one of my coworkers feeling the way I do now.

The term "occupational burnout" pops up in my brain. I've seen it firsthand—watched friends and coworkers struggle with it, manage it, succumb to it, and beat it. And I wonder if that's what I'm up against.

For years, this job has consumed me. I started at the bottom, completed grueling hours of in-flight training, and clawed my way up to become an aerial firefighter. It's been all work and no play, and maybe it's made me a bit of a dull boy.

I've been relentless in my pursuit of this job, and I've never considered taking a break. Hell, I barely even take vacations.

I pause as I pull my socks on, realizing that's not exactly true. In a sense, I have taken a break. I used to spend my winters fighting fires in other parts of the world. Spring, fall, winter elsewhere—often Australia—and returning home to Canada, or down south in the States, for the summer. Fighting fires year-round.

It wasn't until the last couple of years that I finally stepped back to spend the winter working quietly on small contracting jobs in the valley. A gig that gives me a brief break from the death and destruction of natural disasters.

For the longest time, I thought that work was all I had, but now I'm faced with the realization that maybe that's not the case anymore.

I'm terrible at asking for help, but last night, I tried to. And Gwen just *knew*.

Coming home feeling so downtrodden and depleted scared me. It may even be the wake-up call I needed. I fucking hate asking for help, but I'm too old to ignore when I need it.

So I begrudgingly promise myself I'm going to phone our professional firefighters' association and see if there's anyone I can talk to.

But first, food. I'm starving. I didn't eat properly while I was away either. I didn't take care of myself *at all*.

When I get downstairs, I'm met with the chatter and laughter I expected when I first got up this morning. The past several weeks before I left, I avoided joining them, but today I want to.

Gwen and Clyde are both in the kitchen, having a lively conversation with each other. And as I watch Clyde pull a bag of celery from the fridge, moving around comfortably, I can't help but wonder if getting a little sun on his taint really did make him feel better. The improvement, even just in the days I was away, has been exceptional.

"What are we making?" I ask, as I stride into the kitchen.

Gwen turns to face me, knife in her hand, bits of raw chicken dangling from the end. If she looks surprised by my presence, she doesn't show it. "You," she says, "are not making anything. You are going to sit at that counter and relax. And later, you are going to take a nap."

I quirk a brow at her. "I haven't taken a nap after a full night's sleep in years. I'm not a small child."

Gwen doesn't bother staring me down—she just goes back to dicing chicken breasts. "Well, if you can't take care of yourself, then I will have to treat you like a small child. And that means you're taking a nap. Your body needs it."

Clyde watches us with narrowed eyes, gaze flicking back and forth between Gwen and me. "Why is she telling you to relax? I mean, we all know you need to relax. You're wound as tight as a fishing reel. But since when do you listen to what she says?"

I drop onto a stool at the counter and look at Clyde. As irritating as he sometimes is, I have to confess that he's one of my closest friends. So I try something new. I try not to bottle it all up. "Since I overdid it and made myself sick. I've been a little tightly wound, and I think it caught up with me."

Clyde scoffs, grabbing a knife for the celery. "You think?"

I roll my eyes. "Just being open about it, Clyde. Not all of us reap the rewards of putting our perineum in the sun."

He snorts now, grinning down at the celery he's chopping. "I would tell you to try it, except you wouldn't listen to me. You're not enlightened enough."

I shake my head, wondering how the fuck I got to a place where I'm talking about my feelings with the town conspiracy theorist and the girl I got drunk in an airport with.

"But I'll tell you what would be good for you," Clyde starts back in. "Pot."

I go still, head tilting as I stare back at him. "Pot?"

He dips his chin. "Yeah. You know…marijuana. Ganja. Dope. Grass. Reefer. Mary Jane. I don't know what you kids are calling it these days, but it might serve you well. It's medicinal."

Gwen snorts a laugh and covers her mouth with the back of her hand.

"What are you laughing at?" I ask her.

Wide eyes dart up to mine. "Mary Jane. I haven't heard that one in a long time." She can barely get the words out without bursting into a fit of giggles.

All I can do is blink at her.

Clyde turns now, facing Gwen. "You know I'm right, though. It would be good for him."

She rolls her lips together, head tilting from side to side as she considers. All the while avoiding eye contact with me. Finally, she shrugs. "Yeah, probably."

"Aha!" Clyde's hand shoots up in the air, and he stabs toward the ceiling with one of my sharper kitchen knives. "I'm right!" He points the knife my way. "You, my friend, just need to blow a spliff, have a nap, and consider getting a little sun on your perineum."

"Clyde, I will never put sun on my perineum."

All I get for that is an eye roll. But then the man pauses. "Does that mean you'll blow a jay with me?"

I can't remember the last time I smoked pot. Sure, it's legal. Sure, I understand the medicinal benefits. It's just something I've never reached for. And I'm not sure it's something Clyde should be reaching for either. "Clyde, I don't even know if you are medically cleared to be smoking pot."

He waves me off like I'm the unreasonable one in this situation. I suppose I don't have a leg to stand on when it comes to being cleared for something.

"Nah. Grew these plants myself. In fact, while you were

away, Gwen and I took a trip up to my place just to check on everything. Grabbed a little bit. Said hi to my Maya."

My brows furrow. "What's my Maya?"

Gwen's head snaps up, her features taking on a sad expression that has me looking between the two of them. Obviously, she knows something I don't.

"My wife," he says plainly, like this isn't the first time I'm hearing about her. "Got all her pictures up at my place. You've never noticed them?"

I blink at him. No, I hadn't noticed them. I don't think I've ever taken a close look at anything in Clyde's house beyond what was necessary. "I'm sorry, Clyde. I don't think I ever paid close enough attention. Next time we're there, you could show me?" I say, trying to smooth over the lump of guilt in my gut.

"It was a long time ago. She's been gone for forty-odd years now." My throat feels thick as I watch him speak about the wife I never knew he had. "Blood clot got her. She passed peacefully. Though I'll never get over taking her to the hospital and being told it was a migraine. Got sent home that night. She died in her sleep. So anyway, enjoy your life while you've got it. That's what I say. Tomorrow is never promised."

He says it like it's not one of the saddest stories I've heard. Like it wasn't wholly unnecessary.

And suddenly, little bits of Clyde's personality slip into place for me. His mistrust of the medical system. His belief in so many zany things. Why wouldn't he? Why shouldn't he? An event like that would have a profound effect on a person.

It makes me feel bad that he hasn't felt like he could tell me. It makes me question what type of friend I've been to him. I unload all my drama on him, but do I ever stop to listen?

"You could bring the pictures here if you wanted," I say, hoping to make this better. "You don't have to leave just to see your things, Clyde."

I want him to feel at home here. What felt like an intrusion before now feels like me just being a reclusive asshole.

Have I been forcing them to walk on eggshells around me?

"Nah, Maya wouldn't like it here. Her pictures belong there, in our house. We were happy there together, you know. Still one of my favorite places in the world to be. Nobody grew marijuana like my Maya. In fact, I still have some of her strains going to this day. That's how we made all our money, but we still just loved our quiet cottage. Got emergency cash buried in different spots around the property. For safety."

Of course he has cash buried on his property.

My eyes flit between Gwen and Clyde as I take in all of this new information—the unexpected pieces of his life and the strange way we're reminiscing about the way he and his late wife used to grow marijuana illegally.

Deciding this has the potential to be a somewhat wholesome moment, I tap a palm against the island's countertop and announce, "You know what, Clyde? I would love to smoke some of Maya's Mary Jane with you."

At that, Gwen bursts out laughing before dropping a handful of chicken into a sizzling pot. "Yeah, Clyde," she adds. "I too would like to smoke some of Maya's Mary Jane. Let's get this soup ready, then we can all go sit outside and enjoy it together."

The man brightens, standing up taller, his eyes sparkling. "Really? You two would do that with me?"

"Hell yeah," Gwen says as I give him a solemn nod. "You can tell us more about Maya."

Clyde smiles—a rare, genuine smile. Not a smirk, not a mischievous grin, but the kind of smile that speaks to a bone-deep happiness. It's a smile I don't wear often. But, in this moment, it might be reflected on my face too.

I watch as they finish making lunch, chattering away about which ingredients to add to the chicken noodle soup and which ones they should leave out. Clyde approves of Gwen's homemade bone broth but scowls at adding more vegetables. Gwen firmly but gently overrides him at every turn, explaining that if vitamin D is good for his taint, then vegetables are also good for his immune system.

He grumbles, but he doesn't complain. And soon, a warm, rich-smelling soup is bubbling on the stove.

The three of us head outside, the sun heating the front porch head-on this time of day. It's protected from the breeze, which makes it feel more like summer. Light sparkles on the water and that smell of pine trees that I love so much floats in the air.

I take a few deep breaths, chasing that scent and the feeling of solitude that I associate with it. Before long, the scent of marijuana masks the smell of pine.

I glance at Clyde, who is seated in the Adirondack chair

right next to me with his signature cap pulled low to keep the sun off his face, Gwen just on the other side of him. He has a thinly rolled joint pressed to his lips at the tip and pinched between his thumb and forefinger in the middle. He sucks in deeply, and I watch his eyes flutter shut as the smoke billows from his nostrils.

He hands it to Gwen, and she follows suit, a puff of smoke spilling from her lips as she relaxes back into the chair. The way her back arches and the sound she makes is a straight shot to my dick. She's sensual without even trying.

And sitting here has my brain flooding with memories of pressing her against that railing. My lips on hers. Her hands in my hair.

I wish I hadn't stopped.

"You weren't lying, Clyde. Maya was a talented woman," Gwen announces while I try to will my boner away.

He chuckles. "That she was."

Gwen holds the reefer out in my direction, and I reach across Clyde to take it from her. I turn it over in my hand, eyeing it with hesitation.

Truth be told, I've always been a straitlaced kind of guy, and I'm out of my element. Still, I watched the other two enough to mimic their motions.

I lift the joint and take a deep inhale.

Seconds later, I'm coughing, and they're laughing. And not long after that, I'm laughing too.

Clyde sighs. "Maya would have gotten a real kick out of this, watching someone so tightly wound talk about his feelings and smoke her plant. It would have made her happy."

"I live to serve," I joke, taking another puff—this time without coughing.

"Hell, maybe after a few more hits, you'll be out there sunning your—"

"Clyde, don't even go there. Maya sounds lovely, but there's going to be no sunning of anything."

"What about sunning your face?" Gwen suggests. "Just kick back and relax. You can absorb vitamin D through any part of your skin. And vitamin D is hugely beneficial for low mood and a stressed immune system."

Clyde grumbles about absorption rates, and it makes me laugh. My shoulders shake with it.

I take another puff, and my body relaxes. In fact, muscles let go that haven't softened in years.

And so goes the next hour. We share the small joint, and while Clyde stays covered, I slouch back in the sun, letting its rays warm me from the outside in. I absorb my vitamin D appropriately.

Eyes fluttered shut, head swimming, body floating, I let myself enjoy the moment with two people who have become the most unexpected type of friends.

Eventually, our conversation turns to peppering Clyde with whether or not he believes certain conspiracy theories.

"Hey, Clyde, was Elvis Presley's death faked?"

"Hey, Clyde, was the moon landing faked by the government?"

"Hey, Clyde, did they add fluoride to water sources just to make people sickly?"

"Hey, Clyde, is the earth flat or round?"

"Hey, Clyde, who built the pyramids, Egyptians or aliens?"

To that one he says, "Of course the Egyptians built the pyramids, but aliens commissioned them."

Needless to say, the further along we go and the higher we get, the more we laugh.

I laugh until my cheeks hurt. I laugh until my throat feels hoarse. I laugh until my stomach cramps.

I have *fun*.

And god, it's one of the best afternoons of my life.

CHAPTER 27

Gwen

SINCE BASH CAME HOME, I'VE BEEN IN AN INSUFFERABLY good mood.

Between a night spent lying beside him and an afternoon spent getting silly on the front porch, a new sense of camaraderie has grown between us.

It's like he finally opened up, and now I can't help but feel a whole new level of attachment to him. To us. Or, well, to the idea of us.

Last night, I didn't push my luck after watching Bash get high—for the first time in what I had to assume was decades. When we went back inside the house, he scarfed down a bowl of chicken noodle soup, then some fresh-baked cookies…and then a bowl of chips.

After a full attack of the munchies, he walked to the plush couch in the living room, flopped down, and conked out. For three hours, he slept, and I know because I kept checking on him. I draped a blanket over his sleeping form, marveling at how much younger he appears in sleep, without the stern crease to his brow.

When he woke up, he looked better rested than he had first thing in the morning. And seeing his improvement made it that much easier to head out to the studio for a night's worth of teaching.

Even today, my good mood persists. Partially because when I got home from work last night, the sounds of my favorite singing bowls playlist filtered from beneath Bash's room and the scent of lavender oil wafted from beneath his door.

Earlier I had texted him the link to the playlist and then left my speaker and the oil on his bedside table, just in case.

Bash using them should not have felt as good as it did. It was so small, so simple. But it felt like more. It felt like he didn't think I was ridiculous or zany. It felt like he valued the strategies I showed him.

It felt like he valued *me*.

I went to my room with a goofy grin on my face, though a huge part of me was tempted to crawl into bed with him. Sleeping next to Bash had been peaceful in a way that I don't know I've experienced before.

It was a quiet companionship, a soothing connection. It was just *more*.

Everything with Bash has been, since the first time we met.

Now, I prepare the studio for my morning class, brain still hung up on Mr. Tall, Dark, and Handsome.

I lay out blocks and straps at each station, with a full lesson plan in my mind, then I head to the front of the studio so I can greet the students as they filter in.

One by one, familiar faces pass through the door, each a part of the regular following I've amassed. Until I find myself staring into the eyes of someone I didn't expect to see here at all.

Bash.

My mouth pops open and then closes again. "What…" I trail off, shaking my head as my lips curve up into a smile. "What are you doing here?"

The way his gaze rakes over my body, lingering at my hips, my waist, my breasts, makes my body hum. For someone who spent so many years working to find beauty in her body, I don't need to try at all with Bash.

He shrugs, eyeing the studio as though he's never seen it before, assessing the odds and ends for sale on the shelf in the corner. "I had a call with one of the fire association's mental health workers this morning, and they suggested some different ways for me to soothe my nervous system. Yoga was one of them." His eyes slice back to mine. "I told them I knew one of the best teachers around. Figured I'd try it."

My cheeks hurt from how hard I grin back at him. "Yeah?"

"Yeah. So far, every piece of advice you've given me has only made me feel better. So I bet this will too."

I giggle. Yes, Bash makes me giddy.

He wrings his hands together now, a flash of uncertainty

touching his features. "I also wanted to take a moment to…" He scrubs a hand over his beard. "To apologize."

"For what?"

"For being ornery. For the way I've spoken to you since you moved in. My call this morning made me realize this has been a long time coming. That I haven't been myself. And that I have taken out a fair bit of my anxiety on the people around me."

I blink, not wanting to interrupt him. Even though I want to tell him how hot it is to hear him apologize. Too many people walk around never reflecting on their actions, never owning them, never admitting when they're wrong.

"I hate the way I've spoken to you in certain moments, and I wanted to tell you I plan to be better. To work on all these…" His hand goes into a clawlike shape as he rotates it near his chest and his lips draw back as though he's disgusted by the words he's about to say. "To work on all these feelings."

I blink again. Then, I nod. But I say nothing. Honestly, I'm concerned that if I speak, I will laugh over how appalled he looks over having to deal with *feelings*.

"I was a dick. I wasn't myself. Especially that night with the raccoon."

My head bobs. He was a dick about the raccoon. But then he also kissed me stupid, and that part had been a make-out session for the record books.

It hadn't been a healthy interaction, but parts of it had been pretty damn unforgettable. "Yeah, but maybe you don't need to be sorry about *everything* that happened that night."

One of his brows quirks and his head tilts almost

suggestively. "There are certainly parts of that night I am not sorry about."

A thrill races down my spine as my eyes shift to take in the lobby around us, wondering if anyone is watching or listening in as they stroll past.

Bash has no such hesitation; he carries on like he didn't just make me all hot and bothered with one simple sentence.

"I lashed out, and you didn't deserve it. So I'm sorry. If you want to be Gwen Dawson, mother of raccoons, then I won't stand in your way. I support you in that venture. You can be seen *and* heard in my house. And you are welcome to befriend overgrown rodents who may or may not carry diseases. I won't judge you."

I tilt my head to show that I don't quite believe him.

With a heavy sigh, he shakes his head, holding a hand up in defeat. "Much."

I smile broadly. "Yeah, that's more believable."

"Yeah. Okay. I won't judge you *much*."

"Thank you. I appreciate this. And your honesty. And even your mild judgment. If you were too chipper about this exploration of feelings, it would be a red flag."

He gives me an eye roll for that dig and then forges ahead, letting a little cynicism back in. And I'm glad for it. That signature bitchiness is just part of his charm now. "Okay, let's go stretch and shit."

I snort and take him by the hand, long enough to give him a reassuring squeeze as I lead him down the hall. "Let's go get you set up for stretching and shit."

Once in the classroom, I guide him to a spot in the

corner near my mat so I can help him as much as possible. I unroll one of the studio's purple mats for him—part of my ongoing effort to make him look at more purple things—and help him settle into a simple pose while the rest of the class finds their places.

As I lead everyone through the lesson, I make a conscious effort not to only focus on Bash. I start on the far side of the classroom, adjusting positions, whispering reminders to soften or stop holding their breath, to relax their spine.

When I work my way around to Bash, something about seeing him here—trying, being open to giving this a whirl—hits me square in the chest.

I know he's showing up for himself, but it feels like he's showing up for me too.

Either way, it endears him to me even more. This is what makes him different. This is proof that he believes in me and in what I do to make my living. I shouldn't want his approval, but damn, it feels good to have it.

As he moves into Downward Dog, I let my palm glide over his spine. His shoulders are tight, so I apply gentle pressure between them. "Make space here, between your shoulder blades, and drop your chin," I whisper before moving my hand in a gentle circle on his back.

He shivers.

It's way too easy to touch him freely here.

Under the guise of checking his alignment, I let my hands wander. They end up on his hips, straightening him. "Release through your lower back. If it's too strong of a stretch, you can bend your knees, take a deep breath, and then push back into it. Eventually, you'll be able to relax your heels to the floor."

He snorts at that, but he says nothing. In fact, all he does is try. Every time I make my way around the classroom and back to him, his breathing is more even. His muscles, just a little softer. His entire aura, more relaxed.

"You're doing amazing," I whisper.

He chuckles and shakes his head, as though he doesn't believe my compliments.

But it makes no difference to me. I continue giving him praise at every turn, enjoying telling him what a fabulous job he's doing. And the more I do, the more I realize I misread his reaction at first. It's not dismissive. It's…bashful.

It's as though he doesn't know how to accept a compliment—or doesn't buy it. I figure if I keep giving them to him, one day he'll start believing me.

At the end of the class, we move into Savasana, and much like Clyde always does, Bash falls asleep.

As the rest of the class filters out, he finally wakes. Not wanting to stare at him like the obsessed fangirl that I am, I turn my focus to saying goodbye to each student as they depart.

Bree, one of my favorite students, comes up to me. There's a lightness in her body language that wasn't there when she first began yoga with me. Back then, her energy was all turmoil, heartbreak, and sadness, but with time, she's found some balance, and it makes my heart swell to see her in a better space.

From what I know, she'd been through a lot. She hasn't

been at her best, but she's never stopped trying. And striving to be better is one of the best things a person can do.

As such, Bree is pretty badass in my books.

She gives me a shy smile as she hands me a small box wrapped with a pretty bow. "Happy early birthday, Gwen," she says. "I know you're not teaching tomorrow, so I wanted to give this to you today. It's been a hard year for me, but your classes have been a bright spot. I hope you know what a big difference you make in people's lives."

My eyes well as I accept the gift, then wrap her lithe body in a tight hug. "Thank you, Bree" is all I manage, my voice thick with emotion.

When I step back, I squeeze her shoulder, eyes still misty, and smile.

"You enjoy your day off," she says, giving my arm an affectionate rub. "And I'll see you on the weekend."

"Perfect. I'll see you then," I say, watching the woman pad quietly from the room.

When I turn back, Bash is the only student who remains. He's kneeling on the mat, hands clasped over his knees, brow furrowed.

When he sees that I've faced his direction, he lifts his chin, dark eyes dancing over mine in a way that warms me from head to toe. His expression is a mix of both confusion and determination.

"You didn't tell me it was your birthday tomorrow."

I wave him off. "Because it's not a big deal."

Birthdays have always left a sour taste in my mouth, and I don't look forward to them. Usually, I take them as a day to reflect, to practice gratitude, and to think about all the things I would like to accomplish in the year to come. And what I rarely acknowledge is that my birthday usually makes me miss my parents.

Bash stands, shaking his head, his tone of voice slipping back to slightly surly. "Yeah, Gwen, it *is* a big deal."

CHAPTER 28

Bash

GWEN SPENDS THE REST OF THE DAY AT THE STUDIO TEACH-ing. Which is fine, because I spend the rest of the day rushing around planning a birthday party for her.

One that doesn't end with her getting a fucking treadmill.

I stop in at the Bighorn Bistro and beg Tabitha to make a cake or cupcakes or anything that Gwen might like.

I call West and tell him to invite everyone to my place tomorrow evening.

Then I grab a bunch of groceries and head home, mar-veling over the fact that Gwen's yoga class really did make me feel a bit better. A little less stiff. A little less stressed. A little more open.

When I get home, Clyde is sitting on the front porch, tucked into a shady corner. Thank fuck all of his clothes are on because I need to talk to him. I stride out the patio doors and fold myself down into the chair next to him.

"Back for more of Maya's medicine?" he asks, staring out over the water with a grin on his face.

I can't help but chuckle. "Not today."

He grumbles like I've disappointed him.

"Did you know that Gwen's birthday is tomorrow?"

Clyde nods. "Yeah." He's so casual about it. Like I'm an idiot for just now realizing it.

"How did you know?"

"She told me. We talk and don't just make googly eyes at each other from across the room."

I slouch back, already regretting bringing this up with him.

"Or make out on the back deck."

"What the fuck, Clyde?" I throw a hand over my eyes, wanting to hide from this conversation. "Were you watching us?"

He giggles a raspy little giggle, getting way too much enjoyment out of this. "No, I got up to check what was going on because you were barking at her like a police dog who'd found a stash of drugs. Did you forget I live on the main floor? My sliding doors lead out onto this deck. If you guys kept your trysts to the upstairs balcony, I wouldn't have to be subjected to—"

I groan and tip my head back, pressing the heels of my palms into my eye sockets. "Please tell me you were not just hanging out watching us."

He scoffs now. "I'm weird, not a creep." I peek at him from the corner of my eye and his head tilts like he's considering what to say next. "I won't lie. I was pretty pleased with that development. You two are perfect for each other. Remind me of myself and Maya when we were younger."

I keep my face impassive because as much as I love Clyde, I do not want to be like him. The world can only handle one Clyde.

"But." He sighs the word heavily, shifting in his chair. "It seems as though in your mission to be Mr. Good-Guy Hero Man, you've plunked yourself squarely into the friend zone."

"I have not. We're just... We're being mature. It's complicated."

Clyde scoffs. "It's not complicated. You look at her like she hung the moon, and she's the only woman in the world who finds your shitty attitude to be endearing."

"I don't have a shitty attitude."

He turns in his chair to face me. "Kid, you are one big shitty attitude. When I close my eyes and try to envision you, I see a frown floating in the abyss. *Except* when you're around Gwen. So stop pretending this has to do with that prissy little goofball you made when you were too stupid to use a condom."

He reaches forward, one gnarled finger poking me in the bicep. "Because it's about *you*. You're scared."

My mind reels with his assessment. It seems insane that Clyde, one of the least rational people I know, should be the one to see this all so clearly, while I'm stumbling around in the fog.

"I'm not scared," I retort, but it sounds weak even to my own ears.

Clyde responds by fitting his thumbs into his armpits and clucking at me like a chicken.

"Ugh," I reply dramatically, pushing to stand. "Forget it."

"I can't! It's burned into my mind! You've scarred me."

Shaking my head, I move toward the door, wishing to escape this conversation as quickly as humanly possible.

"I've been playing matchmaker for months with you two. Don't squander it! And don't be a chump and forget to buy her a present!"

His words strike a chord as I enter the house. *Months?* Has he been playing the long game with this shit? Meddling and playing innocent?

I decide that's too wild to fixate on. Instead, my brain fixates on a present for Gwen. Or rather *something* for Gwen. Because I understand Gwen well enough to know that simply buying her a present won't cut it. She's not hung up on material items or expensive gifts.

No, Gwen lives for new experiences. And I know which one I'm going to give her.

I wake up early, hoping to get a head start on Gwen. I may not be great at talking about my feelings, but I am great at showing them.

With the kitchen to myself, I get to work prepping an over-the-top breakfast—one that says what I can't. I don't know specifically what she likes, so I make everything. I want her to have it all, everything and anything she likes. Hell,

I even picked up some more lavender from the florist and added a couple of pots to the space. Partly because I know Gwen likes them, and partly because I do too.

They remind me of her.

The counter slowly fills with dishes, each one covered in foil to keep it warm.

Bacon, ham, and sausage.

Waffles, toast, and hash browns.

Eggs—Benedict and scrambled.

Fruit salad and fresh-squeezed orange juice.

Overkill? Absolutely. Do I care? Not in the slightest.

I care even less the second she pads into the kitchen. She's wearing a matching pajama set—shorts and a long-sleeved, collared shirt. Her face is scrubbed clean, and her hair is piled in a loose, messy tumble on top of her head. She still has imprinted lines on her cheek from where it was clearly pressed into the pillow.

She's fucking breathtaking. And the fact that she didn't roll out of *my* bed is downright criminal.

"What is all this?" Her voice is still thick with sleep, and it makes me wish I had been there to wake up next to her. It makes me wish I had told her I wanted her in my bed again. I'd been bold enough to ask her that night when I first came back and too shit-scared to say more ever since.

What I should have been brave enough to tell her is that I didn't want that to be a one-night thing.

I wanted it to be an every-night thing.

"It's a birthday breakfast. Happy birthday."

She clasps her hands at her chest, and I watch her

cheeks flush a light pink as she takes in the spread. "It's too much."

I scoff. "Nah. I enjoyed making it. You eat whatever you want. If there's leftovers, then whatever."

She blinks a couple of times. "No, I meant that you didn't need to do this."

I'm pouring her a cup of coffee when I stop, look up at her, and say simply, "But I wanted to."

She swallows, looking more moved by an over-the-top breakfast than I expected. "Thank you."

I nod and round the island toward her, coffee cup out-stretched in her direction. "You're welcome. Take a seat. Tell me what you want, and I'll serve it up."

With a soft smile, she wraps her palms around the coffee cup and makes her way to one of the stools at the island's counter, gazing over the options.

"Honestly, I kind of want some of everything? It looks amazing." She sounds bashful admitting she wants it all, whereas I'm just thrilled she doesn't hate what I made.

"Coming right up. What my girl wants, she gets."

The term slips so easily from my tongue that I don't even have the time to prevent it. My eyes flit to hers, to see if there's any negative reaction there. Instead, I find her watching me curiously, head slightly tilted as though I'm a puzzle she can't figure out.

And who could blame her? I haven't exactly been straightforward.

I decide not to explain the *my girl* thing away and just carry on plating her food. When I set it down in front of her, she beams. And I can't help but feel like I'd make her breakfast every damn morning to see that look on her face.

I hand her cutlery. "I have a surprise for you after you're finished."

Her lips press together, but I can tell by the way her cheeks bulge that she's pleased—if a little overwhelmed. She then takes a bite of the syrup-drizzled waffle, moaning softly like it's the best thing she's eaten in her life. I puff up a bit, getting off on how satisfied she seems.

I'm standing there making "googly eyes" at her, as Clyde had called it, when he appears in the doorway. He takes one look at the food laid out and then pulls up a seat beside Gwen. "I wish Bash were in love with me. Then maybe he'd make me nice breakfasts too."

I spray my mouthful of coffee into my hand right as Gwen barks out a shocked laugh and thumps a flattened palm on her chest.

At the sink, I shake my hand off, looking down over my plain gray T-shirt and noting the splatter of coffee droplets. I'm about to give Clyde a piece of my mind for being such a meddlesome shit-disturber when the doorbell rings.

All three of us freeze. We've lived together for long enough to know that sound doesn't go off much. And last time it did, it brought along an unexpected visitor.

Both Gwen and Clyde stare at me with wide eyes.

"You guys, eat—I'll go get that."

I head toward the door with a growing sense of dread pooling in my gut. Now and then, a fire starts, and everything just *feels* different. It's like this sense inside me, one that knows when things are about to go bad.

And I feel that now.

Dread creeps up my throat as I flick the dead bolt and pull the door open.

Then I come face-to-face with Tripp.

He's dressed to the nines, hair neatly gelled. In one hand, he's carrying a massive bouquet of red roses and, in the other, a small gift.

I should say something, but I stare at him, dumbfounded. How the hell does he keep showing up just when it feels like Gwen and I are making some progress?

Deep down, I know our situation is not sustainable. Holding out. Hiding it. Keeping everyone happy. But this is the first time I've faced that fact head-on staring at the son I barely know.

"Hey. Sorry to drop in unannounced again." His lips twitch into a sheepish smile.

I clear my throat, searching for words that aren't *what the fuck do you think you're doing here?*

"No, it's fine. You just caught me by surprise. You still got my number?"

"I know, I know. But I'm actually not here to see you."

My jaw pops as he carries on. "Remember how you told me I'd be willing to grovel when I knew it was right? Well, I've been thinking about it a bunch, and I think that it might be right with Gwen."

My stomach bottoms out. "Is that so?"

"Yeah, she…" He looks over my property with a

disbelieving laugh. "She wouldn't even give me the time of day last time. And I want to give her a chance to see how good we could be."

I try not to grimace. This fool doesn't want Gwen. He just can't handle her rejection. But I don't tell him that, and he takes my silence as an opportunity to welcome himself into my house.

"Is she awake? I wanted to make sure I spoiled her first thing."

"Yeah." If cuffing him upside the head didn't make me an asshole, I would do it.

That's my plan. Back off.

But I don't stop him. How can I?

Sorry, Tripp. I'm obsessed with your ex, and I have been since I first laid eyes on her. And now you need to leave because you're ruining my shot with her.

I can't think of a single way to phrase this that doesn't sound fucking awful. So I watch in dismay as he toes off his shoes and heads straight for the kitchen, where Gwen's and Clyde's voices drift out.

His hulking form disappears around the corner, and I inhale a few of the deep breaths Gwen taught us in yoga. I could use a quick Zen moment if I'm about to walk in there and deal with this shit.

When I finally brave the kitchen, my eyes go straight to the small gift bag and the impressive vase of roses sitting smugly on the countertop next to the lavender I chose. My flowers look scraggly in comparison, and an unwelcome pang of inadequacy twists in my chest.

I shake it off, opting to focus on Gwen.

Gwen, who looks downright uncomfortable. And Clyde, who looks one second away from beating Tripp to death with the cast-iron skillet still sitting on the stove.

"I just can't stop thinking about you," Tripp says, facing Gwen with his back to me. "I just think we could give this a go, and you'd see everything you've been missing out on."

I cringe. I want to like the kid, but goddamn, he is just so young and clueless. And so entitled. Talking to her like she's stupid for passing him up.

Gwen's gaze flashes over his shoulder to meet mine. I hold it, letting her see that even though he's here, I'm not leaving this time.

I can't. Walking away almost killed me before. Now, I feel more desperate than ever for her to see me.

It's true—I don't want to get hurt. But nothing would hurt more than missing my chance with Gwen.

"Tripp," she says, finally moving her gaze back to him. "Thank you for your honesty. But these gifts are not necessary. I'm not sure how much clearer I can be when I tell you I've moved on."

He scoffs, a bitter edge creeping into his voice. "What? You're dating someone else?"

"Not exactly." Her eyes shift to me, then back to him. "Not yet."

"But you want to?" Ire tinges his voice now, like her interest in anyone else is a personal slight to him.

"Tripp," she says, calm but firm, "we were very casual for a very short time. We haven't spoken in a year. So you have to forgive me for feeling like this newfound dedication is out of left field."

"Yeah, well, when it's right, you just know." He tips his chin and crosses his arms. "Open the present. Tell me if this other guy can top that."

She grimaces but reaches for the bag. From behind her Clyde mouths, *I hate him*.

My lips flatten to keep from mouthing *Same*. Because right now, I do too. For putting her on the spot like this and taking advantage of her kind nature, forcing her to open a gift that she's been clear about not wanting.

And for making me watch it all go down.

Her fingers tear away the paper, revealing a square, black velvet box. She hesitates, glancing at each of us in turn. There's a flicker of nerves in her eyes, and a part of me wants to swoop in and put a stop to this. The other part of me doesn't want to overstep and blow everything up on her birthday.

When she clicks it open, her eyes bug out for a minute, and then they shutter.

"I can't accept this, Tripp."

When she holds the box out, I catch sight of a diamond tennis bracelet, the light in the house making it almost blinding to look at.

"Sure you can. It's perfect for you."

She closes the box and pushes it across the island as far as her arm will stretch. "Tripp, that's not perfect for me. That right there is proof that you don't know me at all. You telling me to keep my shoes on at your party is proof that you don't know me at all. You thinking there could be anything between us at all now that I know your stories about your dad being a deadbeat are not true is proof that you don't know me at all."

Tripp freezes, all the color draining from his skin as his expression morphs before my eyes. He looks genuinely shaken, and alarm bells sound in my head. "Gwen, you don't know—"

She gives him her palm as she stands. "No, don't tell me how to think, feel, or behave. It pisses me off."

I can't see Tripp's expression, but based on his rigid shoulders, I'm going to guess it's a blend of shocked and furious.

"Nice of you to do this in front of everyone."

Gwen barks out a dry, disbelieving laugh as she steps away from him. "You're the one who keeps showing up unannounced, putting me on the spot, and forcing the issue with other people around. Please, for both our sakes, just stop."

"And you won't even give me a fucking chance to—"

"You know what?" I cut him off. "That's enough. Tripp, take a walk. Cool off. Go put your feet in the sand or something. We have somewhere to be, and the clock is ticking."

"*We?*" he asks incredulously.

I hold my shoulders tight, not backing down, not letting him make this awkward. Because I'm too pissed off to pat his back right now. "Yup. It's her birthday. Pick a different day to do this. Or better yet, don't. Want me to walk you out?"

Gwen turns to me now. Her wide eyes and slightly parted full lips suggest she can't believe I just kicked him out of my house.

Tripp snatches up the flowers and the bracelet, spins on his heel, and stalks out of the room, muttering, "Un-fucking-believable. Both of you."

His departure leaves a deafening silence in the kitchen.

CHAPTER 29

Gwen

I SIT BESIDE BASH IN THE CAB OF HIS TRUCK, STARING OUT the window, the tension between us simmering like ripples above asphalt on a hot day.

He just kicked his own son out of his house.

That's enough.

The firm way Bash's deep voice sliced through the air had startled me. And I didn't miss the way Clyde's eyebrows shot up on his forehead.

Tripp, though? Tripp's expression was pure disbelief. I get the sense he isn't accustomed to being treated like he doesn't walk on water.

I could kick myself for giving him the time of day at all. The version of himself he showed me then didn't seem so… immature.

The strife between them does nothing but cause me instant anxiety. It forces me to think back on the phone call with my mom this morning before I came downstairs. Our annual birthday call where she speaks in hushed tones like my dad might be ready to pop out of hiding and scold her for betraying his edict. We never talk about anything very profound, but I still feel a burst of excitement when I see her name pop up on my phone screen.

On the one hand, I love hearing from my mom. On the other… It always leaves me feeling empty. Wishing for more. Dreaming of approval I know I'll never get.

"I'm sorry he ruined your birthday breakfast," Bash says, pulling me from my thoughts.

I turn my head slowly, my gaze landing on the man seated beside me. Heavily corded arms outstretched, big hands wrapped tight around the steering wheel at ten and two. I can tell by his white knuckles he's squeezing the hell out of it. "He didn't. No one could ever ruin that breakfast. It was the best."

And I'm not lying. Tripp feels like a minor annoyance. One that I washed down with eggs Benedict and waffles—neither of which he would approve of.

In the close quarters of Bash's truck, it's a little too easy to forget about Tripp. I like this little bubble containing only Bash and me. So I resolve to leave this morning in the past where it belongs and let myself be present for whatever adventure we're about to embark on.

Bash's dark eyes slide my way for a beat before focusing back on the road. "You liked it?"

"No." He tenses, and I smile. He's so easy to rile up sometimes. "I *loved* it."

"What did you like the best? So I know for next time."

My heart does this girlish pitter-patter in my chest. *Next time.* God, I hope so.

"I couldn't choose. I loved all of it equally. Can't go wrong. And I'm not just saying that to flatter you."

He lets out a low grunting sound as his hands twist on the steering wheel. "Fine. I'll just make it all again."

I press my lips together, biting down on my smile. This is quintessential Bash. He sounds all surly about it, but he also doesn't bat an eye at making an absolutely ridiculous breakfast spread just because I like it. Hell, if I needed a kidney, he'd probably offer me his remaining one.

I've never known a man with a heart so big. And I think that's the thing I love about him the most.

Love.

My throat tightens, and I brush imaginary dust from the tops of my thighs before changing the subject. "Where are we going again?" We've done nothing but head straight out of town so far.

One corner of his mouth quirks up. "I didn't tell you."

"Right. But now you could."

"Sorry, no can do. It wouldn't be a surprise if I did."

I cross my arms and flop back with a dramatic pout on my lips.

He chuckles. It's deep, low, and feels like velvet sliding over my skin. It makes me want to crawl over the center console and sit in his lap.

"But the good news is…" My attention flicks to him as he brakes, arms crossing over to turn the vehicle. "We're here."

I turn away from him, eyes locking on the driveway we've just turned onto. The weathered sign to our right reads ROSE VALLEY AIRSTRIP in faded white letters. My gaze flicks back just in time to watch him press a button on one of the fobs clipped onto the sun visor.

Now the gate opens.

"You're taking me to an air show?"

He smiles. "No, Gwen. I'm taking you flying."

"What?" The word rushes out on a breath, excitement surging inside me.

"I still have a plane. I had to get my hours of practice in somehow, and now I'm kind of attached to it. Can't bring myself to sell it, even though I probably should." He shrugs shyly. "Plus, I like tinkering with it when I have the time."

All I can do is stare at him, slack-jawed, shaking my head in amazement. "You're taking my *flying*?" I sound incredulous, and it makes him chuckle.

"Okay, good. I'm glad you're not freaked out."

"Freaked out? Are you kidding me? This is amazing! And if I die?" I wink at him. "What a way to go."

He volleys back with my own words: "But what if you live?"

I just shrug, letting a suggestive smile curve my lips. "Guess I'll have to come up with a new great way to go."

He rolls his eyes but fails to bite back on a knowing smirk.

Truthfully, I couldn't be less worried. Bash might be the most capable man on the planet—flying planes, building stuff, making breakfast, kissing like it's an art form. There's no way *this* man is crashing his plane.

The truck inches to a stop beside a quiet airstrip. Sunlight glints off a massive steel hangar to my right. Just beyond it, a few smaller outbuildings huddle in its shadow.

With a firm, "Let's go," Bash jumps out of the truck and rounds the hood to my side. He opens the door before I've even finished unbuckling and reaching for my purse.

When he extends his hand, I catch myself staring at it for a moment. We've held hands before, but I've always initiated the contact.

I slide my palm into his, sighing as the heat of his touch envelops me, and hop from the truck, slamming the door shut behind me. I don't let go of his hand. And he makes no move to let mine go either.

Instead, he leads me to the small door at the corner of the hangar while I try—and fail—not to let my eyes wander down over his ass. His worn black Levi's, trending toward gray, hug him just right, all the way down to his signature black boots. The shearling-lined brown corduroy jacket he's sporting, with its creamy, plush collar folded down around his neck, is unfairly sexy.

He walks into the hangar with utter confidence, and it's hot as hell.

"Greg," he calls out to a man in the corner, raising his hand in a friendly greeting.

"Good to see ya," Greg replies with a nod.

Bash keeps walking, leading me down a row of similar planes until he stops at one in the farthest corner and faces it proudly.

It's small, painted a crisp white with two red stripes

running along the body. A shot of adrenaline hits me as I realize that I'm about to take to the skies in this glorified metal box.

A thread of unease thrums in me, but it's overwhelmed by a consuming sense of anticipation.

Like he can sense my swirling emotions, Bash gives my hand a firm squeeze, and he peeks down at me. "You ready?"

I strum my top teeth over my bottom lip and give him a firm nod. "Ready as I'll ever be. Let the adventure begin."

His eyes hold mine as he repeats the words back. "Let the adventure begin."

Then I stand there, drooling over him as he gets everything set up. I don't know what he does, only that he does it with such easy confidence that it looks like second nature. Eventually, Greg strolls over and opens the hangar's massive sliding doors, exchanging words with Bash about takeoff time and other technical things I don't understand.

Before I know it, Bash has pulled me up into the passenger's seat. "You good?" he asks, leaning in close to reach over my shoulders and strap me in. His breath fans against my damp lips as he talks, and while I should probably be paying attention to what he's saying and thinking about flying, instead I'm thinking about kissing him.

How it felt to be kissed *by* him.

He catches me staring at his mouth, his gaze dropping to mine for only a beat. "Head out of the gutter, Dawson. I'm telling you some of the emergency protocols."

My stomach flips. He scolds me with such endearment. I haven't caught a single word of his spiel.

"Sorry, concentrating is hard right now. Have you heard of competence porn? It's kind of my thing. And you, Bash, are extremely competent."

He shakes his head, amusement curving his lips as his hands work to restrain me securely. "Just trying to keep you safe."

"You will," I say simply. There isn't a single doubt in my mind that Sebastian Rousseau would do anything to keep me safe.

He leans back to assess me and gives my setup a businesslike once-over.

My quarter zip sweater is fully unzipped, showing a peek of cleavage. His eyes pause there for a moment, heat flaring in his dark irises.

"Head out of the gutter, Rousseau. I'm trying to be strapped in safely here."

I get an eye roll as he settles in front of me and lifts an oversize headset over my head. His gaze locks on mine as he grumbles, "My head's been in the gutter since the first time I laid eyes on you."

Heat curls in my gut and climbs up my spine. But he pulls away, acting all casual. Like that wasn't an incredibly bold thing to say to me.

I guess we're both being forthright with each other today. Not wanting to mess with the flirty vibes, I settle back in my seat and watch raptly as he gets settled in beside me, those big calloused hands pressing buttons and flicking levers. He pulls his own headset on, and before I know it, he's turned my way. "You ready?"

"Hell yeah," I say, not able to restrain my absolutely ridiculous grin.

His gaze lingers on my face for a few beats too long, soaking me in. It makes me squirm in my seat, but then he nods—that firm, no-bullshit nod he's always doing.

In a matter of minutes, he's started the engine and pulls out of the hangar onto the single runway. All that's ahead of us is bright-green grass, dark-green pines, and a blue sky.

The warm sun hits my face, and I let out a deep, satisfied sigh. This is fucking incredible.

"I haven't asked you if you've done this before," Bash says through the headset as the plane rolls along. I can hear him clearly over the loud engines.

"No, Bash. You're my first, so be gentle with me," I reply with a smile.

A smile that only grows bigger when I hear him grumble "For fuck's sake" in my ears.

We continue down the runway for a few more moments, and then I hear a gravelly "Cleared for takeoff."

I peer around us like I might never see solid ground again. He's chatting with who I assume is Greg on the channel. Our speed continues to increase until the earth falls away beneath us, and the small plane launches seamlessly into the air.

"We have liftoff."

Excitement fills my chest so full it might burst, and I glance out the window, watching the ground shrink. All that lies before us is wide-open sky—and what feels like endless possibilities.

"Ah!" I squeal, breathless with laughter as I clap enthusiastically. "Look at you go!"

Bash laughs now, the deep sound vibrating through my headset. "Gwen, this is my job. It would be like me clapping when you roll out a yoga mat. Even though when I see that ass in leggings, it makes me want to."

I cough out a slightly surprised laugh at the absurd comparison. "If you don't clap the next time I do, I will be deeply disappointed."

His laughter rumbles again as he continues our ascent, but he never loses focus as we climb higher. I watch him. His profile framed by the blue sky beyond him.

"This is..." My eyes trace his features, just like they did that first night we met.

Masculine. That's what I'd thought then.

Perfect, is all I can think now. The smattering of gray hair at his temple, the strong ridge of his nose.

But it's more than that. It's him knowing me. Knowing I don't want roses. Or diamonds. I want *this.*

Adventures.

With him.

"This is the best birthday gift anyone has ever given me."

His lips roll together, like he's covering an overly pleased expression. Then he presses a button, the headsets crackling to life before he speaks. "If anyone is on this channel, can you wish Gwen a happy birthday?" He sneaks a mischievous look at me before adding, "It's her first time."

I throw my head back and laugh, just as multiple

birthday wishes come through the headset. It's ridiculous, it's fun, and it's a gift I will never forget for as long as I live.

"You are…something else," I murmur, giving him a soft shake of my head before letting my gaze drift out the window.

I knew this valley was beautiful, but there's something about the bird's-eye view that hits me hard. The jagged mountains' snowcapped peaks are spectacular, and the dense forest on their lower slopes makes the sheer volume of trees seem downright impossible. With the lake sparkling at the heart of it all, like a jewel catching the sun, the entire valley is breathtaking.

Rose Hill isn't just beautiful—it's majestic.

"Wow," I sigh. Because no other word seems to do this view justice. "This is *beautiful*."

"Yeah. It is," Bash agrees.

But when I turn back to face him, he's not looking out the window.

He's looking at me.

CHAPTER 30

Bash

I SHOULD BE AWARDED AN OLYMPIC MEDAL FOR SAFELY NAVigating a plane with Gwen next to me.

She's even more distracting than usual.

With flushed cheeks and bright eyes, she fucking *glows*. And to think I had even a small part in making her look like this is the most satisfying thing in the world.

I'd fly around all day just to watch her gaze out the window in awe. That breathy little giggle she makes is music to my fucking ears. I'd sell my soul to hear that more often.

Down on the ground, all the reasons to stay away from her feel insurmountable, but up here, staring at her? They don't feel like reasons at all.

They feel like excuses.

And I can't figure out how I justify continuing to wear them like some suit of honor. The choice seems so simple.

The stakes completely acceptable. The risk of getting hurt again entirely worth it.

I get lost in my head for the rest of the flight, while Gwen gets lost in the view. I take a couple of dips and turns, eliciting gasps, laughter, and firm squeezes to my thigh that do nothing but go straight to my dick.

Eventually, the flight changes from being relaxing to an annoying inconvenience. There's a storm brewing inside me, and Gwen is oblivious to it.

"You ready to head back down?" I ask, my words coming out more abruptly than I intend.

She glances at me, lavender eyes wide and content as she gives me a relaxed shrug. "Sure."

Eager to get back onto solid ground, I loop us back around to the runway, calling our arrival in. Gwen's fingers wrap around one of the handles as we touch down smoothly, and she marvels once again.

"Damn. Should I clap now too? I've been on flights where everyone claps, and the landing was not nearly as seamless as that."

"I hate when people clap on planes," I reply, maneuvering us back toward the hangar.

Gwen laughs, brushing off my comment like it's pure entertainment. "Of course you do. Do you ever secretly judge the flight crew when you fly commercial?"

She peppers me with questions as Greg guides us in carefully, waving me back into my spot in the hangar with safety wands.

"Oh! Actually, I have an important question."

I cut the engine, and Greg salutes me and then heads back to the front office.

"Is turbulence scary for pilots? Or is that just passengers?"

I hit her with a glare, but she's unaware of my inner turmoil, the rush of desperation coursing through me. I unbuckle my harness and toss my headset as she rambles on. "Like, do you worry about that? Or is it just run-of-the-mill stuff?"

"Gwen, stop asking me questions and take your harness off."

She freezes, her brows rising on her forehead. Her expression says *I know you did not just talk to me like that.* But then she turns her eyes downward and clicks the straps loose.

"Oh-kay, buzzkill." She slips her headset over blond strands. "I was going to say thank you for the birthday present, but I guess—"

My hand gripping her thigh brings her up short.

"What?" She looks genuinely confused.

But I'm not. I've hit my limit. I fucking snap. I turn, reaching for her waist. The cockpit is small, so it's not a struggle to pull her to me.

Within seconds, I've lifted her over the small gap between our seats and she's straddling my lap. My hands wrap around her waist, and hers land against my shoulders.

My fingers pulse. I watch them press into her waist and let out a desperate groan as she tentatively lowers herself onto me. My eyes narrow at her jeans like they've done something unforgivable. Because they have. By merely existing.

I want Gwen in my lap. And I want her naked while she is.

"What are you doing?" she says in a low voice, the soft, minty puff of every word brushing against my cheek.

I turn my face up to hers while my heart clashes against the cage of my ribs. I drink her in. Pert lips. Wide eyes. Full cheeks.

Fucking perfect from head to toe.

"What I should have done months ago" is all I say. Then I grip the back of her neck, drag her mouth to mine, and kiss her.

I'm met with zero resistance—only shock. Followed by eagerness. Her fingers move up to rake through my hair as I take her mouth. My tongue tangles with hers as the kiss turns hungry. Her hips swivel, and all my blood rushes south. I grind up into her, once again irritated by the presence of her jeans. I seriously consider ripping them off with my bare hands.

She pulls away, and her heady gaze trails down to my cock, clearly straining against my jeans. Her breathing turns ragged, eyes dancing back up my body. "What about Tripp?"

I hold her gaze but reach forward and flick open the button on her jeans. "He'll have to get over it."

"Yeah?"

"Yeah. Because I'll never forgive myself if I let you get away again."

With that, I slip my hand down the front of her jeans, fingertips gliding over flimsy cotton underwear and the damp heat between her legs.

"Oh," she whimpers, head tipping back as her hips rock forward.

My knuckles bend, pressing into her. Teasing her. Easily finding her clit through the fabric.

"Is that all? Oh?" I ask, circling now, watching a flush creep up her chest and over her throat.

"Yes," she says, chin dropping back down as she presses her pussy against my hand.

I draw it away with a knowing smirk.

"Yes, what, Gwen? I'm going to need you to use your words. Because I'm about to snap and fuck you right here in this plane, but I need to know you want it first."

She eyes me intensely, then drops her mouth to my ear, nipping at the lobe.

"It's about fucking time, Rousseau," her sultry voice taunts.

And just like that, all bets are off.

I yank her panties to the side and run my fingers through her wetness before shoving two fingers in. "You gonna be a mouthy little tease about this, Gwen?"

She cries out, her pussy clenching around my digits.

"You wanna play that game?"

She bites down on her bottom lip. "Yeah, I do."

I groan. Fuck, she's hot. I pull her in for another kiss, hard and fast and demanding as I work the waist of her jeans lower. "Good. Fuck yourself on my fingers and take that sweater off. I want to watch. I'm sick of those perfect tits being covered up."

With a knowing smirk on her perfectly fuckable mouth, she gently tips her hips, easing up slightly, before dropping back down onto my fingers. Then she reaches for the hem of her sweater and yanks it off in one easy motion.

Her hips move again, and her full breasts bounce, pressed up against white lace. With one hand, she flicks the clasp, her bra falling to the side.

My head tips back as I groan, "Fuuuck." She's all soft, pale skin and full, feminine curves. I could look at her for days, spend hours getting lost in this body.

"Like that?" she asks, dropping herself onto my fingers again, a rush of wetness surging from her tight pussy.

"Yeah, baby. Just like that."

I soak her in, loving the way she eagerly bounces on my hand, just like I told her to. I could blow just from watching her like this. "Fucking hell. These tits," I groan before dropping my head and taking one pebbled nipple into my mouth.

When I suck, she whimpers. And it's fucking heaven.

Wanting to give her more, I add my thumb to her clit, spreading wetness up and over it before circling gently.

"Bash," she says on a moan, her hand propped against the headrest behind me, full lashes drawn low. "Careful."

"Careful of what?" I ask as I pull away to take a turn watching where my hand disappears between her legs.

"I'm close."

"Yeah?"

She nods, and I add a third finger, reveling in the desperate cry that spills from her lips. "Good. Come on my fingers. Then I'll make you come while you ride my cock."

Her eyes go wide now, her tongue darting out to lick her lips. "Here?"

I lean in closer, trailing kisses up the side of her neck, my tongue darting out to taste her sweet skin. When I reach her ear, I return the favor and bite down on the lobe. "Yeah. And then at home. In my bed. In my shower. Bent over the balcony with a view of the lake. God, I've dreamed of this ass."

My free hand reaches around, gripping her ass as I continue kissing her neck. My lips glide over her collarbone before I turn my attention to her other nipple.

She seems to have given up talking, lost to the moment.

Her hips swivel, her breaths come fast, and her hands tangle in the short strands of my hair.

It's not until I slide my hand around her hip, over her stomach, and up to cup her opposite breast that she finally lets out the most erotic moan. Her head falls back, blond locks spilling down over her shoulders as I twist her nipple while still working between her legs.

I let myself get lost in her, in watching her. Tasting her. Feeling her. She's soft, warm, and utterly addictive.

"Bash, Bash," she chants before dropping back down and kissing me, slow and lingering. Her hands glide over either side of my neck, her thumbs stroking over my jaw.

Then the moment turns gentle, less frantic, as we find a rhythm together. Tongues sliding, hands exploring, hips pressing.

"Oh my god, I'm going to—" She cuts off, bucking against me and dropping her head to the crook of my shoulder. I feel her come. Her pussy pulses around my fingers, her teeth digging in *hard* on the spot where my neck and shoulder meet to stifle her cries.

Soon, all I can hear is her breathing, and it makes me realize I'm not breathing at all.

After all the time I've spent dreaming of this moment, I need someone to pinch me so I know it's real.

"Okay, your turn," she breathes against my neck as her body stirs back to life. Her hands slide into my jacket and glide over my body.

I only hesitate for a moment. Then I'm all action. Coat gone. Shirt gone. Her hungry eyes devour me as the layers between us fall away.

We're a tangle of limbs. She rips at my pants with a fervor I somehow didn't expect from her. Before I know it, my jeans are pulled down, and she's working on my boxers. One flex of my hips, and they're tugged low enough that my cock springs free.

The way she looks at it and then licks her lips almost makes me finish on the spot. But she reaches forward and grips my thick length tightly. Her palm is soft and warm as she pumps me. Once. Twice.

My head falls back, and I groan. "Lose the fucking jeans, Gwen," I bite out, trying to hang on to some shred of control.

"Or what?" she taunts, twisting her grip again and giving me her best bratty look.

"Or I'm going to blow all over your hand instead of in your tight little cunt."

Her eyes widen, a shocked expression touching her features. But only for a beat because then she's all business. With an eager nod, she pushes up off my lap in the snug space and starts working at her jeans. I reach forward, helping as my patience frays.

Having to wait another single minute feels like fucking torture.

Luckily, Gwen is agile—thank god for yoga—and peels her jeans off easily. All that's left are her white lace panties.

She hooks a finger under the waist, ready to pull them off too, but I reach forward to stop her. "Leave 'em. I can't wait. I'll pull them to the side."

Then I hook two fingers into the soaked gusset of the lace scrap and yank it out of my way. Now I can see her properly.

Curved hips tapering into her waist. Full, tear-dropped breasts heaving. Pussy on display. Puffy lips glistening with her cum.

"I am really regretting this small space because I want to see you from every angle, Gwen."

"Then let's do this thing so we can try again at home." She takes my dick in her hand again, not tripping up at all over the mention of *home*.

She says it like it's ours, not just mine. Like she considers it home too.

Soon, I stop thinking about that altogether because she pushes up higher onto her knees and guides me toward her, lining us up. Bare.

"We need to be safe."

"Yeah, safe. We're safe," she breathes, eyes fastened on my cock. In seconds, she's rubbing my head through her slick core, and my brain short-circuits. I'm too fucking far gone. So I give up on safe. Deep down, I know Gwen wouldn't be anything but.

When she guides me inside her heat, I groan. "Fuck, Gwen. Fuck."

I'm only in an inch, and it's already too much. I don't know how I'm going to hold it together through this.

Every time she eases down a bit farther, it's the most delicious torture.

I watch her pussy spreading and stretching to take me, my heart thundering in my chest.

She cries out when she sinks all the way down, and my fingers dig into her waist—holding on for dear life as my head falls back against the leather seat with a heavy thud.

I can feel her all around me. Warm, pulsing, and so fucking tight. I drag my eyes open to see her, one hand propped on my shoulder and head tipped down, lust-hazed eyes watching us where we're finally joined together.

I drive up into her, eliciting a sharp gasp. My cock comes out wet as I draw back. We both watch raptly, bodies merging and pulling away. Her legs are shaky from her last orgasm, but soon she's riding me eagerly, squeezing my dick.

"Tight as fuck," I grit out, moving my hips in tandem with hers. "I love you like this."

"Like what?" she murmurs, entranced.

"All mine."

Our eyes meet in the dim cockpit. "I am."

And fuck, it's music to my ears.

"Mine," I repeat, increasing the speed of my shallow thrusts.

"All yours," she whispers, pulling me in for another kiss, clenching and releasing my girth as she does.

We kiss. We move. I let my hands roam her body, tracing every curve.

And the friction between us builds. Tension coils in my back, heat radiates in every limb from the strain of holding myself back.

I can feel it in her too. A string pulled too tight, ready to snap at any moment.

"Bash, Bash. Don't stop," she murmurs against my lips. "I'm so close."

My hand curves over her ass, playing with her from behind. "You gonna come for me, baby?"

She just moans into my mouth, arching her back into every bit of pressure.

I press in, feeling her body go taut. I can feel it coming. She rides me harder, skin damp, movements rough.

I bite at her ear again, getting the sense that she likes that.

"Atta girl," I whisper as I press my fingers to her clit. I feel her shiver and smile against her neck. Then my opposite hand grips her shoulder and takes control of the motion. I grit out, "Take. It. All," as I shove her down in one rough motion. Impaling her as she shatters. Pushing her over the edge on a loud cry.

"Oh fuck! Bash!"

The sound of her coming with my name on her lips sends me barreling right off the same cliff. I spill into her tight heat with a deep groan.

We fall into each other, and I give myself over to the instant feeling of everything being right in the world.

CHAPTER 31

Gwen

WE DRESS IN A GIDDY SILENCE. OUR EYES CATCH NOW AND then, and each time, we share a small smile or a disbelieving headshake.

There's no awkwardness, but there is a manic sort of excitement. It's hard to explain.

All I know is that I've never felt like this before.

We leave his airplane hand in hand. And I don't know who reaches first, me or him, or if we both reach for each other at the same time.

I glow, feeling like the cat who caught the canary as I strut through the airplane hangar. That is, until we have to pass Greg in his office, near the exit.

"You two have fun out there?" he calls from his desk.

"I can't imagine a more perfect flight," Bash deadpans, giving nothing away.

The man turns his attention to me. "And you, Gwen? I heard on the radio that it was your first time. How'd it go?"

My mouth pops open, and my cheeks go hot. I know he doesn't know what we just did, but I'm reading it as innuendo anyway.

I let out a nervous giggle, tucking a strand of hair behind my ear. "Unforgettable."

He gives me a wide, clueless grin. "That's what we love to hear."

With that, Bash tugs me forward. "Catch you next time, Greg," he calls, like he can't wait to get away from this interaction.

I tuck my chin as I let him lead me out of the hangar. And it's only when we get outside and close the door behind us that we turn to face each other and burst out laughing.

Nothing about the moment is even *that* funny, but there's something about it that clearly overwhelms us both.

Bash bends over slightly, pressing a hand to his abdomen. It reminds me of that night on the moving walkway in the airport, when he propped his hands on his knees, bent over, and laughed so hard that he could barely breathe.

I hadn't realized then what a special moment that was. I hadn't realized that he didn't create a lot of room in his life for laughter.

I do now, though. So I watch him. I admire him. I laugh along with him.

My chest swells until it feels so full that it could burst. Every limb is deliciously soft. Every lump of anxiety inside me somehow smoothed over. And the knowledge that this is only the beginning of whatever this thing is between us does nothing but feed my excitement.

At the truck, he opens the door for me, and before I can even try to get myself into it, his hands are back on my waist. A flash of what we just did plays in my mind, and a shiver races down my spine as he lifts me into the passenger seat.

"You know I can get into the truck myself," I say, curving a brow in his direction.

He shrugs. "Yeah, I know. But I think I've spent enough time not touching you."

He shoots me a wink and slams the door before rounding the vehicle to his side.

As we pull out of the hangar's winding driveway, he opens the sunroof and warm rays float in, kissing the top of my head. They match the warmth coursing through my limbs.

I close my eyes and settle back into the comfortable leather seat, relaxing into the blissful sensation.

It's one of those days—not quite summer, but so close that you can taste it. Still a light nip in the air, but in the sun, if you close your eyes, it's like you can imagine being somewhere tropical. And after a long, cold winter, there's nothing better.

Well, except sex in an airplane with Bash.

"Does that count as our first date?" he asks, making me smile into the warm light.

"I'd say so."

"Thank fuck."

I glance his way, curious about his response. "Why?"

He shoots me a borderline playful glance from the driver's seat. "Now you have to tell me your full name."

My responding chuckle is raspy. His reasoning transports

me back to that night in the airport. I told him then that my full name was first-date material…and he remembered.

"Guinevere."

I chance a look at him, expecting a joke or offhanded comment. I've always disliked my full name. It seems frilly and impractical, and I've never felt as though it really *fit* me.

But Bash doesn't say any of those things. Instead, he murmurs, "Guinevere," like he's trying it on for size. Then he smiles, reaches for my hand, and adds, "I love that."

The warmth on my face surges through my entire body. I don't think he realizes how good he makes me feel in all the most simple ways. The way he mends my wounds without even trying. No, all he does now is turn up the music and take me for a cruise along the rural road while holding hands over the center console.

He cranks the volume when "She Drives Me Crazy" by Fine Young Cannibals plays. I think I even catch him mumbling along with the words.

We don't talk, but we don't need to. Part of me doesn't know what there is to say. The other part of me is avoiding thinking about the fact that we're heading back to his house, where we're going to have to address how to handle Tripp. Because Bash is an honest man, a loyal man, and if he's going to have me as a mainstay in his life—which I hope he will—we're going to have to tell Tripp at some point.

And I have a sinking suspicion that it will not go over well.

Like I willed the problem into existence, Tripp's rental car is back in the driveway when we pull up. However, in addition to his car, there are also a few more.

The truck rocks as we make our way down the gravel driveway, and I slowly turn my head toward Bash, brows pulled up in question.

"So, about all the things I promised we were going to do when we got home…" He trails off, lifting one hand and scrubbing it across the back of his neck. "We might have to wait until a little bit later."

I cross my arms. "Oh, and why is that?"

I know why. He can see Tripp's vehicle just as clearly as I can. I just desperately want to will it away, pull out an eraser, and remove it from our afternoon entirely.

"It would also appear that Tripp is back."

I sigh and glare at the car and make a wish for it to disappear. He's the last person I want to see right now.

My wishes are not answered. The car is still there, mocking me.

Bash continues talking. "Don't worry. I'll manage Tripp, I know he won't make a scene because the real issue is that I invited our friends over for a surprise birthday party."

I freeze and then bite down on a smile, not wanting to react too obviously. No one has ever planned a party for me. "I don't think you're supposed to tell people that they're about to attend their own surprise party."

Bash scoffs. "Well, these goofs didn't do a very good job of covering their tracks, now, did they?" He tips his head toward where the cars are lined up in the driveway.

"You could have come up with some other excuse. Like… Clyde invited everyone over for a group taint-tanning session?"

Bash looks disgusted. "That's a horrifying visual. But yes, I could have made something up. But you broke my brain. I'm not firing on all cylinders."

I smile. "Bash, this is actually so romantic," I tease. "You planned me a big birthday party? The perpetual bachelor and town loner invited other people to his trash can just for me?"

I get an eye roll now. "Good god, you and Clyde with that Oscar the Grouch metaphor. That really needs to die."

"Why? It's so cute. Everybody secretly loves Oscar. Yeah, he's grouchy, but it's part of his charm. Just like you. If you were too happy, it would just be weird. I would wonder if you were sick or dying or something."

He rumbles a laugh now, shaking his head as he cuts the engine. "What a way to be known: the guy who, if he was too happy, would probably be dying."

He's about to hop out of the car when I reach across the center console, grip the lapels of his jacket, and pull him to me. I kiss him quickly, needing one more before we walk into the house.

He freezes at first but only for a beat, then he softens. Those rough fingers trace the edge of my jaw, fluttering over it like I'm porcelain and he wants to be careful with me.

Less than thirty minutes ago though, he certainly was not concerned about being delicate with me.

And I am captivated by both sides of him.

He kisses me back, so full of longing that it makes my chest ache.

"Thank you," I whisper, pulling away slightly. "I needed that."

He plants one more quick, firm kiss against my lips, and then another, like he just can't help himself. Like he just can't get enough. His eyes trace mine, dropping to my mouth, and then back up.

When he looks at me like this, I feel like I might be the most beautiful thing he's ever seen. I feel like I'm his.

"Always," he murmurs, just before a low grumbling sound rumbles in his throat. Then, "But goddamn it, right now I'm really regretting the surprise party. I should walk in there and cancel it. Tell them all to get the fuck out."

I burst out laughing at that. "Yeah, the best of intentions and all that." I chuckle, planting a kiss against his stubbled chin. "This will just make what's coming later that much better. So let's go get this over with. Start early and end early. Then you can follow through on all the things you said because it would be plain rude to break those promises on my birthday."

His lips curl into the most subtle of smiles. "Yeah, that's probably true. Can't be lying to my girl on her birthday."

I sigh wistfully, pulling myself away from him. Knowing that if I don't create some space, I'll be crawling across the center console for a repeat performance.

He unbuckles himself and points at me before getting out of his truck. "Stay there. Don't spoil my last chance to touch you before we go in there."

Then he slams the door, and I wait because I'd never want to spoil that for him.

We walk in to an eerily quiet house, kick our shoes off, and suddenly I'm glad that Bash did tell me because now I can do my best to control my facial expression.

I pad into the kitchen, the warm heat of him following closely at my back, urging me forward. When I round the corner, a chorus of shouts ring out.

"Surprise!" everyone yells, popping up from beyond the island—except for Clyde, who's seated on his usual stool at the countertop, rolling his eyes.

"You fools all parked in the driveway. She knew you were here."

West clocks him playfully on the shoulder. "Don't be such a buzzkill." Then, "Happy birthday, Gwen!" as he ambles forward to give me a friendly hug.

Beyond him are Skylar, Ford and Rosie, as well as Rhys and Tabitha. Just off to the side of them is a sullen-looking Tripp. On the kitchen table is the discarded bouquet of roses and the box that contains a bracelet that I'd rather not know the value of.

He's smiling, but it's his fake smile. I don't know what antics he's been exposed to in the time he's spent waiting, but something tells me it might have been awkward—not because anyone knows the most recent developments between Bash and me but because they know our origin story.

Tension hits me in my chest as I wonder if how we met ever came up. Tripp doesn't know. Not that he's asked. It's not as though we've kept in touch since I found out that Bash was his father. But I'm desperately hoping that this subject doesn't become a topic of conversation during this party.

That would make things a hell of a lot more awkward than they already are.

My worries are swept away as the rest of my friends rush forward, wrapping me in hugs, dropping the odd kiss on my cheek, patting my back, and wishing me a happy birthday. It's hard not to glow under their attention. Most of my birthdays have been spent alone or traveling or doing something that fills my cup, but not generally being celebrated.

Today, however, feels different, and I kind of like it. I don't bother heading over to Tripp. Not after the way he treated me this morning.

Truth be told, I don't know why he's still hanging around here. I thought he'd have left, and based on the tight set to Bash's shoulders and the way his jaw pulses as his teeth grind, he didn't expect him to come back either.

I wonder if he's figured out all the ways this could go wrong while standing and watching everyone make their greetings.

Seeming to pick up on the tension, Tabitha claps her hands loudly, gathering everyone's attention and really leaning into that executive-chef vibe. "All right, kids, enough milling about. Let's get this party started."

I smile at her gratefully, appreciating how intuitive she is.

With that, she whips everybody into shape. Ford takes over curating the music for the get-together. West opens the front patio doors, letting the warm air blend the indoor and outdoor spaces, then heads off to make drinks for everyone. Rosie and Skylar retreat into the kitchen to keep Tabitha company.

Bash pulls Tripp out toward the front landing, and I watch them go while resisting the urge to follow and eavesdrop. I'm so desperate to know what's being said that I nearly jump out of my skin when Clyde ambles up and bumps his bony shoulder against mine, startling me out of my snooping.

"He came back about an hour after you left. Said he wanted to talk to his dad. Told that little fucker to leave, but he wouldn't."

Anxiety courses through me as I bite down on my lip and nod, my mind replaying what Bash and I were up to while he waited here.

I don't know what to expect when they walk back into the kitchen, but Tripp looking properly chastised wasn't at the top of my list.

He heads straight for me, eyes lifting almost timidly from beneath his lashes. And then, right there in a room full of people, he says, "Gwen, I want to apologize for how I spoke to you this morning. I was out of line and I'm sorry. It won't happen again. I'm going to back off."

There's an edge to his delivery and a level of agitation in his stance that makes me wonder just what Bash said to him. I force myself not to peek over at his dad for any sort of reassurance. It would be too obvious.

And this is all too damn fragile to be taking risks like that.

Instead, I dip my chin and reply softly, "It's water under the bridge." Because the truth is that it has to be.

If Bash and I have any hope of making a future, it has to be.

Tripp offers me a tight smile. "Good. I told Bash I wanted to stay and hang out, get to know his friends a bit. But he said I'd have to take that up with you."

I almost wince. *Awkward*. What am I going to say—*no*? When the man I'm falling for wants a relationship with his son so badly? What kind of woman would that make me?

So I channel every ounce of my inner maturity and give him a casual shrug. "Of course."

Strangely, Tripp looks almost grateful. "Thanks," he says quietly before turning away to join his dad and the other guys on the patio.

His reaction only adds to my confusion, but I brush it off and join my friends.

The afternoon flows from there. Clyde maintains his spot, everyone taking turns coming up to chat with him. They give him an affectionate pat on the head or a side hug, bringing him drinks or snacks, doting on him like he's royalty. What started out as a look of annoyance on his face morphs into one of contentment as the party wears on.

Tabitha cracks open a bottle of wine, and of course, I'm not one to say no. On a hot, sunny day, there's nothing better than a crisp glass of pinot grigio. The four of us—Tabitha, Skylar, Rosie, and me—all get into it, laughing and chatting.

Tripp sticks around. If he weren't so well trained for these types of gatherings, he would be completely out of the loop. Instead, he somewhat gracefully inserts himself into conversations, makes polite small talk, and asks engaging questions.

Still, I catch him eyeing both Bash and me now and then, and I wonder if he can tell *something*.

As I'm sidling up to Clyde, making sure he has everything he needs, Tripp pops into the kitchen in search of another drink.

"And how was your flight?" he asks, affably holding his bottle of beer up in a toast.

Clyde scowls at him, and Tripp just smiles back. I can't tell if he's oblivious or being an asshole by continuing to needle Clyde with his presence. Either way, the strangest thing about the interaction is that he's behaving as though we had no confrontation at all this morning.

I'm inebriated enough to play along. "It was great." I shrug. "I've never done that before. Definitely one for the record books."

"You liked it?" Clyde asks, turning to me with a look of satisfaction on his face.

I grin back at him. "I loved it."

"Ah, well, good. Maybe Bash can take you up there more often."

I take a sip of my wine, humming my assent, because yeah, I'd love to fly with Bash more often. But I can feel Tripp's gaze burning into the side of my face.

He scoffs. "I mean, she's here working with you. Why would my dad take her up in his airplane just for fun?"

I freeze with my glass lifted, my eyes sliding toward Tripp. *Dad?* He never calls Bash his dad. I don't know what he's up to, but I play it off casually. "I'm too busy for that anyway. Between Clyde and the yoga studio, my days are pretty packed."

"Ah, yeah, but the two of you have forged a nice little friendship," Clyde says. "It's good for you to get out a bit."

Fucking Clyde is like a dog with a bone right now. I shoot him a grim smile, inclining my head in his direction as though to say, *Yep, now drop it.*

But Clyde, being Clyde, does not in fact drop it.

Instead, he tips his chin toward the open sliding doors of the balcony. West and Bash both have a hip propped against the railing—the same railing where Bash kissed me for the first time. Beers in hand, they chat away without a care in the world.

I try not to let my eyes linger for too long, but there's something so easy about the way Bash is standing out there. His usually furrowed brow is relaxed, and his typically down-turned lips have taken on more of a natural resting position. Now and then, West says something, and I watch Bash *chuckle*.

I catch myself shaking my head at him, like I can't quite believe the change in him. Then I snap my eyes away, realizing I've been staring too long. I reach across the kitchen counter for a tortilla chip and scoop up a healthy dose of guacamole. Maybe if my mouth is full, I won't have to contribute to this conversation.

"Bash needs a little fun too, you know," Clyde says, looking out toward him and drawing Tripp's gaze in the same direction. "It's nice to see him like this. He works so hard. He's so tightly wound sometimes. Now he's out there getting all wild. Bare feet, shirt buttons undone one too far…"

I smile and nod along with Clyde's assessment until I realize that, without his corduroy jacket, the skin on Bash's chest and neck is far more visible than I realized.

Clyde continues like a steam engine down the tracks. "A

beer in his hand, big old hickey on his neck."

I freeze, but only for a beat, willing myself to act as naturally as possible. Because yes, there is a big hickey on Bash's neck, and yes, I'm the one who left it there.

I came so hard the first time that I thought I was going to scream. So in an attempt to keep my voice from echoing through the airplane hangar I bit down on his neck. I thought it was more toward his shoulder, but in the heat of the moment, I must've shifted up higher. And now he's standing there, talking to his friends with a teenager-style hickey on his neck.

Tripp's brows drop low, eyes squinting as he focuses on the exact spot.

"Huh," Clyde says. "I wonder where he could have gotten that from."

CHAPTER 32

Gwen

THE NIGHT CARRIES ON THROUGH MULTIPLE ROUNDS OF APPE-
tizers, followed by Tabitha's barbecue feast. Conversation flows
and so does friendly teasing, as is to be expected with this group.

But I can't seem to stop checking on what Tripp is up
to. After what went down this morning, his presence has me
feeling more off-kilter than it should. Sure, he apologized
for his fit, but watching him insert himself into this day has
me feeling uneasy, especially since I often catch him staring
at Bash with a slight furrow between his brows.

The expression is all his dad's, which is why I grow worried about what's going on in his head. I wish I could say that
constantly monitoring him isn't affecting my enjoyment of
the evening, but it is.

That nagging feeling that the other shoe is about to drop
won't leave me alone. I slow down on my wine consumption,
not wanting to overindulge and let something slip.

Bash steers clear of me for the most part, which is torture. The occasional friendly smile or holding his beer up in my direction seems to assure everyone that we're on good terms.

Except for Clyde. He looks downright suspicious.

From outside, laughter roars. "Oh shit, sorry," West exclaims between hearty guffaws.

I turn toward the commotion to see Bash standing out on the deck with his arms spread wide, beer dripping from his flannel shirt, a look of shock on his face.

The girls and I watch the spectacle, giggling among ourselves as Ford wipes at Bash's shirt with his bare hands, while Rhys stands nearby shaking his head.

"Please don't kill me," West says. "I really had no idea that one was going to explode."

Rhys scoffs, crossing his arms. "West, you told me earlier that you shook one and put it back in the cooler just to see who would be the one to open it."

West grins, looking exactly like the troublemaker that he is. "Okay, fine, I did do that. That's also why I opened it away from myself." He tips his head toward Bash in apology. "Sorry, Bash."

"You're a big fucking kid, you know that, Belmont?" Bash says, cuffing him lovingly upside the head. "I'm going to get cleaned up."

Tripp observes them with a good-humored expression on his face. He watches Bash head into the house and so do I. But when I look back, Tripp's eyes are on me. Piercing and borderline accusing.

I shake it off and go back to talking with Rosie, Tabitha, and Skylar, determined not to feed into his nonsense. They're deep into discussing wedding plans for Rosie and Ford's upcoming nuptials, and it's a fun conversation to be included in. I never really thought marriage was for me, but seeing these couples, the way they can lean on each other without losing themselves has me rethinking my stance.

Being with Bash has me rethinking too.

It has me realizing that just because the marriage I grew up around wasn't healthy doesn't mean that healthy marriages don't exist.

The conversation shifts to cake flavors, and I seize my chance to follow Bash, making up what is the weakest excuse of all time. "I have something stuck in my teeth that I just can't get. I'm going to go floss quickly. I'll be right back."

Rosie's head flops back. "Ugh, I hate it when that happens."

No one else even blinks at my abrupt departure, and their conversation turns to live music options for the reception. The girls don't think twice about my leaving, and yet the crawling sensation of someone watching me prickles at my back as I head toward the front staircase.

When I get upstairs, I head straight to Bash's bedroom, where I find the door ajar. I don't bother knocking and slip inside with a brisk check over my shoulder to make sure no one followed me.

My heart pounds as I click the door shut. I feel like a kid sneaking into forbidden territory. The risk of being caught is far too real, but here I am, sneaking around anyway.

Light from Bash's massive walk-in closet spills out across the darkened room, and I see his shadow take a couple of steps out toward the main part of the bedroom.

"Hey, listen. I had to follow you up here because…" My words die as Bash steps out of the closet, shirtless and utterly distracting. I lick my lips, scanning the hard lines of his chest, and finish in a breathy voice. "Because I needed to get you alone."

His head tilts, then he trails a finger from his torso up to his face. "Gwen, my eyes are up here."

"Ha!" I bark out a nervous laugh. "Funny. Really funny. Especially funny because I'm pretty sure that Tripp knows something is up."

Bash's head jerks back a bit as his eyes narrow. "Nah. No way. Why would he think anything was going on between us?"

My gaze travels to the purplish tinge I left on his skin. "Well, there's a massive hickey on your neck, for starters."

His eyes bulge, and he turns, striding back into his closet where a full-length mirror adorns one of the cabinet doors.

I step in behind him and watch him stretch his neck, running his fingers over the mark. First, he looks disbelieving, then his eyes heat, and he smirks at my reflection in the mirror behind him. "Have I been standing out there wearing this all night, Gwen?"

I offer a demure shrug, feeling guilty that I left such an obvious mark on him. "I mean, it depended on the angle."

He gives me a disbelieving look, and I go on the defensive. "Listen, as far as I'm concerned, nobody else should be looking at you this closely. That's *my* job."

He scoffs, turning to face me. "Are you feeling possessive after one time, Gwen? That's adorable." His gaze turns hungry, and the way he prowls toward me borders on predatory. "You know what's got me feeling possessive?" he asks with a slight incline of his head, drawing nearer with each measured step.

"What's that?" I whisper.

"Having to stand around all night with all these people here, pretending that you and I are nothing more than friendly acquaintances. You think Tripp's been watching me? Not half as much as he's been gawking at you. I'm supposed to prioritize that kid. I'm supposed to be building a relationship with him."

His fingers slide under my jaw, tilting my face up to his. "But do you know the only thing I've been able to think about all fucking night, Gwen?"

"What?" The fire blazing in his eyes entrances me. He looks vicious, rugged, and downright feral.

"The only thing I've been able to think about is that I don't want him so much as looking at what's mine." His voice drops to a growl. "It's driving me fucking crazy, knowing he's had you."

"He never really had me," I whisper, my voice cracking as I do. "Not the way you do. And I'm s—"

His finger moves up, pressing against my lips, silencing me. "Don't you dare apologize to me for that. We didn't know. How could we know? The only thing that matters is that you're here with me now. We made it back to each other. And as hard as it's going to be, we're going to make this thing work. We're going to give this thing a go. I'm going to tell him. I just—not yet. Not tonight." I nod. Tonight definitely does not seem like the moment to break that news to him.

"But I really don't think I can stand the thought of heading back down to that party without knowing how you taste."

Suddenly, he pushes me back against the door to his closet, and it slams shut. He drops to his knees before me, sure hands tugging at the long, flowy skirt I changed into when we got back.

"I love this skirt," he murmurs. "Such easy access." He hikes it up around my waist, bunching it up in his hand. "Hold this, Guinevere. Keep it out of my way."

I decide my full name doesn't sound so bad when he's the one saying it. My fingers grip the fabric while he tears at my underwear. He's not gentle. He doesn't unwrap me like a gift. He presses me against the door and rips them off, like he's offended by their mere existence.

With a house full of friends just below us, I vaguely recognize that this timing might not be ideal.

But I press my back against the cupboards and lift my skirt higher anyway.

CHAPTER 33

Bash

"Spread your legs, Gwen," I order.

A husky chuckle spills from her lips as she slowly lifts her foot, dragging it along the side of her calf, taking her sweet fucking time like the tease that she is.

"Think that's funny, do you? What about this hickey?" I glance up at her. "Think that's funny too?"

A sly smile curves her lips as she lifts one shoulder in a nonchalant shrug. "Maybe a little bit."

"Then you won't mind if I just…" I drop my head and bite her inner thigh. Hard enough that she gasps. Her fingers flex where they curl into the bunched fabric, her hips thrusting toward me.

"Have a taste?" I finish before kissing the red mark my teeth have left behind.

"N-no." Her response comes out breathy and her teeth graze over her damp bottom lip as she stares down at me with glassy eyes.

"Good," I mutter, unable to look away from the apex of her thighs. The red mark—proving that she's mine.

With a rush of territorialism, I decide matching marks would look damn good on her.

I bite her opposite thigh, sucking on her skin, dick hardening as the closet fills with her desperate little mewling sounds. Her pelvis bucks again, and I watch as another mark blooms on her milky skin.

"Bash," she murmurs, one hand reaching forward so her fingers can rake through my hair. They close and she tugs. "Hurry up. I can't—"

I slip one finger into her, cutting off whatever she was about to say and watching the way she takes me. My cock throbs uncomfortably in my jeans.

When I add a second finger, she tugs my hair again, hissing out a breath as she drags my head closer.

I chuckle, mere inches from her pussy as she physically begs me for it.

"Bash, I am going to lose my fucking mind if you don't put your mouth on me."

This time, when I push my fingers in, I twist. A shiver racks her body. I know I'm driving her wild and I could not care less. Just watching the way she reacts gets me off.

"Frustrating, isn't it? Try being me, having to live in the same house as you while you traipse around in those flimsy fucking leggings, Gwen. Been dreaming of this pretty little cunt for months, so you're just going to have to suffer while I take my time enjoying it."

My words elicit a frustrated growl from her, and I chuckle

in response. I add a third finger, and she pants while I enjoy her pussy stretching to accommodate my touch.

Pulling out, I spread her and rub the slick wetness over her lips. I suck in a breath as her sex glistens before me, making me lick my lips.

"Look at you. Delicious. So fucking tight," I growl as I reach down with my opposite hand to adjust myself in my pants. "So fucking wet." I shake my head in disbelief. As though I can't quite believe I'm here. With her. "You have no idea what you do to me."

I push my fingers back in and almost blow my load as I watch her take me. "Fucking made for me, baby."

"Bash, Bash…" she chants, and it's music to my ears. My name on her lips, my fingers inside her, that raspy fucking voice.

I cave. For her, I fold. Unable to hold back any longer, I drop my mouth to her pussy and take my first taste, the point of my tongue trailing through her seam lightly.

"Oh god," she moans, and I flick my tongue against her clit.

I don't devour her. I savor her and this moment. Much like earlier, we're locked away in a private bubble. The beat of the music pumps from below us and sets a languid pace. My fingers and mouth working in tandem. Her choppy breaths. My heartbeat in my ears. The sweet taste of her on my tongue as I press closer, hiking her leg over my shoulder so I can squeeze that delectable ass.

She grinds against me, and I pull her closer, the fervor between us hitting a fever pitch with every stroke of my tongue. I push into her. I nip at her. I look up and see her chest heaving. I look to the side and see my mark left on her leg.

My cock twitches and I double my efforts.

I turn from patient to demanding. Finger-fucking her harder as my threads of control fray. My free hand explores every curve. Her nails scratch at my scalp. The world around me zeroes in.

All I can see is her. All I can feel is her. All I can taste is her. I'm fucking drowning in *her* and I wouldn't have it any other way.

"Bash," she whispers. "I'm so close. I'm—"

I rear back and take my hands off. "Not yet. If you come, I'm going to blow in my pants."

She nods briskly, gulping for air. Her gaze is unfocused. She looks entirely lust addled. And quite frankly, I feel the same.

Which is the only explanation for what I do next.

I take her hand and lead her out of the closet, looking both ways to make sure the bedroom door is closed before I drag her to the balcony. My fingers flick the dead bolt open and my heart thunders while my dick aches painfully.

"What are we doing?" she asks, voice thick and eager.

I look back over my shoulder at her flushed cheeks and sparkling lilac eyes. "What I told you earlier today I've dreamed of. I have a laundry list of ways I plan to fuck you. And overlooking the lake is at the very top."

"Now?"

I step out onto the balcony, tilting my head to listen. All sounds of outdoor conversation are gone. The low mumble of voices comes only from inside the house.

"Yes. Now. I can't wait any longer. I've waited long enough. And no one can see up here anyway," I say, tugging her out with me.

Her responding giggle is light and airy. Playful and downright alluring. As she passes me, I trail a hand over her hip, placing her directly in front of me as I walk us toward the railing. Her hands wrap around the metal bar, and she folds herself at the hips, hiking her skirt up with a knowing smirk on her lips.

I don't even know where to look first. That face. That mouth. That ass. Do I take a step back and enjoy a pan-oramic view of her bent over for me while the sun sets beyond her?

I feel like a goddamn kid at a fair. Overstimulated. Not sure which ride to take first.

The fabric trails up over the back of her thick thighs, slowly revealing the curve of her ass. "What are you waiting for, Rousseau? You gonna fuck me or just stand there and stare?"

I hold a finger up to my mouth, reminding her to be quiet. "Shh, baby. We're sneaking around here, remember?"

She presses her lips together, understanding dawning in her eyes. But then she widens her stance, pushes up onto her tiptoes, and arches her back in offering.

"Then hurry, I'm so close," she murmurs, reaching one hand down between her legs and making a show of playing with herself.

My lungs seize and my head tips back as I let out a rough, "Fuuuuccckkk." Because this is not making me want to hurry.

It's making want to take a seat and watch.

So I do.

I retreat a few steps, plunk down in my favorite chair. Gripping the armrests, I take in the view. Her pale skin seems to catch the fiery pink and orange hues slashing across the sky.

"Come for me, Gwen," I murmur, keeping my voice low. "Let me watch."

Her fingers still, and her head snaps over her shoulder, eyes skating over my face as though she's checking to see if I'm joking. My expression stays impassive as I undo my pants, tug them lower, and pull my painfully hard cock out. Stroking it while holding her gaze.

Her lips part on a needy sigh and her fingers move again. She swaps between fucking herself and rubbing firm circles on her clit. I stroke myself, marveling at her beauty. Her body. Her confidence. Her willingness. Fuck, she's just so…*fun*.

She's so good for me.

We move in time, and I can see her orgasm build. Her muscles tense, her legs shake. Part of me wants to rush over and help her, the other part is getting off on watching her try so damn hard.

Her panting grows heavier, and so does mine. Precum beads at the head of my cock, and I rotate my fist, spreading it. My gaze fixates on where she rubs back and forth on her clit with increasing intensity.

"Oh fuck, Bash!" she calls out as her flexible body folds forward with the weight of her orgasm. Her puffy pink cunt pulses, and I can't hold back.

Three strides and I'm behind her. With one hand gripping her hip, we're lined up, and before she can even finish coming, she's impaled on my cock.

Her pussy is snug and hot and my brain short-circuits as I take a moment to get my bearings.

"Fuck, fuck!" she cries out again, and it's too loud.

I reach forward, cupping a hand over her mouth. "Gwen, baby, I need you to be quiet. You can scream for me later. But right now, I need you to shut your mouth and take this cock like the good girl I know you can be."

She nods eagerly and her breath fans against my palm as I pull out and push back in. Heat dances down my spine and tension curls in my hips.

"I'm not going to last long after that little show."

She nods again. I thrust again. We both groan.

I move, finding an easy rhythm. Her supple body takes me so damn well. Hot, tight, and made for me. The knowledge that her party is still going on just one floor below does nothing but excite me.

Gwen does nothing but excite me.

My hands grip her full, glorious ass as I lean back to watch where we're joined. The sight of my cock buried inside her almost takes me out. I feel the rush that comes when I'm close to finishing. The desperation. The single-minded focus.

"I'm fucking obsessed with you. Do you know that?"

She mumbles something against my palm, head nodding, as she pushes back into my length. Perspiration prickles at the back of my neck, and my hand grips the globe of her ass.

"I'm going to fill you up so full, Gwen." My words come harsh and fast as I fuck her.

And it's the muffled "yes, please" from behind my palm that sets me off. I unleash, fucking her hard and relentless. She meets my every stroke. Her head bobbles and her body trembles.

She's going to come again. I can just feel it. So I keep my pace, clenching my teeth to last as long as I can. Wanting her to get there again. This time stuffed full of me while she orgasms.

"Yeah, baby. Just. Like. That," I grit out as I drive home, feeling her contract around my cock. And then I explode.

Everything goes tight. My vision blurs. My body pulses. I come so hard, it feels like the world tilts on its axis.

I fall forward onto her back, breathing her in while my body rides the wave. My hand falls away from her mouth and we both suck in harsh breaths as we try to come back down to earth.

"Fuck me...that was—"

"Just the beginning," I finish for her before dropping a kiss to her back.

"Dear universe, I forgive you," she murmurs with a delirious giggle, and I can't help but shake my head.

Yeah, the universe messed with us. But it also gave us *this*.

And we're only getting started.

"We should get back down there," I say, pulling myself back upright and taking her with me.

"Yeah, we really should. I'm missing my own party."

I grunt at that, dropping a kiss beside her ear. "Strikes me that the party just moved up here and no one else was invited."

She shimmies slightly and I pull out of her, biting down on my lip when my cum trails down her inner thigh. I could watch that all day.

Gwen peeks back at me now. "Grab me a towel? Or just stand there and stare again?"

I tuck myself back into my underwear, tugging up my pants as I gawk. "Honestly, I might just..." I step back, motioning like I'm going to take a seat again. Then I shoot her my best mischievous grin.

Her lips pop open, and her eyes flare with faux anger as she tugs her skirt back down. "Sebastian Rousseau!"

"Shame. You're obstructing my view," I quip, taking one last long look over her before I turn and dart inside to get a warm washcloth. The sound of her laughter trails behind me and I find myself smiling at absolutely nothing.

In the en suite, I run the cloth under warm water and catch sight of myself in the mirror. Mussed hair, flushed cheeks. But something else about me looks different. Something less tangible.

Happy.

I squint like that couldn't be right. But it's written all over me, plain as day.

For the first time in a long time, I'm happy.

I blink and shake my head at myself before striding back out to the balcony where I crouch to clean Gwen. She fusses with my hair as I do, putting it back to rights.

"There," I announce quietly before coming back to stand. "She's ready for round three."

Gwen slaps my shoulder playfully before pushing past me. I follow her back into my room and she spins on me. "You go first."

"What?"

"You go back down first. In case there's someone in the hallway. It's not weird for you to be leaving your own room."

I sober at the thought of running into someone and having to explain myself. "I can't imagine anyone would come up here," I reply, buttoning my fresh denim shirt.

She shrugs and pulls me close for a breathless kiss. "Then there's no problem. I just need a minute to get cleaned up."

I give her a sure nod and a quick squeeze on her hip as I lean in for one parting kiss. Her lips are soft, and she smells like lavender. I love just being close to her.

Which is why walking away from her is so damn hard. I glance back over my shoulder as I leave the room. She's smiling at me, looking pleased as punch.

When the door clicks shut behind me, I sigh and step into the hallway, ready to play off my absence like it wasn't unusually long.

I make it to the top of the stairs before I run into Tripp.

"Hey," he says, eyes scanning me a little too thoroughly.

I remember what Gwen said earlier and resist the urge to tug my collar higher over the mark on my neck. "I was looking for you."

"What's up?" I ask, keeping it light as I clap him on the shoulder and turn him back toward the stairwell.

We walk down side by side.

"I'm going to head back to my hotel. I wanted to talk to you about some things, but I don't think it's the right time. I'm sorry if I ruined the party."

Alarm bells sound in my head. *Talk about some things?*

My conscience berates me for how I've behaved today. Like a territorial animal with no forethought. My mood swings fast as I realize how close he came to walking in on us.

"We can talk if you want," I choke out through a tight throat.

"Nah." He waves me off as we hit the bottom landing near the front door. "It's nothing pressing."

Then he turns to face me, his expression slightly defeated. And even though he's been a royal asshole today, a surge of guilt hits me like a punch in the gut. He's a product of his upbringing and I know I see flashes of him trying to be better in his own clumsy way.

"You didn't ruin the party. Maybe we should get together before you head home?"

He shrugs. "I think I might jet early tomorrow. Try to get my head straight. Maybe I can come back again during the offseason?" He turns wide, hopeful eyes on me before adding, "I'd love to fly with you again."

My heart swells, and I nod. "I'd like that," I say. And it's true. I *would* like that.

The problem is, I'm not sure the offer will still stand when he finds out what I've done.

CHAPTER 34

Gwen

I WAKE UP SLOWLY, FIGHTING MY WAY THROUGH THE THICK grogginess blanketing me. Everything feels soft and warm except for something hot and hard pressed against my back. As awareness seeps in around me, my lashes flutter, my toes wiggle, and I eventually crack my eyes open and smile when I realize that I'm wrapped in Bash's arms.

I press back into him, snuggling closer, but as I move, I'm hit with a wave of light nausea. Fuzzy memories take shape in my mind as the day before filters back to me.

The plane ride, the party, the closet, and lots of wine. After Tripp left, the instinct I'd had to stay on guard disappeared, and as lousy as I feel right now, it was totally worth it.

Then Clyde went to bed, and with only the other couples there to see, Bash stayed close to me for the rest of the evening. Our shoulders bumped, our fingers brushed, and after a few drinks, he'd taken to giving my ass a firm squeeze on the way past.

I have no doubt our friends noticed, but none of them said anything. We carried on. Hell, we even played poker, and the camaraderie—the ease and the comfort level—was something that I've never been a part of before.

Moving from place to place has meant that I don't create friendships like that. The kind that are built over years and decades, holidays, favors—a kind of friendship that feels more like family.

I didn't realize until I stood there in the middle of it all that *this* is what I'd been craving. Maybe this feeling is what I've been moving around searching for all along.

It felt surreal, and it made my birthday even more special than it already was.

What's not so special today is realizing that I forgot I'm the one scheduled to open the yoga studio. I have classes starting this morning and running through the afternoon.

Which makes the amount of wine I consumed less than ideal.

I turn over to face Bash, ignoring the lurching sensation in my stomach. Propping myself up onto an elbow, I slide one hand over his thick chest and press a kiss to his sternum, breathing him in.

His cedar-and-amber smell is downright intoxicating.

I kiss him again on one pec, then on the other, and his arms tighten around my back as a contented *mmm* sound vibrates in his throat.

"Bash," I whisper, "I really hate to do this to you... Actually, I really hate to do this to me, but I have to go to work."

He chuckles, rough and lazy. "Did you have too much fun last night?"

I press my cheek against his chest and smile into him, feeling warm, safe, and protected. "No such thing as too much fun," I murmur. "But I think there might be such a thing as too much pinot grigio, and that is what I'm suffering from today. Tabitha told me it was organic, like that made any difference at all."

He laughs and I draw back to glance at him, wondering if I might find any threads of uncertainty in his eyes.

But I don't. Not with Bash.

It feels like we went from zero to a hundred in a matter of hours. But at the same time, it feels like we've been waiting for this, teasing it for months on end. It's been the longest game of foreplay.

We stare at each other for a few beats, not talking, just looking. Soon he pulls me up, dragging my mouth to his and kissing me firmly. Then he closes his eyes and settles back in with a parting shot of "It sucks to be you."

I bark out a laugh, watching him grin even as his eyes stay shut.

And then I ease myself out of the bed realizing that in my drunkenness I'd stripped down bare—my favorite way to sleep. I bite down on a smile realizing that poor Bash had slept next to me all night and not tried a single thing. When I peek back over my shoulder, he's watching me. His eyes race over my naked body, drinking me in like it's the first and last time he'll ever see me like this.

There have been times in my life when I might have felt

self-conscious in a moment like this, but with Bash, every insecurity evaporates. With Bash, all I see in his eyes is love. Or, well, not love but definitely admiration. And certainly affection.

I turn back to him, giving him a view of both sides.

"Hey, Bash," I say, slowly stepping backward toward where his robe is hanging.

He hums, staring ravenously at my breasts. His tongue darts out to swipe at his bottom lip as his lusty gaze travels down to my pussy. Memories of him on his knees in his closet last night pummel me, but I shake them off, knowing I have to stay in motion, or I'll crawl back into bed with the beautiful man who is gawking at me like I'm his favorite treat.

"My eyes," I say, "they're up here."

He grumbles, gaze flicking up to mine but only for a beat. "I know that." He drops his gaze back down again. "I wasn't trying to find your eyes."

I flush, heat suffusing every limb. I spot his T-shirt on the floor and turn to head in that direction. "You want this?" I ask, as I bend over to pick it up.

"Fuck yeah," he practically groans. And I know he's not talking about the shirt at all.

I straighten with a little arch in my back and then peek back to toss the tee at him. "Sucks to be you, then," I reply with a saucy wink.

He swipes the shirt off his face and grumbles something about how he's going to have a boner all day long. And it makes me smile.

With a warm hum in my chest, I force myself into action,

feeling a little green around the gills as I shower, dress, and prepare myself for a day full of pretending to be more balanced than I am.

When I make my way downstairs, Clyde is in the kitchen. He's hunched over a bowl of cereal that he got for himself, and I realize he doesn't need nearly as much help now as he did after surgery.

The moment I step into the room, his eyes search mine. I know he won't find any trace of last night. I've showered, brushed my damp hair back into a tight french braid, and I'm wearing fresh clothes.

Still, he looks me over and says, "About fucking time."

When I come home later that afternoon, I feel like a steaming pile of hot garbage.

I held it together through four classes at the studio and smiled through it all, even though I felt like I'd been run over by a truck. When I greeted Rhys and Tabitha, who looked like they were in fairly rough shape, I pretended I was fine.

But I was not fine. I was tired, grouchy, hungry, and wanted someone to rub my back. And I just generally was feeling a little overwhelmed.

As soon as I walk in the front door, I kick my shoes off and trudge down the hallway toward the kitchen, figuring the first thing I should do is eat.

But when I get there, the smell of something delicious

hits me and I find Bash standing near the stove, chatting with Clyde.

"Hi," I announce before making my way to the fridge.

"What are you doing?" Bash says. "Come sit down. I made you food."

For a moment, I freeze, hand wrapped around the handle of the fridge, then I turn to Bash. "You made me food?"

He shrugs. "Yeah, it was no big deal. I was making something anyway."

At that, Clyde bursts out laughing. "He was not making something else. He's been nervous cooking since he got up. This man is so obsessed with you, he doesn't even know what to do with himself."

Bash scrubs a hand over his face as though he can hide from this conversation.

Me? I'm downright amused. It's helping my mood, so I urge Clyde on with a nod. And he willingly continues. "He made you cookies. He made banana bread—"

"You bake?" I cut in, gaze catching on what looks like a tray of fresh cookies and a pan of banana bread.

Bash rolls his eyes and turns back to the oven. "Clyde, shut up," he says, stuffing his hands into oven mitts before he bends and pulls out what appears to be a casserole. The heavenly aroma makes my mouth water.

"What is that?" I ask, eyes widening when I see the cheese-crusted top.

He places it on a cutting board. "This is the casserole my mom used to make me when I was hungover."

I scoff. "Me, hungover? No, I feel fabulous."

Both Clyde and Bash look back at me with doubtful expressions.

But it's Clyde who can't keep himself from needling me. "That's weird because you look like hell," he announces.

"Only because I'm tired of your shit," I say quickly. But then my attention is back on the food. "Bash, tell me about this. What's in it? I want it."

He tells me what's in it as he dishes out generous servings for each of us—hash browns, yellow curry, cream, sour cream, butter, chicken, peas, and a lot of cheese.

"I think that's it," he says, squinting as though he's trying to recall. "I had to pull the recipe out from an old book, but it definitely brings back a lot of memories of my teenaged years and is still one of my favorites. It's not fancy, but it'll stick to your ribs."

I sit down next to Clyde as Bash slides the plate toward me. I moan when I take the first bite. It's everything I didn't know I wanted.

"Bash, this is amazing," I announce.

Clyde shovels mouthfuls in, nodding along. When Bash takes a seat, Clyde stares at him with a look of wonder on his face.

"Damn," he announces, jabbing his fork in Bash's direction. "If she doesn't marry you after this, I might."

He gets a laugh from me and a groan from Bash. And I have to admit that, for a guy who seems so confused about so many things, Clyde doesn't miss a beat when it comes to the two of us.

Neither of us responds to the *marriage* comment,

though. We carry on, talking about our days. Turns out they were busy. First baking happened, then Clyde's occupational therapy at the hospital, grocery shopping and cleaning up after the party last night, and then there was more baking and cooking.

By the time we're all caught up, I'm full, sleepy, and alarmingly content. I jump up to put the dishes away and tidy, munching on the world's best chocolate chip cookie. As I devour it, I try not to make too many moaning noises, but they slip out anyway.

Bash sidles up behind me under the guise of putting a plate away in the cupboard above me. "If you keep moaning like that, I'm going to be stuck hanging around Clyde while trying to hide a massive boner," he grits out under his breath.

From behind us, Clyde announces, "Well, on that note, I think I'm going to go take a nap or read my new book or just lock myself away from you two."

I drop my chin to my chest, silent laughter shaking my shoulders.

"There's *no way* he heard that," Bash grumbles.

I turn to face him, watching the tail end of Clyde disappearing down the hall. "He's an acquired taste, but I don't think I can imagine my life without him."

Bash's expression turns thoughtful for a moment. "Yeah, me neither," he says quietly.

Watching Clyde leave has a sense of longing surging up inside me. "I would kill for a nap," I say.

Bash tucks a lock of hair behind my ear. "Okay, take a nap."

"But I just got home. I feel like, I don't know. Should we…hang out? I mean, we've kind of just fucked and partied after months of basically hiding from each other."

Bash scrubs a hand over his stubble. "Okay, well, take a nap on the couch. I'll throw on some sports and we can just relax. Together."

My eyebrows raise on my forehead. "Like a normal couple?"

Bash looks rather amused by the concept as he nods. "Yeah, like a normal couple."

We move into the living room, and I have to give myself an internal pep talk the entire way. We've had plenty of physical moments together, heated by passion, fueled by lust, tinged with alcohol. But now here we are, full bellies, dead sober, in a quiet living room.

I take an awkward seat next to him on the couch, feeling like I'm in high school again, sitting next to a boy I like, unsure of how to act around him.

He flicks the TV on and settles back into the cushions. His body relaxed like this is the most natural thing in the world. His arm drapes over my shoulders, and it hits me that we have all this opportunity—now that we've both given in—and I feel paralyzed by the simplicity of it.

"Gwen, stop overthinking this," he says without turning to look at me.

"I'm not overthinking this," I say back.

Now he turns, tongue popping into his cheek like he's got something stuck in his teeth. "I can practically hear you thinking," he says. "You wanted to take a nap. So relax, take a nap."

"Okay, I just… This feels very domestic," I say, a flutter of nerves rearing up in me as I realize that the relationships I've had didn't prepare me for these moments. The quiet moments, the moments of companionship where you just revel in another person's company without having to talk.

And it's like Bash can tell. He reads me so perfectly. It's like he knows exactly what to say.

"Okay, lie down and put your feet on my lap."

"My feet? Do you have some weird fetish I need to know about?"

"Gwen, give me your feet and stop talking." He pats his lap. "Prop that pillow behind your head and take a nap while I watch sports. That's how we're going to enjoy each other's company this afternoon."

I give him a few nods as I turn and lie back, arranging the pillow underneath my head in a comfortable position. "No funny stuff, Rousseau," I tease as I extend my legs in his direction and wiggle my toes like an offering.

He settles my feet in his lap with a smirk and flicks through the channels, eventually landing on a baseball game. The hum of the TV fills the room, and I take a deep breath, feeling my body relax. For once, I'm not thinking. Just…here.

After a few seconds, a thrill races through me because my feet aren't just in Bash's lap. His big strong hands have wrapped around one of them almost absently, his fingers massaging, prodding, twisting.

I smile and let out an appreciative moan, a subtle way of saying, *Please, sir, may I have more?*

"For fuck's sake, Gwen," he grumbles, but he doesn't

stop rubbing my feet, even as the swell of his hardening dick contacts the heel of my foot.

Unlike so many of the guys I've dated, though, he doesn't pounce on the opportunity to make this moment about sex. Instead, he continues massaging my feet with surprising skill.

He rubs them until I drift off from his soothing touch, allowing myself to enjoy being taken care of for the first time in a very, very long time.

CHAPTER 35

Bash

Bash: Hey, Tripp. Checking in on you. Wanted to make sure you made it home safe.

Tripp: Yup.

THE DAYS THAT FOLLOW CARRY ON IN A HAPPY, LUST-ADDLED haze.

Gwen teaches and takes care of Clyde.

I bowl and work on my mental health so that I can be in proper shape to do the job that I love. Hell, I even attend the odd yoga class.

Every day feels better. The combination of healthy eating, exercise, and companionship has me feeling lighter overall.

I would be lying if I said that I'm not avoiding dealing with the Tripp aspect of our current situation. Clyde knows, and aside from the odd incredibly awkward and inappropriate comment, he lets us carry on without judgment.

My room has become our room, and I no longer avoid family dinners with the two of them. Still, knowing that Tripp left town on such awkward terms nags at me. It's been almost a week since Gwen's party, and he hadn't contacted me, which made me wonder if Gwen was right—if he was onto us.

So I figured I'd test the waters by sending him a text this morning. When I got a one-word answer, never has a person overthought the word *yup* so thoroughly.

Part of me had enjoyed having Tripp there that evening. In so many ways, it felt like a step forward. Like something that could be possible. Like Gwen and I could build a life in Rose Hill with our friends around us and Tripp could still come to visit.

Like maybe, just maybe, everything that I wanted was within reach.

I was playing house in my head, avoiding the reality of having to tell him. But now a thread of worry has taken hold. One I can't shake.

My brain circles back to the words I might use to explain how everything got so complicated.

I met her first.

I couldn't help myself.

I tried to stay away.

I'm sorry I didn't try harder.

I want you in my life, but I can't give her up.

Please forgive me.

I met her first.
I met her first.
I met her first.

I keep coming back to the childish retort. Like somehow it excuses every decision I've made since meeting her. But the truth of the matter is I *did* meet her first. It was only one night, but in an endless sea of nights that were only ever numb, she made me feel something.

And that feeling has never left me. I've clung to it almost desperately. A beacon of light that has kept me swimming through rough waters. And only recently have I really had to grapple with the fact that I have no intention of letting that feeling go.

Of letting *her* go.

I've enjoyed living in our happy bubble, and I'm not ready to burst it. After wanting Gwen for so long and being alone for so many years, a large part of me is desperate not to disrupt the peace. That's why I'm sitting on the back deck, waiting for her to come home from yoga, with an absolutely embarrassing surprise ready to go.

"I can't fucking believe I'm doing this," I mutter to myself as I stare out over the darkened water, the shrub-lined edge of the property still and quiet. The day was hot and dry, but the nighttime temperatures still plunge. Spring usually brings rain to the valley, but this year it's like we skipped a portion of the season. We went from early spring straight into early summer.

Soon I hear the crunch of tires on the driveway from the opposite side of the house. Gwen is humming when she hops out of her truck, and it makes me smile. The front door shuts behind her, and she calls out, "I'm home!"

Next, I hear Clyde yell, "That lovesick fool is waiting for you on the back deck."

I shake my head. I thought I saw him peeking out from behind his curtains. Snoopy motherfucker.

I'm met with the soft, rolling sound of her laugh, as though she thinks he's joking. But she still pads toward the back of the house and steps outside.

"What are you doing out here, Casanova? Just being *lovesick*?" she teases before stopping rather abruptly.

I chuckle, peeking at her over my shoulder. "You know me. Just been waiting all day for you to get home."

She scoffs and drops beside me as I reach for the tray covered in tinfoil. I lift it onto my lap, watching her curious gaze dance over the foil as it crinkles.

"What have we got here? Did you spend your day in the kitchen making me a lovesick little picnic?"

I laugh. "Gwen, so help me. If you don't let that one go, you're gonna pay for it."

Her eyebrows shoot up on her forehead. "Now you've got my attention." She salutes me. "Reporting for duty, sir. Ready to pay for it."

I groan. Ever since we started sleeping together, it's been like this. Fun and light and so fucking *addictive*. I look her over, knowing that she's exactly what I've needed. I've been living with a dark shadow covering everything around me, and along comes Gwen, peeling it away, letting all that light in.

With her, the world looks so different.

So much *better*. For the first time in years, I feel excited about the future. With her, anything is possible.

But then Tripp's name pops up in my mind, and I feel sick all over again. Sick because I know I can't truly move forward without coming clean to him.

I push my anxiety aside, focusing instead on the present. Her. Tonight.

"You can pay for it later. Right now, we're feeding raccoons." Her eyes widen as I peel the foil back and reveal a tray covered in small bowls filled with different raccoon snacks. And yes, I spent the day researching on the internet to find out what they like to eat.

"Is this…is this…" She leans closer, her fingers hovering just above the variety of food laid out. "Is this a raccoon charcuterie?"

I chuckle. "It's whatever you want to call it, Gwen. But I picked out an array of options to see if we can get your raccoon friend back."

Her bright eyes flash up to mine, glowing that pale purple color in the dark blue of the night. "You didn't have to do that," she says.

"No, but I wanted to."

A soft smile touches her lips. She doesn't respond to that. I know I've said it a couple times, but it's true. With her, nothing seems like that big of an ask. It turns out that when I care about someone—when I love someone—I'm willing to do anything for them.

Join a stupid bowling team that I never really wanted to. Give them a kidney.

Play Disney Princess with some shitty raccoon.

All just to make them happy. With Gwen, it's especially easy.

"So what have we got here? Can you explain the menu for me?" she asks with a wink.

"Okay, so over here we've got some watermelon. I read they really like that. And then I did some cheese. A little bacon."

She stops me. "You cooked them bacon?"

"I mean, yeah, the internet said they like that. I figured we could try them all." Feeling slightly bashful, I carry on as she looks at me with wonder. "There's canned tuna. Doritos. Marshmallows—apparently they love those, but I feel like it's probably not good for them." I point to the last bowl. "And finally, we have cat food."

Her brows furrow. "Cat food? You went and bought cat food?"

I scoff and wave her off. "No. I asked Rhys if I could borrow some of his cat food. They have a cat, you know."

She laughs, but it's more of a giggle, airy and disbelieving. "Is it weird if I tell you that this is the most romantic thing anyone has ever done for me?"

I eye her carefully. It bugs me that no one has ever done something this simple for her. And I don't need a bunch of accolades for it, so I deflect. "Yes. Because raccoons are the official animal of romance. Nothing says I'm into you like sharing rabies over a bowl of Doritos."

Her elbow juts into my side. "Watch it, Rousseau. *You'll* be the one paying for it later."

And with that, she takes a handful of cat food from the bowl and tosses it across the lawn.

I try to stifle my groan.

"What?" she says, sliding her gaze to me with mock offense. "You're the one who set this up. Now you're gonna make that little bitchy grumble about it?"

"I'm not being bitchy," I reply. "I just… Do you know how meticulously I tend to this grass? The raccoons are going to come around and they'll dig, and they're going to—you know what? Never mind. It doesn't matter. If my lawn is fucked up but you're happy, then it was worth it."

She throws her head back and laughs. But as she does, a rustling comes from the bushes, and Gwen slaps a hand over her own mouth to stop herself. Moments later, a small, masked bandit—who may or may not be carrying rabies—pokes its head from the bushes. Gwen lets out an excited squeal.

"Oh my god, he's back!" she says, eyes lighting like a cartoon character with that diamond twinkle in the corner.

Yeah. Googling raccoon foods and texting one of my friends to borrow a cup of cat food was all worth it to see her like this.

The raccoon's beady eyes land on us suspiciously, but its pointy nose wiggles in the direction of where she threw the cat food. Tentatively, it moves across the yard, picking up a single piece of kibble.

Gwen doesn't rush it by reaching for more food. Instead, a happy smile spreads across her face as she watches the raccoon make his way from one piece to another, his pointy, evil teeth working maniacally at crunching each chunk.

"How was your day?" Gwen whispers softly.

The raccoon freezes, eyes shifting toward us.

"Pretty good," I whisper back, not wanting to ruin the moment for her by talking too much. But she makes a rolling motion with her hand, urging me onward. "I went to a yoga class."

"Yeah?"

"Yeah. My instructor is extremely fuckable. I couldn't stop staring at her ass the whole time."

Gwen bites down on a satisfied smile. "I love this for you. How incredibly motivating."

We share a heated look that has me grinning and hardening in my jeans.

"What else did you do?" she continues, watching the raccoon move forward ever so slightly.

"Talked to the therapist I've been chatting with. They gave me clearance to work again. Might start slow, though. I don't need to overdo it."

She nods. "I bet your yoga teacher thinks it's superhot that you're taking such good care of your mental health."

I chuckle. "What about you? How was your day?"

She lifts another handful of cat food and tosses it onto the grass, just a little closer to the deck. The raccoon startles, then tiptoes forward cautiously.

"Oh, me?" Gwen asks. "My day was great. I kind of want to fuck one of my students though, and that's a first."

I playfully eye her with suspicion. "Is it?"

It's just part of the friendly banter—I didn't mean for it to be about Tripp, but as soon as the sentiment leaves my mouth, that thread of unease stretches between us. He keeps popping up even though I don't want him to. He's ever-present—unresolved.

"I didn't mean—"

She waves me off. "I know, but let me rephrase that. I want to do more than just fuck one of my students, and *that* is a first."

A deep feeling of satisfaction settles into my bones. She's told me before that she's done nothing but keep things casual, that relationships aren't something she's gone looking for. Hell, I could see it the other day—the way she sat on the couch like I was some experiment she had to figure out in real time.

For Gwen, doing the most mundane things might feel more monumental than they should. But those domestic moments...those are what I crave.

The same ones that Gwen hasn't had at all.

I'd be lying if I said there haven't been times when the thought of her with Tripp hasn't kept me up, driven me to distraction, and made me jealous. And yet, it strikes me now that she's giving me something far more precious than what she had with him.

With contentment glowing in her eyes, she reaches for a marshmallow and tosses it across the grass. The raccoon backs up a couple of steps, and I watch as it rubs its grubby little palms together like it's just found something exceptional. It scampers forward, snatches the marshmallow, then sits down on its haunches, rotating the puff of sugar while munching away like you would corn on the cob.

"Oh my god." She sighs. "Is that not the cutest thing you've ever seen?"

I stare at the oversize rodent. I won't lie. I've spent time and energy keeping raccoons off my property by placing my garbage in a shed and generally scaring them off. But sitting here now, watching this raccoon devour a marshmallow, I have to confess, "Yeah, Gwen, it's pretty damn cute."

She hums happily. Like she's relieved that I don't hate her new friend. "Should we name him?"

"You say that like it's a child," I quip.

"Yeah, except I wouldn't name a child Marshmallow."

"Marshmallow?" I ask. "You're naming him Marshmallow?"

She shrugs. "Yeah, why not?"

I watch the raccoon. "I mean, it's just not very dignified. Do you think he's going to run back into the bushes and tell all his friends that the hot blond lady who lives here named him Marshmallow?"

She shakes her head. "You might be overthinking this."

"Gwen, how am I supposed to trust you to name our first child if you can't even give this raccoon a respectable name?"

We both freeze then. God, there's so much unsaid between us, so much implied. I really have to stop stepping in it like this, making things awkward.

But, of course, nothing with Gwen is ever truly awkward.

"Do you remember," she starts, "that night in the airport? How badly I put my foot in my mouth when I went on about us having a night to tell our kids about one day?"

I chuckle softly. "How could I forget?"

She nods, teeth strumming over her bottom lip. "Now we're even."

A low laugh rumbles in my chest as I pull her close and drop a kiss against her hair. I breathe her in. She smells like lavender and coconut. No doubt some oil blend she's using at the studio. "Yeah, Gwen, now we're even."

We spend the next several minutes figuring out what to name the raccoon while tossing him different foods from the tasting menu I created. We settle on the name Sly because she thinks it suits his mischievous nature and I think it sounds kind of badass.

Because if I'm about to become a raccoon dad, you'd better believe it's going to be the coolest raccoon that anybody's ever known.

Out of all the offerings, we find Sly seems most enthusiastic about the watermelon. He comes close enough to reach his grubby little paws forward and take it from Gwen's hands. Her ensuing excitement scares the shit out of him, but he comes back for seconds, so clearly he isn't too traumatized.

Gwen is over the moon.

Watching her tonight makes my heart swell like the Grinch's on Christmas Day. It also erases any lingering guilt I felt about that night I snapped at her.

I may not be good with verbal apologies, but I will go out of my way to make up for mistakes. And it feels like I achieved that tonight.

When Sly ambles off, looking satisfied and ready for a nap, I offer to clean up while she showers. I find myself grinning at absolutely nothing—like the lovesick fool Clyde accused me of being—while standing at the sink, scrubbing each bowl. And by the time I finish putting them back in the cupboards, that grin hasn't faded.

I almost have to pinch myself as I head up the stairs to my bedroom—*our* bedroom. It feels surreal.

And it's made all the more surreal when I step inside our room and find the balcony door open. I can see Gwen. Buck naked, wet hair slicked down her back, bent over the railing.

Waiting for *me*.

CHAPTER 36

Gwen

I wake in the middle of the night to Bash's mouth trailing over my bare skin. We spent the entire evening wrapped up in each other and crashed with the sheets tangled at our feet.

I have no idea what time it is now. All I know is that his massive master bedroom is illuminated only by silvery moonlight and he looks fucking stunning all lit up like this.

He kisses my shoulder and I sigh, trailing the tips of my fingers over his muscled back.

"What are you doing?" I whisper, watching the silhouette of his head move across my chest, lips dragging reverently over my collarbone.

"Admiring you." His words come out quiet, raspy, heartachingly tender. "You looked so fucking pretty. Sleeping in my bed, all these delicious curves on display. I couldn't help myself."

My eyes flutter shut, and I hum with contentment. I feel better about myself than I ever have, but hearing Bash talk about my body like this? It's addictive.

It's healing.

He kisses my breasts. My ribs. My stomach. My hips.

And then he moves back up, hugging me tight and resting his head against my chest. My heart hammers, and I wonder if he can hear it beating wildly under his attention.

"Thank you," I whisper. And I don't elaborate. I don't need to. He *knows*. I think he's always known and he's always seen me differently than my father did.

Where my father found faults, Bash only finds beauty. And he doesn't even need to try. I could tell by the way he looked at me the first time I invited myself to sit down with him.

"I'm always in your corner, Gwen. You ever need a pick-me-up? I'm your guy."

I hug him back, combing my fingers through his mussed hair with a satisfied smile.

I wonder if this is what it feels like to be loved.

And at the very least, I fall asleep feeling incredibly fortunate that this guy—out of all of them—has decided to be mine.

I tidy the studio and my thoughts drift to Bash, as they often have over the past couple of weeks.

It's like my brain has been rewired with constant

thoughts of him, my body reliving memories of the last time we touched. If I thought I was obsessed with him before, I knew nothing. I'm so obsessed that, on a whim, I followed up with the resort in Costa Rica and told them I wouldn't be coming—something I still need to confess to Bash.

All I know is that I have to trust my gut. And my gut says I belong here, with him.

This feeling now? It's incomparable. Consuming. And it's all new. Everything between us feels perfect.

Perhaps just a little too perfect. As life has taught me, nothing really is. There are ups and downs. There are incredibly bright moments, always balanced by the memory of a loss, the feeling of something being incomplete. Or in this case, the constant knowledge that there's an elephant in the room that neither of us wants to look at—let alone talk about.

I stack the wooden blocks on the shelf in the corner, humming to myself as I do, attempting to put myself in Bash's shoes.

He's finally let himself admit he wants this, in his own way, of course. But giving in to temptation—for a man as honorable as him—says it all.

On the other hand, I can't help but notice him checking his phone. Anytime I've asked if he's heard from Tripp since that night on the balcony, his response is somewhat dismissive.

It's always *Oh yeah, we swapped a text* but nothing more than that. I may not have firsthand experience with complicated father-son family dynamics, but I know secrets weigh on a person. I know they are not good for the soul. And whether or not Bash admits it, I know this is eating away at him. Possibly more than he even realizes.

It's something I need to broach with him—soon. But everything between us still feels so tenuous, so fragile and new. Like the slightest gust of wind could push us off course.

I sanitize and reroll the yoga mats, losing myself in thoughts of how I can best support Bash through an awkward moment or a painful conversation.

He is the human embodiment of that old saying *you can lead a horse to water, but you can't make it drink.*

I need to convince Bash he's thirsty, that he needs this off his chest. That much like giving in to the pull between us, clearing his conscience of this perceived deception will only make him feel better in the long haul, even if it doesn't feel very good right now.

I'm mulling this over when a jingle at the front door draws my attention.

"Be right there," I call out, knowing there's no class again for about two hours.

I roll up the last mat and slide it onto the shelf, dusting my hands off on my leggings. When I turn, I realize that the person from the front is now in the studio. And that person is Bash.

Shoulder propped against the doorframe, arms crossed, he watches me hungrily. That electric current I've grown accustomed to feeling around him pulses through my limbs, growing stronger as I take him in.

He's in uniform. I make a show of checking him out, biting my bottom lip as I do.

Navy cargo pants. That matching BC Fire Service T-shirt—the one that hugs his shoulders and biceps in the very best way. Clunky, black boots planted on the studio floor. It should be illegal to look that good and that heroic all at once.

When I finally meet his gaze, I ask, "What are you doing here?"

"Coming to see my girl," he responds, but he makes no move toward me. He just continues standing there, staring at me.

I grin. "In that uniform? You're a filthy tease, Rousseau. I hope you know that."

"Sorry, I've been called out to a bushfire. I don't think I'll be gone too long, but I wanted to come check on you before I left."

"Check on me or parade around in that slutty little outfit?"

He smirks and my panties disintegrate.

I have no doubt that he knows what he does to me. Watching him fly a plane had been hot as hell, but watching him fly a plane in literally any type of uniform would just be over-the-top.

"I don't know. Maybe a bit of both," he confesses.

"How long will you be away?" I saunter toward him, unable to resist the pull. "I feel like I might miss you."

He quirks a brow. "Oh yeah?"

I nod and draw up close, sliding one hand over his rib

cage. With him tucked against me, I turn us just enough to close the door behind him and flick the lock shut.

His face remains impassive, but I can read the question in his eyes. It says *Gwen, what the fuck are you up to now?* Because he knows I'm full of antics, and I think that's one of the things he likes about me.

My hands roam from his waist, running up and back down for a second before reaching for my shirt and tugging it up over my head. My boobs are strapped down tight in a heavy-duty sports bra, but even this setup can't contain my cleavage, and all it takes is one look for Bash to let out a groan.

"Guinevere, what are you doing?"

I smirk and ditch the bra too. "Giving you a parting gift."

"Fuck," he groans. "This is not helping me want to leave."

I shoot him a sultry wink. "Gotta keep you coming back for more."

He sobers for a beat. "I'm never going to get enough. I can promise you that much. I'll always be coming back to you."

I swallow, struck by the sincerity in his words. I've never wanted to stay in one place until now. I don't know what the future holds, but I'm desperate for it to be here. With him.

The realization brings me a sense of peace I've never felt before. Like I'm not just rushing through life, trying to get to the next place. Running from my past and desperately searching for a place I belong. Suddenly, I don't have anywhere else to be.

I'm right where I belong.

And with that in mind, I offer him a soft smile and drop to my knees. "A little extra motivation never hurt anyone."

His head tips back on a groan as I work on his pants. Button, zipper, boxers. When I pull them down, his big hard cock springs free and I lick my lips. I peek up at him again, and he's watching me. Always watching me.

I wrap my palm around his length and squeeze.

"I think the only thing this will accomplish is making me not want to leave, Gwen."

I pump. "It will give you something to think about while you're at work."

"If I think about this, I'll crash my plane," he replies absently, his gaze flitting behind me. I turn to follow his line of sight and realize that he's watching us in the mirror. Him standing above me. Me kneeling at his feet, topless, with his dick in my hands.

With a knowing smirk on my lips, I shuffle, turning us slightly, so he can watch us in profile. Then I take him in my mouth. Palms flat against his muscular thighs, I swallow his steely length, going far enough that I almost gag.

"Fuuuuuuccckkk," he hisses, lifting my hair with his fist and flexing his hips.

My lashes flutter and I swallow, working to take all of him. I love when he takes control like this.

I pull back off with a wet popping noise and stare up at him. His chest heaves, the navy fabric of his shirt stretching in the most alluring way between his broad shoulders, as I open my mouth and stick my tongue out in offering. He turns to take in the view in the mirror, shaking his head slightly as I stay in position.

"You're such a filthy little tease. And it's hot as hell, baby. Never change."

He slowly presses his cock into my mouth, my lips suctioned tight as I hum in satisfaction. Watching him feel so undone over me is the ultimate high.

"This hot little mouth." He thrusts again, my cheeks hollowing out as he does. "Un-fucking-beatable."

I preen, eyes boring into him, saying what my mouth can't right now—that I fucking love this.

I flatten my tongue, letting him use me. The smooth heat of him fills me, bumping into the back of my throat. My eyes water and I meet his every thrust, always eager for more with him. I grip his thighs, holding on for the ride as he smooths his knuckles over my cheeks, looking at me with so much love in his eyes.

"That's it, Gwen. Suck it." His words are choppy, his breathing labored. He glances in the mirror again, as though he can't decide which view he prefers. "So fucking pretty like this."

I hum again, letting the vibration rumble in my throat as I tighten my suction. He makes a soft whimpering noise, and it feels like winning an Olympic gold medal. Making Sebastian Rousseau—Mr. Always in Control—fall apart is my crowning achievement.

I soak in his flushed cheeks, his lust-addled eyes, the way his hands tremble against my scalp as I tip my head back and let him fuck my face.

WILD CARD

He growls my name, and his cock twitches against my tongue. My mouth fills with his cum, and I take my front-row seat to watching him crumble.

And I enjoy the hell out of it.

CHAPTER 37

Bash

"I think I love yoga even more now," I whisper as we walk out of the studio that I'll never be able to look at the same way again.

Heading down the hallway and toward the front desk, I land a playful slap on Gwen's perfect ass. Her only reaction is to throw her head back and laugh. I follow her, drawn to that sound like I have been since day one.

But the perfect moment comes to a screeching, heart-stopping, stomach-dropping halt when I look up and see Tripp at the front reception desk, arms propped against the flat surface. Sizzling fury dances over his every feature.

Gwen and I both stop in our tracks. All the lines I've run through in my head, that I thought would be perfect to explain this whole thing to him, evaporate on the spot.

"Hey, *Dad*." He spits the word. "Good to see ya. And you, Gwen." He nods in her direction without so much as looking at her. She doesn't respond, but from beside her, I can hear her swallow.

I too am at a loss for words because we *know*.

We know that this is about as obvious a way for Tripp to find out as possible.

"I figured I'd come by to pick your brain about some weird vibes I was catching during her birthday. I thought maybe I was out to lunch, thought I was making it all up until I mentioned it to my mom last night. She apparently doesn't tell me much, but she at least had the balls to tell me about my birthday party. That she saw you slip into a powder room with my girlfriend before you tore out of their house in a rampage, leaving a hole in the wall."

My heart stops, turns to concrete in my chest. Fucking Cecilia. Of course, she'd have seen that. And of course she'd have to play the hero by being the one to tell Tripp about it at the worst moment possible.

I give Gwen's hand a soft squeeze as I step in front of her. She returns it, and Tripp's narrowed eyes latch on to the contact between us.

"Tripp—" Gwen starts, but he cuts her off, arms slashing across the air in front of him.

"No, Gwen, I don't want to hear from you. I want to hear from Bash. I want you"—he points at me—"to look me in the eye and tell me you are not fucking my girlfriend."

Rage flashes hot and bright as I step toward him, closing the distance between us. I drop my voice, opting for low and threatening. "If you think I'm going to stand here and let you talk about her like that, you've got another thing coming. So watch your damn mouth."

His jaw twitches as his eyes skitter behind me, and for a moment, he looks remorseful.

But truthfully, I don't even want him so much as looking at her right now, so I draw his attention back with a snap of my fingers. "And I think you mean *ex-girlfriend*, Tripp."

I quickly glance over at Gwen. She's turned the color of a beet and appears as though she would like to run and hide. And god, I can't blame her. This is truly a fucking mess.

"Well, she sure as shit wasn't my ex-girlfriend when you yanked her into a bathroom with you at my parents' house."

"I didn't—"

He forges ahead, fury shaking his voice now. "You think you can just roll back into my life, try to foster some sort of relationship with me, and steal my girlfriend all in one fell swoop? You've got a lot of fucking nerve—"

I lose it then. I cut him off and say the one thing that's been echoing in my head for months now. My voice isn't quiet at all when I confess, "I saw her first!"

Silence descends between all of us.

It's a childish sentiment, and yet it's true. I saw her first. She was mine first. Whether we knew it at the time, that night changed our lives.

"What the fuck is that supposed to mean?" he says, looking utterly disgusted by this entire conversation.

I step ahead again, wanting to put myself between him and Gwen. "We met months before you knew who she was. In fact, the same week that I met you for the first time."

He scoffs now, like he doesn't believe me. "Oh, that's *very* convenient for you, Bash. Nice try."

"It's true." Gwen's velvety voice filters from behind me. She steps slightly to the side so she has a clear view of Tripp, but she doesn't move any closer. "What he's telling you is true. We did meet first."

"Oh, well, how cute for you, Gwen. Bouncing from dick to dick, ticking off the family tree like a shopping li—"

I see red. Every excuse for his behavior flies out the window the minute he spews that venom at her. I reach for him, but Gwen pulls me back. It leaves my hand in the air between us, index finger pointing at him, shaking with rage.

His eyes widen as mine scorch him where he stands. "Finish that sentence and I swear to god not a single thing will stop me from teaching you a fucking lesson, Tripp."

His head tilts in consideration and I glare at him, holding myself back from starting a brawl with my own fucking kid.

"Oh, a lesson, *Dad*? You already taught me that you'll pick some random chick over your own son, so I can't wait to see what else you'll come up with."

"When you act like this, it makes the decision pretty fucking easy," I bite back.

Tripp looks instantly stricken. Like I've laid hands on him when I haven't. I attempt to soften the blow with "Obviously, we all need to talk about this. But if you think you're going to stand here and disrespect her while we do, think again."

"Oh, I'm sorry. Am I supposed to be paying her a ton of respect when she knowingly went after my father?"

I blink at him and lower my hand in defeat, wondering how it must feel to be so sure of yourself. To be so certain that you're right. So absolute in your own innocence.

I can't relate.

"Tripp. How could she possibly have known that I was your father when we all know that the story you tell is that your deadbeat dad decided to show back up?"

His red cheeks go pale and he wipes his hand over his mouth as though pulling away a piece of tape that has been silencing him. "That's what I was told!"

His voice rings through the small studio as my train of thought turns fuzzy. Because what does that mean?

"I spent my entire life being told my dad was some loser deadbeat who didn't want me. They didn't pretend Eddie was my biological dad. They told me I was *unwanted*. That my dad found out about me and took off. Like that was somehow more palatable. So imagine my surprise when you showed up. Started texting me. Taking an interest. That was almost too good to be true. It all felt like one big cosmic joke, one that I was never quite sure was real."

All the air in my chest leaves in an audible *oof*. My palm lands against my sternum as though it can press any shred of oxygen back into my lungs.

"She told you that?" My voice comes out so quiet, so unsteady, and the pounding in my ears is so loud that I wonder if he can hear me at all.

"Yes!" His arms shoot out, frustration spilling from his

every movement. "So in the past several months, I've had to come to terms with the fact that my mom is a manipulative liar and that the man who fathered me did actually give a damn, but I missed years with him because of whatever fucked-up family dynamic I have. I tried to tell you. I *wanted* to tell you. But the timing was never right. Now I find out you're…what, dating my ex?"

He barks out a disbelieving laugh, raking his hands through his hair as he looks around the room like this is a fever dream. "Might as well air it all out now. Because nothing could be more twisted than that."

Nausea roils in my stomach, and Gwen squeezes my hand in a steady rhythm. It feels as though the pressure of her touch is the only thing keeping my heart beating right now.

Silence swells between us as my mouth opens and closes, searching for words that just won't come. The unfairness of how this all played out guts me. I feel like I've been left dangling upside down.

"Tripp, I'm… Fuck. *I'm* sorry. If I had known—"

"You wouldn't have fucked my *ex*-girlfriend?"

I straighten, because as messy as this all is, there's a part of me that wouldn't have done a single thing differently. I do feel bad for him, but I can't undo this either.

"Listen to me. I know what kind of person I am. I know what happened between your mom and me. And you have to believe me when I tell you that if I had known you existed, I would have been in your life from day one. But I wasn't given that choice. It's not fair. To you or to me. The first night I met Gwen was on the heels of meeting you for the first time.

I told her all about *you* and how badly I wanted to be a part of your life."

"*That's* your takeaway from all of this?" Tripp replies, looking absolutely shocked.

"Things are rarely as simple as they seem. I can't explain the choices your mom made. I don't condone them. But I won't spend a lifetime paying for them either. She's already taken enough from me. I want a relationship with you. That's true. But I'm not giving up Gwen. That's also true. I've spent far too long missing out on things that make me happy, and I'm not choosing between these two things. It might take time, and I know we're going to need to have more conversations, but I just… I'm not giving her up, Tripp. I'm sorry."

A weight lifts from my shoulders as I finally admit it out loud. It's a relief to face the reality of what I've known for months now.

I choose Gwen.

He scoffs in disbelief, head shaking as he takes a step back and lifts both hands in surrender. "Wow. This is really something else. Un-fucking-believable if I think about it. It's one thing to be betrayed by some girl I dated for a blink of an eye. It's entirely another to be betrayed by you."

He launches his missile, and it hits its intended target. Me, right in the fucking chest. Because this is a betrayal.

I won't take that away from him.

"Tripp. Maybe we can all go somewhere and talk this out," Gwen says, her voice calm and even. She's being supportive, but the damage has already been done.

He laughs, harsh and bitter. It's a laugh that hurts.

I feel fucking sick, and that feeling doesn't abate when he turns away. I reach for him, but he jerks his arm away from me.

"Don't touch me," he bites out, marching away. "And don't follow me. I can't even look at you." As he shoves the door open roughly, he calls back, "I hope you two are fucking happy together. Have a nice life."

The bell above the door jingles, sounding too light for the weight of that conversation. And when he's gone, I'm torn between wanting to run after him to explain and being too stunned to move.

We stand staring at the door. Through the window, I see his rental car pull away, and I can't help but hope that he drives safely even though he's rightfully distraught.

I turn to Gwen, who looks shaken and a little bit nervous. "Come here," I say, and she does, instantly stepping into my arms. I wrap them around her and drop a kiss on the top of her head. "We're going to work this out."

"Bash," she breathes, "I'm so sorry. This is—"

"No. Stop apologizing when you've done nothing wrong. It's more complicated than either of us knew." I sigh roughly, holding her tighter and breathing in her scent as I confess my feelings. "Deep down, I was prepared for this. For telling him. Maybe not like this—god, never like this—but I've known it was coming and that it wouldn't be pretty. There was just no way around hurting him."

I pull away, cradling her face gently in my hands as I crouch slightly to look her in the eye. "Because what I keep coming back to is this: I can't live without you."

She peeks up at me and swallows, eyes glistening as she gives me a quick nod.

"I hate having to leave you like this, but I have to go." A quick glance at my watch tells me I'm cutting it close.

"I know," she whispers. "We can talk when you get back."

"When I get back." I look her over carefully, searching for any signs of that part of her that wants to keep moving. The part that's scared of settling down, the one I worry might pick up and leave at any moment. Everything here is messy. Costa Rica is on the horizon. Why would she stay? "Don't go, okay? I know everything here is complicated and terrifying. But don't run this time. Please stay. We will work it all out." I give her shoulders a squeeze, getting lost in her pale purple irises, swimming with emotion right now. "For me, just...stay."

With that, I plant one long kiss on her perfectly plush lips. I should try to postpone my departure, but all I want is to flee. I want to work so I can be distracted. I want to process the weight of what Tripp just unloaded on me. And it all feels like too much to unpack. My hope is that, with a few days of distance, it might look more manageable.

I pour as much of myself as I can into this one kiss, begging her to stay, begging her to wait, begging her to make it through this thing with me. Because I have a sinking suspicion that what's on the other side of this struggle might be...everything.

I just have to figure out how to keep it.

CHAPTER 38

Bash

THE JOB DOESN'T TAKE AS LONG AS I EXPECT IT TO. WE HIT the fire hard that night, then run the perimeters in the morning, and by midday, things are mostly under control.

I don't get a wink of sleep. Instead, I spend the time overthinking, figuring out a way forward, and writing a mean text to Cecilia that I continue to delete and retype. I'm given the option of another night in the hotel before catching an early flight home, but my desire to get back to Gwen overrides my desire for extra hours of sleep. My brain is full, my conscience is riddled with guilt, and I can barely keep my eyes open, but in a twist, I still don't leave this fire feeling that same sense of helplessness as I did last time.

Distraught as I am over what's gone on with Tripp, the anticipation I feel at going home to Gwen lightens my mood. For all the years I've spent wishing that someone might be there when I come back, I'm finally about to experience that.

I don't even care what we do tonight. We don't even need to talk. I would settle for lounging on the couch, rubbing her feet. Or sitting outside and feeding a raccoon.

It's with that in mind that I drive toward home from the airstrip. I decide to stop off in town to grab some beer. I even luck out and find the perfect angled parking stall on the street, when getting a spot close to one of the stores is usually an impossible task.

It feels like a positive omen. A sign that despite being deliriously tired, things might actually be going my way. That is until I cut the engine and let my eyes fall just slightly down the block to where some of the bistro tables sit out front of Tabitha's restaurant, the Bighorn Bistro.

Gwen and Tripp are seated at the small metal table and they're embracing. His arms are wrapped around her, his face is buried against her neck. And she's holding him back.

I want to believe that there's a good explanation, that this is a positive thing. But I'm overtired and seeing them out together has every dark, ugly insecurity that I carry with me rearing its ugly head.

I've never been overly concerned about mine and Gwen's age difference, but suddenly I'm wondering: Is it too much? Am I too old? Am I tying her down by asking her to stay? Is she just going to leave? Maybe she'd be happier somewhere else? Or with someone else? Someone like Tripp?

Maybe, like always, I'll be the second choice.

I usually try not to give these thoughts too much credence. I know that they're pitiful and insecure. They make me seem like a more self-loathing sort of person than I want to be. But every now and then, when I'm tired and stressed, they crop up.

I watch them for a beat. The hug isn't a quick side squeeze; it's definitely got more meaning than that. When they pull back, Gwen's hands rest on his shoulders as she gives him a firm and affectionate push.

He *smiles.*

Their lips are moving, but I don't know what they're saying. And I don't think that I want to. Suddenly, all I want to do is be home, and it doesn't matter who's there because I think what I need is to be alone.

When I get back to the house and check the calendar, I realize Clyde is at one of his occupational therapy appointments, which is probably what brought Gwen into town. Distractedly, I put my laundry on, tidy up around my room, and just generally try to keep myself busy so that my thoughts don't spiral too far into a pit of irrational despair. I know sleep would probably give me a good dose of perspective, but I don't let myself relax.

I'm better than this. I know I am. But after being kicked while I'm down so many times, it's just a little too easy to believe I might not be better than this after all.

When Gwen and Clyde do finally come through the front door, I'm an agitated mess. They're chatting away happily, and I feel like I'm storming around with a dark cloud looming over me. I make my way downstairs to see them, and they both brighten at my presence.

It should make me happy, but my head replays the way

Tripp smiled at Gwen, and all I can muster is a frown in their direction.

Gwen must pick up on my body language or, knowing her, just my energy. That smile drops off her face, and her head tilts. But she says nothing other than, "I'm so glad you're back. I had no idea you were coming so soon. Why didn't you tell me?"

I straighten my shoulders, feeling them tense as I do. Anxiety lances through me. She had no idea I was coming back so soon, which is why she was out with Tripp.

Get your shit together, Rousseau.

I don't want to be that guy. I don't want to accuse her of those things, so I give them a very dry "Surprise!"

"Oh boy," Clyde grumbles. "Trouble in paradise. I'm getting the fuck out of here." He moves past me with a slap on the shoulder and then disappears down the hallway.

Gwen watches with a pensive expression on her face. "Everything okay?" She doesn't come nearer, clearly sensing that something is off.

I shrug, moving into the kitchen to busy myself because I'm not really sure how to broach this conversation with her. It makes me realize how fucking terrible I am at talking about my feelings.

But then I realize that with her, it hasn't ever been a problem. I told her about how I was feeling after the last fire. We've talked about Tripp, and we've talked about Clyde. Hell, one of those first nights on the patio, I told her about how badly I wanted to be a dad and the real reason that I built this house—which I've never told anyone before.

The fact I don't want to talk to her about my feelings

right now is only further proof that my head isn't right. That I'm lashing out because I'm tired and overwhelmed. *That's* why I'm trying to walk away from this conversation.

She follows me into the kitchen, calling me on avoiding her immediately. "Bash, I know this is new and very, very tenuous. I get it, I do. But if you're going to turn into a boulder every time that something is a little bit wrong, it's going to make things really difficult. I know we left on awkward, complicated terms and that you've been busy at work, and I totally respect that. But you gotta talk to me."

I walk farther into the kitchen before turning and propping my hands on the island counter across from her. I respect her request for me to tell her what's wrong, so with a heavy sigh, I lift my gaze to meet hers. "I saw you and Tripp out together today."

She sucks in a deep breath through her nose, nodding her head as she releases it. We square off across the top of the island. "Yes, I was out with Tripp today. I would never hide that from you."

She doesn't deny it, and based on the way she squares her shoulders and lifts her chin, she doesn't feel the least bit guilty about it either.

"Why?" I ask. "Because I can't think of a single good reason why you'd need to spend time with him, especially after the way he spoke to you. I'm still fucking furious with him for that. What his mom did is awful, but the way he spoke to you is borderline unforgivable and if I never—"

"If you never what? If you never speak to him again, you'll be fine with that?"

I blink once, shocked by the sternness in her voice.

"You'll just not talk to him anymore? Just pretend he doesn't exist? You and I are just gonna skip off into the sunset like none of this shit ever happened? I was *talking* to him. Trying to explain things in a respectful way. Jesus Christ, Bash. Put yourself in his shoes for a minute."

I swallow. It's like she's read my mind, my internal acknowledgment that I really don't like talking about these things. Avoiding them is so much easier.

"Bash, you and me"—she points between us—"we're not going to work if you can't make amends with Tripp."

I rear back at that, the finality of it hitting me hard across the face. "What the hell is that supposed to mean?"

She sighs heavily and carries on with an edge of exasperation to her tone. "That means that our foundation will always be off-kilter if you can't at least try to work this thing out. You both need to untangle this massive knot. If you don't, it means we could spend the rest of our lives together, but I will always be the person who ruined this for you. I'll be the thing that came between you and the possibility of what could have been. It means that you can't just run and not talk to him. You can't shut down when shit like this happens."

"I highly doubt he wants to talk to me."

"No. Because we hurt him! But he's your son, so you try anyway! And you never, never give up on him!" she exclaims, her own pain flaring in her eyes. I swallow roughly, dropping her gaze because I know this relationship is a tender spot for her. "Man, sometimes you have the emotional intelligence of a gnat, and quite frankly, so does he. Must be hereditary."

My molars grind. "Why is he even still in town? If he's so furious with me and hates me so much, then why is he still here? The amount of time he spends contributing to the economy by staying in that hotel is fucking absurd unless he's still after you."

She scoffs at that. "Get real. He basically called me sloppy seconds. I promise you, he is not after me. But he *is* upset. Tripp isn't just young; he's immature and insecure. He has no idea what he wants. All he knows is that he grew up feeling unwanted—a feeling I know well—and in turn he likes having things that other people want. That's his only interest in me, and we both know it. I reached out to him *for you*. Because I want this relationship for you—and deep down, he wants a relationship with you too. *That's* why he hangs around. But like you, he doesn't know how to say it."

I swallow. She thinks he still wants a relationship with me?

"I wanted to help smooth this over for you. I think Tripp deserved to know how we met and what happened and what a good person you are. And so I did my part to help explain it all to him. *For you.*"

The weight of that statement is almost more than I can bear. I've always thought I wanted fatherhood. I've wanted to be better than the one I had.

But now with the reality of it staring me in the face, I'm... *terrified*.

"Gwen, be real. You two have history. He's here for you. He doesn't care about me."

"See that?" She points at me. "That right there is a problem."

I cross my arms, my brows dropping low on my forehead. "What's a problem?"

"That attitude, Bash. It's all bluster. You're full of shit." She sighs, and I can hear the frustration in it. "I really like you. I like you more than I've ever liked a man before. I think you're it for me, but I'm not spending a lifetime with you tiptoeing around these subjects. We need to lay it out on the table, and if you really are carrying any deep-seated resentment against me for having dated Tripp, then you need to work through it. Because I can't change it and I won't be made to feel guilty for it for the rest of my life. I have apologized. I have shown up. I have chosen *you* at every turn and you throwing that history in my face just to avoid facing your own feelings isn't going to cut it. I won't tolerate it."

A feeling of cold dread crawls down my spine, and her words pummel me as I retreat further back into the old version of myself—the one who believes the universe takes everything away from him.

"And what the hell is that supposed to mean, Gwen?" I say, tightness in my chest making it almost hard to breathe. Every joint feels rigid and my brain spirals, diving down, as I feel her retreat coming.

I realize that this could be the beginning of the end. Over before we ever really started. I'm smart enough to put together the ultimatum in her words, but I need to hear it loud and clear to know where I stand.

"What are you going to do? Take that job and skip town?" I ask, already dreading her answer.

Her lips press together tightly, eyes dancing over my face.

"I'm going to go out and I'm going to leave you to think about this."

"Leave me to think about this?" I repeat. "So is this the end? You just run along to the next stop? Guess you did warn me you don't stay in one place for long."

She rears back like I've slapped her, and I instantly regret my words. I'd like to reach across the kitchen and pluck them right out of the air. Tell her she misheard me.

But she didn't. I can tell by the way she steels herself.

"The end of what, Bash? We're just getting started. You can't get rid of me that easily. The problem is we can't start off properly without you addressing these issues. You can't just sulk and play the victim every time the going gets tough. You need to own your shit. We both know what we have is real. This is it for me and nothing is going to change that. But you still need to reach out to your son and make amends with him. We hurt him, and yes, it needed to be done, but that was a god-awful way to find out. So rather than acting like he wronged you, put your heart in your hand and go talk to him."

She's right.

I hate that she's right.

"And while you're at it, you need to do a little soul-searching to figure out if you can let go of the way we started so we can focus on what we are and what we're going to be. Because I can't handle feeling guilty for something that I would never have done on purpose. I won't sign up for walking around on eggshells in my own home, trying to figure out what's wrong or if I've offended you. It's stressful and unhealthy, and I've lived that story already. I'm not doing it again. I deserve more than that. But most of all, Bash, *you* deserve more than that."

Her words cut deep. They leave me speechless, which is probably just as well because it seems like anything I say just digs a deeper hole.

She looks at me, waiting for me to respond, but I don't. I *can't.*

She shakes her head with a disappointed sigh and then turns, leaving the room. "Excuse me while I *run along to the next stop.*"

All I do is watch as the most precious person in the world to me walks away.

And I don't even blame her.

CHAPTER 39

Bash

"Dude, you're fucking terrible tonight. You're like the new Rhys of the team," West teases.

Ford, Rhys, and Clyde (who came along just to hang out) all get a really good laugh at my expense.

The problem is, I don't feel much like laughing. I feel downright distraught over my argument with Gwen.

It's been several hours since she walked out the door, and the coiling sensation of nausea rolling in my gut has only gotten worse with every minute that's passed.

"West, be gentle with him today. He's already busy beating himself up."

I shoot a scowl Clyde's way. "I'm fine."

He shrugs. "I don't know. Things didn't sound fine from where I was hiding in my bedroom. Gwen laid you out, boy."

I roll my eyes. Fucking Clyde, always spying on us. "I deserved it."

The humor around me dissipates after I bomb everyone's good mood with that depressing take on things.

Four sets of wide eyes gawk back at me.

"What? What are you all staring at?"

Ford takes a sip of his drink, still staring at me. "Probably that you finally admitted there's something between you and Gwen after months of pretending there isn't when we can all tell that there is."

"Yeah," West adds. "I feel like I've been in on a state secret that everybody knows about, but no one talks about. You and Gwen, you're like Fight Club. You know what the first rule is."

I give them another of my signature eye rolls, which they interpret as me finding them funny. Ford, West, and Clyde chuckle between themselves as I watch them make their way to the bar, searching for another drink.

But it's Rhys's intense glare that has my skin crawling.

"What's the trouble?" he asks, his eyes concerned. Sure, he looks like a massive meathead, but underneath it all, he might be one of the most sensitive guys I know.

I glance away, watching other teams take their turns as I search for the right words. "I don't know. Everything feels so messy. You know, when we met, it seemed like it could be so simple. Like, just, I liked her, and she liked me, and we could meet up again sometime. Now it's like my son's involved, right up in the middle of everything, and I want so badly for him to be okay with it. But I just don't know how to make him see that. And the guilt is eating me alive."

I let out a weary sigh. "I said some things to Gwen today that I shouldn't have. I know I hurt her feelings, and I just…"

Rhys's deep voice rumbles across the space between us. "It's just altogether too many feelings, isn't it?"

I look at him, realizing there's a reason why this man is the one I connect with the most on our team. "Yeah, it's just a lot of feelings, a lot of talking, and a lot of things that I haven't felt in a really long time. Like I have something to lose. Like I have something to gain. Like I'm jealous. Like I'm just paralyzed by the realization that one wrong step could leave me with nothing when everything is so close that I can almost taste it."

He nods. "Believe it or not, I know the feeling. Tabitha and I weren't always so clear-cut. I was used to keeping everything to myself, second-guessing everyone around me, never trusting a single soul. And then, you meet that one person who makes you want to break out of your shell. Who it's worth taking those risks for. Who…without them, you'd stay on the same miserable path. Never improving, never changing, never becoming a better version of yourself."

He shrugs now. "Sometimes when you're paralyzed like that, it's not because you don't know what to do. It's because you know exactly what to do. You know what's right, but it scares you. It's not indecision. It's being grown-up enough to know that the world doesn't revolve around you. There's so much in there at play."

I let his wise words wash over me, rolling my beer glass between my palms.

Rhys watches me for a moment, then he chuckles. "I think if you weren't a little scared, you'd probably be stupid. And you're a lot of things, Bash"—he holds his beer up now, clinking it against my glass—"but stupid is not one of them."

I nod and take a sip.

"Don't let her get away," he adds.

Before I can thank him for sharing his wisdom—Rhys isn't a talkative person, and he just monologued some deep advice straight at me—the guys return to our table.

I eye their pinched expressions cautiously because I've got that feeling when you just *know* something is wrong. That feeling rarely leads me astray.

"There's a fire on the back side of the mountain and it's spreading quickly," West says. "We just saw it on the TV."

Sure enough, when I check my phone, I have multiple missed calls. None of which are from Tripp or Gwen. And all of which are from our local Forest Service's number.

I step outside and dial back, quickly hearing the voice of our area supervisor, Dale, on the other end of the line.

"Bash, we need you ready for tomorrow morning," he says.

"How bad is it?" I ask, cutting to the chase.

"It's bad. Windy as fuck tonight, and it's dry back there. No one has burned the underbrush for decades. A dry spring means it's basically a forest floor of kindling and pine needles."

"It's not totally dark yet. I could get up there in time to at least lay out some fire lines. Get a lay of the land. I know the other guys would too."

Dale sighs. "The wind is too much. We're going to battle it from the ground tonight and see if we can stave it off, but it's moving quickly."

"Well, even if I can't do anything from the air, I'm coming down there to help," I say, already marching back inside to grab my keys and say my goodbyes.

"I won't say no to extra bodies," Dale replies. He knows I've got several thousand wildland firefighting hours under my belt. My talents are best used in the sky, but decades on the job give me a level of expertise not everyone has.

"It's heading toward town, Bash. Any help we can get will be an asset."

"I'll be there in thirty minutes," I say, stepping into the bar, where an eerie hush has fallen over the space. Usually, there'd be laughter, bowling balls clattering down the wooden alleys. But right now, there's just the low din of whispered conversation. Most heads are bent over their phones—some curious, some stricken with utter horror.

I reach our table, and the vibe is no different. Clyde and West look especially concerned as they move a map around on West's phone.

"They just issued a round of evacuation alerts," West says.

"Orders or alerts?" I ask. "Because those two things are very different."

"Order for anyone who lives on the back side of the mountain," West says.

All eyes slide to Clyde. His features remain blank, but lines of stress frame his eyes. And it pulls on something inside me. Even heading into a kidney transplant, he didn't look this worried.

He waves a hand. "Good news! I'm already evacuated." His words are meant to sound casual, but there's nothing light about the way he says them.

West adds, "Mine and Ford's properties are under alert, but right on the edge. If it moves down the highway, we'll be ordered too."

I nod at that. "Okay, alert isn't the end of the world. That means you've got time, things can change, orders can be lifted. Nothing is the end of the world."

"Yet," adds West.

The bite in his voice takes me aback, and my features must show it.

"Bash, I have thirty horses on my property. Less than half of them are mine. My trailer holds six. That means at least five trips there and back to wherever I can find that is able to take thirty horses in. And if we move to an order, the time crunch on that is going to mean leaving them behind."

"I'm sure we can work something out," Ford announces. "Let's start making calls, spread word online. People always band together in times like this. My property is easily evacuated. We can focus on helping yours."

West's typically carefree face has worry etched all over it. He shifts on his feet, almost pacing on the spot as he taps his fingers against his lips. "I'm thinking. I'm thinking," he says. "Everyone I know with a trailer will have their own animals to evacuate. I just… I gotta go."

He digs his keys out of his pocket and tosses down two twenties.

"Same," I say. "I'm heading down to the Forest Service offices to find out where they need me. I'm not flying until first light tomorrow."

I toss cash on the table, and West is already heading for

the door. "West," I say, raising my voice to grab his attention. He turns to face me, looking panicked. "I know someone who might be able to help. I'm going to call him."

He nods with a quick "appreciate it." Then he's gone.

I head out to my truck, where I call Emmett, one of my most tried-and-true friends. The world knows him as Emmett Bush, suave, cocky, championship bull rider. But I know him as Emmett Brandt, sarcastic, complicated, long-time friend.

"Call Emmett," I say, already backing out of my parking space. All my earlier worries are now buried by a crushing need to jump into action and do my part for our community.

The phone only rings twice before his voice spills through my truck speakers. Which, in his typical fashion, is to shit-talk.

"Why are you calling so late? Do you need me to sing you a bedtime song to help you sleep?"

"Cute, really cute, but I'm going to cut to the chase. We've got a bushfire burning on the back side of the mountain in Rose Hill."

"Oh shit." His tone turns serious.

"Yeah, and one of my best friends needs—"

"What the fuck, Bash? I thought I was your best friend."

"I said *one of*, you big baby." I can hear the low rumble of amusement from the other end of the line. "Anyway, if you're done being a territorial little bitch, I'll finish my story. One of my best friends runs a training operation, a ranch with thirty horses, and he's currently under an evacuation alert. It's not an order—"

"Yeah, but if it turns into one, he won't be able to get them all out," Emmett grumbles before I can even finish. With a family farm of his own in an area prone to fires, he knows the risks and the issues West faces. "Does he have a place to take the horses?"

"He's working on it," I reply.

"I'd offer up our place, but a trailerful is going to take five hours."

"Yeah," I say with a sigh. "And unfortunately, his trailer only hauls six."

"Shit. Well," Emmett says, and I can hear his feet stomping and the jingle of his keys in the background. "I've got an eight-horse, and I can be there in four hours. Send me the address."

"You just said five hours."

"Oh, nah. That's with a trailer full. Empty trailer, middle of the night, I'll be fast."

For a moment, I find myself smiling because that's just the type of guy Emmett Brandt is. Kind of an asshole, but you don't even need to ask for help before he's promising to show up anyway—shaving an hour off his travel time, no less.

I swear to god I could call him in the middle of the night and tell him I need to bury a body. The only thing he'd reply with is *on my way*.

"You're a lifesaver" is all I say to him before we hang up.

Then I'm speeding down the darkened road toward the office, praying things don't take a turn for the worse.

CHAPTER 40

Gwen

Being out with Rosie, Skylar, and Tabitha is good for me because they are all in fabulous, lighthearted moods, and all I can think about is marching up to Bash and punching his stupid, stubborn face for being so hard on himself.

And in turn, on us. It breaks my heart to see him so down. I want so badly to fix it all for him. But I can't—and that might be the hardest part of all.

I let out a beleaguered sigh and gaze across the bar, wondering if I should turn in and go curl up at home alone to lick my wounds in private.

Tabitha eyes me cautiously, no doubt picking up on my dour mood. But she doesn't call me on it. Instead, she just tops up my wine with a knowing wink.

Between bouts of lively conversation, I retreat into my head. And I think about Bash. It kills me that he's had to learn that people give up on him, that they walk away or use him as a stepping stone to the next best thing.

What's worse is that he can't see that he *is* the best thing for me. The one and only.

I was on the cusp of telling him that I'm in love with him, but I held back because it wasn't the right moment for it. I didn't want to tell him in the middle of a disagreement. I wanted to tell him when he was looking at me like he loves me too, not like my mere existence pains him.

So now I'm sitting at the Rose Hill Reach with my three sweet friends, who can't stop laughing over trivia while I stew over Sebastian fucking Rousseau—the man I love and also want to punch some sense into.

"All right." Doris's voice fills the bar. "The question was: *What is the driest place on earth?* The answer is the Atacama Desert—Team Four, you got it right. But I would like to give an honorable mention to Tabitha Garrison for submitting *Terence's bed* as the answer for Team Two."

Our entire table bursts out laughing. None of us knew the proper answer, so we'd agreed to ragging on the perennial town douchebag as our answer.

Totally worth it. If only to hear Doris's raspy cackle.

I feel my mood improve. It's impossible to watch these women's antics and not feel brighter. It's equally impossible to spend time around Doris without being amused.

Before the next round starts, Rosie gets up to go to the bathroom, and when she returns, her forehead is creased with worry, her blue eyes full of concern.

She slides into the booth and drops her voice low. "Okay, I know we're not supposed to be on our phones during trivia, but I checked mine in the bathroom and a huge fire has broken out on the back side of the mountain. Skylar, West's and Ford's properties are both under evacuation alert." Her gaze slides to me. "And, Gwen, Clyde's house is under evacuation *order*. It sounds like all buildings back in the trees are at risk."

Any lingering amusement I felt snaps, replaced by a jolt of icy dread.

"What?" My voice is thin, matching the shock I feel.

Rosie nods grimly. "Yeah, Bash is on his way to wherever firefighters go, and West is gone to figure out a way to evacuate all the horses off his property."

Skylar's eyes widen in horror, her dainty hand flying up to her mouth. "Oh my god," she whispers. "I have to go. I have to go help him. He's probably freaking out."

Tabby nods, blinking but not giving much away. She's always the practical, stoic one of the group, and in this moment she's no different.

"Okay, let's all go. I'm going to make sure the restaurant is open to evacuees for coffee and snacks and a place to sit, even if it's not as good as their own bed. At least it's somewhere safe to come together."

With that, we all stand at once, heads ducked low as we scurry out of the bar, missing out on the final rounds of trivia night. Doris catches us on our way out, grabbing Rosie by the wrist to stop her.

Her voice drops to a serious whisper. "You girls be careful out there." We nod in unison. "But, Rosie Belmont, if I catch you on your phone again during trivia night, I will ban you for life."

Rosie cracks a smile, a dry laugh, lurching from her throat. "You got yourself a deal, Doris."

We turn to leave again, but Doris isn't done. "And if you run into any hot firefighters out there in need of a place to rest their weary bones, you tell them that food and drinks are on me."

I chuckle at Doris's antics as we leave, but it's fleeting. The heavy weight of what's happening settles in my chest, adding another layer to what had already felt—to me, anyway—like a monumentally confusing night.

When I rush through the front door of Bash's lakefront home, I'm immediately searching for Clyde. I find him on the deck, settled in an Adirondack chair, smoking a joint. Quietly, I pad out the back door and fold myself into the seat next to him.

I reach across, my fingers curling around his hand where it rests against the arm of the chair. My lips part, ready to say *everything will be okay*, but I stop. Because I don't know that. I love Clyde too much to lie to him. And truthfully, it feels like I would be diminishing whatever turmoil he's feeling at this moment if I say something.

So I sit with him in silence, holding his weathered hand while he takes the odd puff. We both look out at the lake, the waves smashing against the shoreline as the wind whips across the water. I don't know if it's in my head, but I swear I can hear the faint crackle of flames spilling through the valley.

What isn't in my head is the smell of smoke, drowning out the fragrant scent of pine. It's unsettling to think that mere hours ago, my confrontation with Bash seemed like the most important thing in the world.

But now, sitting here with a man who's been more of a father to me in the last six months than my own father has been in my entire life, none of that feels like it matters.

When he finally stabs out the butt of his joint and drops it into the dregs of his water glass, I ask, "Want to do some yoga?"

He nods, solemn and steady. I push to standing and retrieve our mats, laying them out on the porch where we can look at the lake and seek a sliver of peace.

We both begin in a kneeling position, and I smile inwardly, watching how freely he moves compared to when we started together. It fills me with a deep satisfaction. I want to do something calming with him, to help keep our nervous systems regulated.

But then, like a hammer shattering a mirror, his raspy voice breaks the calm. "Everything from my Maya is in that house."

If I thought my heart was broken earlier, I realize now that it was only cracked. Because hearing Clyde's voice tremble, knowing he might lose every piece of his late wife, breaks it entirely.

"I'm so sorry" is my quiet reply.

He just nods, sniffing as he looks away, as if he's shielding me from his grief.

We flow through some moon salutations slowly, thoughtfully, leaning on the foundation of our friendship—unlikely as we may be.

ELSIE SILVER

Later that night, I hug him tightly before he goes to bed. He hugs me back the same way.

As I walk away from him, tears prick my eyes. I try to hold it together, but it doesn't work. Once I'm in Bash's bed, I cry.

When my eyes finally dry, I lie awake, tossing and turning. The helpless devastation I feel keeps me from sleeping.

I worry about Bash—who I haven't heard from—knowing he's out there facing this fire. I check the news repeatedly, and the images on social media do nothing to comfort me.

Everything feels terrifying. Everything feels fragile. I feel sad…and useless. Like I need to get up and *do* something.

And when I finally realize that I can't lie here doing nothing, I get out of bed and do something profoundly stupid instead.

CHAPTER 41

Bash

AFTER A LONG NIGHT OF GETTING SWEPT AWAY IN PREPARA-
tion for the morning, tactical meetings for tonight, and
calling in all the reinforcements we can get as the fire
spreads rapidly toward the town site, I am beat. Battling
fires is an emotionally draining job. But it's ten times
more intense when you know a monster like this is barreling toward *your* home.

I'm seated in a chair in Dale's office, where I must've
dozed off. Shaking off the grogginess of sleep, I check my
phone to find a text from Gwen. It appears that it came in
last night, but I'm not seeing it until now.

> **Gwen:** I heard you're going to help with the fire, and I
> just wanted you to know I'm heading home. I'll be
> here waiting for you.

I stare at her words, reading the meaning in them. Knowing her implication. She's not going anywhere—even if I'm being a raging asshole. I smile at the screen, then I'm pulled away by a voice outside that filters in from the side of the building. It's Dale, and his tone sounds stressed. Immediately on edge, I head out of the office and follow the sound.

As I step outside, the overwhelming smell of smoke slams into me like a wall. Light creeps over the mountain's edge, filtering through the dense smoke, creating an eerie, apocalyptic glow over the spring morning.

He ends a call when I round the corner. I nod at him and he starts right in with the bad news.

"By all accounts, shit is bad. And the night was rough. They had to draw back several times. Those trees are going up like matchsticks—forty feet in the air."

I grimace. There's nothing like the whoosh and pop of a bone-dry tree being taken over by flame to make you feel entirely powerless.

"I'll prep and make sure the other guys are ready to go. We've got a big tanker now too, yeah?" I ask.

He checks his watch and nods. "Landing in about thirty minutes."

I let out a sigh of relief. We both know that will make an enormous difference. A plane that size can scoop up a hell of a lot of water from the lake. It's truly ideal.

"Good. I'll get my shit together," I say, clapping his shoulder before turning to leave.

With what little time I have left before I hit the skies, I decide to stop off at West's farm and check in. All I know is that Emmett arrived early this morning, and they've already managed to each get one load out to a ranch about forty-five minutes down the road.

When I pull up, the first thing I see is an exhausted-looking Ford Grant stepping into his Mercedes G-Wagon. He has a small plastic box in his hand. I hop out, coffee in hand, squinting to get a better look. I can see a small, gray mouse inside the box.

When he catches me gawking, he deadpans, "Don't even fucking ask."

I hold my hands up innocently. "I wasn't going to," I lie before changing the subject. "Did you just get here?"

"No," he grumbles. "I've been here all fucking night trying to"—he holds his free hand up in air quotes—"'evacuate' Rosie's stupid mouse."

"Rosie's stupid mouse?"

Ford glares at me.

"You know what? You're right. I promised I wouldn't ask."

"Let the record show that I love Rosie enough to spend all night sitting quietly in a shitty little bunkhouse just so I can catch her favorite rodent."

Telling him about Sly is on the tip of my tongue, but I decide it's not the moment for it. "Is West here?"

"Yeah, your friend Emmett too. They're down at the barn. Thanks for calling him. That's made a huge difference for West. Seems like a good dude."

I nod at that. "Just doing my part."

Ford and I say our goodbyes, and I watch him drive away

with a mouse in his Mercedes before I head up to the stables. Just listening to Ford mention Rosie has my brain circling back to Gwen and how we left things between us.

It's uncomfortable and not ideal, but I know my focus is needed on the fire right now. Once that's dealt with, I can pivot to Gwen and fixing everything that I fucked up yesterday.

Up at the barn, I find West and Emmett strategizing which horses to put into which rig, how much feed to take with each one, and a dozen other things I never thought about.

Emmett stands with his hip cocked and his arms crossed, wearing that signature blank expression on his face. Happy, sad, excited—it's all the same look with this man. Unless, of course, he's spotted a beautiful woman in the vicinity. Then, the most dazzling TV-worthy smile appears on cue. Where I struggle with talking to women, Emmett does not. That much has become abundantly clear in the times we've been out together.

"I say take it all," he carries on. "No point in leaving the hay to get burned if it does end up that way."

West looks ghostly white, like the prospect of everything burning is gutting to him. Emmett faced this years back, when we first met. In fact, fires are a common occurrence in Emerald Lake. So I'm not surprised by the level of detachment he takes in talking about it. For West, though, this is not the norm.

"Okay, yeah," West says, his voice edged with nervousness. "Let's load it up."

Emmett gives him a nod before springing into action, which is when they both catch sight of me.

"You fellas both making out okay?" I ask.

"Yep, got one load out," West replies with a slight hitch in his voice.

Emmett swoops in with a reassuring "And now we're gonna get the rest. It's not even a question. Every last horse is getting out safe."

West's Adam's apple bobs at that. Then he focuses on me. "How's the fire?"

I shrug, not wanting to lie to him but not wanting to add any more pressure than he's clearly already under. "You know, it's not good. But I haven't been up in the air, so I can't say for sure. Once I know, I'll touch base with you. Is there anything I can do? I need to head to the airstrip soon."

Both guys shake their heads just as my phone rings.

When I see Clyde's name, I answer immediately.

His typically creaky voice holds an edge of panic when he says "Bash?" before I've even said hello.

"Clyde, what's wrong?" I don't know why I ask it. All I know is that I can tell something is wrong.

"I can't find Gwen."

My brows furrow. "What do you mean you can't find Gwen?"

"Well, you know, I couldn't sleep, so I woke, figured I'd take a walk down the driveway and see if I could spot the fire over the back rise. That's when I realized her truck was gone, which I found suspicious because we both went to bed at the same time last night. So then I came back in the house, calling for her, and made my way upstairs. Sorry, I looked in your room."

Panic rises in his voice as he lists all the places he's searched, and it's an exact reflection of mine. "Checked her room. Checked the front deck. Checked down by the lake where she likes to put her feet in the sand. I checked *everywhere*. She's not answering my phone calls, they're going straight to voicemail, and I don't think she's here."

My heart drops lower and lower with every sentence until it feels like it might seize up entirely at the prospect of Gwen being missing.

"But the thing I keep coming back to is that her truck's not here. So she has to be out, right?"

I scoff, lifting one hand to the back of my neck as a knot of anxiety pulls tight in my chest. I tug at the short ends of my hair as I rack my brain for where she might have gone. "I don't know, Clyde. I don't know. Have you talked to Tabby or Rosie or Skylar?"

"No, I don't have all their numbers. The thing is…" The way he trails off has my stomach falling down to the floor.

"What's the thing, Clyde?"

"The thing is, last night when she came home, I was… Well, you know, I was feeling down about the possibilities of what could happen to my house. In a dark moment, I kind of said something about that all my stuff was there, everything from Maya. Just sort of having a moment about losing all those memories."

My heart comes back to life but not in a good way. Now it's thudding painfully in my chest, adrenaline coursing through my veins as I travel down the path he's laid out for me.

"Wait, you think she went to your place?"

He makes a soft keening sound. "Fuck, Bash, I don't know. But she looked tearful when we went to bed, and she gave me an unusually tight hug. And I don't know, I just… I'm worried."

My stomach turns over on itself. Clyde left her with a hug, and I left her with *guess you did warn me you don't stay in one place for long.*

Regret pummels me from every direction. Pressure constricting around my skull until I can barely think straight.

That can't be how I left things with us. I never even answered her goddamn text.

But if Clyde is worried, that means I should be very, very worried.

I spring into action. Years of working under pressure snap me back to reality.

"Okay, Clyde, please, whatever you do, stay where you are. Because if she comes home, you're the person who needs to tell me. I'm going to start calling around. I'll stay in touch with you. But I need to go up in the air soon, which means I'll be out of contact for a while."

"Okay, okay," he says, his voice shaking a bit. "I promise I won't go anywhere."

"I mean it, Clyde. Don't even go out on the patio to sun your perineum. Just be ready by a phone, okay?"

"Okay," he says.

"And, Clyde, no matter what, while I'm up there, I promise to fly over your place. I'll check, okay?"

"Okay," he says, voice cracking with emotion. "But, Bash?"

"Yeah?"

"Find Gwen first."

With that, I hang up. Because if I have to listen to Clyde cry, I might lose it too.

I call Gwen immediately, almost hurling my coffee onto the gravel when it doesn't even ring. Straight to voicemail, just like Clyde said.

Needing to keep focused, I pull up my contact list and start going through everyone who might know Gwen's whereabouts.

The first person I check with is Tabitha, because I know she attends Gwen's yoga classes and they've forged something of a friendship.

She answers her phone, sounding tired, but confirms with a nervous voice that she hasn't seen or heard from Gwen. The results are much the same when I call Rosie and Skylar in turn. All nervous. All tired and all pleading with me to give them an update and promising to do the same if they hear anything.

Truth be told, I don't know who else to call. I phone the emergency shelter, but no one with her name has checked in.

As I turn to join Emmett and West, I hear the crunch of tires pulling up to the barn. It's Tripp Coleman, driving right toward me.

He steps out of his car, wearing a sweatsuit, sneakers, and the world's most dramatic eye roll. "My God, you're fucking everywhere," he groans.

"What are you doing here?" I grumble before realizing

he's the only person I haven't called that might know where Gwen is.

"Well, despite the fact that you clearly think I'm a shitty person, I've been up watching the news all night, and I figured I might as well help out since I'm here. So I went down to the community hall, and they sent me here to help load straw bales."

I'm shaken. Why was he even still here? I'd expected him to burn straight out of town and never look back.

He wants a relationship with you too. Gwen's words filter in from my memories.

But all I do is correct him with "Hay bales."

"What-the-fuck ever, man. As if it makes a difference. Just let me do my thing."

He goes to brush past me, but I grab him by the arm, stopping him in his tracks. He looks down at my hand, like I've somehow gravely offended him.

"Don't touch me," he spits, clearly still furious with me for what happened with Gwen.

"Tripp, for fuck's sake, can we please put our differences aside for a moment? I need you to tell me honestly if you've seen Gwen."

"Why would I have seen Gwen? She's made it clear she only wants to spend time with me if it's in your presence."

My breath hitches as my lungs tighten. My god, I've fucked up so badly.

"She's missing," I rasp. "She went to bed at the house last night, and this morning she's not there. Her truck's not there either."

The look of disgust on his face morphs into one of concern. "You haven't heard from her at all?"

"No," I groan, gripping the back of my neck just for something to do with worried hands. "We had a disagreement, and both took a moment to get some air. And now I don't know where she is. She's not answering her phone. Her last text to me said she'd be at home. None of her friends know where she is. I just thought that you might have some idea."

The tension in his shoulders loosens, and they drop down subtly. "I'm sorry, but I don't know where she is. I haven't heard from her since we had a coffee yesterday afternoon."

Both my hands rake through my hair as I turn in a circle, looking around myself as if I might be able to see her somewhere near the tree line or find her at the top of the driveway. Like she might pop up and be fine. But instead, the woman who is the love of my life is missing during a major natural disaster.

It doesn't feel real.

I feel a hand clamp onto my shoulder from behind and turn to see Emmett with a somber expression on his face. "Dude, go. I got this. You have zero game. If there's a girl who actually likes you, you need to go find her."

I press the heels of my palms into my eyes. Leave it to fucking Emmett to shit-talk me at a moment like this. Strangely, it's comforting. If he went all soft on me, it would only stress me out more.

Tripp chuckles and it rankles me, but Emmett doesn't let

him get away with it. "What are you laughing at, pretty boy? The hay bales are over there. Get to work." Emmett points toward the barn, effectively dismissing Tripp before turning to follow him.

And I watch them walk away.

There's a part of me that's surprised Tripp showed up here today. It makes me realize that I don't know him as well as I thought.

Maybe Gwen was right.

And maybe I'll never get the chance to tell her as much.

From up in the air, I have a clear view of the devastation. And while I usually fly feeling relatively cool, calm, and collected, today my heart is in my throat. My nerves are so raw that, even strapped in, I can barely sit still.

When I took off from the airstrip, Gwen was still nowhere to be found. I checked again with the community center, told the other pilots to keep their eyes peeled for her truck, then made my way to the fire service aircraft and got to work.

Without knowing where she is, there's nothing I can do, and feeling this out of control is one of my worst nightmares.

At least if I'm helping, I'm doing something. Because, god, I really need to be doing something so I don't just collapse.

From this altitude, I can see the damage this fire has wreaked. It stretches over the back side of the sprawling mountain, through the valley, and up over the next. It wraps around the side, encroaching on the main feeder highway in and out of Rose Hill.

I don't know exactly how many hectares we're at now, but in the privacy of my cockpit, I curse under my breath, admitting to myself that this is bigger than I thought. So much worse than I imagined.

I should be working on an indirect attack to set our firebreak. We have clear orders—a plan. Create a buffer zone to slow the spread.

But for the first time in my life, I don't give a fuck about being responsible. My focus is single-minded—and it's not on the job. It's on Gwen.

I can't work without finding her. Hell, I can barely breathe, and it has nothing to do with the ominous blanket of smoke. All I can think about is getting a good look at Clyde's place to see if she might be there.

It's not part of the strategy Dale and I discussed before attacking the mountain.

But the truth is, I might let it all burn if it means finding her.

If Gwen is gone, nothing else matters.

Having checked along the highway, I give in to my instincts and turn my aircraft toward the peak of the mountain, knowing that I won't have to go far over that side to get a good look at Clyde's property.

The engine hums and my seat shakes as I fly low over the burning brush and glowing embers. I see the blue tin roof that adorns Clyde's small log house, and I sit forward in my seat, pressing the plane faster to catch sight of it as quickly as possible.

It appears that much of what surrounds Clyde's home has been burned to a crisp. The earth scorched black. The trees reduced to ash…but not his house. The yard surrounding it has miraculously held the fire line.

My limbs feel like lead and I find myself praying for another miracle. Eyes scanning frantically, fingers gripped tight.

I draw closer, and I see it.

Her truck.

Nausea twists in my gut and I have to fight the urge to throw myself from this plane just to get to her. *What was she thinking?*

I drop lower, hoping to catch sight of her, wanting to both shake her and hold her tight in equal parts.

I take one pass over the house, realizing that the opposite side is not as severely burned. It appears the area around the creek off toward the back of his property has been less affected.

Then I catch sight of her—a flash of silvery-blond hair pulled up in a high ponytail. I turn hard, looping back around to circle the property, and based on the way she holds a hand up to her forehead, I know she sees me.

Relief and dread hit me all at once. I found her. But she's closed in. The property is surrounded by flames on all sides.

Frantically, I search the area, wondering if there's somewhere I can land. I want to go down there and pull her out myself, but it's futile and I know it. It's too densely forested. There's nowhere for me to put a plane down here.

Picking up my radio, I call for backup. I share my

coordinates and let the guys know there's a civilian trapped on an evacuated property.

Within seconds, I get confirmation that aerial support is on its way.

I start laying out a plan for how to have her make an exit from the property. The radio confirms that they'll be ready to send a rescue vehicle past the blockade and up in that direction. As long as there's a clear path, they will go in and escort her down.

As I watch the markers for other planes approaching on the radar, I push away the fear coursing through my veins and all the worst-case scenarios playing through my head.

If they need a clear path to get her out, I'll make one myself.

CHAPTER 42

Gwen

AFTER A LONG AND ANXIETY-INDUCING NIGHT SPENT WITH no cell phone connection and an out-of-control wildfire blocking my escape, I take a break from berating myself for being so impulsive and emotionally charged to gaze at the aircraft above me.

Hope courses through me. Like jumping into cool water on a hot day. It soothes, it refreshes, it makes tears leap to my eyes.

"Bash," I murmur, holding a hand to my forehead and watching the plane with a provincial logo flying low overhead.

The relief I feel at the sight of what I just *know* is him is monumental and unlike anything I've ever felt before.

After loading up my truck with every remotely sentimental thing I could find, I spent the entire night adjusting sprinklers and hoses around Clyde's property in a desperate attempt to save his home.

I figured the trees were basically kindling after the dry spring, but the grass was just as dehydrated. Until I got to soaking it.

At some point, I discovered that if I *had* to make my escape, I could leave down the creek on foot and it would take me in the opposite direction of the fire. It would be risky, though. Phone service is out and I have no idea where I'm going and all that would have to change is the direction of the wind…then I'd have a monster of a wildfire pursuing me.

When I attempted driving back down the road that leads here, I found the fire was encroaching on both sides. I realized that if I hit a dead end or a downed tree, I could be stuck in a much more compromising position than I already was.

Ultimately, after weighing my options, I employed the method for if you get separated from your parent in the grocery store.

Stay where you are.

So I sat in my truck, tried to meditate, and failed. I thought about Bash, about our dispute and the tense note we left things on. It made me realize how inconsequential all of that felt in the face of something this terrifying.

I don't want to say those disagreements don't matter. It's just that they feel a lot less important when you're faced with the possibility of dying and leaving the man you love behind.

I don't take back what I told him, but I spent many hours wishing that I hadn't walked out. That I'd pulled up a stool and waited him out.

That I'd been brave enough to stay, that I hadn't given in to my instinct to run.

He takes another low swoop over, and I watch with butterflies in my chest and tears on my cheeks.

Soon, two more planes join him, slightly different in design and size. A voice crackles from a speaker in one, telling me to get in my vehicle.

I wave up at the airplane, showing my agreement, and jog toward my truck. Within minutes, the planes zip over and liquid splatters across the roof. Droplets from it streak down my windshield. I drop my head against the headrest and shame-spiral, feeling guilty for all the resources I'm taking up.

All because I'm a big old bleeding heart with an impulsive streak.

But what's done is done, and I'm not about to turn away rescue when the universe plunks it in my lap.

Time blurs as I sit in my truck. I alternate between closing my eyes, trying to dissociate to ease my fear, and looking out to see if anything's changed.

Eventually, the roar of the planes recedes and everything grows quiet, leaving only the crackle of the nearby fire. Movement at the end of the driveway draws my attention, and a compact fire rescue vehicle careens onto the property.

It stops right beside me, and a female police officer climbs out, along with a man dressed similarly to Bash— only his shirt reads *Alberta Wildfire*.

He rounds the front of the vehicle and jogs toward me as I roll down the window. "Gwen?" he asks.

"Yeah, that's me," I say, trying not to give in to the welling tears in my eyes. There's an embroidered patch over his heart that spells out *Eaton* and I focus on that instead.

"So glad we found you." He smiles, and it might be the most reassuring smile in the world. Something about him screams *confident and capable*, and it eases the knot in my chest.

He reaches a hand toward me. "Hi. I'm Beau. Here to help you out. What do you say we get the hell off this mountain?"

I shake his hand through the open window, grateful. "Sounds like a really, really great plan. You are officially my hero."

"Ah, I don't know if I would take it that far. I just got in from out of province to help out, walked into the station to hear a fella up in one of those planes losing his goddamn mind on the radio over finding you. Figured I could make a detour on my way to the front lines."

I wince. "Sorry. Is he being a nightmare?"

The man grins. "Nah. I'd be the same over my girl too."

I blink at him, too stunned to know how to respond, but he forges ahead, unconcerned by silence. "Are you good to follow us down, or do you want me to hop in with you?"

"Oh, no. I'm okay to follow you down."

"The guys in the air cleared the road, so we should be good to go. It was fine coming up, but we'll want to get down before anything changes."

I nod quickly, reaching for the keys and starting my engine. "Let's go, then."

When the road shifts from gravel and winding to smooth and paved, I heave out a sigh of relief.

With the red truck before me and the fire behind me, exhaustion hits me hard and fast.

Up ahead, I spot the blockade—that wasn't there last night—and two cop cars stretching across the road, lights flashing.

Just beyond it, I see a black truck that I'd recognize anywhere.

Relief courses through me at the sight of the man who comes into focus as I draw nearer. Bash, standing with his hands linked behind his head, his body coiled with tension as he stares straight ahead like he's trying to will me into existence.

The second he sees my truck, he goes from pacing on the spot to gunning for me.

Bash pushes his way past the cars and weaves past the barricades the second we slow. My eyes sting as I watch him run to me. Strong, stoic, and fucking frantic.

The minute I'm close enough to the barricade, I throw my truck in park and open the door, leaving the engine running as I step out onto the asphalt.

Within seconds, he's there. In the flesh. Right in front of me.

Reaching for me. Yanking me into his arms as I wrap my own around his neck. He crushes me against him so tight, it takes my breath away. I don't even mind. It's the perfect reminder that I'm alive.

I breathe him in. And while the air smells like smoke, he smells like him.

He smells like the forest, like trees and amber and gasoline and home.

"I'm so sorry," I cry as he buries his face in my neck.

He says nothing, but I feel his head shake as he holds me in a vise grip.

"I'm so sorry, I'm so sorry," I chant, not knowing what else to tell him.

He still says nothing, but I feel wetness on my neck, a warm trickle rolling down the slope toward my shoulder.

A punch to the gut.

I squeeze him back tighter, pressing myself closer, rubbing my cheek against him. Wishing I could somehow merge myself with him right here and now, undo the hurt and fear I caused.

"Bash. I wasn't… I'm just…" I pull back, wanting to find the right thing to say to him but not knowing where to start.

Tears have clumped his lashes together, and they trickle down his roughly hewn cheeks and freshly shaven jaw.

He looks me over with watery eyes, tracing me as though he's checking for any injury. His hands follow too, fluttering over my arms and across my shoulders. Like he needs proof.

"I'm fine, I'm fine," I say. "I'm sorry, but I'm good. I promise."

God, watching him look so distraught is breaking my heart, and I need to explain myself. "I didn't know. There was no blockade in place when I went up last night. I thought I was—"

"Gwen." The way he says my name stops me in my tracks. It's a plea on his lips, full of so much emotion. "I'm the one who's sorry. I was out of line, overtired, and not myself. I should never have let that all get in my head. I'm just terrified of fucking this all up."

I meet his dark, imploring eyes. He grips my shoulders and gives me a gentle shake, as though checking to see if I'm truly standing before him. His head shakes and his gaze drinks me in. "You're a fucking wild card. Unpredictable and never what I expect. You scare the hell out of me every damn day. But today more than any of them. Because I thought I lost you." His voice cracks. So does my heart. "And I love you, and I hadn't even gotten the chance to tell you."

My heart thuds and my tears finally fall.

He loves me.

There's nothing showy about it. It's not some big declaration, it's not poetic or flowery, but with him it doesn't need to be. Everything with him is dressed down. Beautiful in its simplicity.

He swallows and blinks rapidly, trying and failing to hide his emotion. Another gentle shake. "Never scare me like that again. *Never.*"

Tears tumble over my cheeks as I nod quickly. "I love you too. I do. I have for a long time. And I promise I won't ever scare you like that again. I promise."

I'm finally saying the words that have been trapped inside me for I don't know how long. Words I've mulled over but never spent much time analyzing. Maybe because it just seemed too…obvious. Like, *of course* I'm in love with him. And of course he's in love with me. Why else would we be risking it all for a shot at making this thing work?

He sighs in relief and then he's back to squeezing me. And just beyond him, I see Tripp. Watching from the passenger seat of Bash's truck, looking pale as a ghost. He makes no move to get out of the vehicle, but he gives me a subtle salute with his hand.

"I love you so fucking much," Bash rasps against my hair, hands gliding over the back of my head, my spine, as though having to feel me to know that I'm real. "I didn't know where you were. You could have died. I could have lost you. And all I could think was the last thing I'd have said to you was that you never stay anywhere for long. I told you to wait for me and then I told you to leave. And I… Gwen, I *need* you. Like my next breath. It's… I can't breathe without you. If you leave for Costa Rica, I'm coming with you. Where you go, I'll follow. I don't care where we are as long as we're together."

I squeeze him back harder, feeling my own tears as they soak into his shirt. He'd said that in the heat of our argument, and I hadn't believed him for a single moment. "Okay, but where I want to be is here. With you. I already backed out of that job. I'm staying here. With you. Always. I need you too. That's why I'm never waiting *on* you. I'm living *with* you."

A rough sob lurches from his throat, and he buries his face in my neck, letting me hold him as tight as I want.

"You're my limes, Bash. I'm the tequila. You and me? We're gonna spend the rest of our lives making margaritas, okay?"

I can tell he's about to respond when I hear Beau's voice from behind me. "Ma'am, do you have marijuana plants in the back of your truck?"

Bash pulls back ever so slightly, our watery eyes meeting tenderly as I shrug. "Sorry, I couldn't leave Maya's babies behind."

Bash pulls me in again now, a tearful chuckle getting lost in the strands of my hair. "Like I said, a fucking wild card."

I'm driven back to the fire hall. Tripp takes Bash's truck while Bash drives mine, our hands gripped together over the center console the entire way.

We drive in silence for the first bit, and then, finally, Bash asks me what I know he's been thinking since he found out I was missing. "What the hell were you thinking, Gwen?"

I sigh, my eyes fluttering shut as my head rests against the back of the seat. "I wasn't. I was already emotional from our spat, and then Clyde was just so broken up over his only memories of Maya being at his place. I went to bed. I wasn't going to do anything. But then I couldn't sleep. I thought about how I've moved around constantly and how I don't really have any physical objects that hold any kind of sentimental value to me."

His thumb caresses my hand, and I continue. "And then I thought about Clyde, this funny old man who seems so tough and never worries about anything. He spends all this time alone, and he must have really loved Maya to have never moved on. And it broke my heart. It got me thinking about you and me, and the connections we make in life, and how he might never have that again. But he does have those pictures. And I just went without thinking.

"There was no blockade on the road. I drove straight up, and everything was fine. I packed up the truck, and then I thought, you know, what if I put some sprinklers on? Maybe it could save his place. I knew it would drain the well, but—"

Bash's hand squeezes mine. "It did save the place."

"What?" I turn wide eyes on Bash.

"I'm not sure you realize how close that fire came, but the amount that you soaked the surrounding ground definitely made a difference. It's blocked off now, and I can't make any promises. But yes, currently you have saved Clyde's place—and also shaved ten years off my life."

One stray tear trickles down my cheek, and I brush it away quickly. *Relief.* I feel intense relief.

Bash glances over at me as he continues. "I fucking hate that you went missing," he says, "but I have to confess, if I'd been in your shoes, I might have done the same thing."

"Oh good. We both have a hero complex," I tease as we turn into the local fire hall.

"Let's get you checked over," he says in a way that leaves no room for argument.

And from there, I'm led out of my truck and into the hall. A paramedic checks my blood pressure and my heartbeat. He asks if I've been injured, which of course I haven't. But Bash hovers like an overprotective bodyguard all the same.

He reminds them to check my breathing, to check my eyes, goes on about how smoke inhalation can manifest in different ways. I assure him I'm fine, but until I've been fully cleared, he doesn't back down.

It's only when the paramedic leaves that we find Tripp standing quietly in the doorway, his shoulder propped against the frame. His eyes flick between us, his expression unreadable.

I drop my gaze from him, guilt surging inside me. Bash opens his mouth to say something, but his son speaks first.

"Listen," Tripp says, his footsteps scuffing softly against the floor as he moves toward us in the nearly empty room. Only a foldout table and matching folding chairs fill the space. "I owe you both an apology."

Bash and I both stare at him, surprised by that statement.

"If I'm being honest, I don't know much about either of you. Bash, we've barely spent any time together. And, Gwen, you're right—we were never serious. And I let some weird sense of competition make me act like an idiot. This year has been..." He huffs a laugh and looks away for a beat, wiping quickly at his nose. "A lot. Confusing in a lot of ways. But, Bash, I watched you today, and there was nothing confusing about it. You made endless phone calls. You paced. You yelled. You called in favors. You broke protocol, all just to get Gwen back. And that...that's not something that I can even pretend I've felt before. And more than that, it's not something I'd ever want to get in the way of."

He turns and looks at me now. "Gwen, you're a great person. I do know that much about you. And I wish I knew what it felt like to love somebody the way Bash clearly loves you. So I just want you both to know you have my blessing.

I'm not angry. But I am…" He trails off and lifts a hand, rubbing it over his chin thoughtfully.

I can't help but notice the pieces of hay sticking out of his expensive sweatsuit, and I wonder what he's been up to because he would never be seen looking anything less than polished. But he doesn't seem to care right now. He concentrates hard, silently searching for the words to express himself.

"I'm going to… I don't know. I'm going to need some time to adjust to this. Get my head on straight. I want this to be okay, but it might take me a beat to come to terms with it all."

We both stare at him blankly. I can't speak for Bash, but I know that this is not what I was expecting from Tripp.

"Thank you, Tripp," I say softly.

Bash nods his head in agreement. "Thank you, Tripp. And thank you for your help today. You really stepped up. And I know you've already got a dad to be proud of you, but if you wanted some random guy you barely know to be proud of you too, well, your dreams have come true."

Tripp lets out a dry chuckle, rolling his eyes. "I'll take that. But you really aren't so random, you know. A second dad might be all right. Eventually."

Bash smiles, looking a bit overwhelmed by the moment.

But, of course, Tripp has to offset that by adding, "Gwen, I'm never calling you Mom, though."

I burst out laughing, overcome by exhaustion and the aftereffects of high adrenaline.

With that, Tripp grins and waves. "I'm heading out. See

if they need more help at the farm. You two… I don't know. You two have fun. Or something, I guess."

His face crinkles up, awkwardness tinging the moment, and he turns, leaving us to watch him go. Our breathing is the only sound in the quiet room. The busy chatter of the community center drifts in from the door, a reminder of everything still spinning outside this bubble.

Unexpectedly, Bash drops to his knees in front of me. He rests his head in my lap and wraps his arms around my calves, letting out a deep, heavy sigh. I bow my head closer to his and trail my fingers through his hair. He smells like smoke and engine oil and the soft bristles against my fingertips provide a comfort. He grounds me.

I breathe him in. I breathe my anxiety out.

I breathe him in. I breathe my doubt out.

I breathe him in. I breathe my fears out.

Because with Bash at my side, nothing feels as terrifying.

"I'm never going to run again, okay?" I say, hoping he understands what I mean.

I feel his head nod against the tops of my thighs. "Good, because I'm never letting you go."

CHAPTER 43

Bash

I sit on the front porch, staring out over the lake, but my eyes constantly drop to the left, where I built Gwen a small studio of her own.

I know she's in there, teaching an online class, but I wait and watch for her anyway.

It's been three months since the fire. Three months of us picking up the pieces of our relationship and piecing something together that feels awfully stable. More stable than anything either one of us has ever had.

Gwen promised not to run, and I promised not to let her go, and that's what we've done.

The truth is, I'd follow her anywhere. If she runs, I run too.

But we don't run; we stay.

I built her a studio where she can teach. We even picked plans that would match the main house, and I built it by hand. Every beam, every nail, placed with her in mind. Inside, the floor is heated, and I painted the walls a soft lavender. It's an open space with floor-to-ceiling windows that face out toward the water, flooding the studio with light. It's a perfect, peaceful, sun-drenched retreat for Gwen, as she makes my home her own.

Eventually, I hear the door below open and watch as her flash of blond hair appears around the corner. It's pulled back in a perfectly smooth french braid, and she's wearing a bright-purple matching yoga set—a crop top and leggings that hug her curves in the best way. She's got a water bottle in one hand and a coffee mug in the other, rosy cheeks and sparkling eyes.

She catches sight of me on the balcony and grins. "Are you stalking me?"

I lift my coffee in a silent cheers. "Of course. It's one of my favorite pastimes."

"Creepy." She winks. "But I like it."

At that, she makes her way back into the house, and soon she's seated beside me in the Adirondack chair to my right with her coffee in hand.

"I took a quick phone call after my class in there."

I turn and quirk a brow in her direction. "Oh yeah?"

She nods, letting out a little hum before taking a sip of her coffee. "Yeah, since I'm finally settling down with you, I should put down some roots in Rose Hill."

I swallow. Not sure what to say to that.

She's stayed. She hasn't moved on. She's kept doing what she's doing.

But I have a feeling that she thinks nothing here is really hers.

She moved into my house, become friends with my friends, and took a temporary teaching job at a studio that isn't hers. It was part of the reason I built her the studio, so she felt like she had something all her own. A place she could claim.

Which is why my chest hums with satisfaction when she says, "Kira called from the studio. She was wondering if I might want to buy it."

I freeze mid-sip, not sure how to react to that. "And?" I ask, leaving room for her to go in any direction she wants.

She smiles softly with a subtle shrug. "It might be a good idea. I could see myself doing that. I've got my personal studio here, and I can keep teaching my classes in town. It gives me something to do other than just lie around, gawking at my hot-ass boyfriend all the time."

That makes me grin. "Your hot-ass boyfriend has something to confess."

"Ooh, juicy. Do tell."

"Clyde asked if you could be his date, since I'm in the party for Ford and Rosie's wedding. And I said yes without asking you."

She throws her head back and laughs. "What a chicken-shit! He could have asked me when we were at his place for dinner two nights ago. But is that going to make you jealous if I show up with him?"

I chuckle. "Of course, but I'll keep my temper under control for the sake of appearances."

She taps her lips thoughtfully. "Maybe I could take *two* dates to the wedding. You *and* Clyde. I'd be the envy of everyone there."

I shake my head and grin because this prospect would excite only Gwen. It's one of the many, many things I love about her.

A zest for life.

A glass-half-full attitude.

Her passion for making margaritas out of limes.

She has the special gift of making everything around her better.

Including me.

It's late and the band at Ford and Rosie's wedding is fun and loud and making me feel like an old man. I've been up doing my groomsman duties with West and Rhys all day long, and now at eleven o'clock, I have officially decided that it's past my bedtime.

From where I'm seated at the head table, I can see Gwen dancing with Clyde. Her head thrown back in laughter. She *glows*.

And she does nothing to help with my train of thought. The one that keeps wandering back to what it might be like to be married to Gwen. What our wedding day would be like. What she'd wear. Where we'd host it.

I feel like a lovesick teenager who can't stop dreaming about her wedding day. West even busted me doing a very impromptu online search for engagement rings. Something he's been teasing me about all day now.

Chuckling at the memory of him exclaiming, *Yes, Bash! I thought you would never ask!* I push to stand and sneak out of the massive, white tent. Seeking a little space and fresh air.

I catch sight of the lake, and like always, I'm drawn to it. Like Gwen, it soothes me. The sound, the sight, the smell. Even the color of it when light reflects off the top—light purple.

Stepping down the embankment, my dress shoes hit the sand, and I feel instantly ridiculous. Who the hell wears dress shoes at the beach? Gwen would mock me mercilessly for this. So I crouch down to unlace them, only to come up short when I hear her voice.

"Where the hell do you think you're going? Are you putting your feet in the sand without me?"

I turn and look over my shoulder at her. The pink dress she's wearing is dotted in a small floral print and does the most incredible things for her tits.

Looking her in the eyes—beautiful as they are—has been a struggle all night long. Especially now, with the moonlight highlighting the sinful curve of her cleavage.

"Are you stalking me? Because I hope so," I volley, shooting her a playful grin before taking her hand to help her down the embankment.

"Nah. I just suddenly couldn't feel the heavy weight of you staring at my chest and got to wondering where you went."

I snort at that but don't bother denying it. Then I bend down to remove her sandals before finally ditching my own shoes and socks.

Hand in hand, we walk toward the edge of the lake, the sounds of water lapping against the sand only slightly louder than the band that plays up the slope.

Several minutes pass in a companionable silence. I soak up the calm of the night, sinking my toes into the sand. Feeling the earth beneath me. I relax so completely that the minutes just bleed together, a deep sense of peace coursing through me.

"I love it here," she finally whispers.

"It's beautiful," I reply simply.

"No. I mean here. With you. This life. I love it all."

I turn now, taking in her profile. The dip of her pert nose, the roundness in her cheeks. Her long lashes laid over them as she speaks with her eyes closed.

It hits me that I'd give her anything. Everything. But hearing that she loves what we're building? It fills me with so much pride that I could burst.

"What do you want out of this life together?"

Her eyes flutter open at my question as she turns her heart-shaped face up to mine. Her gaze rakes over my face as though she's memorizing this moment. "Adventure. Big, small. I want to go on every adventure life has to offer. With you."

Our hands pulse as one. Each of us giving the other a reassuring squeeze at the exact same moment.

It's the perfect answer. So perfectly her. An invite to spend my life going on adventures with Gwen?

"I can't think of anything better."

EPILOGUE

Bash

ONE YEAR LATER...

I HOLD THE BALL UP IN FRONT OF MY FACE, GAZE LASER focused toward the end of the lane, and take a deep, centering breath.

I can do this.

I can do this.

I can do this.

I feel Rhys sidle up next to me, lighter on his feet than he has any right to be. "Listen," he whispers gruffly. "I don't want to put any extra pressure on you, but if you fuck this up, I might never forgive you."

My eyes slice in his direction. "Fuck off, Dupris" is all I give him, which only makes him laugh and back away with hands up in surrender. I can hear a chorus of chuckles from our table. Ford, West, Rhys, and Clyde (who is here as our self-proclaimed "coach") sit and watch. Hell, even Tripp came into town to watch this all go down.

Dads' Night Out.

Beers, bowling, and buddies was how West originally sold it to me, and that's exactly what it has become—plus a little bit more.

It's become community, friendship, and a deep sense of shared hatred for Stretch and his stupid fucking bowling team, the High Rollers.

So tonight, I need to bring it home for my team—the Ball Busters. Because if Stretch and his team get a three-peat, I will break something.

It's all down to me in the final, and the odds aren't exactly in my favor. I need a spare to take the win. And though I might be the best on the team, getting a spare under this kind of pressure feels impossible.

I return to focusing on the pins before me. Still, I can feel the weight of my teammates' gazes on my back. We've been at this for a few years now and have finally clawed our way to the championship match.

What do we win? A shitty trophy, a hundred-dollar gift card to the bar, and bragging rights. Which is really what I'm after if I'm being honest.

I square my shoulders and begin my approach. One step. Two steps. Swing back.

Release.

I point my hand straight after the ball and hold my breath, along with everyone else in Rose Valley Alley. I swear the ball rolls down the lane in slow motion, turn after turn, as I will it to hit in the middle of the V.

"Come on," I mutter under my breath. "Fucking do it."

And like I'm some sort of bona fide bowling-ball whisperer, it does.

The ball hits hard—but not too hard—and the sweet sound of pins toppling fills the silent bar. There's a communal intake of breath as we all watch them fall and then chaos.

Everyone in the place—save for Stretch and his shitty teammates—erupts into cheers as every last pin falls.

I turn back to the guys with my arms stretched up above my head victoriously and a shocked grin on my face.

"That's my daddy!" West shouts as he practically launches himself at me, knocking me backward with the force of his hug.

Ford approaches next, giving me a reserved clap on the shoulder, a satisfied smirk touching his mouth. Clyde and Tripp come next, both outlandishly excited for me.

Nothing quite like being congratulated by an actual professional athlete for winning a small-town men's bowling league.

It's Rhys who hangs back, arms crossed, watching Stretch while chuckling to himself.

Stretch, who, in a fit of frustration, has swept all of his teammates' drinks off the table and onto the floor like a child throwing a tantrum.

When Rhys finally does stroll over and join the team huddle, he says, "Goddamn, that was satisfying."

And I can't help but agree. But it's not just the victory—it's that this tradition and these friends have turned out to be one of the most rewarding things in my life.

WILD CARD

TWO YEARS LATER...

"Happy birthday, Gwen!" Greg calls, hopping up from his desk at the airstrip to give my wife a big hug.

We've become regulars here, taking the plane up frequently just for fun. Gwen has come to love it as much as me, it would seem. Except lately, she hasn't quite been able to stomach it.

She hugs him back, giving him a genuine squeeze in the way that only Gwen can. When he pulls back, he looks her over, grinning at us both as she lays a splayed hand over her growing bump.

"Baby Rousseau's first plane ride!"

"Honestly, the morning sickness killed my vibe, and now I'm a little concerned the harness isn't going to fit properly. But Bash was adamant that we couldn't miss the annual birthday flight. Followed by the annual birthday party. Tripp and all our friends are waiting for us, so we won't take long."

"Ah, well, makes no difference to me. I'll be on the radio if you need me. But something tells me if that harness doesn't work, you two will figure out a way to celebrate, even without leaving the ground."

I groan and scrub a hand over my face while Gwen tosses her head back and roars with laughter.

Greg shoots me a sheepish look as he turns to leave. But I still return his departing wave before tossing an arm over Gwen's shoulders and leading her into the hangar with red cheeks.

"I think he's onto us," she whispers, leaning close.

"You think?" I reply dryly. Because yeah, Greg might as well have just said, *Have fun fucking in your plane*.

But Gwen is only amused. Unflappable. Deeply comfortable in herself—so much so that comments like these roll right off her.

I gaze down at her as we walk. Diamond ring on her left hand. Left hand on our daughter, who will be here in three months' time.

Everything feels surreal.

She nudges me with her elbow. "I guess we're not as subtle as we think."

"I am. It's just you."

She turns to me in mock outrage. "I can be subtle."

I quirk a brow. "*Sneak out of the house and repaint the plane* subtle?"

Her mouth opens to say something, but then it slams shut and she turns quickly, searching for our plane. The small one at the back.

The one that used to be white with red stripes.

Now it's the prettiest light purple with darker-indigo-tone stripes.

Her hand moves up from her stomach to lay over her mouth as she walks toward it slowly, shock painting her every feature.

When she turns to glance back at me over her shoulder, her eyes are watery—her smile is too. "Purple?"

I shrug, feeling immensely satisfied with my birthday surprise. "Reminds me of your eyes," I say softly, walking toward her and pulling her into a hug from behind as we both look it over. "Do you like it?"

"Do I like it? I love it. I'm…I'm so lucky to have you. I—" Her head tilts, and she steps away to get a closer look at the tail. "Does that say *Wild Card*?" Her voice cracks and I step up beside her.

"Named it after you too." The script matches the outlandish and perfectly Gwen vibe of the entire makeover.

She blinks hard and fast, turning her gaze up to mine. "This is too much."

I cup her jaw and smile down at her. My wild card. My tequila. My everything.

"Nah, with you, it's never enough," I murmur before dropping my lips to hers. Kissing my wife soundly like I plan to for the rest of our lives.

Then I drag her into our plane.

And we celebrate.

READ ON FOR A SNEAK PEEK OF

FLAW LESS

THE RULES WERE SIMPLE. KEEP MY HANDS OFF HIS DAUGHTER AND STAY OUT OF TROUBLE. BUT NOW I'M STUCK WITH HER. THERE'S ONLY ONE BED. AND, WELL, RULES ARE MADE TO BE BROKEN.

I'm the face of professional bull riding—the golden boy. Or at least I was until it all blew up in my face. Now my agent says I have to clean up my image, so I'm stuck with his ball-busting daughter for the rest of the season as my "full-time supervision."

But I don't need a goddamn babysitter, especially one with skintight jeans, a sexy smirk, and a mouth she can't stop running.

A mouth I can't stop thinking about.

Because Summer isn't just another conquest. She sees the man behind the mask, and she doesn't run—she pulls me closer, even when she shouldn't.

She says this means nothing.

I say this means everything.

She says there are boundaries we shouldn't cross. That my reputation can't take any more hits—and neither can her damaged heart.

I say I'm going to steal it anyway.

CHAPTER 1

Summer

"YOU GOT ONE ANGRY MOTHERFUCKER HERE, EATON."

The handsome cowboy on the back of a huge bull scoffs and shifts his hand around the rope before him. His dark eyes twinkle on the screen, all the hard lines of his face peeking through the cage of his helmet. *"The harder they buck, the happier I am."*

I can barely hear what they're saying over the din of the crowd in the vast arena with music blaring in the background, but the subtitles at the bottom of the screen clear up anything that might otherwise get missed.

The young man leaning over the pen chuckles and shakes his head. *"Must be all that milk you drink. No broken bones for the world-famous Rhett Eaton."*

The easily recognizable cowboy grins behind the cage over his face, a flash of white teeth and the wink of an amber eye from beneath the black helmet. A charming grin I know from spending hours staring at a glossy, still version of it.

"Beat it, Theo. You know I fuckin' hate milk."

A teasing grin touches Theo's lips as he speaks. *"You look cute in those ads with it painted above your lip though. Cute for an old guy."*

The younger man winks and the two men share a friendly laugh as Rhett rubs a hand up the rope methodically.

"I'd rather get bucked off a bull every damn day than drink that shit."

Their laughter is all I hear as my father pauses the video on the large flatscreen, redness creeping up his neck and onto his face.

"Okay…" I venture cautiously, trying to piece together why that exchange requires this impromptu meeting with the two newest full-time hires at Hamilton Elite.

"No. Not okay. This guy is the face of professional bull riding, and he just skewered his biggest sponsors. But it gets worse. Keep watching."

He hits play again, aggressively, like the button did something wrong in this whole affair, and the screen flashes to a different scene. Rhett is walking outside of an arena, through the parking lot with a duffel bag slung over his shoulder. The helmet is now replaced by a cowboy hat and a slim man in dark baggy clothes is taking quick strides to keep up with his target while the cameraman follows and runs tape.

I don't think the paparazzi usually follow bull riders, but Rhett Eaton has become something of a household name over the years. Not a paragon of purity by any stretch, but a symbol of rough and tumble, rugged country men.

The reporter takes a little skip step to get far enough ahead that he can line his microphone up with Rhett's mouth.

"Rhett, can you comment on the video that's been circulating this weekend? Any apologies you'd like to make?"

The cowboy's lips thin, and he tries to hide his face behind the brim of his hat. A muscle in his jaw flexes, and his toned body goes taut. Tension lines every limb.

"No comment," he bites out through gritted teeth.

"Come on, man, give me something." The slender guy reaches out and presses the microphone against Rhett's cheek. Forcing it on him even though he declined to comment. *"Your fans deserve an explanation,"* the reporter demands.

"No, they don't," Rhett mutters, trying to create space between them.

Why do these people think they're *owed* a response when they ambush a person who is otherwise minding his own business?

"How about an apology?" the guy asks.

And then Rhett decks him in the face.

It happens so fast that I blink in an attempt to follow the now shaking and swiveling camera angles.

Well, shit.

Within seconds, the pushy paparazzi is on the ground clutching his face, and Rhett is shaking out his hand as he walks away without a word.

The screen switches back to news anchors sitting behind a desk, and before they can give any input on what we just watched, my dad flicks the TV off and lets loose a rumbling sound of frustration.

"I hate these fucking cowboys. They're impossible to keep in line. I don't want to deal with him. So, lucky for you two, this job is up for grabs." He's practically vibrating with rage, but I just lean back in my chair. My father flies off the handle easily, but he gets over things quickly too. I'm pretty nonplussed by his mood swings at this point in my life. You don't last long at Hamilton Elite if you can't withstand Kip Hamilton.

Lucky for me, I have a lifetime of learning under my belt to brush off his moods, so I'm immune. I've come to think like it's part of his charm, so I don't take it personally. He's not mad at me. He's just…mad.

"I worked my ass off for years to get this country bumpkin sponsorships like he's never dreamed of, and then as his career is winding down, he goes and blows it all up like *this*." My father's hand flicks over at the wall-mounted screen. "Do you have any idea how much money these guys make for being nuts enough to climb up on an angry two-thousand-pound bull, Summer?"

"Nope." But I have a feeling he's about to tell me. I hold my father's dark eyes, the same shade as my own. Geoff, the other intern in the chair beside me, shrinks down in his seat.

"They make millions of dollars if they're as good as this asshole."

I never would have guessed this was such big business, but then they don't cover that in law school. I know all about Rhett Eaton, heartthrob bull riding sensation and mainstay teenaged crush, but almost nothing about the actual industry or sport. One corner of my lips tugs up as I think back on how a decade ago, I'd lie in my bed and gaze at that photo of him.

Rhett stepped up on a fence, glancing back over his shoulder at the camera. Open land behind him, a warm setting sun. A flirty smirk on his lips, eyes partially obscured by a worn cowboy hat, and the pièce de résistance…Wrangler jeans that hugged all the best parts.

So yeah, I know little about bull riding. But I know I spent an awful lot of time staring at that photo. The land. The light. It drew me in. It wasn't just the guy. It made me want to be there, watching that sunset for myself.

"George, do you know how much that milk sponsorship he just flushed down the toilet was worth? Not to mention all the other sponsors whose balls I'll be fondling to smooth this shit over?"

I swear to God I almost snort. *George.* I know my dad well enough to know that he's aware it's the wrong name, but it's also a test to see if Geoff has the cojones to say anything. From what I gather, it's not always a walk in the park working with entitled athletes and celebrities. I can already tell the guy beside me is going to struggle.

"Um…" He flips through the binder on the boardroom table in front of him, and I let my gaze linger out the floor-to-ceiling windows. The ones that offer sweeping views out over the Alberta prairies. From the thirtieth floor of this building, the view over Calgary is unparalleled. The snow-capped Rocky Mountains off in the distance are like a painting—it never gets old.

"The answer is tens of millions, Greg."

I bite the inside of my cheek to keep from chuckling. I like Geoff, and my dad is being a total dick, but after years of being on the spot in this same way, it's amusing to see someone else flounder the way I have in the past.

God knows my sister, Winter, was never on the receiving end of this kind of grilling. She and Kip have a different relationship than mine with our father. With me, he's playful and shoots from the hip; with her, he stays almost professional. I think she likes that better anyway.

Geoff looks over at me with a flat smile.

I've seen that expression on people's faces at work many times. It says, *Must be nice to be the boss's little girl.* It says, *How's that nepotism treating ya?* But I'm trained to take this kind of lashing. My skin is thicker. My give-a-fuck meter is less attuned. I know that in fifteen minutes, Kip Hamilton will crack jokes and be smiling. That perfect veneer he uses to suck up to clients will quickly slip back into place.

The man is a master, even if a bit of a weasel. But I think that comes with the territory of wheeling and dealing the contracts he does as a top-tier talent agent.

If I'm being honest, I'm still not so sure I'm cut out to be working here. Not sure I really want to. But it's always seemed like the right thing to do. I owe my dad that much.

"So, the question is, kids—how does one go about fixing this? I've got the Dairy King milk sponsorship hanging by a thread. I mean, a fucking professional bull rider just slammed his entire base. Farmers? Dairy producers? It seems like it shouldn't matter, but people are going to talk. They're going to put him under a microscope, and I don't think they'll love what they see. This will dent the idiot's bottom line more than you'd think. And his bottom line is *my* bottom line, because this nutjob makes us all a lot of money."

"How did the first recording even get out?" I ask, forcing my brain back onto the task at hand.

"A local station left their camera running." My dad scrubs a hand over his clean-shaven chin. "Caught the whole damn thing and then subtitled it and ran it on the evening news."

"Okay, so he needs to apologize," Geoff tosses out.

My dad rolls his eyes at the generic solution. "He's gonna need to do a hell of a lot more than apologize. I mean, he needs a bullet-proof plan for what's left of the season. He's got a couple of months until the World Championships in Vegas. We're gonna need to polish up that cowboy hat halo before then. Or other sponsors are going to drop like flies too."

I tap my pen against my lips, mind racing with what we could do to help salvage this situation. Of course, I have next to no experience, so I stick to leading questions. "So, he needs to be seen as the charming, wholesome country boy next door?"

My dad barks out a loud laugh, his hands coming to brace against the boardroom table across from us as he leans down. Geoff flinches, and I roll my eyes. *Pussy.*

"That right there is the issue. Rhett Eaton is not the *wholesome country boy next door.* He's a cocky cowboy that parties too hard and has hordes of women throwing themselves at him every weekend. And he's not mad about it. It hasn't been an issue before, but they'll pick apart anything they can now. Like fucking vultures."

I quirk an eyebrow and lean back. Rhett is an adult, and surely, with an explanation of what's on the line, he can hold it together. After all, he pays for the company to manage this stuff for him. "So, he can't be on his best behavior for a couple of months?"

My dad drops his head with a deep chuckle. "Summer, this man's version of good behavior will not cut it."

"You're acting as if he's some sort of wild animal, Kip." I learned the hard way not to call him Dad at work. He's still my boss, even if we carpool together at the end of each day. "What does he need? A babysitter?"

The room is quiet for several beats while my dad stares at the tabletop between his hands. Eventually, his fingers tap the surface of it—something he does when he's deep in thought. A habit I've picked up from him over the years. His almost-black eyes lift, and a wolfish grin takes over his entire face.

"Yeah, Summer. That's exactly what he needs. And I know the perfect person for the job."

And based on the way he's looking at me right now, I think Rhett Eaton's new babysitter just might be *me.*

ACKNOWLEDGMENTS

First and foremost, I would like to thank YOU—the reader—for joining me on this incredible journey. *Wild Card* marks my thirteenth book published and my third series complete. And being able to make writing and publishing my job would not be possible without my incredible readers.

Elsie readers are the best readers and that's a fact. I owe it all to you. Along with a few other people...

My husband and son, who keep me grounded and centered and make me feel so loved and supported every day.

My wildly supportive mom and dad, who have been my biggest cheerleaders for my entire life and show no signs of stopping.

My assistant, Krista, who keeps me sane and organized even though I'm sure that sometimes working with me is a little bit like herding cats.

My agent, Kimberly Brower, who believes in me more than I even believe in myself sometimes.

My sensitivity readers who helped me so much with this one, Kristie and Jill. You are both so wise and so thoughtful and I appreciate you more than you know.

Every editor, proofer, and beta reader who laid hands on this book. The final product would not have been possible without your keen eyes and input.

To my publishers, Bloom Books and Piatkus. Thank you for making my dreams come true.

And finally, I want to give a special shoutout to the sixteen-year-old version of myself who got told she could never do this.

Girl, you did it.

ABOUT THE AUTHOR

Elsie Silver is a #1 *New York Times* bestselling author of sassy, steamy, small town romance. She's a born and raised Canadian girl who loves a good book boyfriend and the strong heroines who bring them to their knees. Her books promise banter, tension, and a slow burn that comes to a screeching halt.

Website: elsiesilver.com
Facebook: authorelsiesilver
Instagram: @authorelsiesilver